The Dark Cry of Aristid

William Brian Johnson

The Dark Cry of Aristid
William Brian Johnson
Copyright © 2022 William Brian Johnson
Published by William Brian Johnson

https://fatherthunder.blogspot.com/

Cover design by Rumination of Thunder Media

ISBN: 9798359168946

DEDICATION

To my father who instilled in me the gift of reading.

To all my friends
that have made this world possible either
through fantasy literature, late-night gaming, critique groups, or
making the mistake of asking me what I'm working on, enjoy.

Special thanks to
Artist's Inc, The National Writers Project, and
The Flint Hills Writing Project
for making me finish it.

CHAPTER 1

The man who burned witches alive stood before Mayor Herrick Blanchfield's desk with an ominous warning. "The knights caught your daughter in Shrinehall, Mayor." Overseer Daniels stopped after addressing him, almost like the title was too bitter for his taste. "The law of the Tower is that no child shall enter Shrinehall without an adult. Even yours. The Temple of Asagrim is not a playground." He leaned forward over the desk. "This is your final warning."

Overseer Daniels, the head of the Tower and the head of a small group of knights stationed in Elta, stood less than a foot away. He had a way of looming over the villagers, making sure his shadow fell across them while terrifying them into submission.

Overseer Daniels' pale blue eyes fell on Herrick, almost eagerly awaiting the incorrect response. It made Herrick sit up straight in his office chair. Herrick had short stature. He was a pudgy, balding, middle-aged man and was no warrior. He adjusted his glasses, cleared his throat, and prepared to speak.

"My apologies, Overseer. My wife and I will make —."

The overseer left without another word. Herrick held his breath until he exited. No warning or excuses next time.

"By the gods, all this and nearing harvest too." He slumped in his chair.

Two knights marched past his office on their regular patrol. He checked to make sure they didn't deposit a squirming red-headed girl not more than six-winters-old at the office door.

Herrick grabbed his cloak and locked up. The village worked

at its normal pace as villagers rushed around in the late summer heat gathering provisions for supper. The aroma of warm bread filled the streets, and spiced meat soon overpowered it, making Herrick's stomach grumble.

He strode around the village square, visiting the different vendors while keeping a wary eye out for his wayward daughter. Some stopped him to offer a hello or to complain about a knight's heavy-handedness or outright abuse. The White Citadel had moved most of the Tower knights to the front lines of a war that has lasted longer than the elders' memory. The remaining knights grew merciless.

A year had passed since the villagers elected Herrick as mayor and the complaints against the knights began. His election nearly caused an armed response from the Tower because their puppet, a man named Loche, was voted out and disappeared that night. In his absence, the Tower sought revenge. Unfortunately, it was revenge against their people.

Herrick crossed the village down to the lower part of the valley. In front of their shops, Valdir, a worn, soot-covered blacksmith, and red-headed Ragnfast, the brash butcher, debated outside their shops. It had already started. Scraps, Ragnfast's massive and weathered wolfhound, ran circles among the two, releasing a low gruff growl until Ragnfast threw him a bone. The two men remained friendly, but sometimes their arguments spun out of control and ended in fists and an occasional dog bite. Other times a knight ventured nearby, making Ragnfast back off his anti-Tower rants and giving Valdir a rare smile due to the fire disappearing from Ragnfast's fury.

Odd that both of their shops were closed so early. They're usually not outside until dark.

The air seemed colder, heavier down here in the valley. Thunder rumbled off the mountains in the distance. The sky, pockmarked with fluffy clouds, appeared the bluest in memory. Not the deadly pale blue of the overseer's eyes, but deep blue like the forgotten sea not far from the Witches Forest, a sign that storms drew near.

"Afternoon, Mayor," Ragnfast greeted.

Herrick looked at the butcher and waved. "Have you seen Allistril?"

"No. No sign of the little firehead. Did you lose her again?"

"Did you hear about Nol?" Valdir interrupted in his usual severe tone.

"He went out on a hunt this morning," Herrick replied. "Did he get anything?"

"They can't find him," Valdir said.

The blood drained from Herrick's face and a feeling ran up his spine like falling through the ice in winter. "What happened?"

"Kordan said they found blood and animal tracks leading off to the Delirium Forest."

Nol's wife, Aurdr, was ready to birth in the coming weeks. "Oh, gods," Herrick exclaimed.

"Ragnfast, Scraps, and I were about to go out."

"Has anyone contacted the Tower?" Herrick asked.

"Hmmph," Ragnfast snorted. "Kordan told Overseer Daniels about it this morning, but you know ..." Ragnfast glanced at Valdir. "Tower business comes first."

Valdir returned with a glare. "The Tower deals with much more than this village. The White Citadel's business is beyond the cares of a local butcher."

"Spoken like the Overseer himself—"

Scraps stood at point issuing a low growl staring to the west. The Tower's bell cut short Ragnfast's reply, two low monotonous gongs followed by the larger bell and a higher-pitched ring from a smaller one.

"That's the gale warning," Herrick said.

They scanned the sky as thunder echoed down Mount Hati. The first wisps of cooler air poured into the valley.

"Storm's coming. You better find your daughter, Mayor." Ragnfast tapped Valdir on the shoulder. "Come on, we'll wait this out in the butcher shop then go looking for Nol."

As Herrick moved up through the lower village, Allistril was nowhere to be found. In the market stood the village healer, a tall brunette in a bright green dress that matched her eyes. She stood alone.

"Herrick?" Della, Herrick's wife yelled.

"Run home and see if Allistril's there. I'm running back to the office."

He huffed up the path to the village square. He took a moment to catch his breath and scanned the village. Thunder roared from the west over the farm fields and black boiling clouds scrubbed the forests that lay behind it.

He scanned the village. The Tower loomed across from Shrinehall, the tall keep that housed Asagrim's knights and the overseer. The village crops lay to the west. Then two places the villager's children were warned to never enter. To the south stood the Witches Forest. It lured villagers by strange dancing lights or an occasional voice beckoning them to enter. Even in the coldest of winters, the trees never lost their leaves. Then where Nol was lost, the Delirium Forest gripped the rest of the village. It was a cursed place that confused its victims and slowly turned them into monsters.

Frantically, Herrick checked the vendors as they slammed shut their booths.

Allistril fears the knights. She wouldn't go to the Tower for any reason. She must be at Shrinehall. By the gods, if Overseer Daniels finds her there again …

His eyes went from the approaching storm to Shrinehall. He jogged to the steps and climbed. The local religious temple for Asagrim, Shrinehall ascended from the middle of the village. Shrinehall gleamed in the sunlight. Its glow continued as the storm swallowed the sun, a sign of the only magic allowed in Elta.

Shrinehall's white marble columns attached to a bright unmarred, clean copper roof stood in stark contrast to the greenish-black clouds threatening from the forest. Herrick ran up the steps as the wind shifted. Little hairs stood at attention on his arms as he advanced up the final steps. The air tingled.

"Allistril!"

The temperature plunged as Herrick reached the top.

"Allistril," he yelled again.

"Daddy?" The voice sounded weak and helpless intermixed with the peals of thunder and blinding flashes of lightning.

Allistril stood in front of Asagrim's enormous statue, clutching its foot. Herrick glanced around looking for Overseer Daniels and beheld the storm moving in. From this height, he saw the monster heading to his village, a large churning summer hailstorm. Fear of the oncoming storm replaced his feeling of relief in finding his daughter.

"Daddy, is it the Wrath?"

Hail tinged off Shrinehall's roof.

"No, child. Be silent about the Wrath." He took a moment to catch his breath and hide his fear. "We are safe." He breathed in the cool air, telling himself that the Wrath was merely a story told to misbehaving children to silence them in church.

He glanced at Asagrim's statue, then looked away. *Einridi, please help us.* He touched the hidden amulet of another god under his shirt. Holding Allistril, he crouched near another god's statue as if divine intervention might save them.

The Tower bells continued their warning as lightning hammered nearby. He stroked Allistril's sweat-stained hair from her face. Her fierce squeeze made his arm go numb until her nails found a home. Hail cracked upon Shrinehall's copper roof and drowned out any other sounds in the valley. Fist-sized stones driven by wind found their way into Shrinehall's hallowed ground. Allistril screamed and covered her ears. The hail's roar, like the saga-rumored sounds of the dying mountain king, drowned out anything else but destruction.

Holes opened in the roof's massive dents. Rain poured into Shrinehall. Cold air breathed through like the last breaths of the damned. The clapping of heavy rain replaced the thunderous roar of hail. Then it slowed to soft gentle rain.

They stared at the ravaged village of Elta below. The storm wasted their winter food. The heavy smell of harvest and earth filled Shrinehall.

Once again, the Tower sounded its warning. Herrick's gut clenched as he realized it was more than a warning. It was a plea to Asagrim for help. A strange noise made him look up. The miracle of Asagrim went to work sealing the holes in the copper roof, popping out the dents, and making the metal shine. All while crops, livestock, and villagers died below in the shadow of Shrinehall.

CHAPTER 2

Della stood in Shrinehall finishing her prayers as the rising sun warmed her tired bones. She had bandaged and balmed the wounds of Elta's injured in the three days since the storm. Now she breathed. Below the bellows of those needing help were the cries for the dead. Fourteen died in her care, ravaged by a storm that might end up killing them all. She dared to close her eyes in one last murmured prayer. Waves of exhaustion attempted to consume her as she filled her lungs and looked at Elta below. The hail swath left a cruel scar that cut right through the village and stopped at the Delirium Forest.

The crops and storm-ravaged bodies lay in the fields. Livestock remained where they'd fallen because the butcher, hunters, and villagers processed what they could before rot set in. The fallen and livestock bloated in the late summer heat.

Her glance went to the fallen in the fields. Her dead villagers and friends, people she'd served, remained until Overseer Daniels found time in his day to drag himself from his Tower to say final rites. No matter how she wished them removed, interrupting a church ritual proved deadly. Only after Overseer Daniel's rites would the bodies be moved to the mass pyre and then the remains placed in the graveyard.

Della's thoughts strayed from the dead to the living and the soon-to-be-born. Aurdr waddled down the street from her house toward the Delirium Forest. The hunters, exhausted from their days of saving and preparing the winter meat, walked along its edge shouting for their missing comrade. The hailstorm spared the broken trail where Nol walked in.

Kordan formed a human chain with the hunters he led and pressed into the forest as the others held tight to keep him from becoming lost. Cold air blustered through Shrinehall as shouts called out from below. The hunters pulled Kordan from the madness just in time.

She sat on the tiled floor and turned her attention to those moving through the ruined fields. Herrick toured battered crops, empty livestock barns, and stores with dwindling supplies. his hunt was as worthless as the hunters searching for Nol on the other side of Elta.

Below, the hunters had broken out their waterskins and provisions. Some hunters lay asleep on the ground, except for Kordan who embraced Aurdr, maybe out of exhaustion, sorrow, or out of the fruitlessness of their search.

Herrick spent the rest of the afternoon calculating and recalculating the inventory numbers. Just as feared, not enough food remained for winter. Such news proved deadly for a self-sustained village. He sighed and sat back in his chair. Outside the window, followers trod up the steps to Shrinehall for afternoon prayers. Light reflected off the copper roof and blinded him.

Herrick shielded his eyes and watched Overseer Daniels conduct the rites. The overseer lifted a mead horn to Asagrim's statue, poured a libation at the statue's foot, then passed it to the families as they approached.

What could Shrinehall do for us in this time of need?

Herrick gathered the farm reports and left for Shrinehall. He nodded and sidestepped the families returning home. Most of them, the true-believers, ignored his greetings and stared through him as if he was a ghost.

How did I ever get elected?

The true-believers were a small dwindling population. For many winters, a cruel man had led Elta, nothing more than a hand puppet for Overseer Daniels. Under Locke, the number of burnings for witchcraft, jail for heresy, and expulsions from the village rose to historic levels.

As a simple merchant, the Delirium Forest trapped Herrick when "The Seizure" occurred. The Tower did not find him important enough for an amulet that provided passage back. He'd met Della and soon after married. Unable to travel as a merchant after it sealed off the safe-passage forest roads, Herrick took odd jobs. Soon his family grew beyond him and Della. The people welcomed him, but he kept quiet about his beliefs to keep the church at bay with the approaching elections. Talking and listening to people had always come easy to him. So did politics, but he was unprepared for the enemies made in standing up to the White Citadel. To them, he was a mosquito, but a mosquito with a deadly virus. The elections were a landslide and Locke disappeared into the night. A fate that Herrick wondered would happen to him if he was ever replaced.

Herrick joined the line still waiting to be received by Overseer Daniels. A few followers glanced or glared at him. Herrick gazed at the roof and inched forward. Finally, the family before him said their invocation and drank from the horn. Overseer Daniels took the horn back, bowed to Asagrim, and returned the horn to the statue's feet.

"And a visit from Elta's mayor. What brings you to Shrinehall this afternoon?" Overseer Daniels asked.

"A plea for help."

Overseer Daniels turned to the statue and closed the rite. He picked up the horn and passed it to Herrick with a glint in his pale eyes. The horn, full when placed at the statue's foot, was now dry.

"Asagrim was thirsty, and you have his answer," Overseer Daniels said. "Hail to the Allfather."

Herrick recoiled from the answer like a slap. "The village will

13

not survive the winter. We have food for two months if we severely restrict the stores."

"Go pray to your god then, Blanchfield. You are a heretic here. Your wife and family show up on the Seasonal Rites and for the Tides of Life, but you ... always at your office."

"I know you and I have issues, but this is for the survival of the village."

Under the overseer's gaze, Herrick felt his voice shrink and break.

"You worship the Thunderer. I've seen the idols carelessly hidden in your house when I visit. The Thunderer is responsible for this destruction, and you come to me for help?"

"It was a summer storm," Herrick replied hesitantly. "Nothing else."

"Begone!" Overseer Daniel's voice boomed through the empty Shrinehall as if he was in the middle of a sermon. "You are a boil on this village, and I will see you fail. This is Asagrim's country. You are a stranger here. State who you follow before Asagrim, Mayor Blanchfield. Make the claim."

Rage seethed in Herrick's chest. "You will kill this village because I am not a follower?"

"The Church has their issues at the moment, wars on several fronts," Overseer Daniels paused a moment then stared directly at Herrick. "Your issues are beneath us."

"These are your followers."

Overseer Daniels took the ritual tools and meandered off.

"Or is it because the Allfather provides for his armies, so you no longer need food or drink?"

A pop echoed through Shrinehall. Overseer Daniels had left and teleported to the Tower. Herrick stared at the papers in his hands, the village death sentence. He wanted to yell at Asagrim's statue, tear up the reports at the statue's feet, but Mayor Herrick Blanchfield understood his position.

He left Shrinehall, ignoring the confrontation that boiled in his chest. His was a position of power taken away from the church. It ran against the church's authority and the village reaped the consequences. As Mayor, he kept his head low and went about the daily business. He let his family worry about religious duties in a futile effort to keep the peace.

Herrick slumped back to his office, shuttered the windows, and moved a secret panel in his closet. He took out the idol of the god worshiped in his old country, Einridi, the Thunderer. He pulled small stubs of tallow out of his desk and lit them. For the first time in winters, Herrick prayed to his old god, the god of the people and not the ruling class.

CHAPTER 3

urdr spoke to the gatherers at the village square that evening. There were little amounts of grain here and there that they'd discovered, but the hailstorm had ravaged most of the fields. With the grain scattered, they needed more hands to collect it before it rotted. Though gathering was her job before children, Aurdr was useless in her condition. When the others talked about needing help, she absentmindedly rubbed her belly for the baby that was due. One more mouth to feed.

The hunters called out on the edge of the Delirium Forest. Many stared forward, seeking a scrap from Nol's clothes or a sign he was near.

Kordan walked over to Aurdr. "The baby will be here soon. You need to be home resting. I told you if we found something, I'll send word."

"I wanted to tell you to stop, Kordan. They've been up all night. Nol would not want this much fuss over him."

"I know." Kordan paused to look over his hunters. "We're all exhausted and only an hour before sundown. I'll send them home then."

Aurdr wept. Kordan wrapped his arms around her. "Sister. You are not alone here. I will take care of you and the children until we find Nol. The baby needs you to rest. You need to rest. Go home."

"I think something's wrong, Kordan. I've not felt her move today, and she's so low."

Kordan patted her on the back. "Let's go get Lofn or Della.

I'll take you."

"No. Stay here. I saw Della in the market and will talk to her." Aurdr held on to Kordan for a moment. Then turned to walk away, not looking into the Delirium Forest.

It was cooler in the village but walking up the hill tired her immensely. Aurdr took little sprints of steps, then after thirty steps, she needed to stop and breathe. Pain radiated to her feet. Her legs hurt from walking and standing all day. She watched the square, wishing to see Della. A bench in the village square almost called out to her. She heard a voice call her name.

She stopped about midway, the pain reached up her abdomen and held her still. A hand landed on her shoulder. Through tear-stung eyes, she saw the village midwife call for a cart. Aurdr leaned hard against Lofn's small frame to find relief, but she bore the weight easily.

"She's coming," Aurdr pleaded, "and something is wrong."

Valdir pulled up with a cart when he saw Aurdr in trouble. Then towed it alongside Lofn to her house. He stood back, staring at Aurdr as Lofn ran into the house to prepare. Within a moment she returned, helping Aurdr up and into the house while he hesitantly followed.

"Go start the kettle. I need hot water," Lofn instructed, her soft touch on his soot-covered shoulder shook him from his horror. Lofn lit some herbs, waving the smoke into Aurdr's face. "Breath deep. You are in a safe place."

Aurdr inhaled. Her face released the tension. Lofn's glare moved Valdir's feet. He ran outside, drew water from the well, and then placed it over the fire. He fled to the porch not wanting to be part of what happened inside. Several people looked oddly at him as screams erupted from Lofn's house.

He nodded at the villagers and wished them well while his stomach churned. "By Asagrim, I have things to do today."

He peered around the door into the house. "The water is on ... can I leave?" His gaze locked on Aurdr, who leaned forward in her chair with teeth clenched.

"Not yet, I still need help. When this passes, you need to keep Aurdr balanced on the chair."

Valdir waited until Aurdr fell back. Lofn pressed hard on the swollen belly, her hands searching for something.

"I have –" Valdir started.

"You will stay here and help. This baby is in distress."

The smithy shifted his weight awkwardly. Lofn stomped across the wood floor.

"I've heard you bellow war stories over mead for many winters. If a woman's blood upsets you, I'll have some new stories to tell at the next feast, Valdir the Boneless. Now go stand at her head. This is the job you must do right now."

Lofn hadn't even looked at him, but Valdir moved behind the chair. The smoke eased his tense shoulders as well.

"Smithy, don't get too relaxed," Lofn barked. "We have work to do." She grabbed a clean rag and a tightly stoppered bottle from the shelf. "Comfort her. I have to prepare something."

She disappeared into the other room. The smithy tapped Aurdr's shoulder, repeating a mantra, "Everything is going to be fine, Aurdr. Everything is going to be fine."

Aurdr grabbed his hand, squeezed it tight, and rolled forward on the chair huffing. Valdir panicked and yelled for Lofn and shouted, "Nol, where are you?"

Lofn returned with the rag soaked in a foul-smelling liquid.

"You've talked about taking on entire villages. This is just a baby. Stand back." Lofn held the rag up to Aurdr's mouth. "Breath deep, Aurdr. This will help with the pain."

Aurdr took a deep breath, and then her head fell back against the chair. Lofn held it to her for a moment, then threw the rag into a bucket nearby.

"Hold her tight. She's going to fight us."

Valdir moved up and grabbed Aurdr's shoulders. Lofn moved to her stomach. She placed her hands on the belly, pushed in, and rotated. Aurdr's screams filled the room as she struggled.

"Hold her!"

Valdir pressed on Aurdr, holding her to the chair as the midwife worked. The door cracked open with a squeal.

"Not now!" Lofn yelled.

"It's Della." The mayor's wife entered the room and moved to Aurdr, looking to Lofn for instruction. "I'm here to help."

"Baby is feet first, but something else is wrong. Comfort her and help Valdir hold her down through the worst of the pain."

She eased the pressure as Aurdr's belly shifted. Lofn grabbed a sheet and covered Aurdr before cutting away her clothes. "Valdir, go get my water and put it in a clean bucket."

The smithy scampered gratefully out of the room.

It seemed cooler outside like those days when he'd stayed too close to the kiln, and his thinking went strange. He looked at the steaming water, wondering if it was ready. Lofn yelled his name from inside.

"On my way," he said, grabbing the bucket.

Inside, Lofn took some instruments out of the drawer and placed them in the water amid the cloud of steam. "Back at her head, Valdir, unless you want the show of a lifetime."

Valdir glanced at the wrong time and felt the blood drain from his face.

"Gods, Lofn," Della smirked. "He doesn't have the stomach for this."

"Berserker, go stand behind the chair and do what I have told you. I need the village doctor's help." Lofn kicked him in the back of the leg. Valdir swore to himself while his stomach did flips. He refused to be shown up by the womenfolk. He took Della's place at Aurdr's head and breathed in some of the herb smoke.

Lofn took a pair of tongs and placed the instruments on a

clean sheet. The women spoke in hushed tones as they went to work. Valdir relaxed and leaned back against the wall. The smoke made him drowsy. Though the women's talk grew more animated, they seemed oddly sad.

"Della, this isn't going to be natural childbirth. Be patient. I will do everything to save her and the baby. Valdir, do not talk to anyone about this."

"What?" Valdir asked, rousing from the smoke.

"Give me your hand."

He stared at her questioningly as she grabbed a small knife from her belt and cut her hand. Then Lofn made a fist over Aurdr's belly.

"I need your hand, Valdir."

He stared at the blood dripping on Aurdr's belly, then his thinking cleared.

"Witchcraft … is outlawed."

"Would you like her and her baby's blood on your hands or just your own?"

"She could die too?" he asked and paused a moment, then slowly gave his hand to Lofn. "Do it."

The slight cut was little more than a pinch before she joined his hand with hers, and their intermingled blood fell.

"Della?" Lofn passed the knife. Della made a quick wound and then added to the blood pool.

"I hope it is enough," Lofn said. "Or we will lose them both."

The chant began in a low tone followed by quick words and movements. Valdir looked at Della in a mixture of fear and wonder. Della nodded, took his hand, and squeezed them over the belly. Lofn's chant increased in volume and speed. She shouted unfamiliar names then stopped. She smeared the blood with her wounded hand into the shapes of runes that he had only seen in the church. Valdir gasped as Aurdr's belly stirred, and the baby kicked.

"We must move quickly," Lofn said.

She tented the sheet over Aurdr and went to work. Soon blood welled. Lofn placed a small, gray female baby on the sheet, still tethered with a cord wrapped around her neck. Della dropped Valdir's hand and released the infant from her natural noose. The baby squirmed and choked. Lofn held it upside down and cleared the fluid from its mouth. Soon, cries filled the room, and the baby pinked up.

Valdir burbled as tears spilled from his eyes, causing clean rivulets to form down his soot-stained cheeks. "Never have I seen such magic, my lady. This truly was a blessing from the gods. Your secret is safe with me."

"Then I take that as your oath of silence to Asagrim, Valdir. You have already spilled blood here to help us. Don't be afraid of it. No harm will come to us if it is not discussed. If it is spoken aloud, blood will be spilled again. But today we saved this baby's life."

Valdir nodded as Lofn gave the infant over to Della. Lofn continued to work on Aurdr as the smithy hung his head and wept.

CHAPTER 4

Bera heard the door open about the time Valdir came home from the forge. She'd long ago learned not to expect him home earlier because most evenings he worked late, argued with Ragnfast, or went to the mead hall and drank. Her husband usually walked in, bellowed, and grabbed her in a fierce embrace. Tonight, he stood by the door. His soot-covered face had rivulets of tears carving lines through the grime.

"Valdir, what happened?"

"I… I saw something."

An odd, bitter smoke wafted in with his entrance. "What did you get into, fool?"

"No, woman. Listen to me." Tears dissolved into a whisper so unlike her strong husband. "There are witches among us."

"Valdir, what are you going on about?" She waved a dismissive hand and returned to cooking. "Go clean up, supper is almost ready."

He walked into the other room. She heard the pitcher's water stream into the bowl and him splashing about. Then silence.

She took the pot off the fire and sauntered into the other room. Valdir stood looking out the window, his voice strained.

"I know there are certain potions for healing that the Tower allows, and I know it's different at the White Citadel. Healing isn't true magic when it's done with bandages, potion, and herbs. But they did something, something wrong … they used my blood."

Bera was used to her husband's stories, but tonight, something seemed different. He looked panicked. The man that raged and took on armies was deeply and truly afraid.

"They used my blood in the rite." He stared at the wood floor and shook his head. "The Magistrate will know, and I'll be burnt at the stake. They will strip away all I own and leave you to fend for yourself."

Bera put her arms around him. "Tell me what happened. Who are these witches?"

A shuddering breath. "Della and Lofn. They revived an infant."

"Whose?"

"Aurdr's."

"Aurdr had her baby?" Bera squealed. "Was it a boy or girl?"

Valdir spun on her and grasped her arms in his viselike grip. "A girl ... a girl I think, woman, and I don't care. Listen to me."

"No, you listen to me." She shook him off and took his face in her hands. "Come eat your supper. There are no knights at the door. No one is coming to get you. Calm down."

Valdir grabbed a clean tunic and stalked away to the cooking fire.

Bera slowly followed, arms reaching around herself. "So ... you saw a birth today. No wonder you are so shaken. Sorry, love. This was something I never gave you. It's just something people don't talk about it until you're with child."

He turned away to sit at the table while Bera grabbed bowls and filled them with soup.

"I know how people have babies, Bera," he grumbled as she set the soup before him. "I am no fool."

Valdir stared into the soup bowl.

Bera got herself a bowl and blew into it. "You are a fool. You know war and are good at it. There are things in the home you know so little about." She ate and left Valdir to stir. He bolted from the table, nearly knocking the chair over. She watched him pace the floor until he moved to the fireplace and threw another log on the fire. He took the poker and stoked the flames. Then took a long look at the poker.

"Valdir, no," Bera commanded. His cold stare made her step back. Valdir rushed into the back room.

When Valdir made the fire poker, he added something a little different. An iron lock stood out among the floorboards in the back of the house. The only way to unlock it was with the special fire poker.

She heard the lock release and then groan as he pulled the floorboard back. As she walked into the room, he stood above it for a while as if he stared into a grave. His hand brushed the box inside. Then he drew out the contents he'd kept hidden for decades. The old wooden box had held up well. He pressed the secret release and opened it.

His old short sword. His hand brushed the hilt.

"Don't wake *it* up, you fool. Or the Magistrate will come for you," Bera whispered.

He carried it into the other room almost knocking Bera out of the way. She followed him. Now the fool had it in his hand. The platinum runes glinted in the firelight. Valdir's sword from his berserker days. The sword that carried him from continent to continent to voyage, learn, and plunder.

"Put it away, Valdir. You are safe." A cold sweat ran down her back. The sword had great power and would not be ignored by the Tower. "Should we go see the overseer?"

"No!" He shouted. "No. Give me a moment." He stared at the weapon a moment longer then pressed the flat of the sword to his head. Bera waited in fear for the old runes to flare to life, but Valdir took a deep breath and placed it back into the box. He stood a moment, deep in thought, then placed it into the floor and closed the floorboard. The lock engaged making her jump. Valdir kneeled on the floor with his hand placed on the secret lock for a moment. He stayed there for a heartbeat more, then rose.

"Let me eat in peace. Then we can talk."

Bera cleaned up her dishes and went to wash them. She didn't hear Valdir behind her until he embraced her.

"I did see the birth. I wasn't ready for that, but I am not losing my mind. Aurdr's child was still."

Tears gathered in her eyes. "You mean the baby died?"

"No," Valdir replied. "It arrived still, and the witches brought it back to life."

CHAPTER 5

Days later after Aurdr recovered from her hard birth, Lofn slumped in the pew of Shrinehall and shivered against the early morning air. This baby's birth required more magic than she had used in many winters and the after-effects still haunted her. The arrival of Della and the rest of the Blanchfields propped her up against the pew as Della slid in and embraced her.

"Gods, you are freezing."

Lofn smiled at her. Della removed her cloak and covered them both. Della's hand brushed against Lofn's, and the warmth flowed through her body.

Lofn sighed at the shared power. "Be careful, my friend."

Della flashed a smile and whispered, "Allistril wanted to see you all week. If I don't give you a little anima, you'll drain her when she jumps on your lap."

Lofn was about to warn her of public displays of power when Overseer Daniels appeared from behind Asagrim's statue. His dark mauve robe always reminded Lofn of a cancer against the statue's marbled stark white. The overseer approached the large stone altar before those gathered as the sun erupted onto Mount Hati.

His presence made Della's grip a little harder. Lofn tapped her hand and released it.

"Asagrim, we request your divine presence at this child's naming." Overseer Daniels lifted a horn of holy mead to the sun, then to Asagrim's statue. "This rite has begun."

Lofn stilled beside her stone-faced friend, amused at how

much Della feared the overseer. Beside her sat Herrick Blanchfield. He usually attended the naming of children and the seasonal rites but remained absent from the day-to-day worship. Allistril sat forward next to Herrick and stuck out her tongue when she noticed Lofn's glance.

She loved the Blanchfields, but this little one was special. Herrick tapped Allistril on the shoulder and pointed to the front. Lofn not wanting to cause her little soulmate more trouble, sat back and watched the villagers, many of whom had used her services in the past.

In her time as a midwife, she had presided over infidelities, disease, infertility, hard births, and the occasional stillbirth. The previous one, sweet and gentle Allistril, took Lofn down for a week. Della remained conscious, fighting all the potions to beg for her daughter's life, and Lofn answered. She'd poured so much anima into the baby, she sometimes wondered who Allistril truly belonged with.

Della had remained close to her and kept her secrets. She studied in secret under Lofn after the stillbirth and increasingly showed some power.

"Aurdr and the newborn … approach Asagrim," the overseer called as he poured part of the drinking horn into a trench at Asagrim's foot. A humble sacrifice to the god and his earthly incarnation, the Allfather. The mead disappeared before it landed in the trough. Magic to some, a divine blessing to others, and a sin punishable by death if a common person made the wine magically disappear.

Under the church's political arm, the Magistrate had outlawed magic used by common folk decades ago. With most local practitioners wiped out or forced to join the Order of Ord, she had to maintain her guard. Aurdr's baby had revived by supernatural means. Luckily, Aurdr survived her ordeal with only a few memories of a black-faced man, possibly a dwarf, looming over her and crying.

Della practiced magic with her. Valdir watched her from three aisles over, still grimy but in a clean tunic. Worse, his ursine-like wife stared too. The local bread maker spoke to Valdir in a low whisper until the overseer's pause forced all eyes forward.

"What is the child's name, Aurdr?" Overseer Daniels asked.

Aurdr shifted from foot to foot before the congregation. She stared at her older daughter who sat in a pew as Kordan approached her. He put his arm around Aurdr, whispered, and both looked out to the Delirium Forest.

She held out the baby, facing the forest as her whisper traveled throughout Shrinehall. "You got another daughter, my love. Come home."

"The name, Aurdr."

She turned, tears streaming down her face. "Why won't you help them find my husband, Overseer Daniels?"

The overseer's expression never changed as he waited. Kordan spun Aurdr to him and talked quickly, fear evident in his eyes. The congregation strained to hear, but then Aurdr interrupted with a name, too soft to hear over Kordan's mutterings.

The overseer appeared startled for a moment. "Repeat that name?"

"Austri."

Lofn smiled at the overseer's reaction. Austri meant luck. The name of a godlike dwarf that held up the eastern heavens, once popular until the war with the dwarves started over a hundred winters ago.

"Did I hear you correctly?"

"Yes. I name this child for luck," Aurdr said, standing straighter. "For luck on the upcoming winter, for luck that we continue to have food for our families, and for luck that they find my husband unchanged by the forest."

Shrinehall grew very still. Aurdr did not dare say more. Kordan returned to his seat next to his older niece while Overseer Daniels continued through the naming ceremony with the passion of a farmer clearing his destroyed crops.

The baby's wails filled Shrinehall as Overseer Daniels rubbed

Asagrim's rune into the baby's forehead. Austri, a strong name in these trying times even though her wails made Lofn wonder how hard the overseer pressed.

Instill fear at an early age, you ormstunga. Lofn glared at the overseer.

Asagrim's statue loomed above the masses in Shrinehall. Lofn looked up at the statue as its head creaked from looking down at the overseer and turned to look down at Lofn. Then its arm dipped from the rising sun to the ruined crops below.

"Lofn?" Della took her hand.

Lofn blinked, then stared at her friend before glancing around. The statue's shift appeared unnoticeable to the masses as they huddled around the new baby.

She smiled not showing Della her fear. "Let's go see little Austri."

Lofn almost pulled Della to the baby. As they gushed on little Austri, the fine hairs on Lofn's neck stood up. Nearby, the cowled overseer stared through her.

The unexpected feast that followed the naming ceremony remained sparse. An error from the smokehouse ruined the meal, a son with no experience trying to take over for his fallen father. Too much fire. Too much smoke.

Lofn felt more eyes upon her at the dinner, but as she wandered through the crowd, more people stared at their empty feast. She spent time with the Blanchfields and played with Allistril to shrug off the statue's omen.

There had been a few times that Asagrim animated. Once to warn of an unknown southern invasion from the giants. Once when Locke had disappeared. No one had seen the movement, just noticed that the statue had shifted. Maybe her need for anima caused visions. Of all things, why would Asagrim give her a sign? From the village's square, the statue appeared to be looking to the mountains once again. Lofn glanced at Shrinehall as she walked about with Allistril in tow. Those that sat with Valdir and his wife, the true-believers, frowned.

"Why do people stare, Lofn?" Allistril asked. "It's not nice."

"It's because they think your head is on fire with all this red hair." Lofn said, tousling the child's strands.

Allistril giggled and swung Lofn's hand around, but the feeling of unease spread like untamed wildfire.

Many of the locals decried the baby's feast even though they choked down the burnt meat. As the days passed, prices rose while the sacks of wheat, butcher's meat, and produce were visibly shorted and stored for the hard winter coming.

Lofn walked past the bakery, drawn in by the scent of bread. Bera slid a couple of loaves from the stone oven and set them to cool. The bread didn't appear real. It looked like bread-colored rocks stacked to cool.

"Greetings," Lofn said.

Bera looked up in shock. "Good day, lady," she replied flatly.

"Valdir lets oathed secrets fly like the sparks on his forge," Lofn said. Bera turned red.

"He said you have the ability to do certain things." She bit her lip in hesitation. "This from an old warrior that's seen many lands and oddities in his travels. He's frightened from what he saw, but the dolt never did understand women."

"Aurdr's baby, Austri, was still."

"That he said."

"Aurdr was going to die."

Bera went to a rack next to the oven where a regular-sized loaf of bread cooled. This one was golden and soft.

"This was for the Tower and their men that watch over the village," the baker said. She extended the loaf to Lofn, "but I think it would be a proper gift to you."

Lofn stared at the fragrant bread then shook her head. "I can't accept this."

"This isn't a gift, my lady. It's my plea. My grandmother had her magics. I ask you ... beg you, heal the fields like you did that sweet baby."

Bera's tears swiftly flowed. As other customers strolled in, she hid the loaf and wiped her eyes. Lofn stepped back. The customers looked at the small rock-like bread on the serving racks, turned, and left without so much as a greeting.

"Gods, we are doomed," Bera said.

"Magic is outlawed. I only know how to help in births. For the crops to come back would announce to the Magistrate that magic lives here. That is far beyond what I can do."

"You know enough, and we will die without food." Bera slammed her fists onto the tabletop.

"Not so loud, Bera. The Magistrate would come. Hope that the Tower will help."

"Mayor Blanchfield said that wasn't an option. We're on our own."

Lofn spread her hands helplessly. "I don't know what to do."

Bera leaned over the counter. "Magic came naturally to my grandmother. She listened to the land and did as the nature gods instructed."

Lofn sighed. "Have you told anyone else what Valdir saw?"

"No, my lady."

The way that the true-believers glared at her said otherwise.

"Keep your bread, Bera. Send it to the Tower and hope that it brings us relief."

Lofn left the bakery. She understood natural magic, but something of this scale could kill her. There were other magics practiced, shuttered from the outside intrusion, but not this.

Something like this would bring the Magistratus and the full power of the Magistrate. They burned people alive for this, although the church used their magic with impunity on the open battlefield and within its walls. Without this miracle though, the villagers would die.

Lofn told Della she was unwell and needed to rest. She pleaded for her not to visit. Then spent three days locked away in her house in preparation for this night. Burning herbs filled the atmosphere and empty potion bottles littered the floor. Heat built in the cottage, pushing away the cold that threatened outside.

The heavy trance didn't allow for communication if the magistrate's knights stormed in, but the trance was the only thing that revealed the way. She removed her clothes and dug into the earthen floor. The earth accepted her, and she fell harder into the otherworld.

Shadows crept into the cottage, throwing images of Elta's murdered witches onto the walls. Voices screamed in their tormented agony and then fell away. A whisper interrupted her state at the twilight between unconsciousness and death. The lantern cast shadowed messages throughout the cottage. In a stupor, she crawled to it, fumbling to interpret the strange meanings.

Her hand burned as it brushed against one of the symbols. A transfer of energy like Della had given her but hundreds of times more powerful. This animus arose from the ancients. She stumbled through the house trying to flee the fire in her veins. A multitude of voices commanded her in languages she didn't understand until an elder crone's voice stood out among the concert. The elder's voice stood out, so high-pitched and weak that the other voices quieted out of reverence. As she instructed,

Lofn's nails scratched runes in the dirt. As she completed one magical circle, another voice became translatable.

She completed the words, overlapping circles and runes. She translated the seventh runic circle and stood, shockingly sober and aware of her surroundings. A strange wind blew through her cottage erasing the herbs in the air and the runes carved in the dirt. Lofn's heart pounded as the wind whistled through the shuttered windows. A single thought echoed in her mind.

Outside.

She grabbed her heavy boots and fur-lined cloak to cover her nakedness as she stepped from the house. Light from the full moon rose above the Witches Forest and gave a cold white surrealness to the landscape. Something moved within the rows of dead bent-over cornstalks. Lofn shuttered the lantern and stepped inside, locking her door, afraid of what she had summoned.

CHAPTER 6

Overseer Daniels droned about faith and the Allfather during the service. Lofn hung her head. She didn't sleep after last night's rite. Her head throbbed, hungover from potions and herbs. Even though the smell of the herbs had left her cottage, they marked her this morning. The cold morning's bath hadn't washed it away, and stares needled her at Shrinehall. Valdir and Bera were absent, but now others in the mass watched. Overseer Daniels stopped the sermon, and the villagers met his gaze hesitantly.

"Let us pray," he intoned. "Asagrim, give us the knowledge to make it through the dark season, help us ration our supplies, and fill our empty bellies."

Her stomach raged in anger like the burning corpses of the storm dead. Lofn stood before Overseer Daniels continued.

"What can Asagrim do for us?" she challenged. "Ease the starvation? Stop our sorrow as we watch family die?" Lofn walked out from behind the pew and pointed at the opulent robed figure. "You stand there well fed from the White Citadel magic, but you refuse to pass this power onto the village you serve? These are your people, Overseer, and they will die all around you while you do nothing more than watch from your gilded perch telling us how we need to pray harder to the Allfather." She cast an outstretched arm toward the statue. "Or are we meaningless in the eyes of Asagrim?"

Overseer Daniels arched an eyebrow and stared at her. His answer was monotonous.

"The Citadel supplies their war-burdened with food. I have contacted them for help, but there is nothing they can do. The Allfather's strength barely sustains his followers."

"Then beg," she commanded. "State how our grain stores are not enough. We've marked horses and oxen we need for butcher. Ragnfast has added so much sawdust and bonemeal to stretch the remaining meat, it's inedible. The local game that's found is lame or diseased." The villagers stared at her in awe. Lofn continued, "We are trapped here by the Allfather's accursed Delirium Forest. We cannot leave. Tell the White Citadel that their tributes from Elta will dry up, and their prized Shrinehall will surround a graveyard."

Overseer Daniel's mouth pressed into a thin line of silence.

Lofn approached the statue.

"Asagrim, hear my words. Fill the fields and bring back the game, or stand aside and let us find a god who can." She turned and stared hard into Overseer Daniel's eyes. "This I demand."

Lofn stormed out of Shrinehall as the shouts and arguments erupted. Overseer Daniels yelled for order as his staff slammed into Shrinehall's floor and echoed throughout Elta like a magistrate's gavel sentencing death. The arguments persisted and flared.

Lofn descended Shrinehall and sprinted to her house. A basket sat on her front porch. She hesitated, grabbed it, and entered. The blanket covering the basket hid food and goods with a note from Bera:

Help us.

She grabbed potions, a waterskin, and slid on heavier clothes. The heavy cloak covered her walking staff and short sword. The Tower's knights would hunt her soon. She gazed at her short sword and decided against certain death. She was no fighter.

Outside the arguments intensified. Villagers were hungry and tired of the passiveness of Asagrim's true-believers. She exited the back of the house, daring one last glance.

Herrick huffed up to Shrinehall as people stood waving their arms and launching accusations at each other. A few people traded blows, but Overseer Daniels had fled. Horns sounded from the Tower.

"Gods, why did I speak up," Lofn wondered aloud. She looked around to make sure the overseer didn't ready a spell to blow her into the next world.

She snuck down the hill, running between houses and down into the empty valley. She glanced behind to make sure no one followed. The southern Witches Forest, that people were too superstitious to enter, stood a brief run ahead.

There were tales of witches and fay folk that inhabited the haunted woods, but wasn't that what she was? A witch? A midwife that dared use a little power to save a dying baby, tried to save her village, and stood up to an overseer? What would a place of monsters and old crones be compared to a village where the knights searched to add her to the kindling? Survival in the Delirium Forest was impossible without the Tower's or White Citadel's magic. The Witches Forest seemed almost inviting. Wasn't that what she was now? A witch?

The dead crops surrounded her, and the smell of rot sat heavy. *Lofn, get down.*

She dove into the stalks and covered herself with her cloak, wondering where the deep voice came from. The earth rumbled as knights galloped down a nearby path before she peeked out to see them ride away. The Tower wanted her now.

Something glimmered out in the Witches Forest, a small blue beacon that summoned her. *Come, child. Let us welcome you, for we have watched you.*

With no hunters or knights in sight, she rushed forward. The forest covered her like an awaiting lover on a cold morning.

CHAPTER 7

A couple of weeks had passed since Lofn disappeared and Shrinehall descended into chaos. Lofn was now wanted by the Tower. Arguments between Asagrim's true-believers and the villagers intensified until fights broke out in the streets. The knights announced and enforced a curfew since Overseer Daniels had fled to the White Citadel. The people openly debated Overseer Daniel's abandoning his starving people. Others insisted he sought help for a starving populace. All the while the knights threatened order and kept a sharp eye on Lofn's house. Della answered the heavy knock at the door.

"Lady Della, is the mayor in?" Kordan stood in a heavy cloak with a cart full of freshly killed deer, grinning from ear to ear.

Herrick came up beside his wife in shock.

"Kordan, how?"

"I don't know, Mayor Blanchfield. Maybe Asagrim heard Lofn and thought her sermon was better than the overseer's."

"Lofn's done more for this village than …" Herrick squeezed his wife's shoulder before she committed heresy.

Kordan glanced at her and laughed. "Herds are standing around just waiting to die. We came to drop this off to Ragnfast and call out all hunters. Game is at hand, and we are saved."

"Ragnfast will be pleased. I'll gather the folk," Herrick said while collecting his cloak and bow.

He ran out the door and went house to house. One of the hunters tossed him the hunter's horn. Herrick blew three quick notes and ran off to join the others. The villagers ran from their homes, cloaks, and weapons in hand as they rushed toward the Witches Forest.

Della sent Allistril over to Aurdr's and hiked toward Shrinehall. An ogrish form in plate armor loomed near, but his attention focused on the forest. Sir Solveig stood near Lofn's house but paid little care. Della didn't want to stoke the brute's anger being so close. The brief afternoon twilight gave ample shadows to hide in. She crept farther down the hill, staying vigilant as she approached, not wanting to deal with Sir Solveig's infamous anger. Truth be told, he was a dullard, although a brutish dullard. He did not notice if she was careful. Near Lofn's house, notes were posted announcing a reward for her capture.

Della snuck around deeper into the shadows and watched the edges of the fields. The wild game stood bewitched. The local hunters stopped wasting arrows and simply walked from animal to animal, slitting their throats. When the call went out that there was too much meat, they walked them into enclosures. Even with the protests of those nearby to stop killing. It didn't take long for Sir Solveig and his great sword to whack the head off a deer.

Della watched disgusted.

A warrior without a war is a terrible thing. Too bad the front lines didn't call you, Solveig.

She glanced around before approaching Lofn's back door. In the distance, the dead fields appeared to be coming back, greening up, the stalks tried to stand like exhausted knights at attention. Della peered around to see if anyone noticed her before slipping into Lofn's cottage. She stood in the stillness of the house, keenly aware of another's presence.

"Lofn?" Della whispered into the gloom.

She pulled a small knife from her belt and prowled the rest of the home to find Lofn, exhausted and dirty in her bed. Della scanned the house, removed Lofn's mud-encrusted boots, and covered her with a thick blanket. Then with knife bared in the dark of the house, Della set on the bedside and waited.

CHAPTER 8

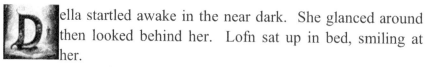ella startled awake in the near dark. She glanced around then looked behind her. Lofn sat up in bed, smiling at her.

"My protector." Lofn reached out touching Della's shoulder.

A spark leaped from her finger before Della felt the shock. It paused her before she spoke. "Are you crazy coming back here?" Della tried to control her anger as she whispered.

Lofn fell back into bed. "How long have I been gone?" She stretched out on the bed almost kicking Della.

"Two weeks since you sent Shrinehall into chaos."

"Gods. Only a couple weeks?" Lofn bolted upright.

Della arched an eyebrow. "Were you not aware of sunrise and sundown? Where did you go?"

Lofn face stilled and darkened. "What has happened?"

"Overseer Daniels has fled to the White Citadel. The knights are everywhere and going through the village looking for you. You are wanted. There should be a guard outside, but Sir Solveig walked out to the edge of the forest."

"Has anything ... changed?"

"Are you responsible for this? Gods, Lofn. You will bring the magistrate to Elta."

"What happened?"

"We hunted and couldn't find anything. Now the herds are standing on the village's edge.

Thunder rumbled in the distance. Lofn closed her eyes and relaxed.

"What is happening?" Della asked.

Lofn opened her eyes and stared off into space. "The less you know at this point, the less in danger you are. I will return to the forest."

Della felt the blood drain from her face. "Oh, let the trolls take you. You were in the Witches Forest? Gods. You went to the Witches Forest?"

Something leaned heavily against the door. Both women stared at each other, only broken when Lofn slid from the bed and pointed to the back door. They silently crawled for it.

Lofn stood grasping the handle as Della slapped her hand.

"Did you bring anything back? Do I need to worry that you're something from the forest?"

Lofn embraced her. "It's me, sister. I want to see Allistril and Herrick more than anything. You are my family. You are my home. What I did was to protect you, and I feel I've been lost for so much more than one week."

Della pulled her key and held it to Lofn's arm.

"Did you just Iron-truth me?"

Della pulled the key away and looked at Lofn's skin. "Before I take you to my family, you better believe it.

"I'm not a fay—"

The front door opened, and the beheaded carcass of a deer flopped through the door. Both Lofn and Della were outside before they saw who brought it in.

"I don't want to put you in danger," Lofn whispered.

"We're all in danger," Della said as she moved past the house. Thunder rumbled close by. A cold gentle rain fell.

The villagers stood outside their houses, staring at the carcasses as the hunters brought them in. Della walked calmly in the open checking to see if anyone was watching as Lofn sprinted from house to house behind her. Soon they entered through the back of Della's office connected to her house. Quietly, Della snuck ahead to make sure they didn't have company. Allistril sat at the table drawing.

"You're supposed to be at Aurdr's," Della said.

"She was busy with the baby," Allistril replied. She half glanced up at Della, recognizing the figure hiding behind her. Allistril's shrills of Lofn's name made their blood run cold.

Allistril ran to Lofn and hugged her.

"We must be silent, firehead. The knights are looking for me," Lofn said before giving Allistril a strong hug and a kiss on the forehead.

They went upstairs into the sleeping quarters, then climbed into the attic.

"There is a mattress over there on the boards until we figure out what we're going to do with you." Della walked over to the window and looked down. "Allistril, stay here with Lofn until I get back. I'm going to find your father and get this figured out."

Herrick converged a meeting of the Thing later that evening. The usual conference of village elders and businessmen met at Shrinehall to discuss goings on in the village, but this was different. They met to discuss whether to protect Lofn or let the Tower have her. Some of the true-believers were refusing the meat. Herrick needed the discussion and stood along the edge peering down at the knights patrolling Elta. They had almost refused this meeting and went house to house collecting the meat unsure of its origin.

Will we die of starvation or by the hands of the Tower?

Herrick stayed deep in thought, then looked around, counted those at the table, and smacked a small hammer onto the surface.

"Has the witch been captured?" Orn asked, one of the village elders and a true-believer.

"Witch?" The word caught Herrick off guard. Wild game surrounded the city. The crops had greened. Their grain looked ready to harvest. They were saved. "You called her a witch?" Herrick fell into his chair.

"This is not natural, Mayor. Her words caused a riot at Shrinehall that the knights had to put down. Then she disappeared. The crops came back, and animals stand bewitched waiting to be slaughtered," Orn said, arms crossed as he finished speaking. "She is a witch."

"I don't think Asagrim did that," Ragnfast said. "Asagrim hasn't done much in my lifetime."

"Praise Asagrim that I am upwind of you, Ragnfast," Valdir said.

"Oh, may the trolls take you, and that stench came from Scraps," Ragnfast snapped and reached under the table to pet his dog.

Herrick slapped the table to bring order. "Maybe the Tower came through and did … something?"

Several chuckled around the table.

"Overseer Daniels is at the White Citadel."

"Then maybe I should ask old Asagrim for my own kingdom," Ragnfast added.

Valdir flinched from the comment. He stood, then sat glaring at his friend, the butcher.

"Raven starver," Valdir called under his breath.

Herrick held up his hands before another fight erupted among Shrinehall's walls. "The question at hand, elders and businessmen, is what we can do?"

"The meat is good. I've checked everything butchered," Ragnfast stated. "All this food surrounding us, we would be idiots to starve and watch it rot. Someone needs to take over the dead farmer's fields so we can harvest. We need to release the meat in storage to the people."

Valdir nodded at Ragnfast's words. "I believe in Asagrim, no matter what my idiot friend here says to provoke me. I want to eat and believe this is his miracle." Valdir looked up at the statue and sighed. "Asagrim has changed since the storm. He no longer points to the sunrise, but at the very fields themselves."

"Who cares what caused the miracle?" Ragnfast interrupted.

"I care, Ragnfast." Valdir smacked the table which brought out a low growl from Scraps. "I care, as do many of the elders here. The true-believers, I've heard you call us that when you don't think we're paying attention. My friends, Elta was founded for the believers of Asagrim and a southern outpost of the Allfather. We are his distant children here, like it or not."

Several conversations broke out as Herrick tried to maintain order.

"I will not eat that which is ill-gotten gains," Orn stood. "I am a religious man. I'm not changing that in the winter of my life. Lofn is a witch, and she used dark arts to bring this about. Please keep this new meat and grain separate from anything left over from before this … miracle."

"There is not much left but a horse that we slaughtered. However, that meat is aging rapidly. In a week, we will have nothing," Ragnfast said before adding, "We have one more horse and an ox, but we need the ox for the fields."

"I will not eat sacred horse flesh," Orn said

"Then starve," Ragnfast spat.

Several of the men chuckled as Orn stood and walked to the statue. He touched Asagrim's foot and paused. "Mark my words, you heathens. The witch will bring nothing but pain to you and your families."

Ragnfast laughed. Orn went to the stairs and left.

"This is a village that once faithfully worshipped Asagrim. Yet now we sit at His table and mock Him?" Gaut, the other elder at the table and patriarch of one of the largest families in Elta, released a shuddering breath. Lines etched his face like old, weathered markings on tree bark. He was the eldest of the village by fifteen winters. Some thought this coming winter was his last, while others were convinced the man would never die. "What Lofn did upset the way of

things … of nature itself. Magic is outlawed for a reason.

Overseer Daniels might return with an army seeking her capture and what are we going to do? Stand in their way with full bellies waiting to be sliced open by a knight's sword? Isn't that what this meeting's about, Mayor?"

"No," Herrick begged. "Orn protested the food's origin. I fear others might follow his lead, so I am here to know the will of the village. We can either trust what has occurred or starve."

"Orn's left. With him out of earshot, are you proposing we move against the church?" Valdir asked.

Gaut laughed at the ridiculous question.

"Gods, no," Herrick answered. "How could we in the outer territories survive? We are alone, and they would burn us to the ground."

"Then what do you purpose, Mayor?" Gaut wheezed.

"That we address this matter to the Tower. If they refuse, we take it to the White Citadel."

"Politics. The Tower has a death warrant on any witch or wizard that is not their own," Ragnfast said. "I've seen many placed on the pyre over my life. Some only because they went against the Tower's will."

"How will you get a message to the White Citadel if the Tower says no? Go through the Delirium Forest?

Herrick shrank back a little in his chair. "I don't know. I hope to have this matter resolved and the entire thing based on a miracle of Asagrim."

"Asagrim's Miracle?" Ragnfast asked.

"That gives Overseer Daniels some clout," Gaut said.

"Otherwise, we can hold the yearly council, rule Lofn head of the council, and hope the Tower and White Citadel recognizes that harming her goes against the will of the people," Herrick said. "If that even matters."

"A pardon from burning that lasts a year," Valdir said.

Ragnfast shook his head. "Or the ashes of a village we once called home."

CHAPTER 9

The morning's weak light bathed the large cold iron gate in reds, oranges, and gold. Once strong enough to withstand a giant attack, it now held back a meek politician. Already he'd waited for some time since his knock. Then he pounded on the door seeking some response other than his echo mocking him. The Tower stood silent.

Hours passed until the late fall sun blinked above Mount Hati for the last time that year, briefly stopping the chill of oncoming winter. This was why the elders had named the mountain Hati, after the mythic wolf that chased and devoured the sun at the end of the world. Mount Hati cruelly swallowed the sun during the coming winter months. Herrick took a deep breath and let the rays hit his skin, before it disappeared, just like his hopes to talk to the knights. He looked below to the busy town's square where Elta came out to watch its final peak.

He tired of a morning of complete inaction and a heavy gut of fear. Several scenarios played out in Herrick's mind, each one not ending well for Elta, Lofn, or his family. He was not a brave man. He'd never pulled a sword in anger and only killed during a hunt. He'd tried to defend a few from the pyre after the overseer laid down his law, but the Tower always overruled him. He knocked one last time.

"Raven starver," Herrick said it out loud. It was an insult that Valdir had issued at Ragnfast, but it also cut Herrick to the bone because he was no warrior and would never be. His discussion could not lead to war.

He stepped away from the gates and stared at the villagers below. So much to lose. So much to lose quickly. Had he built much of anything during his time as mayor? The people stirred among the vendors, but as the crowds began to shift, in the center of the square stood Overseer Daniels next to a large pile on the ground.

"People of Elta, you have been warned." The overseer's voice boomed across the valley. "The Shrinehall is not a place for children to play." The overseer knocked his staff against the cobblestone and suddenly disappeared.

Herrick's blood ran cold. His daughter had been home asleep when he'd left in the dark hours before morning.

Something moved behind the gate. A horse? Was it armor? He stepped forward and pounded the gate again.

"Stand clear the gate!" someone yelled.

The heavy iron gate swung open, knocking Herrick out of the way. The four Tower knights exited and surrounded Herrick as he stood up and dusted himself off.

"I have business with the Tower," he cried. "I demand a council with Overseer Daniels."

Once again, silence. Two knights watched him while the others went into a defensive stance around the gate.

"I demand a council with Overseer Daniels!" Herrick repeated as the knights went to their swords.

"I am here, Mayor. What can the Tower do for you today?"

Overseer Daniels emerged from the gate. His eyes also looked over Elta, tracking down to the pile that one of the shop owners approached cautiously. Steiner, the stonemason, poked the pile, then dropped to his knees and pulled a small child from it.

A splash of red hair stuck out of wrappings.

"Allistril?" The words fell out of Herrick's mouth.

"No, not your fireheaded daughter … not this time," Overseer Daniels replied.

Herrick stared at the knights that watched him. "Let me go."

"Not yet. There is a lesson here, Herrick."

Steiner called out as other shopkeepers surrounded him. One shopkeeper ran off, then another. In moments, Della appeared and pulled back the rags that covered the child. Herrick saw the redden cut skin that covered the child's back.

"Is that Jahan? Ivanar's son?" Herrick asked.

He squinted to see a flash of red hair run out of the village boundary from his quest to find Nol, rage quickened Ivanar's pace, his skin matching the fire color of his top-knotted hair.

"This will not bode well with the villagers," Overseer Daniels pointed to the butcher shop. Valdir stood in front of Ragnfast as he fought to approach the village's square. Herrick heard his bellows from the Tower.

"Soldiers, protect the Tower." Overseer Daniels gave the order as calmly as if he'd told them to accompany him on a ride through the village.

Several crossbows creaked around Herrick as they were drawn. Heavy bolts slipped to rest on the crossbow string, bolts capable of going through full plate armor. The four knights pointed at the crowd gathered below and waited for the overseer's command.

"Jahan!" Herrick yelled.

The boy was one of Allistril's playmates and the only other fire-headed child in the village. Ragnfast's nephew began to squirm and scream.

Della stopped working on the boy and glared toward the Tower. Herrick didn't know if she had seen him there or not. She yelled to Ivanar and Ragnfast as they approached, and they quickly shielded her and the boy.

"An armed rebellion? Will you and your people march against the Tower, Mayor Herrick Blanchfield?"

"No, that isn't what we discussed."

"You called the Thing and met with a group from the village last eve in Shrinehall. What did you discuss?"

"The miracle."

The overseer snorted. "The witch's grain and meat?"

"We are starving, Overseer Daniels. A hungry belly doesn't care if it's fed by a farmer, or by Asagrim's grace. Even His statue points to the fields now."

"A signal that witchcraft has occurred."

"What if this is a blessing?" Herrick implored. "A true blessing of the Allfather who heard the prayers of his followers."

Overseer Daniels walked forward and looked about. Herrick stepped up, but two knights quickly grabbed him and threw him to the ground.

"Your wife is staring up at us, Herrick. What do you suppose she is thinking?"

"She hopes that you let her treat the child. She is the healer."

"Ivanar and Ragnfast are protecting her and the child. With two bolts, I eliminate the majority of those who speak against Asagrim's rule. With a third, I may eliminate them all."

"You would start a rebellion against the Tower, Overseer Daniels."

"Give me names …"

"No. I'll give you a simple offer."

The overseer stood next to the knight and checked his aim. "Your wife is at the end of this bolt flight."

Herrick's pulse thundered in his ears as he stared at his wife, Ragnfast, and Ivanar below. He swallowed hard, then cleared his throat. He cautiously stood. "Let us eat. Call this Asagrim's gift.

Make those who are starving believe again."

"And the witch that is at your home?"

He stared and no words formed on his lips.

"Yes, Herrick. We know she is with you."

"Let her live." His voice sounded weak in his own ears.

"If we go to your home and burn it to the ground, what will you do if your precious daughter is inside?"

"I know you want me to follow Asagrim. I will openly pledge myself to his rule and follow the will of the Tower. Just don't harm my family."

Overseer Daniels looked back down into the valley at the village square. "Any dissent will be dealt with swiftly by the hand of the Allfather."

"Agreed." Herrick took a deep breath and steeled himself. "And Lofn?"

"Excommunicated from Shrinehall at the least. If she dares enter, she will be cast out of Elta." The overseer bent close. "Or I make you responsible for lighting the pyre that cleanses her from this world."

Overseer Daniels flicked his hand, and the knights pulled up their crossbows. They marched to the gate entrance.

"Make sure I am understood, Herrick. Any dissent will be crushed. If I find you or your wife in any part of it, I will personally burn you and your family as well as the witch. Come tomorrow at daybreak and we will discuss Lofn's survival."

Overseer Daniels turned and disappeared inside the gate without another look. Herrick stared down below. Della held Jahan. Then with a quick nod, ran along the street toward her office with Ragnfast and Ivanar close behind.

CHAPTER 10

Della dressed the final wound on Jahan. The boy's groans visibly agitated his father. Ivanar reacted as if her very touch tore into his spine.

"Why is Mayor Blanchfield talking with the overseer?" he asked, voice rising against the cramped office.

"Did you see his knights?" Della asked, wiping the ointment from her hands. "Did you see them aiming at us through their crossbows? Ready to shoot us like dogs in the village square."

"It would have started the uprising."

"It wouldn't. Overseer Daniels knew his audience and in a show of force, put down the two biggest idiots that have ranted against the Tower."

"Are you saying no one would fight for us?" Ivanar asked.

"No, I'm saying it was the exact response they were looking for."

Ivanar stretched back and stared out the window. "Has the poison been made?"

Della sighed. "It's made. It's not yet been tested, but I'm convinced it will work."

Ivanar looked at his brother. "Do you still have the stash of meat for the knights?"

Ragnfast nodded. "It's awfully suspicious, but the normal meat is almost gone. The roast will be in one of their last deliveries.

"Then all is ready to begin."

Herrick entered the house and placed his coat on the hook. He walked over to Allistril and gave her a long hug.

"You're home early," she said.

Herrick clung to his little one, unable to speak after all that he'd just witnessed.

"Daddy, is everything okay?"

He kissed her head several times, then held her for a couple heartbeats longer. "Go upstairs, Allistril. I'll call you down later."

He smiled broadly as Allistril climbed the stairs. When she disappeared, he let the mask shatter as he fell into his chair. He closed his eyes and sat there for several moments, replaying in his mind the knights aiming crossbows at his wife.

"What happened?"

Herrick opened his eyes to see Lofn descend.

"Herrick?"

He allowed the issues of the day to finally defeat him as he hung his head. "Gods, Lofn," he sobbed.

She approached and knelt in front of him. "What happened?"

He nodded. "Jahan was found in Shrinehall playing alone. The overseer dropped him off in the village square ... after they lashed him, of course."

Lofn sucked in a breath.

"Jahan, Ragnfast's nephew. He is only six ... Allistril's age. They whipped him simply for playing."

"May Asagrim show his wrath," Lofn spat. "I delivered that child."

"Della has him at the office."

"I have stayed here too long and put this village in jeopardy."

"Lofn, no. Please don't say that." Herrick rose. "I met with Overseer Daniels at the Tower today after waiting at the gate. This was his reaction to the Thing last night. We spoke about protecting you, and revolution was mentioned more than once." Herrick leaned over the table, tears clouding his vision. "A rather short-lived revolution, I'm afraid."

Sobs wracked his breathing.

"I will leave, Herrick. There is no point in putting you and Della at risk any longer."

"No." Herrick snorted. "We're all at risk just being in Elta. I only wanted to approach Overseer Daniels on several topics. We've been at odds for too long, and it's time to come to peace."

Lofn frowned and shook her head. "Overseer Daniels won't be at peace until another incompetent *skreyja* sits in the mayor's office."

"Did you bring the crops and animals back, Lofn?" Herrick asked.

Her eyes widened, and she retreated a step.

Herrick nodded, "Thank you."

"Herrick, I—"

"There is brewing anger toward the Tower and White Citadel for refusing to help after the hailstorm. If we don't find some way to appease them, we all may perish. By hunger, by sword blade, or just by our stupidity."

"The Overseer—"

"The Overseer's been to my office complaining of Allistril playing in Shrinehall. He's marked her. At least he came to me about it first instead of flaying the skin off her back." He shuddered. "I thought it was her at the village square. I don't want to look out my office window and see her thrown down because I didn't act. If anything, you saved this village. So, no more of this talk of walking into the wilderness, please."

Della entered the house from the kitchen that connected to her office. When she came around the corner, she stared at Herrick with fury and sadness. Words were unnecessary as they embraced.

"I'm sorry, Della."

"Sorry about what?" Lofn asked.

Della lifted her head from Herrick's shoulder. "The four

soldiers at the Tower this morning. They aimed crossbows at me as I shielded the boy they'd flayed."

CHAPTER 11

Lofn woke in the morning, alone in the Blanchfield attic. The leaden press of exhaustion hung on as if she hadn't slept. She had in fitful moments, then slight panic woke her up several times. Groans from the house settling as colder weather set in unnerved her. An occasional pop made her sit up in bed thinking a knight was at the door.

The spirit of conversation and arguments went through her head as she woke up. The debate went late into the night with Della and Herrick, sometimes heated while other times it was just Herrick holding them both telling them everything would be okay. Lofn finally dozed off for a moment when her thoughts went silent.

She woke when the door clicked downstairs. Looking in the bedroom below, Della and Allistril slept in bed, but Herrick was missing. He left before anyone else rose to beg the Tower for her survival. She hated hiding out in this sanctuary and putting the Blanchfields at risk. If it was the Citadel's all-powerful will to put mages and witches to death, then so be it. Let the overseer's hands wash in *her* blood, not the blood of the family protecting her or the fields that guaranteed their survival through the winter.

The Blanchfields had risked much protecting her. Although Herrick had a vocal promise from the overseer that Lofn would survive, the Tower knew where she was. Even after they argued last night, they huddled upstairs, waiting for the magistrate to appear in force. Even Allistril took watch at the windows, waiting for the knights to storm the house, but they never came. Herrick approached the Tower to argue for Lofn's life from the same people that had Della in their crossbow sights yesterday.

Lofn sat up in bed. The simple action spun the room. She leaned forward to find something to focus on. She tried to blame it on the time shift from the woods. Ultimately, she knew what it was, and the lack of her monthly course confirmed her fears. A rabbit might be trapped to complete the prediction, but continuing nausea told the story. How much time had she spent in the forest? It wasn't weeks, it felt like years.

She centered herself and the nausea stopped. Soon Della and Allistril were up and cooking breakfast. Lofn went down to join them in easy smiles and simple conversation. Nothing prodded the argument from last night. Lofn worried about how much Allistril heard and how much she worried. After a hurried breakfast, she rushed upstairs to her attic hiding spot to retch and barely found a chamber pot in time. Della followed, and Lofn realized this was no longer a personal secret.

"How?" Della asked.

"You're a healer and a mother, you know how it happens."

"That's not what I meant. You were gone for a week?"

"To you, I was gone a week. To me, I thought it had been at least a season."

It was late before Herrick reappeared. His shoulders fell heavy with the message he carried, and bloodshot eyes only stared at his chair. He mumbled pleasantries to the family and warmed himself with the night's fire.

"Lofn?" His gaze locked on the fire for too long.

Lofn approached. Herrick took her hands, they were cold like an old ice giant.

"You are no longer wanted by the Tower. You are free. There will be no sentence."

"Gods, how?"

His gaze finally rested on her. "Overseer and I came to some agreements on local matters. There is one problem."

Gods, Herrick. What did they do to you? "Problem?" She finally asked.

Herrick paused. "You are banned from attending Shrinehall."

"What?"

"You are to be cast out from the church, but you may remain in the village."

A knock on the door stopped them from talking further. When Herrick answered, Ragnfast appeared surprised. He entered with a slight limp. One eye was swollen shut, and he moved carefully.

"I thought you would still be at the Tower, Mayor."

"What happened, Ragnfast?" Della asked, moving quickly to Ragnfast's side.

"I got a little wordy with the knights after Jahan was found. This was their answer." Ragnfast motioned to his bruised face. "They almost killed Scraps while trying to protect me. They jailed me. It was a long night in the Tower until Sir Hakon approached me and said that the mayor freed me." He glanced at Della and Lofn then lowered his head. "I talk like a great warrior to the knights. Like I could take them on in combat. But Jahan's treatment angered me, and I went after them like a drunken fool. I wanted to thank you, Mayor. No telling what would have happened if I had been there much longer."

He shook Herrick's hand and glanced at Della.

"Let me check your bruises and make sure nothing is broken," Della said.

"No, I'm fine, just a little sore. I need to get back to the shop and see to Scraps. They took the last of my regular meat stores last night. It wasn't much … just a roast. Now, it will be the remaining horse and oxen, then we have to eat the new meat."

"They took a roast?" Della questioned.

"Of course, they wouldn't touch the new meat until someone else ate from it."

"Go prepare the new meat, Ragnfast. We have a holiday coming soon enough," Herrick said.

"Thank you again. Valdir will help me lift the animals to the butcher block."

He turned and left. Herrick sighed after the door shut.

"He was arrested last night after bawling out a knight. Rumor was that Kordan had Ivanar searching for Nol all night to keep him busy. Ragnfast was with him earlier but snuck out."

"You wagered our freedom for a pat on the head from the overseer?" Della's outrage seethed under the surface of her words. "We still have bolts aimed at us."

"I wagered to save Lofn from the pyre," Herrick replied.

CHAPTER 12

Several days passed in hunger because the overseer wanted to hold the Deep Winter rite before releasing the new meat. Lofn had gone back to her house, and they spent the days trying to conserve their energy. Light disappeared a little more from the waning sky and bed came earlier. Sleep slightly comforted their roaring bellies.

Della woke several times that night listening in the dark for Lofn and remembering that she went home. Then she laid in bed waiting, too tired and hungry to move. She heard something faint at first and set up in bed.

The Tower warning bells clanged to life in the middle of the night. She reached over to Herrick when a heavy knock sounded on the door downstairs. Herrick stirred but didn't move. The knock reverberated through the house.

"We need the healer," someone shouted from outside.

"Mommy?" Allistril whispered.

"Stay here." Della got up, lit a candle, then put on her robe. Half-awake, she maneuvered down the stairs to open the door. A gloved hand reached in and forced it open.

"Mistress Blanchfield, I need you at the Tower."

"One moment." Della shrank back as Sir Hakon pushed the door open.

"Now." He demanded as he entered the house, grabbing her arm. "We have two men down at the Tower."

Della pushed his hand away. "I need my potions and ointments."

She grabbed a small packet of herbs as Sir Hakon grabbed her by the waist and had her to the door before she protested.

"I need my things! Allistril, wake your father!"

Outside Sir Hakon lifted Della on the horse, then mounted. "We have potions there." He sped off into the night with her trapped in front. She looked back to see Herrick staring out the window.

Della demanded answers from Sir Hakon, but he was too focused on the road, too focused on getting to the Tower as fast as possible. Up the hill they flew. She held on tightly around the curves to keep from flying off the horse. On the top of the hill, the iron gate that kept Herrick at bay previously stood wide open. They came to a halt by the entrance to the Grand Tower. Sir Hakon vaulted from the horse and hauled Della from it. He pulled her toward the Tower with the tension of a child showing a hesitant parent a terrible thing.

They passed the main gate into the stable area. The Tower stood before them. Della tried to focus, but the hunger and tiredness blocked her. As they drew closer, the battlements came into view.

"What is this? What is going on, Sir Hakon?"

Della tried to take it in. Most village folk that entered this part of the Tower were rarely seen again. They entered large ornate metal-crafted doors that glowed with their magics. Tapestry and statues filled the main hall with stories of war and heroes frozen in marble and brass effigies. Their remains entombed under the base that held the statues. She tried to remember the story of the tapestries as Sir Hakon moved her past. They entered the great hall with its roaring fireplace. Magical daylight flooded through the false windows, showing a daylight view of the village below. They walked into the main hall of the Tower. The scent of fresh-stewed meat stopped Della in her tracks.

"Gods, you have food?" Della asked.

Hakon removed his helm. He looked younger in his panic than his twenty-some winters.

"Something is wrong with it. The knights went down after they ate it."

Della did her best to hide her guilt. "Asagrim's blessing. When did the knights start eating again?" The Allfather's blessing made it to where his knights and servants never had to eat or drink, unless his power was no more.

Sir Hakon watched her, almost as if he silently asked the Allfather for permission. "Do not take my words beyond this room … under pain of death."

Della nodded.

"The Allfather's power is waning," he whispered. "The butcher has been holding aside meat for the Tower. We have to eat and drink now as well for the Allfather's power no longer sustains us."

"You took from us all while the village was starving?"

Sir Hakon led her around the tables near the fire. "This is our payment for it."

Two knights lay on the carpet dressed only in their tunics, almost nude in appearance without their armor. Their bodies lay contorted, clawed hands reaching out for some unknown and unseen salvation.

Even with two people before her in obvious need of medical attention, her head swam with the savory scent of cooked meat. Her hunger held her in place.

"Della Blanchfield, treat them!"

Della came out of her meat trance and looked around the room. The grand hall was empty save for them. "Where is Overseer Daniels?"

"He was called again to the White Citadel. I'm here alone with them. Sir Solveig and Wagonmaster Thron went with him."

Della sensed panic in the words. She glanced down at Sir Torstein, a knight with a usually heavy hand. Foam dripped from his mouth. His wide, angry eyes stared into nothing. She diagnosed that the poison used worked perfectly.

She moved cautiously through her examination. She had

talked to Ragnfast about several excuses. The easiest was spoiled meat and the symptoms of the worst type of food poisoning. The healer in her knew that the reaction would not be as severe, but the overseers usually didn't deal in diagnosis. Their glut of healing spells immediately cured and allowed the injured back into battle. They didn't care about cause.

Della removed a potion and poured the contents into Sir Torstein's mouth. It washed the foam away, but the knight did not swallow. Della touched his neck and felt around for a pulse. There was nothing.

"Sir Torstein's life has passed into the arms of Asagrim. He will sit at his table tonight. I am sorry."

"That is not possible," Sir Hakon shouted. He backed up as if to hit her then stumbled in shock. When he used the table to steady himself, she carefully moved to Sir Geir.

He was normally a gentle knight, one that occasionally played with Allistril, but the memory of him staring down at her through a crossbow filled her with enough rage to complete this ruse. Bubbles formed in the foam dripping from his mouth. She felt a slight pulse and poured the remnants of the potion into his mouth. His muscles were rigid as she tried to set him upright.

"Help me," Della said.

The knight tried to get him to bend, but the rigidness won. Sir Geir gasped heavily and then breathed no more.

"Are there any potions or relics stored here?" Della asked frantically.

"No relics are accessible without the overseer's presence, but there are potions here."

Sir Hakon rushed her into a nearby room that stored several elixirs, bottled in the Citadel's runic script that Della understood. Each one should glow as if bathed in moonlight, but these refracted no light and were dull and lifeless.

"Are even the potions dying?"

"Yes. Anything infused with the Allfather's blessing is ruined. Soon our Order will be in chaos." At a clatter from the next room, Sir Hakon rushed out to attend Sir Geir.

Della tottered between the potions. She found one brewed for ingesting toxins that might work. She hesitated to let the poison work until Sir Hakon yelled for Della from the other room. She grabbed the potion and moved in.

He sat on the floor with Sir Geir in his arms. "There is no need, healer. He is gone."

Della felt for a pulse and agreed. "Asagrim received two knights this evening."

Della bowed her head and sat silently with Sir Hakon near the fire.

They sat for several moments until a small door opened from across the great hall.

"I thought you said you were alone," Della asked as a gaunt young woman entered the room.

Her dirty white dress hung on empty shoulders. She might have been blonde at one time, but her hair was now dark, unwashed, and fibrous.

The girl bowed staring at the floor. "Sir Hakon?"

Sir Hakon's expression contorted from grief to anger. "What is it?" he grunted.

"The others in the thrall quarters."

"Thralls?" Della asked. "You have slaves in the Tower?"

"What about them?" Sir Hakon gently laid Sir Geir's head on the floor and stood. He stared at the young girl. "What about them? You should be on duty."

"Sir, they took some of the meat. Something is wrong."

Della's eyes widened. She grabbed several of the potions, her bag, and ran toward the thrall. "Show me."

"No," Sir Hakon shouted.

The girl stiffened, paralyzed with fear.

"Did you eat any of it?" Della asked.

The girl glanced in silence at Sir Hakon.

"Answer her," he shouted.

She flinched as if slapped. "No, I ate none of the meat. The others removed hunks of the meat and shared it."

Della looked back at Sir Hakon. "Thralls or not, they need help."

Sir Hakon sighed and waved her on with his gauntlet. The young girl slumped back through the door and down a long staircase. Della thought this was the dungeon area but found a small hall lined with cots. The thrall's living area.

Seven bodies lay on the floor in different states. Two men and one older woman lay with bulging purple faces and empty eyes staring back. Another two men frothed at the mouth in the final stages of the poisoning. Along the side of the room, a young boy and a young darker-skinned girl curled up on the floor.

They rushed to the younger ones who hadn't fallen into the latter stages of the poisoning. Della handed one of the potion bottles to the thrall. "Make him drink this, support his neck like this." Della opened the potion bottle. She sat the dark-skinned girl up, then tipped her head back, slowly pouring the potion into her mouth.

"Not too fast or you will choke them."

The girl in Della's arms convulsed. She laid her out, letting her continue the fit.

"Aren't you going to help her?" the thrall wailed.

"There isn't much I can do until she stops."

She walked over as the thrall finished pouring the potion into the boy's mouth. The flushing rose to his neck. It may already be too late.

The girl Della worked on curled up in a ball and threw up. Della rushed back over and cleared her mouth. "Can you hear me?"

The girl nodded but didn't open her eyes. In the flickering of torchlight, Della noticed fine hair under her chin that went up to her sideburns.

"A dwarf? I'm giving you a potion to drink, you may survive this yet. Take as much of it as you can." She finished giving her the bottle and pulled some herbs out of her pocket. "Chew these."

The girl bit and made a face. "Don't spit it out. I know it tastes terrible. Chew it and don't stop."

The thrall across from her placed the boy's head down. He frothed at the mouth, head fully flushed.

"Come help me. Nothing can be done for him."

The thrall slumped over and sat down at Della's feet. Scars framed her haunted deep-set eyes. She was older than Allistril, but years of neglect and starvation aged her unnaturally.

Della examined the dwarven girl. The redness had not spread to her neck. She checked under her tunic and did not see any redness around her limbs.

"Keep chewing; you may yet survive this."

The other thrall stared at the ground.

"What is your name?" Della asked gently.

"Theim."

"Theim?" It was an old word in the old language. Them. "What is her name?" Della asked, gesturing to the dwarven girl in her arms.

"Theim." She said. She pointed to the bodies around her. "Theim. Theim. Theim. Theim. Theim. We are the thralls from the White Citadel. We do not have names."

Armor scraped down the stairs. The thrall walked over and placed her head against the wall. The dwarven girl in her arms recoiled. Her panicked eyes fluttered open.

"Sir Hakon is coming," she whispered.

The knight reached the bottom of the stairs and glared at the bodies on the floor. "Theim, take them to the roof for the ravens."

Della choked back the urge to tell her to stop. Dead birds may further suspicion. The thrall walked from the wall and dragged an older woman down the dark corridor. Della protectively held the girl in her arms.

"No more potions will be wasted on Theim."

Della waited until a door clanged down the corridor before unleashing her anger on Sir Hakon. "Thralls were outlawed."

"Thralls were outlawed for the commoners," the knight

corrected. "The White Citadel still uses the war won."

"War won?"

"Your usefulness here is at an end," he said, ignoring her question. "Thank you for helping me, but you must go."

The girl in her arms sat up. A moment later she rose on shaky limbs. Della hadn't noticed how short the girl was at first. She stumbled over to the wall and faced it, steadying herself.

"I need to make sure she is ok."

"I've caught her eating rocks before. She's fine."

Della opened her mouth to rebuke him but was silenced.

"This isn't a debate, Mistress Della. It is time to go." Sir Hakon's hand migrated to his sword handle.

Della watched as the blonde thrall dragged another body down the long corridor. She gathered up the potions and her bag, walked to Sir Hakon, and dropped the remaining potion at his feet. The bottle exploded. The weakly glowing medicine ebbed and faded.

"Next time you need a healer, go elsewhere."

She glared at Sir Hakon before striding past, up the stairs, and away from the thralls.

CHAPTER 13

The days grew dark in Elta, and so did the mood of the Tower. Overseer Daniels returned as soon as news reached the White Citadel over the deaths of the two knights. Edicts were announced, there was the regular fanfare to honor the fallen knights, but no blame was issued forth. As per the knightly "Brotherhood of Thekk" tradition, a large pyre was built in the village square, and the bodies of Sir Torstein and Sir Geir were laid out on display.

On the first morning of Mani, the first day of the new week, with the moon high in the sky, the knight's bodies burned on the pyre, and their souls traveled to the hereafter to dine with Asagrim. The Tower bells tolled the long, low tones, and the villagers emerged from their houses. They gathered solemnly at the square, hungry and huddled from the cold. Overseer Daniels stood before the pyre with his remaining knights Sir Hakon and Sir Solveig flanking him.

"As the Ravens of Asagrim welcome the newly dead, may Sir Torstein and Sir Geir feast at the table of Asagrim in the great Valhal," Overseer Daniels exclaimed and began his lengthy sermon.

"At least someone eats today," one of the villagers commented.

Ravens circled above, occasionally landing on the roof to gain their fill, and it disgusted Della. Spells upon the bodies of the fallen knights kept them looking as they did in life and forced scavengers away. Those on the roof were not so lucky.

The two thralls did not leave Della's thoughts, nor did the lifeless stares from the Tower's basement. She even begged Herrick to go with her back to the Tower and check on them, but Herrick only shook his head.

Della avoided eye contact with Ragnfast. Even in the dark, his grin threatened to give their deed away. They would all burn if the overseer ever discovered what had happened.

Overseer Daniel's words trailed off as she thought about Sir Geir's final moment. She was a healer that had become a murderer, several times over. Overseer Daniels tapped his staff three times. A bright flame rose from it. "Pass into the arms of Asagrim and prepare for the final battle."

The overseer held the staff to the wood. The hungry fire ignited the full pyre. The populace of Elta watched the pyre burn as its smoke rose into the starlit night sky.

Orn softly spoke an old poem, learned by each child at a young age. "Cattle die, kinsmen die; the self must also die. I know one thing which never dies ..."

"The reputation of each dead man," the crowd droned together.

Overseer Daniels muttered the last of his prayer. The raging fire consumed quickly, drowning out his last words. He paused, backed off, and watched. Soon the fire was the only light in Elta. He slammed his staff into the ground once more, and a beacon of light emerged from Shrinehall's roof, completing a spell usually withheld until Deep Winter's Rite.

The light illuminated the villagers' gaunt and hungry faces. Della wondered about their survival, but only Overseer Daniels, Sir Hakon, and Sir Solveig now stood against them. Unless the plot was revealed.

She had blood on her hands, but if it freed the village, it was necessary. This was Elta, a small village on the southern frontier, a small village that did not matter in the larger scheme of Asagrim or the White Citadel.

But Elta mattered to her.

CHAPTER 14

Huast, the season of darkness, eased into Elta with the first snowfall. During this time of darkness, the sun's rays were too weak to wink the stars from the sky, and darkness oppressively ruled for several weeks through winter. Only torchlight and the Tower's magic kept the streets and Shrinehall lit. The light alone from Shrinehall made it difficult to ignore. The loss of two knights gave pause to the Tower, and they withheld releasing the wild game.

Della had come to Lofn's several nights, upset but refusing to say why. She'd recounted about trying to save the knights from apparent food poisoning and the discovery of the thralls. However, something else lingered beneath Della's words. Something unspoken.

The villagers had survived off broth soups from the old bones and herbs Ragnfast had unearthed and ground up. A horse was offered up to slaughter, but the meat quickly ran out. Overseer Daniels demanded more inspection before the storehouse opened, and the people starved, though food was plentiful. Overseer Daniels demanded that Deep Winter's Rite occur before anything else was released. Finally, at Herrick's request, the Tower released small quantities of grain and food for preparation, but not to be consumed until after the festivities at Shrinehall.

Lofn eased quietly back into the village life. On the morning of Deep Winter's Rite, she watched neighbors, friends, and babies she had birthed into the world, climb the hill to Shrinehall. Lofn, the midwife, stayed on her porch and watched the folk go to the god's shrine that abandoned them in their time of need. This seasonal rite was the time for family, and the Tower forced her to watch it from the steps. Even though Asagrim's statue prompted her for action, it remained silent now, ignoring her blaspheme and staring out to the mountain as if waiting for the sun to return.

She didn't look to the hill again. The magical lights made her eyes water, or that's what she told herself. At least her heavy winter clothes concealed the bump that quickly grew in her belly. Quicker than any pregnancy she had witnessed before.

The warm savory scent of Solstice Bread wafted from Bera's Bakery, but she avoided the place. Bera and Valdir passed her house on the way to Shrinehall without a simple hello or gift of bread. All from the woman that begged her to descend into witchcraft to save the village. She watched them climb.

Then out of the corner of her eye, past the harvested and winter-planted fields to the woods where the supposed witches lived, a small orb of blue light appeared and floated between the trees. Lofn stepped from her porch. She walked down into the valley, passing those coming to Shrinehall, the true-believers that damned her still.

Blue lights danced through the trees of the Witches Forest.

Join us, Lofn. It has been too long.

The voice caressed her as a slight wind pushed her along. Those walking to Shrinehall watched as their outcast savior strode into the Witches Forest.

Overseer Daniels returned to the Shrinehall and gave a triumphant speech on miracles, darkest hours, and loss. The true-believers sat and watched transfixed. Several of the others, ravenously hungry and fatigued, dared glances into the Witches Forest on the edge of their village and whispered about Lofn going in.

At the blot, the sacrifice to Asagrim and the ancestors, Herrick emerged leading a powerful ram, one found on the edge of the forest and unknown to most of the congregation, a symbol of his god. The ram's tranquility surprised most of the churchgoers as it approached the shrine and fell to its knees.

Overseer Daniels handed a knife to Herrick. He made the quick cut across the ram's throat, then held a bowl gathering the dropped blood. It swayed and fell after giving the last of its offering.

"Thus, begins the great feast," Herrick announced. "All praise to Asagrim and the ancestors." He stood holding the bloody bowl.

Overseer Daniels dipped the sacred drinking horn into the blood and raised it high, then poured it into the sacrificial trough at the great statue's feet. Overseer Daniels smiled as the blood mysteriously drained away, a sign that Asagrim was happy with the sacrifice.

Herrick glanced to the overseer and spoke as a trembling ran underfoot like shifting uneven ground. The very pillars of Shrinehall shuddered.

The villagers retreated from Shrinehall as Asagrim swayed on his pedestal. Overseer Daniels's hands raised above his head, and he dropped the sacred drinking horn. Before the horn fell to the ground, it rocketed across the shrine spraying blood onto the fleeing villagers.

"Asagrim has passed judgment! The food is tainted!" screeched Overseer Daniels.

Herrick stared wide-eyed at the blood-stained statue as he realized the grim fate of his village.

In the darkness of Deep Winter Rite, the Shrinehall called families to come to praise and worship. Villagers stoked the hearth-fires and the scent of spiced meat and bread filled the village. Villagers moved from house to house in celebration, sharing food and mead and spirits, no matter the weather. If it were a balmy winter night or in the middle of a blizzard, the reveling lasted until the next morning's bell toll from the Tower. When the bells rang out, all visitors, no matter if a true-believer or those that did not step into Shrinehall, were equally welcome.

Tonight, on this night of planned celebration, Herrick Blanchfield kneeled near the alter of Shrinehall and watched the panicked villagers of Elta run to their houses. The usual bright lamps that lit the hosts' homes were extinguished at once. They lit the hearth fires and burned the food. Ragnfast had snuck and distributed more meat than what the overseer dealt out. Bera took in gifts of grain from the villagers and began cooking. Now it all burned in sheer panic.

"This is my fault," Herrick whispered.

He walked over to the fallen ram and went to his knees. His hand rested on the animal's head. He bowed his head and searched for the words of a proper prayer.

"Einridi, Einridi the Thunderer? Have I betrayed you? God of the people, my sacrifice of faith was for the village. I tried to reason with Asagrim, to give us a chance."

His voice disappeared between sobs.

A hand brushed his shoulder. Della kneeled, embracing him.

"Herrick, listen to me. This was not Asagrim—"

Her awkward pause made Herrick glance up, Overseer Daniels stood next to Allistril. Her white dress and coat splattered with sacrificial blood. The overseer's crimson robes spread out almost framing her, and his hand casually fell to her shoulder as if claiming another sacrifice. Allistril looked as if a creature from the Delirium Forest touched her.

"What were you about to say about Asagrim's will, Della Blanchfield? From what I saw, from what I felt, this sacrifice was rejected. Don't you agree?"

"How will our people survive the winter?" Herrick asked.

"The knights have already been dispatched to the grainery and the lockers. Even the butcher will be visited to make sure this meat does not feed our people and for a list of those who received meat before it was cleared. The enemies of Asagrim have sent wicked magic to torment us in our darkest hour." Overseer Daniels gazed down over Elta. "Even now, it smolders in the chimneys up to the heavens."

Herrick felt the burn of Della's anger as her fingers dug into his shoulder.

"Choose your next move wisely, Herrick." Overseer Daniels patted Allistril on the head and with a simple word, disappeared.

Herrick leaned over his sacrifice and wept.

Della grabbed Allistril and headed home. Sir Solveig and Sir Hakon already going door to door. Chimneys belched the food meant for Deep Winter's Rite. The sight froze Della on the steps.

When the goods arrived that morning, Della quickly cooked up several different meals that Allistril and her ate. She made her daughter wait after each tiny bite to ease the digestion. They didn't need to be sick during the ceremony.

When Herrick left the house to prepare for his sacrifice, he was almost as nervous as his first public speech. Color had returned to Della's and Allistril's cheeks compared to the true-believers who still retained their ashen complexions.

She admired Bera for being able to withstand eating the bread before it came out of the oven until Bera waddled past them down the stairs of Shrinehall with her dress knotted so she could run.

"All that damn grain wasted on the witch. The knights are at the bakery, and there goes all that bread up the chimney. Curses on Lofn, the witch."

Della watched Bera pass. Lofn was in danger. Overseer

Daniels dared the village to hope they would eat again. He'd made sure the village knew they were wrong—and who was to blame.

Before Della and Allistril moved, a small mob of the true-believers arrived outside Lofn's house. Torches in hand and lit it on fire. Flames engulfed the place that birthed their children.

CHAPTER 15

Lofn emerged from the Witches Forest. The passage of days or weeks were a mystery. She climbed up the valley and walked past the houses to find the cold ashes of her home. She stared at the ashes, dirty, flushed, and feral, dumbfounded by this new information.

"The witch returns."

A rock clipped her in the head, knocking her forward into the snow. With her head reeling, someone cast a game net over her. Several of the true-believers rushed forward and threw her into a cart.

She yelled, fighting the game net, but only tangling it further. No one spoke to her as they trudged up Tower Road.

At the gates, Sir Hakon and Sir Solveig undid the netting and fit her with shackles and a claw-like mancatcher around her neck and hands. The tightness of the shackle around her neck stole her breath as Sir Solveig forced her up against the wall. Sir Hakon stripped her clothing and threw buckets of icy water on her. She convulsed from the cold but was forced to the overseer's chambers. The shape of her body gave the knights pause.

Huge wooden timbers etched with runes suspended a high ceiling above a large fire pit. A stag cooked on a spindle above the pit. Sir Solveig forced her close enough to the fire that her skin tightened. The heat should have been excruciating, but oddly enough, Lofn did not feel pain.

"The witch ... Lofn." Overseer Daniels spat.

Sir Solveig forced her around, exposing her naked body for

the overseer's raw appraisal. Overseer Daniels lounged on a large, oaken throne perched on a raised dais. He took bites of an apple, slowly chewed, not giving Lofn a transient glance.

"Um, Overseer Daniels?" Sir Solveig requested.

Overseer Daniels snapped his fingers, and Sir Solveig forced Lofn face down to the floor. She fell to her hands and knees with a grunt. The mancatcher choked and threatened to snap her neck at this angle.

Overseer Daniel's fine robes swished as he descended and circled her. "Bowing at the feet of the church you tried to overthrow," he taunted.

"I did nothing."

Sir Solveig forced her to stand.

"You almost single-handedly started a revolution. Asagrim knows better. The grain, the meat, and you are cursed."

"What have you done?"

"Your meat and grains have been quarantined and you ... are to be cleansed by fire."

"Overseer Daniels," Sir Solveig interrupted.

The Overseer's pale eyes glared at Sir Solveig. He simply nodded toward Lofn. Overseer Daniels scanned her body. "By the Allfather, are you with child?"

A grin nudged at the edges of her lips. "Yes."

Overseer Daniels' eyes lost focus as Lofn felt a whisper of power. "This cannot be," the Overseer choked out. The color drained from his face and made him as white as the snow that fell outside. His back went rigid. Tiny beads of sweat broke out on his face. "Knights," he whispered, then shouted, "Knights!" His eyes focused back to the Tower and he stammered, "Gods, who sired this child?"

"Look to the forest, Overseer," Lofn whispered as she felt the power in her belly. "This is not of your simple understanding."

The Overseer stepped back. "Knights! To the dungeon with her. I must contact the White Citadel immediately."

Lofn stared at him as a slight smile visited her lips. Even with the choking mancatcher fastened around her neck, her echoing laughter filled the hall.

The knights forced her into the dungeon. Old, withered bodies hung in the cells, a ghastly parade for those marched through to their doom. Sir Hakon opened a cell, and Sir Solveig forced her to the wall. They traded the mancatcher's shackles for those of the cell.

While most prisoners faced outward, the knights placed her facing the wall and tightened the shackles to completely immobilize her. The clang of the cell door cast her in frigid and utter darkness, but Lofn had no fear or discomfort.

CHAPTER 16

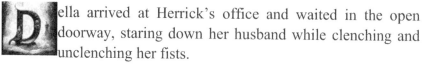ella arrived at Herrick's office and waited in the open doorway, staring down her husband while clenching and unclenching her fists.

"They are going to burn her. Do something."

"I've done all I can," Herrick said in a small voice, head in his hands.

Della stared at him through a veil of tears that matched those trickling down his cheeks. She ran from the office to the village square, shadowed by Shrinehall's intense light. Snow fell freely upon the village, giving it a blanket of innocence.

Up ahead, Sir Hakon and Sir Solveig walled off a stack of wood. A single wooden pole waited in the center. Sir Solveig stepped aside to reveal Lofn chained to it and dressed in white robes. Tension thrummed through the square.

The villagers milled about. Some of the true-believers chanted "burn the witch" while others appeared distraught, hungry, and retaliatory. Ragnfast still carried his butcher blades and watched Della waiting for some sort of signal. The scruff around Scrap's neck flared as he growled, ready to attack. Toward the back of the crowd, Ivanar had his hunting spear and sword still at his side. Kordan appeared with his hunting bow loose in his hand with no arrow notched.

Lofn was one of their own, a member of the folk that had delivered most of the children here, and the cause of an uncommon miracle that they were not allowed to touch.

Ragnfast talked about a possible assault while the people had some strength left, but his words were hurried and vengeful. Della knew the small group was too weak. Valdir argued with him loudly in the village square, but the knights were too busy to care.

The knights surrounded Lofn and steadied polearms against anyone that dared approach. Della had already killed two knights and didn't want any more blood on her hands, but she would not lose Lofn.

She walked to the knights' perimeter and stared at her friend. Overseer Daniels trudged toward them through the snow, his mauve robes appearing as old blood against the white bandage of snow. He stepped near the pyre and unwrapped a scroll.

Della stepped back into the crowd and glared at Ivanar until he returned the look. Her glances at him then to Overseer Daniels only brought Haveldan, one of Kordan's seasoned hunters over.

"I can try to hit him, but I can't guarantee a kill," he murmured. "His magic will get us before I can take him down. There are too many people here, Della. He's not a deer in the forest."

Warm tears fell when she looked back at Lofn. "Do we have anyone else with bows in the crowd?"

"Kordan's got his bow. Not sure what he would do if I ask. I'm sorry, Della. There is no time."

"Ask him and wait for my signal."

Haveldan hesitated, then nodded, moving back through the crowd.

Overseer Daniels's voice boomed across the village square as if he read about the rebirth of the Allfather. "I call you here, residents of Elta, to bear witness. Witness what happens when you move against the White Citadel, consort with demons, and engage in witchcraft. Against you, Lofn the Midwife, I pronounce you guilty of these charges. Those found guilty of devilish work against the White Citadel are to die by purifying fire by the rule of the Allfather."

Overseer Daniels took his staff, struck it three times against the ground, and fire rose from it.

Della searched for Ivanar, Kordan, and Haveldan. She glanced back to the overseer who stood there, staring at something behind her. Kordan readied an arrow but then stopped. She turned to find Herrick moving through the crowd, moving past her and approaching Overseer Daniels.

Della yelled at Herrick to stop, raged at him, calling him less than a man. She yelled to whoever heard to take the shot.

"Della." Lofn's voice rang out in her head and her voice broke her.

"Sister," she sobbed and turned to the pyre.

Lofn stared down at her. "Forgive Herrick. He has no choice. You don't know the nightmares the overseer has threatened him with. Run, sweet Della, and prepare." She closed her eyes and leaned against the pole.

Wind howled through the valley from the Witches Forest as Overseer Daniels lit the torch in Herrick's hand. Herrick froze in place until the overseer whispered something to him. He looked up at Lofn, tears visible, and muttered for forgiveness. Lofn nodded as he put the burning torch against the wood. The wood smoldered like it was green and freshly felled, not its current aged condition. Overseer Daniels struck the staff again against the ground, and flames roared, burning white from the staff.

"Afraid to do your own work, overseer?" Lofn shouted.

"Move, you fool." Overseer Daniels shoved Herrick out of the way.

Herrick crumpled to the ground, torch spinning out of his reach. The overseer held his staff to the wood, yet the fire did not catch. The snow fell heavier, creating tiny vortexes as it fell around Lofn.

"Your powers are worthless," Lofn taunted.

Herrick scrambled back into the crowd as Overseer Daniels stepped back. Anger flared in his eyes. "The witch will die now."

He pointed the staff at Lofn as the crowd heaved back. He howled the word of activation, but the staff's flame evaporated.

"Damn you, witch."

Lofn's tiny laugh flowed through the crowd as they dispersed from near the pyre. Overseer Daniels backed away and withdrew three stones from a pocket within his robes. The knights fled as Overseer Daniels blew into his hands until a glow escaped them. Then he hurled them toward Lofn. The stones exploded into fireballs and streaked toward her only to turn and fly in different directions before their target. Two veered to Shrinehall, and the last returned to Overseer Daniels.

He stared after those heading to Shrinehall. When the one rebounded to him, he called out the Allfather's name as the stone exploded. Overseer Daniels, surrounded in flames, withered. Twin explosions came from Shrinehall as the magical light that filled Elta suddenly extinguished.

The village plunged into darkness as fire erupted between Shrinehall's pillars. Asagrim's statue crumbled and crashed into the altar. Sir Hakon and Sir Solveig pushed villagers away from the overseer while the true-believers ran in the direction of Shrinehall.

Ragnfast headed toward the knights. Ragnfast pulled hard on Scraps' lead, who didn't know what direction to run in the chaos.

"Go to Ivanar's now." Della tapped Ragnfast's back. Others attempted to extinguish Overseer Daniels. His robes fused to his blackened skin, then fell away while a burnt, clawed hand reached out to an unseen savior. Della stared at the carnage as Lofn waited on top of a cold pyre with a slight smile on her lips.

That evening, the villagers gathered at the darkened ruins of Shrinehall. Pieces of the copper ceiling had melted away leaving a hole above the remains of Asagrim's statue. In the past, any damage to Shrinehall mended. Now the magic had died here.

Herrick climbed one of the tables and attempted to call order, but the conversations in the crowd went from the cursed food to killing Lofn themselves. He tried several times to gain attention, but too many people argued in the crowd. Fights broke out. The villagers were too hungry, frightened, and mad to listen to reason. Orn approached the ruined statue of Asagrim, knelt, and wept. Gaut crept behind him, laying a hand on his back.

"There will be no saving us now," Orn said.

Herrick heard several distinct pops over the current roar. He peered at the Tower. Its beacon roared to life, signifying an imminent attack. The low-pitched horns sounded from the Tower, quieting the chaos around him. Moments later, bright red portals hummed in the Delirium Forest.

Gaut stared up at him. "The village has shown defiance against Asagrim. Now we will pay for it."

The villagers fled for the imaginary safety of their houses while Herrick waited at the crumbled leg of Asagrim. Would he be added to the kindling of the next pyre?

Additional horns sounded in the distance. A contingent of knights passed through a portal near the Tower. An armored wagon appeared with the standard of a black raven on a pool of red. The magistrate entered Elta. If the villagers paid for this, it would be tonight.

CHAPTER 17

Herrick commanded Della and Allistril to lock themselves in the attic. Several plans ran through his head, but each one ended up in the slaughter of the village. He extinguished the lamps as several shapes charged by the window. Shouts and occasional screams echoed in the night. Herrick picked up his bow, readied an arrow, and aimed for the door. The bowstring bit into his fingers and his aim bobbed wild.

Einridi, I have forsaken you, but my need is just. Protect my family in their time of need.

A thunderous knock pounded against the door, the blow from a mailed fist. Herrick set the bow and arrow down as a second knock threatened to tear through the door if not immediately answered.

The tarry scent of the signal fire drifted into the house as Herrick opened the door. A knight loomed over him on the porch. A black robe concealed his armor, rendering him almost invisible in the darkness. The signal fire highlighted his red hooded mantle. Twin black ravens embroidered onto the shoulders stared forward, their ruby red eyes glowed in the firelight. His attention dove deep into those rubies.

"Mayor Herrick Blanchfield," the knight stated.

"Yes." Herrick stared into the red eyes, unable to defend his house.

The knight pulled him from the house. Della bounded down the stairs, but the knight simply closed the door and waited, his hand resting on his sword's grip.

"Della, stay with Allistril. Do not leave the house," Herrick begged, his head suddenly clear. "I'll be fine. Do not open the door."

Her sobs filtered through.

"I am Sir Talbot, and I am your handler," the knight said and pushed Herrick up the street toward the Tower's entrance. Out in the darkness, the magistrate's knights rushed like a congress of ghosts through its streets, capturing anyone foolish enough to be out. Their wispy shapes moved unnaturally fast, almost gliding instead of running.

In the village square, a portly, black-robed knight read from a scroll. An unnatural light surrounded him, but there was no source. His high-pointed hood drew Herrick's attention. Then his voice rang out like he was next to Herrick, telling him the new rules.

"No villagers are allowed on the streets of Elta until sunrise. No exception unless it is magistrate business. Those found on the street after dark while this is decreed will be put to death without trial."

He repeated the message as the other knight forced Herrick up the hill. The black knight's voice steady in his head as they moved away from the village square.

Herrick continued up to the Tower's gate. Several villagers gave anxious glances as he stumbled by.

"Ragnfast?"

The butcher lay crumpled on the ground. He groaned but didn't reply. His left eye was swelled shut, and several fresh bruises covered his arms.

The knight pushed Herrick through the open gate into the Tower's courtyard. Archers lined the stairs with arrows at the ready. The signal fire's light made it difficult to tell what was real and shadow.

On the far side of the courtyard, a magical white orb floated above a knight seated behind a large ornate table. Herrick focused on the orb instead of the several archers ready to release their volley of arrows upon him. The knight glanced up and rose. His mantle was white with a black raven glancing sidewise as if to get a better look. "Sir Talbot, bring him here."

Sir Talbot pushed Herrick forward.

"I am Master Agmund, grand commander of the magistrate. I am in command of the Tower and Elta. Any questions or requests are to be brought to me while I am present. Do you understand, Mayor Herrick Blanchfield?"

"Yes."

"You are to go to your mayoral office and wait. The Magistratus requests an audience. The request is simply a formality, and you will be at your office as he is prepared." Master Agmund pushed an ornate scroll across the table.

"The Magistratus is here?" Herrick asked, flinching as he stepped back into his keeper knight.

Master Agmund continued, "You are abstained from this curfew. However, this does not mean your family is allowed out. Carry this scroll everywhere you go." He extended the rolled parchment, which Herrick took with trembling hands. "It will be your right of passage to the magistrate. You are the voice of the village to the White Citadel until we take our leave. You will be our eyes and ears. You are now dismissed."

"Eyes and ears?" Herrick questioned. Master Agmund's gaze went back to the table to a list of names. "You are dismissed."

Sir Talbot grabbed him by the shoulder and forcibly redirected him to the gate. Ragnfast was no longer there, and the others refused to meet his gaze. Sir Talbot stopped at the gate.

"Find me if you need to speak to Master Agmund."

Herrick nodded and returned down the path to the village. Cloud cover hid the moons and starlight. Only the odd floating orbs of magical light reflected from the pavestones.

The streets had emptied during his short time at the Tower. Herrick flinched at every sound as he descended to his office. Sweat poured from his brow even though the cold night air made him shiver. Secretly he begged for something to appear, a villager fleeing their house, a knight stampeding toward him on horseback. Anything but the horror that soon descended upon his office.

Lofn still hung facing the wall. Any movement pinched her wrists and her neck, but there was calmness. A sense of power. The knowledge that they could not hurt her. The acrid scent of burnt meat and hair filled the Tower. Overseer Daniels' groans and screams punctuated the cold night air.

"Is he going to die?" she asked. She felt her heartbeat pulse through the chain wrapped around her neck. "Is he going to die?" Lofn shouted this time.

"What matter is it to you, witch."

Someone was there. In the shadows. Watching her. But the chains prevented her from seeing the presence that filled the darkness.

"We will find a way to end your threat." The voice called out.

Overseer Daniels screamed in some far-off part of the Tower. She didn't hear this odd voice move away, but the weight of the presence dissipated.

The chains were tight, almost painful, and they choked her. She took a couple gulps of air, then chains suddenly slacked. Lofn moved her neck around and shook her wrists. The chains fell and clattered to the floor. In relief, she lowered her arms and chafed wrists, healing them as she rubbed them.

Lofn sighed and relaxed her head against the wall. All this power thrumming through her, she had no control over it. She tormented Overseer Daniels while he tried to execute her, ultimately burning himself with the fate he had planned for her. She did not regret his demise, but the destruction of Shrinehall was a misstep. She didn't want a rebellion against the god. Only a rebellion against the overseer and this wretched Tower.

She turned around to Sir Solveig's startled face before he ran down the hall, yelling for the commander. The overseer was simple. Sir Solveig and Sir Hakon were a buffoonish afterthought, but now, she faced Asagrim's army.

The oil lamp burned low, etching deep shadows in the wall that moved in rhythm to Herrick's pacing. He adjusted the flame and waited, wanting as much light as possible when *it* entered his office.

"Hello?" Herrick whispered to the darkness thinking it had arrived. He whispered a quick prayer in his family's name as a slight breeze fluttered the farm reports across his desk. The flame's undulation forced the shadows to dance in the room.

Horses stopped outside his door. Unseen voices gave quick commands. The office's temperature plummeted, and the mayor's chest tightened. Two knights with the magistrate's mantle entered his office, all with spears at the ready. They shut the door and locked it. Then the knights walked in precision around the room, checking as they went, and finally addressed Herrick.

"Mayor Herrick Blanchfield of Elta, the Magistratus demands a meeting."

Herrick stared at the spear points. "Y-Yes," he stammered and backed up. "Is he here?"

Shadows poured from the wall. Their inky blackness spread through the room as if searching, then it gathered before his desk. The shadows rose from the floor, swarming into long velvet robes. From the top of the mass, a tight, nearly skeletal face emerged. A hand rose from the robes and placed a wide-brimmed hat on its head that framed its intense dark eyes.

"Magistratus," Herrick croaked.

It stared through him. His scalp tingled and burned as if

unseen hands massaged his head, then plucked out individual hairs. One spot in the middle of his head felt like a maggot burrowed into his skull and spit ice into his brain. The Magistratus' mental intrusion commenced. Herrick understood its words before they were spoken.

"You have received aid from a witch," the voice scraped inside Herrick's mind.

Herrick steadied himself against the desk. The Magistratus' presence pulled the life from him. He tried to speak but couldn't.

"You consulted with a witch, received aid from her, hid her, and now she is heavy with child."

The Magistratus' hollowed eyes widened. Their dark pools reflected the lamp like hellfire. Herrick fought against the darkness of the thing's eyes but did not resist its call.

"She meant no harm. She's innocent ... she's ... she —."

Herrick fell into the abyssal eyes of the Magistratus. The wraithlike thing caught him by the jaw and pulled him across the desk. It floated several feet above the ground and took Herrick with it. A torrent of invisible hot tendrils spread through the mayor's brain seeking information. Herrick tried to scream, but the Magistratus's thin hands felt like frozen iron and locked his head into place. The inquisition.

They spoke in unison.

"I am not the sire. I am innocent of this crime, but tongues have wagged. Rumors, the witch consorting with a demon in the forest. No demon, it saved us all. She won't tell me who the father is ... who the father is ..."

A slight cry escaped from Herrick as blood seeped from his nose.

"Help us," they murmured. "Starvation. We begged for help. The crops withered in the fields. We are going to die of hunger this Winter. The Tower and White Citadel refused aid. We are starving."

The mayor struggled, gritting his teeth. Pressure from behind his eye sockets threatened to burst if he tried to separate from the gaze. It was impossible.

"We should burn the fields and watch your village die for the crime of magic," said the Magistratus. "While the populace watches and chokes, I will have you flogged in the village square along with your daughter and wife. It will be quite the festival."

The Magistratus hesitated and studied him. "You had no hand in this, so you are innocent of the crime of magic. You are to be a puppet of the White Citadel. This child will be born from great power, and he is to be ours. This is the only solution."

"Th … There is only one solution." Herrick's voice died as he slumped in the Magistratus' hands. It cradled Herrick's head and whispered in his ear.

"Notify us when the witch is giving birth, or we will burn this village to ash and put you all in unmarked graves. We will not suffer the witch to live, nor those denizens that support her, but the witch will not die until the child is born."

A shadow flowed from the Magistratus' mouth and burrowed into Herrick's ear.

The Magistratus threw Herrick across his desk and into his chair. Herrick fell back into the chair, bounced, and his head slammed against the desk. A small pool of blood formed under his nose. The Magistratus dipped his thin claw-like hand in the gathered blood and stared at it in the lamp's fire.

"Attend to this fool, so he doesn't choke. He has work to do."

A knight lifted the mayor back into his chair. The Magistratus removed his hat and disappeared into the shadows as they returned to normal from the candle's flicker. The knights quickly exited. Even unconscious, Herrick seemed to relax.

Heat seeped into the office as the mayor snored in his chair. Blood smeared across a speech where he implored the use of quarantined grain and meat to survive through winter and the farm reports that said nothing else remained. The magistrates' arrival had sealed their fate.

"Another," Master Agmund ordered and watched Sir Hakon strain and place another rock on the pile. A small mountain of rocks had formed. Master Agmund waited for a plea or a scream or even a whimper. No witch had survived beneath this many before, but apparently, Lofn was resting comfortably. Sir Hakon nearly stumbled but placed it on top.

In silence, they waited for a sign. A scream or plea. Nothing.

"Another," Master Agmund commanded.

Sir Hakon glared at the commander while he struggled off the pile.

They had tried swords, axes, and hammers to no effect. Almost as if the metals had a heart of their own. Even Master Agmund's sword refused to come out of the scabbard in her presence. Three wars, countless battles, and the master of the magistrate had never seen anything like this. Even his Magistratus refused to emerge in her cell.

"Another," he said from the far side of the room, leaning against the wall.

"There are no more." Sir Hakon kneeled, exhausted. "You want me to climb on and jump?"

"Is this some joke to you?"

Sir Hakon laughed. "We've lost the temple and our overseer, and yet we can't touch this witch." He hopped a couple times on the rocks until he lost his balance and fell.

"The overseer has been transferred to the White Citadel. He is not lost yet."

Sir Hakon steadied himself and stood. "And what of the Allfath—"

"Do not talk of such things in the presence of this witch." Master Agmund left the wall he had propped up watching this idiot knight work. This village was a backwater, somewhere that should not even hold his attention. Yet here he was, trying to crush a witch that for all he knew might be enjoying their muted bickering.

"Master Agmund." One of his magistrate knights approached.

"Two men, brothers, tried to attack a couple of knights."

"The redheads. Ragnfast and Ivanar, I reckon," Sir Hakon spoke up. "Ivanar's been wanting to attack the Tower for years and his brother developed a mouth.

"They waited until we arrived to attack?"

"Not necessarily. Overseer Daniels wanted to send a message to the village and found Ivanar's boy playing in Shrinehall."

"Did he kill him?"

"No, Master Agmund. We lashed him."

"Overseer Daniels's brittle ego shows again. Fine, let us talk to these heretics."

Master Agmund placed his hand on his sword's pommel. He stared at it a moment wondering if he could unsheathe it if needed, sighed, and walked out of the cell.

Sir Hakon carefully stepped off the rocks to the cell door and stopped. He scanned the pile for any sign, any movement of stone, any odd gasp or groan.

"Lofn. Please give up the ghost." He stopped and rubbed his raw, bleeding hands. "There is a monster here that will eat your poisonous soul, and probably all of ours. If you die, they will go away."

He waited, proud but angry for what the day had cost them until the floor trembled and the stones tumbled down the pile. Sir Hakon shut the cell door and rushed to catch up to Master Agmund.

CHAPTER 18

Several hours passed since the knight took Herrick and marched him off to the Tower. In the dark of their house, Della sat on the couch. Her only company was the clank of armed knights moving outside in their heavy mail, highlighted by the occasional piercing scream that sent ice through her veins. Herrick's bow and quiver sat next to her. Thoughts tromped murderously through her head.

Della almost started the revolution after the knights seized Lofn. While her husband organized the elders to beg for forgiveness, she spoke to those tired of the Tower's heavy-handed rule and Overseer Daniel's mostly empty threats about rebellion. The level of anger and animosity surprised but incited her defiant thoughts. Most were ready for an uprising, but there were always two sides in Elta: those standing with her, angered that the Tower left them for dead, and those against, the true-believers who would die at Overseer Daniels's charred feet. If he survived.

The magistrate's arrival brought many problems. If the Magistratus was in Elta, one glance from the monster confirmed the uprising, then her daughter might accompany her to the pyre.

"Mommy?" the soft voice called from upstairs.

"Come down here, Allistril."

In the Tower's ghostly warning light, Allistril appeared like a fairy descending the stairs. Her red hair splayed out wild over her white nightgown.

"Where's Daddy?"

"He hasn't returned, love." Allistril snuggled in next to her.

The warmth of her little body made Della rethink the entire rebellious plan.

"Let's go find him," Allistril said.

Della glanced out the window. Tears begged for release, but she refused to let her daughter see them. The knights were still out there, waiting for anyone who dared leave their home.

"We can't, baby. We're trapped."

Hours passed in darkness as the Tower sounded its morning bells. Since the sun didn't pass Mount Hati the long nights seemed endless. Della moved her sleeping daughter cautiously and rose quietly from the couch. She touched the hardwood of the bow, wondering how far she could escape before the knights ran her through. She crossed the floor, waiting for something to stir outside to give her a sign they were still under siege. Allistril's heavy breathing and her own heartbeat were the only sounds.

She left the bow where it lay. She breathed deep and went to the door. Her hand barely brushed the door handle.

"No one out until curfew is over!" someone shouted from behind the door.

Defeated, she went back to the couch and waited.

Della awoke to the Tower's horns of midday. Low bass notes rumbled through the village like approaching thunder. Della grabbed her cloak. She opened the door and searched the darkness. The snow outside had finally ceased falling.

"Allistril, stay here. If anything happens, go to Aurdr's house as fast as you can run. Do not trust the knights, and do not come back here unless I come to get you."

She left before the child answered.

Horse and mail-footed tracks, drag marks, and blood disrupted the snow blanket and told of Elta's occupation. The villagers assembled in the square. Della rushed through them, searching frantically for Herrick but didn't find him.

The massive gates of the Tower opened, and the magistrate knights proceeded toward the village square. Several villagers followed, torn, bruised, and tortured. Della found Ragnfast toward the end of the group, barely able to keep up with the crowd. Leaning as he walked and holding his side. The bruises that covered his exposed flesh told the story of his night in captivity.

Some moved to the village square. Others hobbled home. Della stood among them appraising wounds when Allistril's scream ripped through the village square. She appeared frozen near her father's office, staring in the window.

Della rushed through the throng of villagers only to be divided by the knights on horses. Several of the magistrate surrounded her. She tried to weave past to grab her daughter.

"Hold." A large red hooded knight dressed in a black tunic stared at her but talked to the knights around her. "Let her go."

She stumbled past the horses and knights to make it to her daughter. Allistril didn't move from the window.

"I told you to stay home." Della shook her daughter's frail shoulders. "This is not a game."

"Daddy is in there on his desk." Allistril pointed at the window.

Della opened the door and found Herrick face down on his desk. Old blood smeared the paperwork before him.

She reached for the side of his neck, searching for the telltale beat of his heart. The rhythm was slow and shallow.

"Herrick. Herrick, wake up."

She pushed him to lean back in his chair. His eyes flickered and closed again. Flecks of grey covered his dark hair like dust, and his skin hung from his face.

"Gods, Herrick. Come back to me."

Like a sleepy child, Herrick slowly opened an eye, then the other. They fluttered wildly side to side before settling upon her. One eye focused on her while the other pupil remained large.

"I thought you were a battle-maiden coming to take me home," Herrick said.

"You almost died behind a desk," she scoffed. "They wouldn't fetch you."

Herrick gave a weak laugh.

"What happened to you last night?" Della asked.

Herrick closed his eyes and relaxed in the chair.

"Is Allistril safe?"

"She is at the window."

"Did they come for you last night?"

"No. They refused to let me leave the house."

Herrick sighed. He slowly opened his eyes again and looked outside. Allistril's face was barely visible in the lamplight but remained plastered to the window.

"Get me out of here, Della," he gasped. "Only bad news will come today."

"Come then. I won't leave you here."

She forced him to stand and supported him as they walked out of the office. Every step through the snow made Herrick groan.

Light emerged from the village square where a heavy knight with a pointed black hood read proclamations. After Della passed him, she noticed the silver embroidery on his cloak. A silver outline of a cawing raven. She felt the tingle in the air even this far away from the knight. His voice sounded as clear as if he was next to her, telling her all the things that had gone wrong in her village. She paused for a moment. They were here investigating magic by using magic. Knights on foot kept the crowd back from the speaker, but the knights on horseback surrounded them and kept the villagers from escaping.

Della ignored them as they moved back to the house, but she felt the pleading stares from the villagers upon them. Allistril ran to the house to open the door and stir the home fires. Closer to the house, Della practically carried Herrick. Several villagers waited at her office door and glanced up as she approached. She shook her head.

"Walking through the cold and dark, just like before we delivered Allistril," Herrick said weakly.

Della crossed the house's threshold and sat her husband down near the fire. She wanted to rage about Lofn, but now was not the time. Allistril followed with the heaviest blanket in the house.

Outside the crowd gathered in the square shouted and argued. The fire inside Della stoked. She needed to be among them, but her husband needed her now. No telling what horrors he had experienced.

Abruptly the shouting stopped. She grabbed her supplies and started assessing Herrick. She wanted to go outside, but he was in a grim condition. Even under the blanket, his skin felt ice-cold, his stare far away. Occasionally the eye with the blown pupil turned in and watched her as she cleaned the blood from his face.

CHAPTER 19

In the early evening, Master Agmund ascended the steps to the top of the Tower. "Where is the sun in this accursed country? Old injuries that had not hurt in years flared up again. He felt hunger and thirst. First, it affected the lower soldiers, but now the entire army needed to eat, and there was limited food available. At first, he thought it was disfavor of the Allfather until it affected all the clerics, warpriests, and even the magistrate. The Allfather's days were running out. This backwater village's starvation and their simple overseer's egotistical reaction caused more problems than it was worth, but the witch's power gave Master Agmund pause.

On the Tower's roof, the moon appeared like an orange smear just over the horizon. He blinked and rubbed his eyes, part smoke of the signal fires, part from total exhaustion.

The ravens had nearly picked clean the bodies on the Tower's roof. His presence startled the ravens working on the bones. They took flight, croaking their cries at his interruption.

He approached the thralls' remains and noticed a couple of dead ravens lay next to the bodies. He interviewed the butcher, a troublemaker that spoke out against the White Citadel. His soldiers roughed him up, but he had remained silent. There was an element of uprising in this village, and Ragnfast and his brother seemed to be the cause, spurred on by the abuse of their boy. Soon enough the Magistratus would regain its strength and go visit Ragnfast's brother, Ivanar.

Master Agmund returned to the edge of the roof and gazed

down into Elta. He waited long enough until the ravens didn't perceive him as a threat and landed. He pulled a gem from his pocket and whispered a rune over it. A small hum of power awoke. Agmund pulled his cloak around him and whispered another word. The eyes of this mantle flashed to life. One raven croaked and hopped toward him. It watched for a moment, then took flight. Agmund held up the gem and looked through it.

The village of Elta showed clearly before him as if in full daylight. The Delirium Forest that surrounded Elta glowed a fiery blue. To the south, the so-called Witches Forest showed as if it was burning down. The raging pink fire flared and ebbed, threatening to engulf the village. The firestorm edged close to the trees, then the flames snuffed out. The forest cinders wavered, danced, and the embers formed together. A brilliance within the heart of the forest reappeared. A small sun formed, emanating energy back into the Witches Forest before it fell apart again.

A forest god was present. That explained the sudden return of the beasts and the fields.

Agmund lowered the gem. He peered through his natural sight at the Witches Forest, then skyward. In the pale moonlight, the raven wheeled through the sky. Agmund motioned downward, and the raven dove. It flew past Shrinehall, by the Witches Forest, and around to the shops on the outer part of the village. It came back toward the village center and Agmund lifted the gem once more.

He found landmarks. The pink fire stopped at the edge of the Witches Forest as tendrils of blue ran from the Delirium Forest under the entire village like a root system. Agmund whispered on the gem again, and the light disappeared. He placed the gem back into its pouch. He deactivated the magic of his mantle and pulled a necklace out from beneath his armor. Quietly, he spoke, "One," and waited.

The gate, the easy transportation between this backwater and the White Citadel, should have opened. Something was wrong. There was a small clap in the space behind Agmund, and he spun around with sword in hand.

"Forgiveness, Master Agmund. I am Mangata Soren. We will bring you home."

The scholar wizards, the mangatas. Whose names meant the sea's silvery reflection of the moon on water, or the moon's path. A group of master wizards that refined the raw magic of the world for the White Citadel and used the madness of other dimensions for inspiration. Mangata Soren pulled a stump of charcoal from his purple runemarked robes and drew a large circle around them.

"Something is stopping us from leaving this area," Mangata Soren said.

"It's in the forest and watching us," Master Agmund commented.

"Another?" The scholar pushed up his glasses. "Are we in danger?"

"No, it stays to the forest. Get me to the White Citadel, and I will make my full report."

"Yes. Of course. Let me see what I can do." Mangata Soren drew near the dead. "Oh, whose bodies?"

"Nevermind them. Get me to the White Citadel."

"Hmmm. They appear poisoned."

"Mmm-hmm," Agmund agreed as the mangata scribbled runes and sigils into the ground as quickly and flawlessly as Agmund wrote his name to writs and orders.

"There is great energy below us as well. Is this the witch?"

Agmund considered the blue tendrils running underground. "Yes, but I fear the Delirium Forest may be spreading."

"By the stars and their madness. Let me see what I can do." The mangata laid down a few more circles in quick, concise patterns. Agmund wondered if the geometry was as perfect in the drawn circles as they appeared. The scholar commanded the magic from the center, a wry smile crossing his lips. "Yes, that should last long enough … no, already the runes on the outside are disappearing. The energies here are chaotic."

"Can you get me back?"

"Yes. Apologies. I may come back and study this."

The scholar fell into a rhythmic chant, and Agmund felt as if he moved at incredible speeds. He shut his eyes tight. Otherwise, nausea slowed down his report.

He took a stabilizing step forward. His armored foot stepped onto a soft pillow. When he opened his eyes, he found other copies of Mangata Soren all dressed in different colored robes, reading scrolls, books, or grabbing wands to defend against the sudden intrusion.

"Master Agmund, we have arrived. Due to the energies working against us, I moved to my quarters, or we may have been injured in the process."

Agmund studied Mangata Soren, a pleasant man he had only briefly worked with before and around at his army of reflections. As a man who worked to stomp out magic, to be surrounded by it uninhibited made him uncomfortable.

"Thank you, Mangata Soren. Figure a way for my magistrate to leave as soon as possible. Foul things are happening in Elta, and we can't afford to lose any more soldiers.

CHAPTER 20

In the deep night, Della awoke to the sound of the door almost getting kicked in.

She rose and left Herrick in a deep sleep. It remained dark outside except for the illumination of the signal fire and the small orbs wandering the streets. Without Shrinehall's beacon, time was difficult to tell without seeing stars.

She felt heavy, weighted as if someone was in the room with them. She lit her lamp, waved it around the room, but did not see anyone.

The hammering on the door continued. She crept down the steps unsure of what to do. She was not about to open the door to the knights.

"Della," a familiar voice mumbled through the door.

She rushed to open it. Ragnfast collapsed into the house when the door fell open. His face was so swollen that his shock of red hair barely identified him. She immediately pulled him in and shut the door. Then she closed the curtains and shuttered the lantern.

"Gods, Ragnfast. What are you doing out? What happened to you?"

Ragnfast mumbled. "Go get Ivanar. He's dying."

Della wondered if his jaw was broken as swollen as it was. She walked him through the darkened house into her office. "What happened?"

"Magistratus." Ragnfast struggled, held by pain. "Damned thing threw me into the wall. Ivanar's hurt bad." Tears fell.

"It's a death sentence if we are out." Della pulled on her cloak anyway. "Stay here. You are too injured to fight if we're caught."

"Jahan," he croaked.

"Gods, is Jahan in the house?"

Ragnfast nodded. "Della. Help us."

"Don't follow me," Della said as she extinguished the lantern. "I will protect Jahan, but I can't protect you as well. You will be on your own."

"No." Ragnfast struggled against her.

She touched his ribs, and Ragnfast yelped.

"Get your ass on that cot, now. The only thing you will do is get us caught."

Ragnfast hesitated.

"One hit to your ribs and you are dead. Sit down!"

Ragnfast crept over to the cot and sat.

Della moved to the office's back door. The clouds were thick tonight, plunging the valley into deep darkness without moon or starshine. Strange, small orbs of light patrolled the streets, but Della did not see any magistrate.

Panic and the need to get to Jahan replaced starvation and fatigue. Della pulled up the cloak's hood and moved low around the houses.

She found a dark place and watched. A knight stood guard on the street, his hand gestures moving the orbs around him.

She closed her eyes and concentrated on her anima. She whispered "here" into her hand and threw it. Down the street from Ivanar's house, the word sounded out from the shadows. An orb of light followed it and brightened. The knight pulled on the tunic's hood, his figure shimmered and flew down the street. Della stared as he moved, never seeing a knight in full armor move so fast. Their insurrection was over before it had started, and Della realized their doom.

She ran to Ivanar's house and went around the back. She pushed open the draft access grate under the house and crawled in. She pulled it shut and waited. Waited to see if some spectral knight reached in to grab her. Della waited in the dark with her heart hammering, realizing the job she had to do. She maneuvered by touch, letting memory guide her, feeling a familiar bag of swords that Ivanar had stashed for the uprising. Maybe the uprising would have worked against the slow, dim knights of Elta. This invasion was something so different and beyond what a mangled Ragnfast, a damaged Ivanar, and a village healer could hold back.

Della took a deep breath and moved past the swords. Light trickled from the floorboards above and showed a small tunnel to her left. She crawled into a wooden box. Above her was a false bottom to a bed Ivanar had built. This was a place for them to hide or to get in and out of the house unseen if needed.

There was silence in the darkness. She dared to push up the mattress. Jahan stared at her from across the room, backed up against a wall.

"No," he whimpered as Della peeked from below the bed, tears streaming down his cheeks.

She scanned the room and didn't see anyone else. She pointed to her eyes. Jahan shook his head no and pointed to the floor. She pushed the mattress and the plush pillows out of the way and crawled out.

A sharp exhale came from the floor below the bed frame.

"Oh, gods," Della exclaimed.

Ivanar arched his back as he gasped ragged breaths. Della moved to the floor next to him. Black ichor traced the veins on his legs, leading up to his clothes. Della ripped his shirt off and found the marks centered all the way to his chest, his heart became a large black mass near the center. Ivanar's body arched again as he pulled in a sharp breath. This time his eyes opened. There were no pupils left, just darkness that reflected a terrible starless sky.

"No," Della wept. She was useless to him now.

No potion could help him. No healer would apply a balm. Not even the overseer could drive out this evil. She had only heard about it in old wives' tales and stories to scare the children, but here in front of her, Ivanar was lost to living death and transformed into a monster. Della focused her anima again, reached out, and touched Ivanar's head. It was intensely cold almost like the frozen bodies they would find in Deep Winter.

"Sleep," she whispered.

His body relaxed, and he fell to the floor.

"Jahan, now," Della said as she pulled up the bed. Jahan paused.

"I won't leave him," he said in a small voice.

Ivanar pulled a deep raspy breath, his dark eyes fluttered open again, but this time it locked on Della.

"Now, boy!" She yelled.

Someone hit the door.

"Who is in there?" The voice demanded from outside.

Jahan ran into Della's arms.

She grabbed Jahan and dropped him into the bed frame and followed. She slammed the bed down as the door shattered, followed by the hard steps of a knight. Ivanar stopped his ragged breaths. They lay in the darkness, Della barely breathing, praying for Jahan to stay silent.

"I know you are here, boy." The knight bellowed. "Show yourself."

The knight continued through the house. "By the Allfather," he exclaimed.

As quietly as possible, Della pushed Jahan through the tunnel and followed. The knight above them screamed. Intense cold washed over her and drove the air from her lungs. She felt her anima drain away.

Gods, what is happening?

She pushed Jahan quickly through the dark, wanting to get away from what happened above them. As they moved out of the back of the house, she covered Jahan in her cloak and fled between the houses.

They snaked between the houses as horns sounded around them. The lighted orbs streaked toward Ivanar's house, intensifying with light. The shadows melted around them as the orbs rose in the sky. Della pushed back into the remaining shadows as the ghostly magistrate knights flew past them.

She waited for the last knight to pass. The shadows had lost their secrets, and as tired and hungry as Della was, she would make mistakes.

"Now," Della said as she pushed Jahan down the street.

When they were close to the house, Della peered out as a knight shouted down the street. The sudden light blinded her.

"Jahan, I can't see. Can you?"

"No," Jahan sobbed.

The knight's shouts continued but seemed focused on Ivanar's house.

Della grabbed Jahan and sprinted across between the houses, fully illuminated in the magistrate's light. They ran around to the back of the house, sneaking in the remaining shadows and into her office. Ragnfast, battered and bruised, grabbed Jahan as he ran to the bed. In the silence, Ragnfast held his nephew, then wailed at the fate of his brother.

"Stay here," Della said as she went to the draped windows and peered through.

Figures moved as her eyes adjusted. Further down the street, knights surrounded something that muted the very light around them. Another horn blared.

Behind the knights, the black knight, the herald with the proclamations, emerged. The knights surrounded him defensively, their weapons drawn and glowing. As the black knight spoke, power thrummed through Della's chest. Every word, every syllable caused him to absorb the failing light around him. The symbol of Asagrim that he held before him brightened like the summer sun. She felt his words continue, then the power released. The light orbs dimmed, and Della gasped.

Ragnfast's weak voice came from the darkness. "Are you okay?"

"I'm fine," she said, looking into the darkness of the room. When her eyes adjusted, she looked back through the curtains.

Down the street, Ivanar's form floated in front of the knights. His skin as black as the deep darkness, his extremities more shadow than real. Whatever the black knight did, stunned it. But Ivanar floated there changing, becoming more shadow, more monster.

"Knights!" the black knight roared.

They advanced with weapons ready. Whatever Ivanar became reared backward and disappeared into the darkness. The knights gave chase as they disappeared behind the houses. The black knight lowered his holy symbol and watched them for a moment. He then turned and approached Della's house.

She ducked under the window. "The knights may know we're here."

Ragnfast groaned, "We're done."

She glanced out the window. The black knight was almost there.

"Be silent," Della commanded as she moved through her office into the main part of the house.

She made it into the kitchen as the knight knocked. Della hung up her cloak and wiped her feet. Suddenly realizing the prints she left in the snow.

"Who is it?" Della called from behind the door.

"Lady Della, we require your husband. There has been an incident."

She cracked open the door.

"Ah, good morning," the black knight addressed as he removed his hood. "I guess it is morning. So hard to tell in this part of the country." He was a sizeable portly man with a close-cropped, white, stubbled beard and hair, who inhaled large gulps of air before he spoke.

"Herrick is very ill," Della replied.

"I am aware, and that is why I sought him out here instead of making him walk to the Tower," the knight said. "I request you wake him and make him presentable. I need to speak with him now. I am Sir Baleindin. I am the herald of the magistrate, and he needs to be aware of what has happened."

"Please let me dress," Della asked.

Sir Baleindin smiled. "Please don't take too long. It's cold out here, and there may be monsters about."

She shut the door and locked it. Then grabbed her cloak off the hooks and quickly went back to her office. She had a warm coat she kept there for the late-night patients before she had a chance to warm things. She exchanged her cloak for the coat and quickly put it on. Ragnfast was asleep next to Jahan.

"There is a knight outside," she whispered to the boy. "Remain silent." Della didn't know if Jahan heard or understood as he stared into space. She grabbed a blanket and covered the boy, being careful not to put weight on Ragnfast. "Cover up, my sweet. I'll be back."

When she reentered the house, Sir Baleindin examined Herrick's chair, a light orb illuminating the area around him. "Your husband, Lady Della?" Sir Baleindin gently tested the chair before he sat.

She stared at the knight, knowing she had locked the door. Next time she had to bar it. "One moment," she said, rushing by him and up the stairs.

"Mama?" Allistril sleepily called out from the dark.

"Go back to sleep, now. I need to get your father up."

"Where have you been?"

"Allistril, go to sleep," Della said in a forced whisper. "We have a knight in the house."

Della moved to Herrick and lit the lamp beside the bed.

"Herrick," she said, putting a hand on his cheek.

He still felt cold. She had never been in the presence of a wraith like the Magistratus before and just being in the same area of his lesser, felt the effects. How did Herrick survive? She checked his hands for signs of the shadow, then him carefully. He startled. Herrick sat up immediately, wide-eyed and panting, with his arm out defensively to hold back whatever evil came in his dreams.

"It's Della, calm down." Herrick reached for her and

whimpered. As she held him, she felt the thump of his panicked heartbeat. "We have a knight in the house needing to talk to you."

"Oh, gods, no. No. Not again."

"Herrick. Calm down. Something happened."

The tension melted out of his shoulders, and he breathed easier.

"Give me a moment. I will get dressed and make it down," Herrick said.

Allistril shoved her head into the pillow, but Della didn't have time for explanations.

Sir Baleindin appeared to have dozed off in Herrick's comfortable chair, but he sat up when she stepped on the first stair.

"Please give him a moment, he's frail," Della asked.

"I understand," Sir Baleindin said and relaxed again into the chair as it groaned.

Della walked down the steps, staring in wonder at the magic orb. It had no vessel that contained it but appeared to be a sphere of light.

"You are a doctor, I understand?" the knight asked, interrupting her assessment.

"Yes. I am Elta's healer."

"Did you work with the witch?"

The question reached out and lashed her. Was he here to talk to her husband or interrogate her? "She is a midwife. Of course, we worked together."

Sir Baleindin adjusted himself in the chair and sat forward. He was about to say something when someone knocked on the door.

"That's Sir Talbot. Please let him in," Sir Baleindin asked.

As Della opened the door, her eyes struggled to see in the dark. She stepped aside as the knight walked in.

His cloak was still active, making his body shimmer and appear out of place. Being this close to the knight, Della understood the magic. You could not tell where the knight was completely, making combat very difficult. He removed his red hood, and the magic ceased. There was a raven on his tunic that had brilliant rubies for eyes that she was drawn into. She felt the magic of the tunic and broke off from inspecting it as it tried to draw her in. They stopped talking and Sir Baleindin watched her. She glanced up at the staircase to find Herrick waiting at the top of the stairs. He hesitated, weak and staring at Sir Talbot with Sir Baleindin. Della rushed up the stairs to steady him.

"We chased the wraith into the Delirium Forest, but the forest magic was too strong to follow. The woods will claim it," Sir Talbot said.

"Double the watch. Have the others return to the Tower. Master Agmund will return soon."

"Wraith?" Herrick asked from the stairs as Della helped him down into the room.

"Ah, greetings, Mayor Blanchfield." Sir Baleindin rose from his chair. "Yes, an unfortunate side effect. You have a wraith loose in your village. The knights chased it into the Delirium Woods, where hopefully it will be claimed and not turn into something," Sir Baleindin paused then added, "more horrific."

"Who?" Herrick asked.

"I will let your wife fill you in on that later. I do believe she witnessed the transformation." Sir Baleindin's smile was as pleasant as sunlight returning to the valley. He then addressed Della, "I do believe you have patients waiting, healer. Please see to them."

"Della? Who is here?" Herrick glanced around. "Who else is here?"

Rage held her silent. When she finally spoke, it was through gritted teeth.

"The Magistratus killed Ivanar." She choked back a sob, "in front of Jahan, and left him in the room to watch the transformation. Ragnfast was thrown into a wall. His ribs and jaw are broken."

"Della?" Herrick stared at his wife with that one ungodly blown pupil.

"Which broke our laws about curfew," Sir Baleindin said with a knowing grin. "Master Agmund will have to be made aware, but the magistrate understands. You are a healer ... and these are your people. Go to your patients, Della Blanchfield. As for now, the Mayor and I have things to attend to."

Della slowly walked toward her office under the panicked stare of her husband. Ragnfast's injuries might be calmed by potions. Jahan's were more of the mind, but all of them were now under threat of the magistrate, and no treatment or balm healed that.

CHAPTER 21

don't know if it is safe. The witch is distorting the way," Mangata Soren said.

Master Agmund closed his eyes and fell back into the chair. "The magistrate needs to evacuate Elta by moon sign. I'm sure you know that is three days away."

"If I send you back now, you could end up in the Delirium Forest or worse, near that center of power you tracked."

Agmund shifted, checked his sword, amulets, and cinched up his robes over his armor.

"I have protection against the Delirium Forest, so that is of no concern. I need to get back."

"Fine, you take the risk. Then you must move the witch as far away from the Tower as possible. I will have spells ready to go as soon as it is done."

"Then make haste." Master Agmund rose from his chair.

"One last question, Master Agmund. The populace of Elta?"

Master Agmund turned and looked at the mangata. "They have consorted with a witch. The portal. Now."

Agmund felt the portal wrap around him, then appeared in the Delirium Forest not far from Elta and the Tower. Waves of dizziness made his head swim, but the warmth of his amulet took over and righted the world. It was dark, but he could see the flames of the Tower's signal fire in the distance.

The trail reached out before him. The pathway righted itself as long, gnarled branches pulled back to open the way. Above his heart, he pressed a small pin in his armor into the skin.

"Baldr," he whispered. Orbs of light appeared and swarmed around him. Simple hand gestures finished the spell, commanding the orbs to spread out.

Agmund's hand went to his sword handle ready to unsheathe, its activation word ready on his lips. The hair on his neck rose before he heard the ragged growl.

"Herteitr," Agmund spoke as he pulled his sword.

A figure leaped past him from the trees. The being, something twisted from the forest, landed in front of him.

"Help me," it rasped as Agmund moved. Dressed in a ragged hunting tunic, it appeared more wolf than man.

"Get back, shepherd," Agmund commanded as he passed by. The monster hesitated. Agmund whispered a word, and the raven's eye on his tunic blazed. "In the name of the White Citadel, you will allow me to pass." The shepherd, a lost soul swallowed by the Delirium Forest, fell aside, forced by the tunic's magic.

"My wife," the monster growled, shaking its head. "Is she alive?"

The monster backed down the trail, moving out of the orb's light. In the darkness, its amber eyes blazed. This one was new. Fragments of its humanity were still there, and it made him more dangerous. This must be the reported lost hunter, Nol. It was far too late for him.

"She is fine, monster. Begone."

It hesitated, then the glowing eyes winked out. The light orbs flashed over to the shepherd's last position. The branches of the Delirium Forest groaned and covered its absence.

Agmund placed the orbs into a defensive mode, orbiting near and far from his position. The silence of this forest was maddening. Slight noises escaped the village during the occupation, but mainly he listened to his heartbeat, breathing, and the wind above clipping the treetops. At the edge of the Delirium Forest, a slight crunch in the underbrush made him strike.

"Bring her to me!" the shepherd yawped. It surged and jumped at Agmund. The orbs streaked, silently striking the shepherd, then exploded. With patches of hair on fire, the shepherd fell hard onto the forest floor. Agmund sliced a length through the flesh of the shepherd's arm. The cut immediately turned black and festered. Agmund sheathed the sword and walked out of the Delirium Forest. Knights and archers lined the path to the tower and stood ready to protect him if anything chased after him.

"The shepherd is near," Agmund said as he sheathed his sword.

The shepherd would last only hours as the sword's sickness claimed it.

A few moments later Master Agmund stared within the prison cell. Lofn lounged comfortably on the stones.

"When?" he asked the knights around him.

"Just after you left, Master Agmund," Soren commented in the corner, or rather a shade of him did, floating in the corner, taking notes. "The stones lifted, and she simply crawled out."

Agmund approached Soren's form, his notes seemed to move on the page in an unknown language.

"Have you figured out how to get up the gate?"

"As I suggested, we move it away from her." The mangata studied the witch, taking a moment to adjust his glasses. "She is not commanding her magic. This child is warded stronger than anything I have ever seen."

Agmund stared at the witch. "Send the knights to find a site for her. We need to do this soon. Then we will leave this for the Overseer and his remaining knights to deal with."

CHAPTER 22

The summoning bell rang from the Tower as dawn barely peaked above the mountains. Villagers crowded the main road, as the Tower gates swung open. A procession of knights marched with Lofn in chains before them. The orbs preceded them, lighting the way. Lofn's bright white gown that she wore at the burning had been torn. Her exposed skin appeared as white as the snow-covered streets, making her appear like a ghost floating by the gaunt faces that watched her pass. They marched toward Dead Man's Trail.

A single beggar's shack stood at the edge of the village near the Witches Forest. At one time, it housed the sick and diseased.

"If they put her there, why not just release her into the forest?" someone said behind her.

"Are they going to release her to get rid of her?" someone else asked.

"Feed us!" someone begged.

Lofn stopped, and the precession almost tripped over her. Her chains fell to the ground.

"I did. You are too stubborn to lift it to your whimpering mouths." Lofn said, then her stare went directly to Della. "They can't kill me. They've tried."

Della felt a rush of power when Lofn spoke that almost knocked her off her feet. Della refocused on the crowd and tried to steady herself. Sir Hakon took Lofn's arm and forced her along.

"Your death will be the cruelest." Lofn said to Sir Hakon as she was led away.

Della wanted to talk to Lofn, but that would be nearly impossible now. She tried peering over the heads of those around her and found herself whispering, "What have you become, sister?"

They marched her to the beggar's shack. Elta's two remaining knights stood guard by the door as Lofn entered the shack. Sir Baleindin returned to the pyre in the village square with his pointed black hood pulled low. Light erupted from the village square as he unfurled a new set of orders.

"By order of the magistrate and the White Citadel, the witch Lofn is to be held under house arrest on the furthest point from the Tower. Any citizen aiding the witch will be put to immediate death.

Della held back tears. She glared at the magically induced knights that were in Elta. Any revolution would be put down brutally and quickly without any sense of accomplishment or any chance of change.

The wind changed direction, suddenly blowing back on them. It tickled her ear.

"I'm safe, Della. Have faith. We will be reunited, and they will soon be gone."

CHAPTER 23

As the midday horns blew, Della put the last of the bandages on Ragnfast and tried to get Jahan to sleep. The boy would nod off, then awake, screaming. She was thinking of using a couple different sleeping potions when there was a knock on the door. Herrick had left earlier with the knights, so she ignored it. It happened a few more times until it sounded at her office door. She went to open it and found Valdir waiting.

Della paused, then carefully opened the door, and slipped outside.

"What do you want?" she said, refusing to look him in the eyes.

"I'm looking for Ragnfast. I can't find his brother or Jahan anywhere. There was a fight at Ivanar's house."

She stared at him, seeing the concern on his face, but the anger surged within her.

"You shortwit. *Vitskertr.*" She spat in the old tongue. "You are the cause of this, your *kerling* wife. You brought this to Elta. Ivanar is dead. Claimed by that Magistratus monster and released into the forest." Della slapped Valdir. He recoiled from the slap but continued to listen. "They beat Ragnfast like a dog."

"That's why I'm here, Della. Scraps is dead. I found him stabbed through this morning."

"He's lost enough today. Don't burden him further."

Valdir rubbed his cheek. His next words came slow. "We are all starving. I gutted Scraps this morning and will prepare him." Della lunged at Valdir. He grabbed her before she hit him again.

"Damn it, woman. Stop. I never imagined this would happen. I heard this morning that the magistrate are leaving as soon as the witch's magic is cleared from the Tower. They will leave us to starve."

"Then die alone," Della said, wrenching her arm from his grasp.

"It's no secret that you've led this secret rebellion against the Tower for years. Ragnfast boasted about it all the time. It's this village's worst secret. They knew." Valdir's eyes locked with Della's. "They knew."

Valdir turned red, the same shade of crimson that developed when Ragnfast and he debated. "I didn't want any of this to happen. I heard rumors about what the Magistratus did to Herrick. He had no part in your stupid plots. Please let me help."

"Against the knights?" Della asked. She said it too loud and glanced around to see who was nearby. No one was on the streets, not even the knights.

"No, you've seen them. What they can do. In my old days, I could do some things, but not like that."

"You used magic?" Della spit the words.

"When I plundered in the old days, I had a special sword. Then I found Bera, she calmed me down and made me put *it* away." His voice broke almost as if he was talking about an old lover lost to the sea.

"Then what will Valdir the Boneless do for us?" Della asked.

He paused for a moment, taking the taunt. "I have a feeling something will happen to the stores before the magistrate leave. Ragnfast showed me a secret way to get in once by accident. I want to move some of the food into his cold storage before they leave, just in case."

"If you get caught?"

"Then it's all on me. I will bring the available meat before I start. You distribute. Then if I'm caught, at least someone will have a full belly and that damn dog will serve a final purpose."

He walked off before Della could answer.

By late day, the horns blew from the Tower. Sir Baleindin arrived on the pyre once again, reading a list of punishable crimes. Valdir dropped off what appeared to be a roast and several steaks. Della wondered who the cooking fires and even simple aroma of food would summon. She walked around the village, talking to several trustworthy people who hauled wood, kettles, and water to the steps of Shrinehall. Before the fires even started, the true-believers arrived. They watched, not knowing what to do and careful not to engage Della's anger. No knights, not even the Tower knights, were visible.

Several nervous glances went to the Tower as they cooked, then as the meat hit the grills and kettles, Aurdr called out. "The signal fires are extinguished!"

Della glanced up to the Tower as the dense smoke wafted away from Elta toward the Delirium Forest. She felt a strange tingling up her spine and felt something similar the night the magistrate arrived. She peeked back at the beggar's shack. Sir Hakon stood guard but suddenly rushed up the road to the Tower.

Master Agmund caught him near the village square. Della could hear Sir Hakon begging to go with them, shouting at Master Agmund, then bellowing, "No." The raven eyes on his tunic shined, and Sir Hakon turned and slumped back down Dead Man's Trail, almost as if Sir Hakon's body rejected every single step. Master Agmund followed Sir Hakon until he saw Della.

Master Agmund watched him walk a little further and turned to Della. "Your husband is at the Tower. He is fine. We had to discuss some terms before the magistrate left. He is safe and will be home soon. Good day to you, Lady Blanchfield."

He bowed, turned, and walked back to the Tower.

Aurdr approached Della. "Is this it?"

"I don't know."

Pops emanated from the Tower, then silence.

Della glanced up toward the gate moments later. Herrick emerged. His walk was purposeful but exhausting. She left the fires and walked up the hill to meet him. Although her belly felt as if it was about to gnaw out through her skin and go back to the meat.

Herrick stopped, unsteady. Della rushed up to meet him.

"They're gone. Leaving back to the White Citadel."

"How?"

"Master Agmund said the investigation showed we supported the witch, but nothing else would be done. If she stays imprisoned, we will be spared."

"That's Lofn you speak of."

She watched Herrick talk, almost trancelike due to hunger or trauma, Della didn't know.

"We have a little meat."

"We will not touch the quarantined meat. It's cursed."

Della closed her eyes, not wanting to yell at Herrick in his current condition.

"The knights killed Scraps."

"Oh, then let's eat." Herrick stepped and almost fell over. Della grabbed him and steadied him, then helped him down Tower Road. "It smells wonderful."

Villagers assembled chairs at the foot of Shrinehall. Della sat Herrick down and steadied him.

The thin strips of meat brought people out of their houses. Aurdr and the others cut the steaks up into smaller pieces. They had to thin this out to make sure everyone ate. There was a village of the starved to feed tonight.

A slight amount of light brightened the horizon, then quickly disappeared. They still had time before the sun peaked up over the mountains, but this was a time of hope. The sun would brighten more each day until it finally emerged. Kordan gathered torches and lined them up on the street. With the knights leaving, there were only a few orbs on the road, except for the large glowing orbs that hovered over Sir Hakon standing watch at the beggar's shack and a few lights from the Tower.

The crowd seized the meat as it came off the grills. It wasn't a typical meal, but the starving did not care. One roast was already taken from the kettles and cut up. Any bones were thrown back into the kettle pot for a broth that may sustain them for a few more days. The people had this meal and maybe a few more.

Valdir, Orn, Gaut, and a few other business owners surrounded Herrick. Another loud pop came from the Tower. The tingling in Della's spine ended. The magistrate was gone. A small man in red robes stared down at them from the Tower's roof. Della finished her food but felt that she was being watched. When she looked up at the Tower, he simply stood there, watching. She felt compelled to go to him.

"Aurdr, this is the last of it. Take a double portion so you can feed that baby. Make sure Allistril eats and go take some of this to Ragnfast and Jahan in my office. Tell Ragnfast that the provisions came from the quarantined meat. I will talk to him as soon as I return."

She walked up Tower Road and could see the massive iron gate still open. The courtyard appeared worn and empty. Horse hoofs and wagon tracks stamped into the dirt along with old blood.

The man on top of the Tower had disappeared. She wasn't going to enter the courtyard further for fear of it being a trap. When Della turned to leave, she found the small, long-haired but balding man standing beside her, appearing in rather severe concentration.

"Hello," she said.

He smiled through his spectacles and bowed slightly, but his concentration seemed broken. "I knew you could feel the presence of magic. You are Elta's healer?"

"Yes," Della replied, not sure how to answer a direct magical question by someone possibly magistrate.

"I am Mangata Soren from the White Citadel."

"I've heard of the mangata but have never met one."

"Dark times are ahead for your village, I fear. The damage has been done by the magistrate, and Elta will feel winter's grip for a while. I wanted to give you these." He held out a small bag and a large bottle. "I think you know what they are."

Della held up the bottle and could see the soft, red pulsating glow inside.

"A fairly powerful healing potion. I thought the potions were beginning to fade?"

"Yes, they are. The mangata have found other ways. That bottle holds several doses. You have many injured down there."

Della riffled through the bag. Several herbs, some plants that she couldn't identify, and a tightly wound scroll were inside.

"Those are components and instructions to make other potions." The mangata seemed to be searching for the words. "A … gift to your village."

"Thank you, Mangata Soren."

"There is one more thing. A small rock underneath it all. It's special. When the time comes, you will know what to do with it."

"I'm sorry. I don't understand."

Mangata Soren smiled. "I can see the pathways of magic pooling within you. You are a natural-born practitioner. There are traces of it on your hands where you used it the other night."

Della took a step back.

"I am not of the magistrate, Della Blanchfield. I am of an order of wizards seeking enlightenment." The mangata paused and laughed. "Of course, surrounded by a contingent of knights seeking to destroy all magical works. Your friend in the beggar's shack is becoming something wonderful and powerful, but she may end your village."

"By the food in quarantine?" Della asked.

"No. I'm sure the food is quite fine. Your friend Lofn, the midwife, is the vessel for immense power. The sire of the child is something of the forest and older than the ground we stand on. Prepare for the baby's arrival and beware of those coming to claim it."

"The magistrate?" Della asked.

"In its many forms, but I have probably said too much, and my absence is surely being noted. Child, a quick question?"

Being called a child threw Della. "Yes?"

"If I offered you to come to the White Citadel to train in magic, what would you say?"

"Elta needs me. This is my home and my people," Della said it too quickly, an automatic reaction to anything from the White Citadel.

Mangata Soren's brow furrowed. "This will not be the simple Order of Ord, where the simple practitioners go. This would be under the mangata."

Della paused, then shook her head. "No."

Sadness shadowed Mangata Soren. "Of course. This village needs its healer. Your people await."

Della glanced at the gate as Aurdr walked in.

"Everything okay, Della?"

"Yes, I'm talking to …"

Glancing back, Mangata Soren was gone.

"Ragnfast can't open his jaw to eat and keeps asking about where the meat came from."

"I'll go calm him down." Della gripped the bottle, bag, and walked back with Aurdr.

"I think just about everyone in the village has shown up. Not sure how much will be left."

"Let's get back to them. I need to check on Herrick," Della said.

Herrick sat talking the politics of the Magistrate, his answers were prepared, almost taught. Della walked past him to her office and found Valdir talking to Ragnfast, who was struggling to get out of bed.

"This half-troll won't let me leave," he muttered when Della walked in.

"This half-troll is probably saving your life. Relax," Della commanded.

She grabbed a cup and poured some of the potion into it.

"Drink this," she said as she pushed the cup into Ragnfast's hands.

He took it, smelled it, and, even with his butchered face, winced.

"Just drink it, Ragnfast."

Ragnfast struggled to open his mouth. He drank deep, then threatened to spit it out.

"Swallow it, you fool. That's worth more than your life at this point."

Ragnfast did. The effects were sudden. The bruising melted from his face. The swelling fell, revealing Ragnfast's natural shape. A loud pop came from his jaw, making him wince and grab it.

"How do your ribs feel?"

"Still hurts to breathe." His voice was stronger.

Della was about ready to pour another dose when Valdir touched the bottle.

"Wait. That's a very strong potion, give it a moment," Valdir said.

Ragnfast pulled up his shirt. Bruises cleared, and as Ragnfast moved the bandages, lacerations sealed up and closed. Then on his side, a large bruise and swelling drained away. Part of his chest popped out. Ragnfast yelled, "*bikkja*."

Della slapped the bruise as it disappeared. Ragnfast yelped and winced.

"You don't use that language in here," Della said.

Ragnfast laughed and fell backward, the bruising on his face and swelling almost disappeared. Even his lips returned to normal.

Valdir looked at Ragnfast. "I'll stay here. Those potions can have some odd aftereffects. He will feel like he can take on the world, and this idiot might try, then crash hard and sleep for a week."

She poured another and stoppered the bottle. She walked

outside and placed it in front of Herrick. The food remained in front of him untouched as he stared off into the distance.

"Herrick?" He seemed to snap out of it.

"Della, I think we are free. We've done it. They're gone."

"Take the drink, Herrick." She watched the large eye stare at her, then it settled on the cup.

"What is this?"

"Something that will make you feel a little better."

He sipped at it, made a face, then downed the potion.

"It will take a moment and might make you feel a little warm, but you will feel better."

The color returned to his cheeks. Della wondered what damage the Magistratus had truly done to him. How close did he come to Ivanar's fate?

"Mayor Blanchfield?" A familiar voice called out.

Della felt her spine go rigid.

Herrick focused behind Della. "Hello, Master Agmund. I thought you had left." He stood like the potion had taken twenty years off his life. *Not too fast, Herrick. Don't let them know I have the potion.*

Master Agmund slightly bowed to Della as she turned around, then stared back at Herrick.

"We have completed our investigation and will report to the White Citadel. Please let me know if anything changes with the witch."

"Very good, Master Agmund." Herrick walked forward, almost bumping Della out of the way, and shook the magistrate's hand a little too forcibly.

"As Sir Baleindin instructed, beware of the grain and meat until we respond. You look well, Herrick."

"Very well, sir."

Della's stomach churned. Something was going on here, magic involved. She glanced at the jewels on the tunic. Their gleam sent her mind spinning.

"Excuse me. I don't feel well," Della said as she stumbled

away from Master Agmund.

She walked back to her office and shut the door, quickly moving to the potion bottle and bag that the mangata had given her. The bag made the slightest move. She picked it up and opened it.

The intense floral smell made her wince. At the bottom of the bag through all the herbs was the simple stone. She picked it up.

"I am amazed you heeded this so soon." The stone vibrated. A voice exploded inside her skull.

"Mangata Soren?" she said aloud.

Valdir talked to Ragnfast in the other room. He yelled out, "Who are you talking to?"

Della rushed to the door. "Master Agmund is right outside talking to Herrick. It would take nothing for him to come in here and find Ragnfast healed."

Della shut the door, then moved out of the office into the kitchen. She glanced outside. Herrick stood in rapt attention to Master Agmund.

"What did Master Agmund do to my husband?" Della said aloud.

"The mayor is bewitched by the magic of Master Agmund's tunic. Each knight has certain powers they can control. Master Agmund can control the mind. There may be something else, Della. Those that the Magistratus enthrall have a bit of the creature still in them. It gives the magistrate a chance to know everything that's going on."

"His blown pupil?"

"Ah yes, then it does watch."

"What about Ivanar?"

There was a pause before the stone vibrated again. "If you speak about the one that the Magistratus turned, any knowledge becomes part of the Magistratus and Master Agmund, who is in full control of the creature."

"Oh, gods."

"It fled into the Delirium Forest shortly after being turned if the reports are correct. If that did truly happen, the transfer of knowledge may have been limited. It was told that he resisted the Magistratus and died due to the intrusion. I am sorry about the loss of your friend."

"Me too."

Della stood in the silence of her house, thinking of her old friend. Finally, the stone's vibration brought her out of it.

"I have one request."

"Yes?"

"I am interested in the transformation of your friend, Lofn."

"You mean *the witch*?" Della said it too forcibly.

"No, child. I mean your friend Lofn. The child she is carrying is going to be wonderous."

"Everyone here just refers to her as the witch and has forgotten her."

"She is a unique woman that I wish I had the power and time to understand and befriend."

"Why has the White Citadel banned magic, but yet the magistrate uses it in plain sight?"

"Magic is power, power corrupts, and absolute power corrupts absolutely."

"You don't agree with their methods?"

There was a long pause, Della thought the connection stopped. She went to the window when the stone vibrated once again.

"The old ways powered by the Allfather have become corrupted. Those that practiced it, and drew power from him, accelerated this corruption. It had to be limited."

Della stared at her hands. "I'm corrupting the Allfather's magic?"

Laughter rang throughout the room. "No, child. Your magic is based on something older. The power of life. This is why I wish to train you." Della relaxed a little as the mangata continued. "Your friend has tapped into something even older. I am part of the mangata. We are the scholars of magic and now where it ends. The White Citadel has allowed us to live when they put every other witch, warlock, or wizard on the pyre. It concentrates the power as we research other sources, but I have already said too much."

The pause in the conversation forced Della's next question. "Are we going to die here? Is the magistrate going to doom us?"

"Your friend Lofn did something of incredible power. In doing so, she brought something to the Witches Forest. Elta may have to deal with that."

"What is it?"

"The father of her child. Which brings me to my request."

"Yes, Mangata?"

"If I send you something, I would like for you to place it within 50 lengths of where Lofn is staying. Press it into the ground with your foot."

"Will it harm her?"

"No, child. I have no wish in harming her, just to study her and the magic fields near her. Will you do that for me?"

"I will."

"Hold your hand out."

Della moved her hand out. A small, red portal formed in the air above it. A small gem dropped from the air into her hand. She could feel some power within it. The portal shimmered and disappeared.

"This evening, the magistrate will be gone. In three days, there will be a fog moving in at high moon, go and plant the gem then."

"What about the knights?"

"The two remaining knights are all that stay in Elta. Your Sir Hakon, who was placed on watch this afternoon, and Sir Solveig, who refuses to leave Overseer Daniels in his current state."

"Why is Overseer Daniels back in Elta?"

"We did all the healing we could here." Suddenly the mangata sounded agitated. "Goodbye, Della. Keep the stone nearby." Della felt the stone cool to the point it got cold. She placed it on the table as frost covered it. Not wanting Herrick to find it, she placed it in a cup and moved it back to her office.

She opened the door. Outside, at the table, Herrick stared at the beggar's shack. "A part of the Magistratus remains," she said out loud.

Someone stirred behind her, and she turned as Ragnfast cautiously sat.

"The meat." Tears began to fall down his face, and Ragnfast took a couple of quick gulps. "I took one look at it. Those *bikkjas* killed Scraps."

CHAPTER 24

Master Agmund took his final walk through Elta. He surveyed the area, taking notes, and occasionally stopping and holding a gem up to his eye. The villagers in Elta watched him trudge up Tower Road nearing the gate. He gazed across the land and at what had become of Shrinehall. He slowly nodded to himself and disappeared within the gate. There seemed to be a collective sigh that went through the village as the boom echoed through the valley.

Herrick walked around meeting with the villagers, calling the council together at Shrinehall to discuss the matters of the village.

They gathered a couple of hours later.

Torches cast odd shadows around the ruins, and Herrick's eyes bored into every one of them. When a torch would flicker, he cringed.

Valdir helped Gaut up the steps. Gaut was the eldest, a true-believer, and refused to eat any of the meat. Not even Scraps as he was passed around.

"No matter how dark the times," his words came slow and halting, "I won't eat a pet. My time is near, just like the Allfather's." He steadied himself on Valdir. "Let the hungry have it."

"Goodbye, níðingr," Ragnfast said, standing at the edge of Shrinehall and looking out at the Tower.

"Tough words to call Master Agmund after he left," Valdir said.

Valdir walked Gaut over to a chair and sat him carefully

WILLIAM BRIAN JOHNSON

down, then took the chair next to him. Ragnfast eyed Valdir and sat across from him.

"Funny, I don't believe he killed your brother and your dog. But I did notice his boots were nice and clean when he left. Your doing?"

"Want another nip off the old healing potion? I would be glad to be the cause."

"Enough." Herrick stood. "Before the magistrate left, the laws were set that denied—"

"Mayor, we have food." Ragnfast rose from his chair. "We have meat and grain. The magistrate flexed their muscle and said we all collaborated with Lofn. Then they left. They have worse problems than a small village trying to overthrow the White Citadel."

"They will be back, Ragnfast. Do you want to have the Magistratus ask you where it went?" Valdir asked.

Ragnfast's face reddened, he started to say something but straightened his stance and breathed deep. "You know how I will vote, Mayor. I've got an orphaned nephew that wakes up screaming at night for his father. I don't know if it's for his loss or what he saw his father become." Ragnfast patted his leg and winced, realizing Scraps was no more. He glared at Valdir. "Go ahead and make fun of that, hearthfire idiot. I'll slit your throat like a sacrificial ram." Ragnfast walked down the steps of Shrinehall and disappeared into the night.

"See, Mayor," Gaut wheezed. "We don't even need the magistrate to tear us apart."

"The laws are clear—," Herrick said.

Gaut interrupted, "I have lived too long, Mayor. I am not afraid of my meeting with Asagrim when I pass, but I don't need to watch everyone around me die." Herrick tried to interrupt, but Gaut held his hand up. "I move to let those that want to eat the food do so. Let those of us that have decided against the food go before Asagrim with a clear conscience. That is all I ask."

"Ayes" surrounded Herrick except for Gaut. Orn also sat back

130

in his chair, silent, appearing more dead than alive.

"We should test the lots just to make sure. One man, one woman, one child. That way we can see if anything is wrong with it," Steiner, the stonemason, said.

"I'll go first," Valdir said. "I'm hungry and ran my mouth too much tonight."

Heavy snow fell overnight, but it wasn't enough to keep the village from gathering at the foot of Shrinehall. The villagers stared at the fires as Herrick created the lots. Steiner showed up and placed tables. Valdir took his seat like a condemned man.

"What are you doing, Valdir?" Bera yelled. "What are you doing? This is the witch's meat. It's cursed. The magistrate said no."

He sat watching the fire, ignoring his wife's words.

As the sun neared the peak of Mount Hati, Herrick cast the lottery. Two names of true-believer's were drawn. After much bellowing and teeth gnashing, Ragnfast arrived with meat.

"I refuse to let this idiot die a hero. I will take a place." Valdir smiled as Ragnfast sat next to him. The two traded insults as Steiner also sat with them.

"I checked the meat and checked it again for any rot," Ragnfast said. "This is good meat. Let's cook it. I am hungry,"

Goat, boar, and deer sizzled on the grill. Ragnfast stood, walked over, and pulled a knife. He cut into a steak and breathed it in. "Maybe this is magic," he said after taking a bite. "Because it is wonderful."

"It's cursed meat, you fools," Bera said.

Ragnfast looked at Bera. His face reddened, he grabbed his throat, dropped to one knee, then laughed. She walked off swearing Ragnfast's name. He got up and chopped up some of the meat on the grill so it would cook quicker.

He took pieces to Valdir and Steiner.

Valdir inspected the meat and inhaled it.

"Oh, that's good," Valdir said as Bera yelled at him from across the square.

"Ragnfast, could you put that on the grill a little longer? I don't like my meat as rare," Steiner said.

Ragnfast arched an eyebrow. "Eat this now, Steiner. Or get stabbed in the lip with the fork."

Steiner ate the bite off the fork and smiled. "I agree. It's good."

Ragnfast returned to the grill, cutting off slices of meat and tossed some to Valdir. Then it became a rhythm. Take a bite, throw a bite to Valdir, and stare at Steiner until he asked nicely for a piece of meat.

Herrick stumbled around the scene.

"The magistrate said that the food will not be eaten."

"You need to talk to my wife, Mayor. You sing the same song," Valdir said.

As the smell of cooked meats spread across the village, several villagers decided it was their sacrifice as well and took the meat as it came off the fire. The true-believers stared at them in sorrow, then as a group, left. Ragnfast tore into the goat's shank and smiled at the mayor. Valdir devoured a deer steak as his wife shouted curses at him. Steiner wept at the taste of fresh boar.

"Oh, this is so good," he muttered through his tears.

Some stood back and watched those that had eaten. After an hour, they too begged for meat. For the first time since the great hunt, laughter echoed through the village. Valdir, after hearing enough from his wife, tore a hunk off a shank and shoved it in her mouth.

"You know, love. People are right. You can be a *kerling*. Eat, laugh, or go get some of that grain and bake."

Bera stared at her husband in shock. Her jaw was working, trying to make words, but she stormed off to the grainery.

"Uh-oh, Valdir. Looks like a cold night in your hovel tonight," Ragnfast said.

Valdir shook off the comment and returned to his meat. "There are many cold nights in my hovel."

Della watched the commotion from around the cooking pits and walked down the hill to Lofn's confinement. Sir Hakon noted Della as she approached.

"Lady Blanchfield, why are you here?"

"An invite from the mayor. The curse has been lifted, and the food tastes like any other. The entire village is feasting near the village square."

"The food is off limits, but I am here to guard the witch." Della noticed Sir Hakon struggling, trying to push past something. "I will arrest you all … but I can't move past this post."

"Master Agmund's command?"

"More than that. He's done something to my body. Some spell. I start to think about leaving here, going to the Tower to sleep, and I feel like a drunkard. My mind swims. Master Agmund did something to me. I passed out here last night and woke up nearly frozen. Even when nature calls, I can't move from this point."

"We will make you a shelter."

Sir Hakon stepped forward, his demeanor had changed.

"Thank you for the invitation, Lady Blanchfield. You need to leave the area and not come down here again."

Della nodded. The knight stared.

"She will bring ruin to your family if you do not leave," Sir Hakon said.

"My husband informed me of the proclamation that the magistrate made, but that allows me to check on the wellbeing of a villager."

The knight's hand migrated to his sword. Della backed up.

"I would be careful meeting with a witch. Overseer Daniels barely survived his encounter. You will not be so lucky."

Over the knight's shoulder within the shack, a figure huddled close to the fire inside. If she were to see Lofn, it would have to be another time.

Della returned to the village square. Half the village sat around meat drunk as the true-believers returned. They passed the crowd and ascended the ruins of Shrinehall for afternoon prayer. She watched them. They were gaunt and haunted, half too weak to make it to the top. She walked around the table to Valdir, who sat back in his chair with a big smile and full belly.

"You know them. You need to say something." Della asked.

"Yeah, I've got history with Orn's family. Gaut and Orn are on the council with me. Bera's close to some of the others."

"Plate up some food and take it to them. If they refuse, get some grain from your wife and take that. No need to watch them starve."

He nodded somewhat sleepily. Della kicked his chair walking past, almost tipping it over. She took a couple steaks, plates, and knives, and climbed Tower Road, knowing all eyes were on her.

She approached the Tower gate which still stood open. No archers came from the empty shadows and drew on her presence, but some blood remained in the dirt. The Tower loomed above her like a forgotten behemoth as she walked around it. At the back of the Tower, a staircase and door led down to the basement.

Della descended the stairs, took a deep breath, and opened the door. It took a moment in the poor torchlight to see them, but on their cots lay the thralls. The two girls stared at her in the doorway. Della held her finger up to her lips and pointed to her eyes, then pointed outward. Both girls glanced around, the dwarven girl's eyes reflected the weak torchlight. Finally, they shook their heads no.

She walked over to the cots and sat the meat down.

"Don't get caught with this, but enjoy a meal. I will try to bring more," Della whispered.

She could see fresh bruising on the dwarven girl's face.

"If you want to come with me, I will hide you."

Both girls shook their heads no. The blonde girl never looked away from the food, but the dwarven girl reached out and took Della's hand.

"Thank you."

She touched both girls. "The meat is safe, we ate it in the village. No one is getting sick from it. Eat it slowly, I will wait."

They picked up the meat with no need for utensils. The dwarven girl smiled, something Della felt didn't happen too often. "It's good."

"Take your time. Give your body a chance to get used to it."

"Theim!" someone shouted from upstairs.

They both wiped their hands on the bedding and stood.

"We must go. Sir Solveig summons us."

Della stood. "Come with me, please," she whispered.

Both girls got up and ran for the steps as he bellowed for them again. Della felt little sorrow for Sir Hakon, but for Sir Solveig, there would be none.

No one became sick after the meat, and a day later, Bera milled the grain and cooked up a batch of her famous bread. No one had taken ill, died, or became inflamed with the pox. There was no curse on the food. Shops opened again for the first time since the magistrates' occupation. Three days had passed since they left. Although the air felt thick and warm from the day's snowmelt, Della felt the sharp tug of winter on her as she shopped through the square with Allistril.

"Shrines cannot be rebuilt on empty stomachs," Bera said as

she handed out loaves of freshly cooked bread, a big fake smile plastered across her face.

"The gods should curse us all for the way we treat those responsible for the miracle," Della said under her breath and kept walking. Down the street, she scolded Allistril because she had snuck a bite from the warm loaf.

"She does know how to bake even though she is a terrible woman," Allistril smiled.

"Allistril, don't say such things," Della said trying not to smile.

They strolled through the village square. Every once and a while, Della glanced at the beggar's shack. It was impossible to approach without Sir Hakon staring at her. She took him a heavy blanket, but even when she approached, he threatened her. She left it in the snow, and it was still there. Without any official business, she would be aiding Lofn and put to the stake as well. Her husband warned her several times that if she went against the magistrate's order, her life would not be the only one in jeopardy.

Sir Hakon was starving. The full bellies they possessed would already be a death sentence, but Sir Hakon stood anchored to his spot. Sir Solveig and Overseer Daniels had not emerged from the Tower since the magistrate left.

Della scuffed up the street. Herrick walked among some of the vendor tents, but he passed without a glance. Allistril took the silence in stride, poorly sneaking another bite of bread. They walked closer to the house.

"Go play, Allistril," she said and went to the door. "I'll call for you later."

Della entered the empty house and placed the market goods in the pantry. She stopped and hung her head. Guilty plans flowed, some that would have them all put to death if there was any sort of knightly presence left. She needed to know Lofn's condition and what could be done for her, no matter what she had become.

She left the other goods on the table and walked out. The humidity left a wet film on everything. Fog oozed from the

Witches Forest. It made the trees dance among the clouds.

"What are you doing, Della?" someone called out.

She turned. Several villagers stopped on the road, watching her next move.

Della decided to wait until the fog had set in.

Della made sure the smell of stew flowed through the house. Allistril was dancing with a bowl when someone put a key into the locked door. Allistril retreated to the dinner table as Herrick walked in. He approached the fireplace, sticking his hands out to warm up.

"Feels like snow, again. That fog has snuck in from the Witches Forest."

Della placed three steaming bowls of stew at the dinner table.

"I'm warm enough." Herrick removed his winter cloak, walked up the stairs, and disappeared.

"We're going to eat," Della called up. Allistril took her seat and blew on the second bowl of stew. Della sat as well and took a bite. It was hot, but the richness of the broth made her sigh.

"The magistrate proclaimed that the food is off limits," Herrick called from the room above.

"We all heard what the magistrate proclaimed. We just don't care. If you don't want to eat, starve. I'm tired of hearing you drone on about what the magistrate said."

"The Magistratus almost killed me," Herrick said as he came down and sat on the steps.

Della softened for a bit. "I understand, and I know what happened to Ivanar, but I will not live in the shadow of the magistrate and starve when there is good food in the lockers. There is more than enough for us to eat. I'm not afraid that something will happen."

"If it doesn't, it will when the magistrate come back."

"To here? They couldn't wait to get out of here. I'm sure they have more important matter to deal with at the White Citadel."

"Master Agmund didn't seem to think so. He will be back."

"Then we will greet him with full bellies instead of tombstones.

Della took a big slurp of stew and Allistril joined her. They remarked on how good it all tasted.

"Enough you two." Herrick disappeared back upstairs.

"Allistril. Go grab the bread from the counter."

Allistril walked into the kitchen and brought back the bread loaf. Two small hand-sized hunks were missing.

"Herrick, I think we have a hungry child or large mice," Della yelled.

Allistril giggled and handed the bread over. Della removed a hunk and placed it in the third bowl.

"Go take this to your father."

Allistril took the bowl and moved up the stairs.

Herrick sat in the dark.

"Daddy?" Allistril asked.

"I'm here on the bed, Allistril." Herrick reached over and hit the fire striker, sending a shower of sparks to the wick of the lamp. It caught and flared up.

"I brought you something to eat."

His eyes moved around to the shadows in the room, then back to Allistril.

"Take it downstairs, child."

"Daddy, this food came from a miracle. Maybe Asagrim didn't accept it, but I do. So does mommy. Maybe Lofn did this, and she loves us. She wouldn't hurt us."

"Enough. Take it downstairs!" Herrick yelled.

"I thought you were dead in your office. I don't want to find you dead up here."

Allistril went down the stairs, tears forming but not yet falling from her eyes, and put the dishes on the table. She waited for a moment head hung down, then cleared her bowl from the table, no longer hungry.

Herrick walked downstairs and kissed her on the head. Allistril hugged him hard. He reached over her head and took the bowl.

"Let me go so I can eat, child."

Herrick took it to the table and stared at the food in front of him for too long.

Della cleared her throat, and Herrick shook his head and took a bite.

"How is it?"

"As good as I remember. It has been too long since I've eaten."

Someone knocked at her office door.

"I wonder who that could be? I'll be back." She moved through the house and made it to her office. She lit a lantern and walked to the door. She opened it into the pea-soup fog that blanketed Elta.

"Hello?" she called out to the darkness.

The thickness of the fog stopped Della. Sudden thoughts of running into Ivanar and those shadowy hands reaching out stopped her cold. She had a dagger in the office and swords under Ivanar's house, but this thing he had become needed something stronger.

"Lofn, I need you," she whispered.

Something seemed to move in the fog.

"Hello?" she called out again. Stepping out of the door, she couldn't see anyone, much less the businesses and houses nearby.

This is foolish, she thought and shuttered the lantern. She moved in the dark, pocketed her dagger, and put her cloak on. She hurried into the house.

"Aurdr's baby has a rash. I'm going to check on it and take Aurdr some stew."

Herrick was staring at the stew again. "Tell them I wish them well," he said flatly.

"Herrick," Della said. He looked up and smiled at her. "Eat."

She waited until he had eaten a couple of spoonfuls. Otherwise, he might stare at it all night.

She quickly filled a basket with food.

"Keep an eye on Allistril. There is a heavy fog that's fallen. I don't want her leaving the house."

"I will be here."

Herrick went back to staring at the stew, then would take a bite, then returned to staring at it.

Della climbed the stairs. She found Allistril playing. "Go sit with Daddy, remind him to eat."

Allistril nodded and went back downstairs with her.

Della left through the office, grabbing the gem the mangata sent. Then she closed and locked the door behind her. Growing up in Elta had its benefits, like knowing how to maneuver around the village nearly blind. It was dark. The heavy fog made the nearby torches almost useless. There was the occasional torch on the street that provided a small beacon of light, but it would appear and disappear as she moved through the streets. She stopped and listened for anything. It seemed as quiet as when the magistrate occupied the village and she snuck out to see Ivanar. Della felt for her dagger at Dead Man's Trail. The magistrate chased Ivanar into the Delirium Forest opposite of where she headed, but she didn't know what to expect.

Something glowed in the snowy grass beneath her feet. She bent down and a small firebug flashed. She picked it up and cradled it in her hand. It was too soon in the year for them to be out. Usually, they didn't emerge heavily until midsummer and disappeared by early fall. With it being early spring, they should be frozen in the ground. The firebug took off and streaked in front of her, leaving odd blue lines in the fog. It took off down the path toward the beggar's house. Della slowed her approach, took the gem, and planted it into the ground. She listened to the darkness. If Sir Hakon was out here, he would be very near.

She watched the bug's path as it stopped in mid-air and

waited. Not hearing anything, she moved forward. The bug guided her forward until the outline of the shack became clear. Suddenly, a strong odor hit her.

"Who is out there," Sir Hakon commanded. Orbs of light flashed near him and moved. His voice was raspy, dry, and upset. Heavy-armored steps echoed in the mist, followed by the shink of his drawn sword. He stood on the far side of the shack, but Della knew the fog hid her well. A sound in the opposite direction forced him away. The firebug startled her, almost hitting her in the face, and buzzed behind the shack. Della followed, keeping an eye out for Sir Hakon. The firebug landed, flashing excited pulses of blue. A board on the back of the house hung loose. She pulled it away, glanced inside, and stepped in toward the hooded figure in front of the fire. She waited in the shadows as the light orbs passed outside, lighting the cracks in the boards. Sir Hakon was still searching.

Della put down the basket and reached out. Her hand passed through the hooded figure.

Magic. Della backed up, but the image never wavered. Lofn was not here.

She looked out of the missing board. Moving quickly and staying away from the light of the fireplace, she escaped. The blue bug appeared again, leading her away from the house. Sir Hakon's heavy boots tromped on the ground not far from her. The bug flew away from the shack and down to the edge of the Witches Forest. Della stopped, not daring to go further. The bug returned to her, then to the edge of the forest.

"Lofn?" she whispered.

The bug flew back to her, then back to the trees. Suddenly, stars erupted from the forest. Countless firebugs lit up. Della stood there in wonder. The ground behind her lit up and the clanks of armor came closer.

"Halt!" Sir Hakon croaked.

Della ran back into Elta. She glanced back, the wall of bugs grew more intense. The wall of blue ascended, blinked, and winked out of sight. Della pressed into the fogbanks as a lost knight searched the valley.

In bed that night, Della hung between sleep and wakefulness. The hazy moon stared at her from outside the window. The fog's encroachment made the moon a dead, callused thing staring at her from beyond the veil. Sleep took small sections of the night away, but she awoke several times, yet the moon did not move. Finally, the moon broke through the fog. Herrick snored in bed next to her. Allistril slept across the room in her bed, but there was another presence.

Della sat up as the moon fully revealed itself. It lit up the room and the shadow near the wall. She gasped and fell back as the shadow drew near.

"Do not fear me, Della," it said.

"Lofn?" Della's voice choked.

Moonbeams penetrated the female's form as it came closer, rendering it translucent.

"Spirit Folk," Della whispered and glanced at Allistril in horror.

"Pay no heed to legends of the past. Those monsters are long departed." It reached out a hand and touched Della's cheek. It felt electric and warm. "Lofn gave us a message to deliver."

Herrick stopped snoring and bolted upright. Della could only stare at him in the moonlight. The voice hung within the cool atmosphere of the moon-bathed room.

"Come."

CHAPTER 25

As the faint dusk broke over the mountain, Della walked down Dead Man's Trail with another basket and a pail. Herrick followed, carrying a tent and torches. It was dark near the shack and the orbs that hunted nearby were gone. As they ended Dead Man's Trail, they found Sir Hakon collapsed near the shack. Had he died of exhaustion or had something from the forest gotten him? There was no blood visible in the snow. She stared at the forest until Sir Hakon startled awake and cautiously, slowly, stood, hand on sword.

"Halt," he croaked and fell over.

Della hurried down the trail. "Sir Hakon, we are here for you."

He pushed himself up, then gobbled a handful of snow. He strained, trying to stand. "No one shall approach ... the witch."

Della put the basket down and approached with the pail. "You need water."

Sir Hakon stood and stumbled while trying to unsheathe his sword.

"Halt!"

He fell back over in the snow.

"If you don't stop, I will leave this water here. You will just stare at it all day."

"Please, Lady Blanchfield," Sir Hakon begged. "Help me."

"Set the tent up, Herrick. This may be difficult."

Herrick found a flat piece of earth and began to assemble the simple square tent.

Sir Hakon remained in the snow. He rolled over to his knees and relaxed. When his hand moved off his sword, she stepped forward. Immediately, Sir Hakon fell forward and yelled, "Halt!" Herrick stopped putting up the tent and approached. Della held out her hand.

"Wait a moment." She watched Sir Hakon as he relaxed and took his hand off his sword.

Della moved away from him. Took several steps to the side and approached him again.

Sir Hakon tried to stand but stumbled from his anchored spot. "Halt," he shouted. It came out raw, trailed off, and Sir Hakon collapsed.

"Herrick, take his sword," Della said. It took him too long to process. Della grabbed the sword, unsheathed it, and tossed it away.

"No," Sir Hakon bellowed. His face red with cold and fury. His eyes settled on Della. "What have you done?"

"Unarmed you. I'm trying to break the spell."

He lurched for his sword, then landed flat on his face. Della put a knee in Sir Hakon's back as Herrick walked over and took the sword.

"Take it to my office. Otherwise, this will continue. Now, Herrick, go."

Herrick walked up Dead Man's Trail back to the village. Della barely had to wrestle Sir Hakon to keep him down.

Della waited for Herrick to crest Dead Man's Trail before rolling Sir Hakon back over. The armor made it almost impossible. She wiped the snow from his helm.

"I thought this armor was supposed to be lighter."

"The Allfather's blessings are gone. He seemed to relax as his sword went further and further away. "Remember what I said about the potions?"

He lay there breathing slower and slower.

"Please. I lay here in my waste, but all I can think of is that water."

Della grabbed the pail and brought it over. She pulled his helm off and lifted his head. She dipped the steel cup and held it up to Sir Hakon's dry, cracked lips. He drank greedily. Della pulled the cup away. "Slow it down." She held it back up, and he drained the rest of it. She poured a cup of steaming broth from a kettle in the basket. "This is next. We need to ease you back into food." She sat the cup next to her in the snow. "I have soap unless you think you can walk to the Tower now."

"Hah. I'd freeze with a soap and pail bath out here." Sir Hakon's eyes opened a little wider. "My sword?"

"We had to make sure you didn't run me through. It's back to you as soon as you are ready. I want you to sit up now." Della helped Sir Hakon sit up. "Do you want me to remove the armor?"

"Yes, I'll have to scrub it down sooner or later."

"There is that blanket I gave you, but you'll look like a beggar walking down the street."

Sir Hakon dropped his gauntlets and fiddled with the straps of his pauldrons.

"My fingers are too cold. I can't." Sir Hakon sighed deeply, then shudders escaped his chest. "We're lost," he said as he started to cry.

Della guessed it was probably the hunger, the exhaustion, or just the loss of will. So much had changed in the last couple of days, so much had fallen into her and the village's favor. Maybe this would all be worth the sacrifice of Ivanar. As she removed his pauldrons, Sir Hakon wept.

"It will be like the old Elta before all the Tower knights were sent to the frontlines," Della lied.

"The old Elta? Shrinehall is in ruins. The magistrate has passed judgment and left us on our own. They left us here to die. They didn't even bring rations to the Tower."

"We have food and your curse is broken," Della said as she removed the first pauldron.

"The master of your order didn't leave you in the snow to die." He wiped his eyes. "Could I have that broth?"

Della passed it to him. He sipped. "I hate broth. Even when I was a child and ill."

The second pauldron came off easier. Sir Hakon finished the cup greedily.

"This is from the cursed food supply?"

"It's broth from the boiled meat. I have real food in there but wanted to make sure you could stomach this," Della said and worked on his gorget.

"From the cursed supply. If the death that took my brothers-in-arms claims me, at least I won't go to Asagrim hungry."

"The food is safe," Della said.

"The Allfather no longer blesses us, but I stopped being hungry after the roast killed Sir Torstein and Sir Geir. I should have died too, but I was on watch, and they mocked me about how good it tasted. It was my brother's last words to me."

Sir Hakon stared at Shrinehall. Della could tell he was looking at the fallen statue. She removed the gorget and worked on the breastplate straps.

"When I leave, stay away from the house. Please, I beg of you." He took another drink of the broth. "There are dark, twisted magics here. I don't want you or your daughter falling into them. When I was guarding this place half asleep, I could hear them. They taunted me from the Witches Forest, calling my name and saying that Allfather will die soon. I could see their faces in the night, and they gave me visions of the Tower and White Citadel in flames."

"Who did you see?" Della asked.

"Witches that I had put on the pyre."

Hooves exploded on the trail. Sir Solveig approached with sword in hand.

"Why does the mayor have your sword, Hakon? Why is his wife undressing you?" Sir Solveig demanded. He threw the sword into the snow near them.

Della filled the cup again and gave it to Sir Hakon. "What did you do to the mayor?"

"Nothing. He gave it to me without a problem. Now, Sir Hakon. Explain yourself."

"He's water-starved. You left him out here with no relief. We found him collapsed this morning and under the spell from the magistrate," Della said.

Sir Solveig turned up his nose. "There is no spell from the magistrate, that was his orders from Master Agmund himself. Orders I fear you have disobeyed."

"Master Agmund placed a spell on me that I could not stop defending the beggar's shack from those that approached."

"There was no spell. This was the witch's doing."

"I need sleep, Sir Solveig. I've been out here for days with no break, and I am exhausted and frozen."

"Your weakness saddens me, Hakon. March to the Tower at once and clean yourself up."

"Let me change out of my armor."

"You are a Knight of the Brotherhood of Thekk. You losing your sword should deny you of that heritage. Lose your armor, and I will stab you where you stand."

"Please, Sir Solveig. I am filthy. Do not make me march through Elta.

"Now," Sir Solveig commanded, his face burned and mailed fist bunched up ready to strike.

Sir Hakon rose with Della's help. He paused at his knees, struggling to rise. Sir Solveig dismounted and grabbed him under the arm, forcing him to his feet.

"You smell like a charnel house! You mock us all with your appearance. March now," Sir Solveig said. He walked back to his horse and mounted. "Lady Blanchfield, we will be back soon. You are to stay away from the beggar's shack. If we find you any closer to it, you will be arrested."

He stared at her too long, and it made Della's skin crawl. Della wished he would have been present when they ate the poisoned meat.

"Walk quicker, Hakon."

They walked up the trail, Sir Solveig bellowing at Sir Hakon along the way. A small crowd of villagers came out to watch them with awkward stances and unsure stares. They didn't know how to react after the magistrate's occupation, but Sir Solveig made it a spectacle.

Della finished putting up the tent. There would be no doubt Sir Solveig would make Sir Hakon come back down and freeze, watching the shack while he sat in luxury as the handmaiden to the crispy overseer. The thought made her laugh as she shook the snow from the blanket. She needed an ally in this fight or at least one that might hesitate before running her through.

A big snowflake landed on her face. She sighed and finished up her work. Della gathered up the broth and water cups and looked again at the shack. She knew Lofn was still not there.

"Sister," she whispered to the forest.

The snow fell harder. A sudden wind roared toward Elta. She could no longer see the Tower. Shrinehall and even the torches that lined the street disappeared. The wind howled through the Witches Forest, driving the soft snow into a pelting blizzard, threatening to rip the tent away. She stepped inside it. Then silence fell over the valley.

As Della peeked outside a cold fear welled in her belly. The snowflakes hung suspended in the air. She left the tent and grabbed one. It felt cold and melted in her hand. She pulled a dagger from the basket left on the ground.

"What in the name of Asagrim."

"It's not Asagrim, sister."

A lone form stood in front of the beggar's shack. The woman had the skin of luminescent limestone in the dark, dressed in the same white dress of a prisoner ready to burn at the stake, and was heavy with child.

"By the gods, Lofn."

Della rushed forward and embraced her. Her belly had grown since her captivity. Della stepped back and stared at it, her hands moving to touch Lofn's belly.

"It will be soon. This has not been a normal pregnancy," Lofn said.

"How?"

Lofn smiled "Time runs differently in the Witches Forest. Even though it's only been days since I've seen you last, I've spent months there. This birth will be very soon, sister."

Lofn grabbed Della, embracing her. "So much has happened. So much has changed. Please come with me."

Della hugged her back, and there was a steady thrum of power in her. Della cautiously stepped back.

"I will not hurt you, Della. Do not be afraid. Please. Please come with me."

"I can't, Lofn. So much has changed here: the magistrate, Herrick's attack by the Magistratus, Ivanar was killed, and Jahan saw it. Herrick needs me, Allistril needs me, Jahan needs me, Elta needs me."

"Allistril needs me. Bring her." Lofn's voice went quiet.

"What?"

"I will take you both into the forest. Our new lives will start there."

"What about Herrick? What about Jahan? You birthed him!"

She slowly shook her head, "My sister, they cannot enter the Witches Forest."

"Then no, Lofn. I do not know what you have become, but I cannot support leaving Herrick and Jahan."

In the profound silence of the valley, Della could feel her heart hammer. "Herrick sacrificed himself for you. I can barely get him to eat now. He's become like a child. I've healed all his wounds, but there are wounds I can't see. He was attacked by the Magistratus."

"Because he stood up to the overseer," Lofn said.

Della stepped back. She closed her eyes, wanting all this to stop, to go back to the way it was before the hailstorm. Her anger rose.

"Because of what you did to Overseer Daniels." The last part came out quiet. Too quiet, almost like a child describing a monster in the room to a parent. "This has been the strangest revolution, but there is a new age about to come to Elta. The Overseer hasn't been seen since he tried to burn you and you burned him."

Lofn stood emotionless, "I summoned back the crops and the beasts to feed the people, then I was pushed out. Your family, my family, is all I have left."

"What about the children?"

"In time."

"In time?" Della paced. "In time. We have given everything for you to survive. All the work and stupid maneuvers Herrick tried against the Tower to keep you off the stake, and you want me to leave him. Even now I catch him staring at the wall, waiting for the Magistratus to come out."

"Then decide, sister. Are you the healer of Elta or the ruler?"

"He sleeps so much, then wakes up screaming."

"Bring him to us. We will heal his mind."

"Us? Who is with you?"

"Sometimes thousands, sometimes just Him."

Della stepped back. "I don't understand."

"The witches of the past, present, and future. I see Allistril there. She will become a witch of immense power."

"Who is him?"

"There are things I cannot explain. You will have to see."

"No."

Lofn reached forward and touched Della's forehead. In the past, Della had traded mana with Lofn. A sharing of power that tingled through them if one felt low. This was not a sharing. This was a flooded river breaking the dam. This was the ice giants pushing a mountain over on a village.

Della wanted to scream as pure power burned through her body. She felt more alive than she had ever been.

"Just come with me and see, sister. Awaken," Lofn said gently. The faded light above Della turned black, and the hidden stars exploded into nova overhead.

CHAPTER 26

Bera checked herself every morning for pox, sure that the witch's food would be the end of her. Her dolt of a husband just laughed it off as superstition. Valdir lay snoring next to her. The sudden blizzard was a good reason to stay inside and sleep, but once it gave up, she needed to go get more witches' grain to grind. It exhausted her, checking every grain before milling, but if the grain looked odd, it was her duty to call out the witchcraft involved.

Valdir snored again in loud gulping breaths. There was a big fight last night before bed and it still stung. Valdir thundered about taking his sword with him, saying the knights no longer protected the village. Since Sir Hakon guarded the witch and Sir Solveig stayed with Overseer Daniels, nursing him back to health, she understood Valdir's fear but doubted his intentions.

With that sword, Valdir fancied himself as a fighter that could stand up to any threat. His damned magic sword. The thing would put the old warrior on the stake. The arguing went on for hours until Bera went to bed, having enough. She woke overnight to see him staring at it with the floorboard open. Had he awakened the magic? She threatened him that if the magistrate came back, it would be him on the stake and her with the torch. She was done with it.

She got out of bed with a loud groan, loud enough she hoped to make Valdir flop over. He stirred enough that she could yell at him for going against the White Citadel's degree of no magic. She would report him to the Tower if she had to, and she had to go there today anyway.

She moved through the house, changing out of her nightdress and into her work clothes. Then pulled her big boots on, she had work to do today. Sir Solveig secretly came into the bakery yesterday, asking for a large order of meat pies but said that no one else be told. That was her duty today, to cook for the knights and protect them in their time of need. Everything had to be doubly inspected. Especially the meat, so another accident would not claim them. It would be a long day because she trusted nothing she was about to make. She lit a lantern and prepared for the cold outside.

Bera opened the door. The snow had stopped, but the clouds threatened more. For such a windy spring storm, it didn't add much to the snow on the ground. She went around the house and grabbed the cart, gently brushing the snow from the boards. She stopped by the mill to grab some sacks for the wheat while humming a tune about the Allfather's glory. She tried not to think too hard about the grain and meat while swearing several times along the way.

She neared the grainery and found Ragnfast pulling meat from his lockers. It was too early for discussions, especially with Valdir's "friend."

"Good morn, Bera," Ragnfast called.

"Good morn, Ragnfast. How is Jahan?"

"Still staring at the floor."

"Hmmm. Good luck with that."

She passed him with the cart. Ivanar and Ragnfast had their little rebellion against the Tower and paid sorely for it. It was the way it should be. To go against the overseer and the Tower was to go against the White Citadel. It hurt her to even think about what that witch did to the overseer. Many nights she thought about taking a torch to the shack and watching it burn.

She ended up at the grainery and unlocked the large doors. Inside the dust has risen a little. Care needed to be exercised not to spark a fire. Bera scooped the grain, trying to check each scoopful in the weak lantern light for any sign of curse. Each scoopful came with a prayer and a watchful eye. On her last scoopful, a light seeped from under the grain.

"Witchery," she said and stepped back. She thought about getting Valdir, but it would be another reason to pull his sword. It glowed a pale white like what the magistrate knights had around them when they were in Elta. She watched it and scooped the grain away from it. Maybe it was a message from the magistrate that she could take to the people. The orb slowly rose, and she poked it with the scoop.

The resulting explosion echoed through the valley.

CHAPTER 27

S ir Solveig had enough of watching the overseer. The White Citadel's healers showed him over and over how to clean off the dead skin, then treat the raw areas with bear fat, mead that had turned to vinegar, and potions. The smell would not leave his nostrils. Almost like drunken pickled pig's feet. The overseer had slept soundly for several hours, and there was over another hour before he needed to rub the balm on his failing skin. He would patrol and wanted fresh air. His armor awaited.

"Theim!" he bellowed.

The dwarf cautiously approached. Her bruising faded from when she stole the poisoned food.

"Armor."

As the dwarf helped him buckle his armor, his mind drifted.

The village remained silent since the magistrate left. He missed them and wished they would return and deal with the witch once and for all, but as Master Agmund said, there were more things going on in the White Citadel than Elta's problems. They would account what they had found, make judgment, and report back. It wouldn't be good though. Any judgment returned would lead to the loss of the villagers. Since the way through the Delirium Forest closed, travel was impossible, especially since the magic was failing and becoming more chaotic. Sir Solveig tried to impress the magistrate during their stay, but Master Agmund ignored most of his questions and just requested he go out and fetch more for interrogation. Sir Solveig did mention Ivanar and Ragnfast being trouble but didn't expect Ivanar to die.

"Loosen that strap, Theim."

Sir Solveig needed a new village. These villagers were beaten and starving. He appreciated that they had already broken magistrate rule and ate the witch's meat. It was punishable by death, but no one had turned to toads or rats. So, he placed an order with Bera for meat pies. The magistrate had to expect the knights to eat to protect the Tower and village, to protect Overseer Daniels. He would starve since they lost the blessings of the Allfather.

Theim buckled his armor into place and moved away. Sir Solveig slapped his breastplate. He'd been cooped up too long and needed to go around through the village. It took more strength and less armor to mount the horse. He missed the blessings of the Allfather, the lightness of the armor, and wished the current host would depart so a new Allfather would be born. Someone like himself. Sir Solveig would rule with a strong and mighty hand just like the magistrate.

Once on, he kicked the horse to get it going, wondering how long this one would last before they ate it. He left the Tower gates and moved down the trail toward the village. In the distance, coming up Dead Man's Trail was Mayor Herrick Blanchfield, carrying something odd. He galloped down the trail. The mayor carried a sword through the village.

The horse grunted with his repeated kicks. "Move it, you dumb beast."

Herrick held it like he didn't know what to do with it. Sir Solveig squinted, making out some of the White Citadel's markings on the sword. It was one of theirs.

"What in the name of the Allfather?" Sir Solveig shouted. He thundered down Dead Man's Trail, and when he got close enough, kicked the mayor down. Sir Solveig dismounted with a grunt and snatched the sword from Herrick's hands. "Why do you have this?"

Herrick rolled on the ground. "My wife … is helping Sir Hakon. He's ill."

Sir Solveig looked down the trail to the beggar's shack. Sir Hakon was down, and Lady Blanchfield was removing his armor. Sir Solveig made it back into the saddle after great strain.

"This won't be the end of this, Mayor, you go wait in your office." He kicked the horse again. Hakon looked conscious, almost willing to have the witch's friend remove his armor.

"Bewitchment."

He kicked the horse down the trail. Its grunts told him to ease off or he was getting thrown again. Lady Blanchfield was loosening his breastplate when Sir Solveig arrived.

"Why does the mayor have your sword, Hakon?" Hakon was in a stupor. It caused Sir Solveig to yell the next words. "Why is his wife undressing you?"

He threw the sword into the snow near them, wanting the mayor's wife to dive for it. She remained on her knees and filled a cup for Sir Hakon.

"What did you do to the mayor?" she asked.

Sir Solveig laughed to himself. There was no threat. Then the stench hit Sir Solveig.

"Nothing. He gave it to me upon my approach." Sir Hakon barely made eye contact as he sat in his soiled armor. Sir Solveig had seen similar things happen on the battlefield but not on simple guard duty. "Now, Sir Hakon. Explain yourself."

The mayor's wife babbled before Hakon even took a breath.

"He's water-starved. You left him out here with no relief. We found him collapsed this morning and under the spell from the magistrate," Della said.

She had no right to speak when he accused a knight of his failed duty. Sir Solveig turned up his nose. "There is no spell from the magistrate, boy. That was his orders from Master Agmund himself. Orders I fear he disobeyed."

Hakon stirred in the snow. "Master Agmund placed a spell on me. I could not stop defending the beggar's shack from those that approached."

Sir Solveig felt his anger well up. "There was no spell. This was the witch's doing."

"I need sleep, Sir Solveig. I've been out here for days with no break, and I am exhausted."

Now Solveig wished that Lady Blanchfield would make a move toward the sword.

"Your weakness saddens me, Hakon. March to the Tower at once and clean yourself up."

"Let me change out of my armor," Hakon pleaded.

How easy it would be to strike him down, take the Overseer to the White Citadel, and leave these sinners, start over.

"You are a Knight of the Brotherhood of Thekk. You losing your sword should deny you of that heritage. Lose your armor, and I will stab you where you stand."

"Please, Sir Solveig. I am filthy, do not make me march through Elta."

"Now," Sir Solveig commanded, his boiling red face and mailed fist threatening violence.

Hakon struggled, not strong enough to rise on his own. The witch's friend helped him. Once again in a huff, Sir Solveig dismounted and grabbed Hakon under the shoulder, forcing him up. He wanted to slap Hakon but was sure the weak knight would be back in the snow.

"You smell like a charnel house. You mock us all with your appearance. March now," Sir Solveig said. He walked back to his horse and mounted. It was a struggle. "Lady Blanchfield, we will be back soon. You are to stay away from the beggar's shack. If we find you any closer to it, you will be arrested."

He stared hard at the woman. Rumor was Ivanar called out her name near death when the monster, the Magistratus, forced him to tell who the accomplices were. Hakon took several quick steps like he was about to fall.

"Walk quicker, Hakon!" Sir Solveig bellowed.

Hakon started the slow trot of an exhausted thrall. Sir Solveig rode directly behind him. If Hakon stumbled and fell, the horse would take care of the situation, but the smell downwind was awful. He kicked his horse and galloped past Hakon. "Praise Asagrim, you *veisugalti*. I swear to the gods above that you smell worse than a cesspool hag." As Sir Solveig rose over the hill, some of the villagers were out working. He yelled, "*Veisugalti*," at Hakon again, startling the villages who just stared at Hakon as he passed.

"Move it," Sir Solveig said. "I think we're going to build a *niðstöng*, a scorn-pole, and tie you to it at the base of Shrinehall. Let the people of Elta have their way with you."

He looked around at his audience. "Eh, Steiner," he called out to the stonemason. "You have a long enough pole? About four lengths tall?"

Steiner turned and walked away from the knight.

Sir Solveig laughed at the reaction. The villagers were still scared.

"Run, *Eldhúsfífl*"

Sir Hakon stopped.

The first flakes of snow fell.

"Enough of this rubbish." Sir Solveig grabbed Sir Hakon's breastplate and dragged him while kicking the horse. The horse bolted, quickly closing the space between the village square and the Tower's path. Hakon yelled stop several times until Sir Solveig slowed then let the knight go. Hakon collapsed to the ground and rolled.

"Get up, boy." Sir Solveig spurred his horse forward. The horse came forward, close to Hakon, and neighed. Hakon slowly stood.

"Your horse won't trample me," Hakon said. "Who do you think feeds him and brushes him out."

Sir Solveig kicked the horse hard. It grunted and reared back, knocking Sir Solveig off. He landed with a grunt in the snow. Sir Hakon patted the flank of the horse, sending it on its way. Sir Solveig lay in the snow looking up at Sir Hakon. He wiped the snow out of his helm and sat up. "Let's get to the Tower," he finally said.

Sir Hakon extended a hand and helped Sir Solveig up. "We are in dark times, brother. It's only you, me, and a gravely injured Overseer. I know you don't want to hear it, but Master Agmund used magic on me. If we turn on each other, this village is dead."

"Hurmp. If the magistrate returns, this village is dead."

"What should we do?"

"Lock ourselves up in the Tower and wait for Bera to deliver meat pies."

"And you called me an Eldhúsfífl?"

"Watch your tone and get cleaned up."

Sir Hakon, relieved of his soiled armor, soaked in the hot tub. The dwarven thrall stared at the armor. Sir Solveig walked in and noticed her turning her nose up.

"I bet it's not the first time a dwarf found a turd in the armor. Your history is probably full of it."

The thrall stared at the floor. Her gaze moved to the armor. She gathered it, never looking up. Sir Solveig grabbed a bucket and dunked it in Sir Hakon's bath water. He waited for the girl to turn, then dumped the water over her head. "Here you go, get a start on that armor."

The thrall stood still, then stormed off. Sir Solveig watched her leave down the hall. "We will get more of them soon."

"More of what soon?" Sir Hakon asked.

"Dwarven thralls. I guess the White Citadel is mounting a large assault on the mountain."

"Yeah, I heard from the magistrate. I also heard we were taking large losses and relying on renegade wizards."

"Bah. We've got enough magic," Sir Solveig said.

"No, the Allfather's magic is gone, that will cost us in the war."

"Don't speak like that in the Tower, boy."

Sir Hakon soaked for a moment, near sleep. He spoke drowsily, "What even started the war, Sir Solveig?"

"Arguments and anger. Some say it was the beginning of the Allfather's mindsickness after he crushed the giants. The Dwarf King began mining outside of the mountain. They had found a vein of that special metal of theirs, and it ran shallow and for miles. So instead of simply burrowing like the rodents they are, they tore huge gaps out of the land.

"Was it their land?" Sir Hakon asked, head back on the tub.

"What the Allfather sees is the Allfather's. They had their diplomats meet, more of a request for numbers of those in the mines rather than what they did. Then the Allfather left the White Citadel and called for a meeting with their king. He was away on a trade mission in one of the other kingdoms. His son gave the Allfather a tour of the mines. Then the dam that held Lake Laogi back from the mines broke."

"That's not what I heard?" Sir Hakon said.

"It's not, boy. It's not. The Allfather erased the dam, entirely winked it out of existence, and watched from the bottom of the mine as Lake Laogi emptied into it. The Allfather lost his dwarven diplomats and his guard that day, but the dwarves lost thousands."

Sir Hakon silently thought about his old teachings from the White Citadel. "That's not the history I was taught."

"The losers of a battle rarely tell the tale," Sir Solveig said. A hint of sadness in his voice.

"What's wrong?" Sir Hakon asked, sitting up in the tub.

Sir Solveig remained oddly quiet, shifting in his chair. He stood, paced, and said, "I think of our stories. Other knights have banners on these walls telling of their greatness several generations later. I think we are forgotten by our own people."

Sir Solveig nodded to Sir Hakon and walked out of the great hall. Maybe he left to go see to the overseer, but Sir Hakon thought maybe, this would be the first time Sir Solveig would go and quietly contemplate.

Della's world seemed full of fire. She saw glimpses of people, some she remembered being burnt at the stake. Witches. She was surrounded by children, by adults, by the infirm. Some were people of power whose presence made her soul crackle and burn. Some were those who were ignorant of witchcraft, but an errant neighbor blamed them for a seizure or pox. Now, they were beings of power. They came to her in memory. Della almost named them, then they disappeared. In the distance, the branches of the forest spanned forever, blotting out the sky. A massive wildfire erupted from the center of the forest. Then in the fire, the branches moved. They formed elk-like antlers on the head of a forgotten god. The antlers spanned the night sky. Waves of power washed over Della. She was hot, and her sweat formed a barrier that was indifferent to this power. She had to strip off her clothes to cool down. This colossal form rose before her. The antlers rose and knocked the stars from their old orbits. Della screamed and retreated. Darkness overcame the vision as Della stepped out of the Witches Forest. Della went from feeling the heart of the sun to a cold, snowy morning.

"Gods, Lofn. Is that the father?"

Her answer came as a rumble thundered through the valley. The roof of the grainery flew past the Tower and landed in the Delirium Forest. Della stood in shock. The villagers rushed from their houses as she shook herself into the now. The grainery walls had blown out, had toppled from their stilts, and the grain was on fire. Villagers stood like cattle unsure of what to do. Kordan and his hunters were at the well already drawing water.

"Is anyone hurt?" she asked as she moved.

Steiner walked over the blown-out boards and portion of walls.

"Here!" he called. Steiner tried moving the portion of the

wall. Valdir pushed through the people.

"Bera! Bera, where are you?"

"Valdir, over here!" Steiner called.

They tried moving the portion of a wall, it budged enough to reveal a burnt arm. Valdir reached down.

"Gods. It's her."

Ragnfast moved people out of the way Steiner ripped the boards off the wall. His gloved hands protected him while Valdir's callused hand tore and bled. He attacked the wall like a berserker, flinging boards out of the way until he reached his wife.

"Della?" he asked as his voice failed.

Bera lay below. Her hair singed and gone. Her skin swollen and bright red. The force of the blast pushed her out of the grainery, then the walls landed on her. Valdir held her limp hand.

Della fished in her bag, pulling out the potion bottle knowing it was too late. She lifted Bera's head and poured the potion into her mouth. Blood and potion washed out and fell to the ground. She felt on Bera's neck, looking for anything, a pulse, a ragged breath, but there was nothing. Della had a flashback to the Theim that passed in the Tower.

"I'm sorry, Valdir. She is gone."

Herrick arrived with Kordan and the other hunters following with buckets. What was left of the grain was still on fire. They threw the water on the grain, then quickly rushed back to the village well. Several villagers worked the pully to pull the water up out of the well as fast as possible. They transferred the water, running back to throw it on the grain. Steam and smoke rose.

Valdir looked at the Tower and to his wife.

"Where are the knights?" he croaked.

"What did you say, Valdir?" Della asked.

"Where are the knights?" he yelled.

Valdir stood, his face burned more than from the slights of Ragnfast, redder than his burned wife. Rage bellowed in his heart. He stomped off through the crowd.

"Steiner, can you remove the rest of the boards?" Della asked.

She watched Valdir as he disappeared into the crowd. Herrick simply stood in the middle of everything, observing. Aurdr had taken a couple of the buckets from the hunters and filled them with the wet grain untouched by the fire.

"Bera is dead," Della said. Herrick looked at her, then looked back at Aurdr filling the grain. "Herrick." Her husband looked back at her. "Do you understand me? Bera was killed by the explosion."

"Aurdr is getting the grain," Herrick replied and went back to watching Aurdr work. His large pupil looked wildly around, taking everything in. Valdir left his house and walked up the hill toward the Tower.

"You need to stop Valdir before he does something stupid."

Herrick looked up the hill.

"The knights will stop him if they need to," Herrick mentioned.

"By Asagrim, the knights will kill him if he attacks, you fool."

Della ran up the hill after Valdir.

"Valdir, stop!"

She ran up the zigzagged path. Valdir was nearly at the top, but his gait was slow. He walked like he carried Bera's body on his shoulders.

"Valdir, she wouldn't want you to do it."

He spun around with a glowing short sword in his hand. The back of his eyes reflected the same glow.

"I will face them, Della." His voice was strong, and another, almost otherworldly voice spoke in unison. "They are responsible. This is what happens when we go against their will."

"You fool. Extinguish the sword, or you will bring the full fury of the magistrate back to this village."

Della expected him to jump and slash at her. He looked back at his sword. He whispered a word, something old, arcane. The light dimmed from the sword until it faded into the dark.

"The magistrate are responsible," Valdir said.

"That might be, but now is not the time."

"You know the time, don't you? I know Ragnfast and you talk. I know Ivanar was killed because of what you've talked about, but I also know my wife was innocent. She was doing what I told her to do. I told her to get back to work and bake. She loved the White Citadel and the Allfather, even the idiots in the Tower. She would have starved along with the true-believers if I had let her."

"Help us get her body out. We need your strength."

He looked back down at his sword. Valdir's hands bled, but the sword was clean. Della's heart was in her throat. She couldn't stop him from attacking the Tower. She couldn't stop him from attacking her.

"Valdir, please. Come down, now."

His grip on the sword relaxed. He took a deep breath and closed his eyes as tears fell. "I'll help, but soon there will be a reckoning."

Della watched Valdir, but soon something else took her attention. She climbed to the top of Tower Road. Behind the tower, where the roof of the grainery went, the Delirium Forest was on fire.

Della told Kordan about the fire nearing the Tower, and the hunters ran up the hill to contain it the best they could. Several of the villagers cleared the grainery debris and were able to retrieve Bera's body. They wrapped it in a white shroud and took it to the village square. Lofn's pyre stood and next to it the burn marks where Overseer Daniels fell. Valdir climbed the pyre and removed the pole.

"It seems wrong to make this her pathway to Asagrim." Valdir said, "but it's here."

Valdir rearranged some of the wood, then picked up his wife, and laid her in the center. He sat with her for a while as the villagers milled about, picking up grain and debris.

"We don't have to do this now," Della said as she walked to the pyre.

"We do," Valdir replied. He sat there for some time and held Bera's body. "This wasn't the life I promised you. For that I am sorry."

Steiner and Ragnfast approached.

Valdir nodded at them but stared at the body.

He moved and laid Bera's head down softly.

Valdir looked to the Tower a few times, took a deep breath, then lit the pyre. It caught and immediately blazed. "Pass into the arms of Asagrim and prepare for the final battle. Or go work in the bakery and make the old gods fat." He stood stoic as the wood caught and spread.

The villagers and true-believers surrounded Valdir as Bera's embers rose into the sky joining the stars. Orn approached Valdir. A hand on his shoulder transformed into an embrace. Valdir held him, his large body framing the old man.

In a broken voice, Valdir said, "Cattle die, kinsmen die; the self must also die. I know one thing which never dies ..."

The crowd began to reply, and Valdir continued, "Wait for me in *Valhöll* with my kin, beloved. I will be there soon enough."

CHAPTER 28

Ragnfast cut some simple steaks and threw them on the grill. Words had not been easy between him and Valdir since Ivanar died. Even now with the embers of Bera's pyre dying, he ran several conversations through his head. In the morning, he would go dig the ashes for him. An extension to the old graveyard formed deeper in the valley from the storm dead, the knights that passed, and soon for the true-believers if they didn't start eating. Ragnfast sighed. This part of the graveyard was new and already held too many marker stones. He needed to make one for his brother, even though his body still floated about the Delirium Forest as a monster. Ivanar. Thinking about what happened was like the magistrate knight kicking in his ribs repeatedly.

Valdir was his friend. That was the only way to explain what they had. They had constant quibbles where peace was made over the ale that Valdir made. They were both hurting. The last thing they needed was to fight with each other. Food was the solution. Sometimes, the best conversation is not having one while stuffing one's belly.

The simple act of butchering and cooking relaxed Ragnfast immensely. He watched Jahan staring at the fire. Ragnfast tapped the grill, making little embers jump up, but Jahan's expression did not change. He walked out and looked up the hill at the village square. An orange glow lit up the night's sky behind the Tower. Below at the village square, Valdir was still at the pyre. A few people made conversation with him, true-believers. Orn shook his hand and embraced him. Ragnfast didn't know how they survived. They had been without food for too long now and showed it with their gaunt and skeletal forms. Their appearance looked ghostlike, almost wraithlike in the shadows.

The thought stung Ragnfast harshly. He closed his eyes and took a deep breath. "You hungry, Jahan?"

The boy didn't answer, only stared into the fire.

"We will eat well tonight, little friend."

Ragnfast walked into his house and retrieved some wooden plates, a platter, and utensils. He stepped outside in time to flip the meat, then walked to Jahan and held him tight. He patted the boy and messed up his hair, uncombed and unwashed for several days. You smell like the back end of a yak, boy. When we get home tonight, you bathe. Jahan clutched onto Ragnfast.

"I know," Ragnfast said, holding him tightly. "I miss him too."

They held on to each other until the steaks had to be removed. A little too done for Ragnfast's taste but a sacrifice made for Jahan. He put them on the platter and handed Jahan the plates, forks, and knives.

"Let's go eat by the pyre."

They climbed the hill as the true-believers were leaving. They didn't look at Ragnfast with any interest, nor any contempt, their gaunt faces pulled over tight skulls passed him as if he was an object on the trail and nothing more. At the back of the group, Orn walked painfully slow. He stumbled, and Ragnfast grabbed him almost dropping the steaks.

"Thank you," Orn said. He watched the steak a little too long.

"Eat this, old man. I have a ridiculous amount more." Ragnfast helped Orn back on his feet.

"No. No, thank you, Ragnfast. Asagrim provides."

"Then believe that Asagrim provided this. Why die when food is plenty?"

Orn laughed. "Because the witch made the food with her magic."

"What if I told you the knights are eating it too?"

Anger flashed over Orn's face and dissipated quickly. "The food is not natural. Thank you for helping me, Ragnfast. Good evening." Orn steadied himself and then walked off, disappearing into the night. At the village square, Valdir stood over the hot ashes, picking at a couple pieces of still burning wood.

"I'm not hungry," Valdir said to Ragnfast's presence.

"Yes, you are." Probably slept late and hadn't eaten anything all day.

Valdir looked at him and grunted. Jahan handed him a plate. They took the steaks over to some setting stones and ate them.

"Wearing the sword?" Ragnfast asked.

"Yes."

He cut into the steak, taking a bite. Ragnfast waited. He could feel the anger rising.

"This wasn't an ordinary explosion. The magistrate did something to the grainery to make it explode if anyone tampered with the grain."

"Are you sure?"

"Skofnung told me."

Ragnfast made a face at the name.

"Gods, Ragnfast, you make a face like a dog hearing a whistle." Valdir realized his words. "I'm sorry. The sword told me. It's been warning me for a while something was going to happen."

"How long have you been talking to your sword?" Ragnfast couldn't contain his laughter.

"Longer than you've been cutting meat. I was cutting the heads from those trying to stop our conquest. It holds the ghosts of many."

"Bera wouldn't want you doing that," Ragnfast said, suddenly serious.

"Don't put words into my dead wife's mouth," Valdir shouted. Jahan startled, almost dropping his plate.

"Valdir, you unsheathed the sword. Didn't you?"

Valdir took a deep breath. "Maybe." A wry smile crossed his face.

"Did *he* come through?"

"Yep. Magistrate didn't come back, did they?"

"That's a bold move."

Valdir was silent for a moment. "We talked last night about it. How no one is left to protect Elta. I said I would do it, but I wanted my sword. She was mad and went to bed in a huff. She was gone this morning before I woke."

A soft wind blew through the valley. Valdir grabbed a plate, and they all ate in silence, watching the fire approach the Tower. A howl sounded from the forest.

"Nol?" Ragnfast asked.

"I hope not. The flames may be driving him toward Elta."

Valdir unsheathed the sword. Ragnfast had seen some runes on Shrinehall, the knights, and Overseer Daniels staff, but never in the hands of a commoner. These runes were different. They bled light. It also seemed to pulsate while Valdir held it.

"Is that alive?" Ragnfast wanted to run like a lamb from the butcher.

"Yes, raven starver. It's alive. Don't be uneasy around it. It senses weakness."

"Put that away before the magistrate comes back, you fool."

"So, do you think the magistrate will come?" Valdir stood, holding the sword in front of him. "Skofnung, awaken." The sword lengthened. The blood-red runes intensified until the sword blazed white. The glow washed over Valdir until it reflected in his eyes. Valdir turned and held the sword over his head to the Tower. "Where is your magistrate now?" he shouted. "Maybe the Magistratus will come back too. I'll take him out for both of us."

"End this now, Valdir."

Valdir suddenly turned around. His eyes glowed with the same light as the sword. "Ragnfast Ketilsson. Ketilsson … that's not right. That was on your mother's side. You should be Ketilsdóttir." The voice was not Valdir's. Ragnfast backed away.

It was an insult that should have made Ragnfast attack. It was an old family story of embarrassment that his great-granduncle stole the name from his wife. Ketill was a great explorer and warrior. The granduncle's family were fishermen and trappers and had the clan name Óttar, after the animals they trapped. He had never told anyone in Elta.

"Óttar's a cute name for you. I will call you, Óttar." It was in Valdir's voice, but stronger and more capable.

"How, how do you know this?"

"The sword's power. It knows things, and it tells me. Sleep, Skofnung."

As the light waned in Valdir's sword, it shrunk back to its normal size. The runes continued their pulsation, and the light bled.

"Valdir?"

"Easy, Óttar, you don't know magic. It can be a bit much to see for the first time."

"Bera wouldn't want you using the sword."

Another cry broke the night. Both turned and looked at the Tower. A colossal shadow lifted above the forest, then crashed into the ground by the Tower. The hunters cautiously approached. The beast's screech rang through the valley.

"Is that Cody running down?"

"The forest burns and the flames come this way," Kordan yelled as he gathered the hunters. "The fire heads to the Tower. Get the shovels."

There was mumbling between them.

"We won't enter the forest. Remember the lesson of Nol."

"Nol? Remember the lesson of Ivanar!" Haveldan the hunter yelled.

Someone else yelled, "Let the Tower burn."

"The magistrate did that to Ivanar," Kordan said.

"And our knights did nothing to stop it."

Kordan shouted over them, "We must start digging a trench before the Tower to stop the fire."

"There's not enough room for a fire break, Kordan." Haveldan yelled back, "We'd have to enter the forest. Not one of us will do that again."

"If the Tower catches, the embers will rain down on the village. Then what? Curse the knights as our homes burn?"

There was a shout from the Tower above them. The knights had installed a bolt thrower on the roof. A long javelin sailed from the Tower roof, then something screamed deep within the forest.

Within the Delirium Forest, other shadows advanced backlit by the coming flames. The trees themselves seemed to uproot and move, clearing a path. Almost welcoming them. The odd sounds, bellows, screams, and howls, made the hunters stop in their path. They drew their bows and nocked arrows. A figure walked away from the other beasts.

"Nol?" Kordan whispered. It moved in front of the fire, then turned to face the hunters. The figure had lost an arm.

"Or is that Loche?" Haveldan asked. Kordan recoiled at the name of the old mayor who disappeared.

"Loche was a smaller man. That's Nol. Look how he stands. He's changed."

Several hunters babbled around him.

"What happened to his arm?"

"Do we bring him out?"

"He's not Nol anymore. If he approaches, he will attack," Kordan said.

"What of Aurdr?"

"She misses him, but he is a shepherd of the forest now. If he returns, we are doomed."

The figure glanced back at the fire, then ran from the flames back into the dark forest.

Cody, the youngest of the hunters, stepped back, "They fly!"

They backed up and watched figures fly from the top of the trees, gaining height then falling in slow, lazy loops, scanning the prey below.

"Hold your arrows unless they fly to Elta," Kordan yelled.

Another bolt soared overhead into the forest.

"Fools," Kordan yelled, "Hold your arrows."

The remark took a few of the hunters by surprise until they looked and a few of their number had notched arrows toward the roof.

"Fire's shifting. Back off from the Tower, now. Let the knights have their play. If they bring something from the forest, let them take care of it. Otherwise, we will protect Elta. You, boy, Cody. Go get Valdir. If he is sober, tell him to come."

"He lost his wife today," Haveldan said.

"All the reason to get him into a fight. Cody, get Ivanar's brother, Ragnfast, as well."

As Cody ran, the hunters moved to an open spot on the Tower grounds. Shadows flew in the night sky but not beyond the borders of the forest. Something large erupted through the trees into the night sky, unearthing a scream that even the hunters themselves feared. It took large loops. Leaving trails of smoke in the moonlight. Sir Solveig stood on the Tower above them, aiming with the bolt thrower, and took a shot. The shadow screamed and wheeled in the sky. With each wingbeat, it fought to gain height, until it crashed before the hunters. In the weak Tower torchlight, the beast stood out, the scorched feathers and the exotic skin of its head, large, looming, and swollen.

"Asagrim, have you ever seen anything like that?" Haveldan asked.

"It's been twisted by the Delirium Forest. Haveldan, don't go near it." Kordan said.

The creature lay face down, sharp ears turned toward Haveldan's approach. A quick succession of chirps and growls came from the beast as it rose, dwarfing Haveldan. The beast's crimson face looked like that of a burnt hairless wolf. Its maw was a nightmare of muzzled teeth and deformed beak, burned, mutated, and rebuilt by a mad god. Its sick, yellow eyes glowed in the torchlight behind Haveldan. It hissed with the voice trailing into a low growl that reverberated in the thing's chest.

It flexed its wings on the ground, the javelin-like bolt firmly wedged into the wrist of the wing, and blood fell to the ground. The monster slowly brought its wings up, barely missing Haveldan. The beast tested its wings with a couple of slow flaps. Then it rushed forward and lept into the air. The wings thumped in the heavy night air as it attempted to gain height.

"Beware those wings. They are not feather," Haveldan yelled. The knights and hunters both aimed at the beast. It hovered, then flicked its wings forward. Shards of the odd feathers sang through the air and embedded into the Tower, ground, and Haveldan. He stood for a moment, then lost his footing and fell back. The hunters and knights fired at the beast. Several arrows and a bolt hit. The monster veered back into the forest and crashed into the treetops. The hunters watched with bows at ready for the thing to charge through the cursed trees as Kordan assessed Haveldan.

"Fool, I told you to get away from it," Kordan said.

The hunters walked back as Ragnfast and Valdir joined them.

"What was that thing?" Valdir yelled.

"Something cursed from the forest. It went down in the trees. We need to get Haveldan to Della now."

"What was wrong with you today?" Della asked as she removed the plates from supper.

Herrick sat in his chair hunched forward. "I don't know. I was watching what was going on after the explosion, I just couldn't think, couldn't act. It was like something else was in control. I was just watching."

"Couldn't think? You had the hunters pouring water on the fire."

"That wasn't me, that was Kordan. I watched. You told me Bera had passed. It's like it was a dream."

Della stood watching him until Herrick looked up. That strange pupil was still blown out but moved with his other eye. "How do you feel now?" she asked.

"Like myself," Herrick said, crossing his arms and looking at the floor.

She continued watching him, wondering if she should even speak about what happened. She knew the monster listened.

"Today after Sir Hakon and Sir Solveig went back to the Tower, Lofn appeared to me."

"Della, no!"

"Something is about to happen. She told me we should leave."

"How can we leave? We're trapped."

"I don't know. She told me to come into the forest."

"The Witches Forest? Della, you can't. I don't want you to go near that shack."

She crossed her arms. She wanted to tell Herrick that Lofn offered to reverse what the magistrate had done to him. Then it just came out. "She also wanted Allistril to come."

Herrick stood, fist clenched. "No. I won't lose my daughter to that forest."

"It's not the Delirium Forest, Herrick."

She was ready for him. Herrick did not have the nature of a violent man. It was unusual for him to even stand in an argument. He usually shied away.

The sudden knock on the door defused the coming argument that Della did not want. She answered the door. Ragnfast stood out of breath, pointing to Valdir and Kordan carrying Haveldan.

"Are we under attack?"

"Something from the Delirium Forest attacked us."

"Take him over." Della shut the door and rushed into her office.

She ran through the kitchen and opened her office door as Valdir and Kordan arrived. They moved Haveldan to the bed. Three odd, metal shards protruded deep from his leg, shoulder, and the third lay on his ribs. Della rushed about gathering ointments, rags, and potions, including the one that Mangata Soren gave her.

The dagger against Haveldan's ribs fell out as he was placed on the bed.

"What is this?" Della asked as she picked up the shard.

"Part of the creature's wing," Valdir said.

"This came from an animal?"

"It was not like any animal I've seen," Haveldan said. "The horror of that thing's face."

Valdir took the feather. "It feels like brass. Sharp too, better edge than I can make."

Kordan described the beast as Della carefully pulled out the dagger from Haveldan's shoulder. Blood filled the wound and spilled. She carefully and quickly stitched it shut.

"I can't give you the potion until I get this last one out. I don't know what it would do otherwise."

"Della, I need to go rejoin the hunters in case that beast comes back," Kordan said.

"Go. Ragnfast can help."

"So, I guess we're freely using magic in Elta now?"

"Shut up, Valdir. You have your sword, and she's used potions for years," Ragnfast said as he stepped up to the bed.

"Óttar," Valdir called.

"Boys, the potion was given to me by one of the White Citadel's wizards. It works well, and healer potions were always allowed by the Tower. I've not seen one work this well before."

Della took a deep breath and looked at Haveldan. "The shard is near an artery. I'll have to be quick and careful."

"Do what you need to, Della." Haveldan raised his head and watched her. "I've made my peace if a battle-maiden comes to find me."

Della touched the protruding blade. It gently throbbed. The blade itself was on the artery she thought. "Ragnfast, get that potion ready. Haveldan, drink what he gives you as fast as possible. Valdir, you may need to apply pressure."

She grabbed her old tourniquet and banded it around Haveldan's upper thigh. She used a wooden rod to twist the silk strip tightly on his leg. "Valdir, give that three more twists."

Haveldan yelled.

"No one else dies today, Haveldan." She looked at Valdir as he twisted the rod three more times. Haveldan grunted, clawing at the sides of the bed.

"We will do this quickly," Della said. She pulled the blade straight out and could see the artery within the leg. Even with all the pressure, the artery sprayed from the wound. "Now, quickly the potion."

Kordan poured it into Haveldan's mouth who coughed and sputtered.

"Della!" Valdir yelled as the rod in his hand cracked and broke. Blood poured, then shot across the room. Haveldan's head hit the bed.

Della tried to twist the tourniquet, but blood still sprayed from the wound. She dropped the tourniquet, pointed at the wound, and yelled "Ber-Isa-Elhaz!" The room filled with red light. Runes appeared, cutting the air with their incantations, and dove into Haveldan's wound. Ragnfast and Valdir were blown off their feet to the back wall. Haveldan was still. Then slowly he coughed and raised his head.

"I thought I died."

Valdir and Ragnfast could only lay on the floor and stare at Della.

CHAPTER 29

Herrick threw another log on the fire as they waited for word on Haveldan. He glanced over at his daughter. "Go on upstairs and get ready for bed. Mom will be back soon." Herrick froze and stuttered on the last words. He turned and stared at the wall where Della's office was. Two thumps hit the wall.

"Daddy?"

"Go upstairs, Allistril." The words were distant, flat, almost dreamy. Herrick stood and moved toward the kitchen as a growl reverberated through the house.

Della screamed.

"Stop it, Valdir!" Ragnfast yelled.

The door slammed in the office, then a loud crash shook the house.

"Daddy!" Allistril yelled upstairs, but Herrick was unable to call back. He continued walking to Della's office.

Thunder struck outside, and a roar shook the valley.

"It's not the season for lightning. This is unnatural," Herrick said to himself. "Crimes of magic." He wanted to run. This eccentric stroll was all he could command his body to do. The hallway was dark, but oddly he could see as if it were lit by unfettered moonlight. There was a moment of panic as his hand opened the office door. A surreal nightmare flashed through his mind that would end up with him staring at the Magistratus when he entered, but he could not stop himself. Slowly, his hand grasped the knob and opened it. His eyes scanned the office and the gap that stood where the door was. Broken like something huge had gone through it. He reported to no one in particular.

Ragnfast had a bow and a quiver. He looked at Herrick with panic in his eyes. "It's Valdir. Valdir … became something. He's going to kill Della. Get your bow. I don't know if I can stop him."

Herrick stood still and stared.

"Gods, Herrick. Can you hear me? Get your bow!" He ran out the front door. Lightning flashed and thunder roared nearby. Another roar echoed through the valley.

Herrick walked through the large gap where the office front used to be.

The Witches Forest glowed with the same intensity as the fires raging in the Delirium Forest, but this was not destruction. The blue firebugs lit up the Witches Forest and swarmed in a vortex around Della. An enormous bear, greater than any grizzly, towered over his wife.

"There is a cave bear in Elta. Cave bears were thought to be extinct." Herrick said coolly as it stood ready to swipe at his wife.

"That's Valdir!" Ragnfast yelled and shot two arrows in its back that merely fell to the ground after they hit. Kordan's horn blew in the distance from the Tower. The hunters ran down the road. Della pointed at the beast. An unearthly green glow surrounded it as its hair stood on end. A lightning bolt discharged from the forest, striking the bear and sending it flying back.

It laid on the ground, fur and skin burnt to the bone. Della turned and ran to the forest, the blue glow of the forest intensifying around her and quickening her movements.

Ragnfast ran at the bear, nocking an arrow and aiming at the cave bear's slacked jaw. The lightning wounds tugged themselves together and sealed. New fur sprouted around the healed wound like wild grass. Herrick stood nearby.

Ragnfast shouted. "No, Valdir! Let her go. Please."

The bear stirred.

Ragnfast stepped in front of it, "No."

The bear rolled over and stood. Ragnfast loosed the arrow. It whistled and struck Valdir in the open maw.

Blood poured from the wound, but Valdir snapped at the arrow until it fell out. Ragnfast stood before it, bow slack at his side. He reached for an arrow as the bear roared. It looked up and watched Della enter the Witches Forest. Its raging eyes then focused on Ragnfast, who simply spoke, "Jahan."

The bear swiped at Ragnfast, claws entering his torso and ripping viscera away. The next swipe threw him violently to the side. The bear charged toward the forest and Herrick approached where Ragnfast lay dying.

"Mayor … take care … of the boy," Ragnfast struggled to say.

Herrick stood, watching the lifeforce leave Ragnfast. He then strolled to the edge of the Witches Forest. Valdir roared at a curtain of firebugs circling along the entrance. When Valdir got too close, they attacked. The bear would swipe and roar at them, then retreat. The hunters entered the valley and drew arrows.

Kordan walked to Ragnfast's corpse. "Gods, did Valdir kill Ragnfast?"

Herrick stared ahead at the bear trying to enter the forest.

"Yes" came his dreamy far-off response.

"Kill it," Kordan commanded. Arrows screamed through the night, hitting the target. The bear roared, still galloping and finding its way into the forest blocked. The other arrows seemed to bounce off this beast, but he remembered hunting the Grizzlies with his father as a child. Kordan drew his longbow and waited for the bear to pass in his field of aim. He grabbed a curved broadhead arrow that Valdir made especially for him, just in case a large bear interrupted his hunt. He watched the front legs. When they passed his chest, he fired.

The arrow struck Valdir's inner leg and he roared at Kordan.

Its pace lessened. Valdir's gurgled roar answered back as it drunkenly charged through the firebugs into the Witches Forest.

The hunters gathered near where the bear entered. The blue firebugs slowed down in their flight, hovering and making a wall to the hunters.

"What do we do, Kordan?" Cody asked.

The bugs parted and created a large opening. Cody almost walked in until Kordan stopped him. Valdir's naked human form flew out of the forest over their heads and landed hard on the ground, rolling to a stop. The forest itself writhed, split, and opened. Branches, evergreen in the deepest of winter, knotted together to create the form of a man. The firebugs themselves swarmed upon it, giving an immense hand flesh. It emerged holding Valdir's glowing sword by the blade. A large figure exited the Delirium Forest. Draped in the skins and skulls of beasts and man, its elk-like antlers reached to the sky above as in almost prayer. His body pulsed with the blue glow of the forest as he stalked out before Valdir.

Kordan dropped to his knees in reverence followed by the other hunters. Only Herrick Blanchfield, quiet and observing, stood. The slow, blue light ebbed within its body, turning to a red glow that crossed his entire form and highlighted his silhouette in the dark. He took Valdir's glowing sword in his hands and snapped it like a weak branch. The light bled from the blade as he dropped it in the snow at Valdir's feet.

It stood and stared at Valdir. "Herrick Blanchfield," its voice echoed through the valley like thunder. Herrick stood almost 100 lengths away from the forest god. The god's massive head turned toward Herrick and it reached out. Herrick sailed through the air by an unseen force, then stopped before him. It grasped Herrick's head and said, "You are unnatural, enough of this." Its words echoed by every creature in and near the Witches Forest. Red light overwhelmed Herrick's small figure. The god laid Herrick down as he retched darkness into the earth. A black shadow flowed from his mouth and faded. Herrick collapsed to the ground, unconscious.

Horns bellowed from the Tower. The being moved to the fallen form of Ragnfast. Its hands passed through Ragnfast's chest and lifted a shimmering form. It raised its hand and the ghostly form fell apart like glittering snow.

Kordan dared to look up as the being approached.

"Ivanar Ketilsson, I summon you." Its voice boomed.

In front of the beggar's shack, a small white light erupted from the ground. A gem rose in the air and hovered as a white-hot beam of light shot out and pierced the being through the chest. It looked at Kordan in shock as the firebugs exploded and the wooden supports split and fell to the ground. The blue light ebbed and faded away.

On the edge of the Witches Forest, a wraith appeared, ignored by those that just watched a god die.

CHAPTER 30

In a darkened spire room at the White Citadel, Master Agmund remained seated in a large chair. A small candle illuminated the Magistratus' hands on his temples. The Magistratus flinched and howled, releasing Master Agmund's head.

"That is all, Magistratus."

The wraith disappeared into a small velvet-lined box that contained a skull and pieces of bone. Master Agmund closed the box and whispered a locking rune over it.

"Elta is lost," Master Agmund said, slumping in his chair, exhausted. "The forest god severed my link to Mayor Blanchfield."

Mangata Soren sat at a table across from him, drinking from a horn. "There are other plans." He pulled a potion from his robes and drank it. "I need a moment for this to work."

"Take your time. Wake me if it's important."

"You will want to remain awake for this." Mangata Soren stood and walked to the middle of the room, his hands dancing before him. The air shimmered as runes on the floor burned around them. Mangata Soren tapped the floor like a trapped rabbit and a golden circle formed. Quick shouted words erupted from his lips as an image appeared between them. The forest god held something in his hands that fell apart. The god looked at one of the hunters.

Quick staccato spells flew from the mangata's lips, each one like a slap to Master Agmund's ears. In the image, a beam shot out and struck the god. His form fell apart, and the room went dark. Something collapsed in the room.

Master Agmund picked up the candle and lumbered over to Mangata Soren's form on the floor. He reached out and checked for a pulse. The mangata lay unconscious.

Master Agmund opened the chamber door and called for a thrall. A young man appeared wearing his simple white uniform. Magical runes tattooed his arms, some for location, some for harm if he disobeyed. This was their Theim.

"You will take Mangata Soren back to his study. Inform the others that he has committed great magic and will need time to recover. Also, move the Magistratus to my office. I retire this night."

The Theim bowed low and moved the unconscious wizard's form.

Master Agmund slipped down the back stairs, the need for sleep dragging him down to the quarters. He entered his humble room and stumbled to his bed while removing the vestments. The bed called and he embraced it, pulling the covers up. He skipped his evening prayers to the Allfather. His visit to the chambers today made him unsure if Asagrim's earthly form even heard them anymore. Elta would fall in ruins.

Earlier today, Master Agmund requested an audience with the Allfather. When he was a young knight, this place held a fervent energy. You felt unstoppable, but a single glance from the Allfather either emboldened the victory or let a warrior know his time had come. Like Shrinehall, this place felt like a ruin. A single guard opened the great doors to let him enter. Inside, a shaft of sunlight illuminated the old relic. The once great war table assembled knights, warpriests, mangatas, and magistrate to sit with the Allfather. This table supported conquest but had grown silent and unused. Now, dust scattered across it like the ashes of the great knights it held within its wood.

Master Agmund's exhaustion made his mind race. Earlier, he announced his findings on Elta. In the past, after such a report, the

Allfather would feebly proclaim to burn the village and salt the earth. Now, he lay in his deathbed like a shriveled fetus. His daughter, Lady Eira, sat on his throne and listened with great concern. The strangest look came from her when she mentioned the pregnancy and possible sire. She excused Master Agmund to commune with her father.

He left the room and waited in the antechamber. Sir Gregory, the champion of the White Citadel, walked past Master Agmund and entered the room. Hours passed before he was summoned again.

Sir Gregory and Lady Eira sat at the table together, but Lady Eira chose every word. "We will spare Elta. The overgrowth of the Delirium Forest will be punishment enough."

"We leave the village intact?" Master Agmund dared to ask.

"When the child is born. The overseer will take it and return the infant to the White Citadel. Then the witch will burn. Any in legion with her will die at the hands of the local knights."

"Even the knights are eating the tainted meat and grain. This was against our orders."

"The war, Agmund," Lady Eira answered. "We need all resources here. The way to Elta is dangerous and difficult to maneuver even with the most powerful of our magics. I will work with the mangata to have a path cleared through the Delirium Forest by the time the child is born."

Sir Gregory nodded. "I will meet them outside the Delirium Forest and bring the infant back."

"Is Overseer Daniels well enough to complete this mission?"

"Well enough," she nodded with no look of concern on her face.

"Then thank you, my lady. I will await further instruction." Master Agmund bowed and turned to leave but froze when Lady Eira spoke.

"At this point, Agmund. Forget about Elta. We have other needs of your skills elsewhere."

"Yes, of course." Master Agmund smiled. "I await your

command." His entire journey to Elta was fruitless. He fretted over her words, "needs of your skills elsewhere." Which meant one thing. They were going to the Dwarven Siege of Mount Suðri.

CHAPTER 31

Every nerve on Valdir hurt as he awoke. He stirred, grunted, and lay still. It had been twenty years since he went into full berserk with the sword's influence. Now he had to face the ones around him with the monster he was.

"It's not right what you did."

The voice made him open his eyes and look around. He was in a Tower cell. Steiner stared at him through the bars.

Valdir groaned. "What are you doing here? Why am I in here?"

"You don't remember?"

"I berserked." Valdir stiffly sat up. "I don't remember when I change. Did I hurt Della?"

"What are you?" Steiner asked.

"A man that in a moment of anger did something stupid."

"Are you a demon?"

Valdir scrutinized Steiner, but the question made a flood of memories hit. Flashes of light and pain. Images of a horned man from the forest. He shook his head trying to clear his throbbing headache. Valdir laid on the cot. "Get me some water."

"You will have no such comfort."

From Steiner, that was an oddity. For someone who moved stones all day, he had a rather gentle demeanor and always avoided conflict.

"What happened, Steiner?"

"You mauled Ragnfast."

The words struck Valdir. "What?"

"We're meeting tonight. Mayor Blanchfield can't wake up. His healer wife ran into the forest when you chased her. Only Orn, Gaut, Kordan, and I remain on the council. Orn and Gaut are talking about leaving. We're meeting about hanging you."

Valdir stood and stumbled to the cage. His limbs drunk and heavy from a berserk hangover. He grabbed at Steiner who stepped back.

"Get me out of here."

"I won't release you, monster. You are in here for murder. The overseer is not well, not enough to cast judgment, so the council will do it. You put Elta in danger and will be judged."

Steiner lifted his chin and scowled at him. Any other time and Ragnfast and Valdir would have found it hilarious. "Abomination," Steiner said and walked away.

Valdir howled. The loss of his wife, the loss of his friend, Ragnfast, flooded onto him like a burst dam after a storm. His yells and screams reverberated through the empty cells of the Tower and remained unanswered. Della used magic, and it enraged him to become the monster he denied for so many years. Bera, his filter, was gone.

The sun climbed closer to the mountains but didn't appear over the peak. A fire burned to drive off the cold, but its fingers still crept among the ruins of Shrinehall. Steiner sighed and gazed out toward the beggar's shack on the edge of the village. Outside of the Witches Forest, a large, new tree grew, with a trunk that appeared to be a man. Steiner shook his head. This was too much for him.

"Is the witch even still in there?"

He turned to the table and glanced at Orn and Gaut, who had to be both carried up to Shrinehall by the hunters. They slumped in their chairs completely overtaken by their hunger. Kordan sat, sharpening his sword.

"Then let's start this. I don't remember how the mayor did this in the past, so let's just make our decisions and go," Steiner said.

Sir Solveig climbed the steps. He arrived unarmored in a simple tunic.

Steiner stared at his assent. "This is village business. Does the Tower reject our meeting?"

Sir Solveig held his hands up. "I know the Tower has not been a part of the Thing before, but you don't have anyone here. Can I join?"

"You can join, but you have no vote." Steiner shrugged, "Welcome. Where is your armor?"

Sir Solveig sat. "I wanted to be here as a citizen."

Kordan sat back in his chair. Steiner noticed he placed the blade on the chair next to him and didn't sheath it.

"Has anyone become sick from the food?" Steiner asked.

Kordan shook his head, throwing a glance at Ragnfast's chair. "No one has become ill."

"Then what would it take for you and yours to eat?" Steiner asked. "Even the Tower eats."

Sir Solveig stared at the table. "We do. We eat the damned meat and grains."

Gaut remained motionless in the chair. Orn seemed startled awake by the question. "Then that is on your soul, Sir Solveig. There is a path through the Delirium Forest that the fire has burned." Orn paused a moment. "Tomorrow, my kin are leaving for the White Citadel."

Steiner laughed. "You won't make it. You can't. We can't allow your women and children to die because you don't like what's happened here."

Orn leaned toward Sir Solveig. "Is there anything stopping us?"

Sir Solveig shook his head. "No. No rules keeping you here.

We used to have trade routes until the seizure occurred. That's how the mayor came to Elta. How is he, Kordan?"

Kordan answered, arms folded at his chest. "Aurdr is looking after him, Allistril, and Jahan. She's got her hands full. There has been no change since last night. He's in a deep sleep he can't wake from."

"What about Della?" Sir Solveig asked.

Kordan looked up at Sir Solveig, watching him like a beast in the arrow's path. "No sighting of her."

"You are a fool if you leave," Steiner said to Orn. "You will die on that path."

"My great-grandson scouted the path this morning. He entered the fire's path near the Tower. He did not feel the change coming on him. One of the old trails is visible to White Citadel. I think they could make it over a week."

"You are not strong enough and will be simply claimed by that evil forest, just like Nol," Kordan said. "We fought something from there that I still can't believe was real. There were other things inside, waiting."

"Asagrim and the Allfather will protect us," Orn said.

"Like he protected Nol," Kordan said.

"Eat something, get your strength back before you go, or just stay," Steiner said. "Gods, I wish Herrick was here."

"Thank you for your concern, Steiner," Orn said.

"Then let's do what we came together for," Kordan said. "Valdir's fate."

Steiner gathered his thoughts. Kordan spoke up. "I was there last night. I wounded him before he could hurt Della."

"Della Blanchfield went into the Witches Forest?" Gaut whispered from his chair. "She is in league with the witch."

"I don't know. I heard things about last night. Heard the thunder. She ran there to get away from Valdir or whatever Valdir became," Steiner said.

"I'm too new to this table to know how all this works and apologize if I say something that goes against what you do here,"

Sir Solveig interrupted. "I was originally at the White Citadel, and I know of some things not seen in Elta."

"What is Valdir?" Steiner asked.

"I talked to him this morning. He's a berserk. Sword enhances it. He can take the form of a bear and fight." Sir Solveig said as a matter of fact.

The table stared at him.

"Valdir used to be in a special unit of the White Citadel army. A very exceptional unit that most people don't know about. They trained him. It's uncommon, but in large battles, you see groups of them. They're unstoppable."

"So, it's natural?" Steiner asked.

"I wouldn't call it natural, but they have different ways of doing it. Some have to kill a bear, then there's a big ritual under a warpriest, others are cursed. Valdir didn't tell me that much. I think he's probably cursed."

"So, the man that told everyone about Lofn's magic used to use magic," Kordan said. "Fitting."

Sir Solveig waited for Kordan to finish. "Either way, they are incredible to watch in battle. Even if they call themselves cursed, they are Asagrim's blessed."

"He used a magical sword," Gaut said.

"Yes, he did," Sir Solveig interrupted. "Which Valdir procured in his time under a king of the White Citadel. He was part of his special guard. That king was assassinated and his people scattered. That's when he became a plunderer. If the magistrate had found it, they would have figured out who he was. That thing in the forest snapped it in two."

"And now that the magistrate is gone, are we freely using magic?" Orn asked.

"I am not the overseer. I am a soldier. Valdir got the sword in his time at the White Citadel, so I have no issue. My sword had magic qualities and so did my armor."

"Then we vote to hang him, all in favor?" Steiner blurted.

Orn glanced over at Gaut. "We will abstain from this vote.

Our kin leave in the morning, and we will not vote on the death of a man."

"Steiner, hold on." Sir Solveig stood to address the group. "There are things out in the forest that we don't know or understand. The fire showed us that yesterday with that bird-thing that almost killed Haveldan."

"That was no bird," Kordan said.

"Then what was it? How do we fight it? Weaponized feathers? Is this a new breed or something that the chaos of the forest caused?" Sir Solveig asked.

"I'm a hunter. Nothing more," Kordan replied.

"Then be more or this village won't survive." Sir Solveig glared across the table. "You know animals, you've hunted them since you were a child."

Kordan nodded.

"Then figure it out. Find the weakness of this new creature." Sir Solveig stood. "This is where I have to ask something of the council, something outside of Tower rule." Sir Solveig looked at everyone gathered and stopped on Kordan. "Spare Valdir. Let him fix his sword. We will keep him at the Tower and under guard while at the forge.

"He killed Ragnfast in cold blood," Steiner yelled, hitting the table.

"There are things in that forest that will kill this entire village," Sir Solveig said flatly. "Sir Hakon and I are all that's left. Overseer Daniels is at the Tower, but he's barely alive. That's it. The magistrate told me no more knights or overseers. There's a war going on and it's not ending soon. It's not going well either." Sir Solveig's attention went elsewhere until he finally spoke. "We are alone here."

"So, are you the new voice from the Tower?" Orn asked.

"For now. This is why I am here."

Silence took over the table.

"I've been friends with both Valdir and Ragnfast for years," Kordan spoke. "We've lost Ivanar, Bera, Ragnfast, and we don't know about Della, Lofn, and Herrick. We've lost too much. If Valdir is a berserk, we don't know what set him off. Della used magic. I saw it. She used lightning to strike Valdir. If Bera died by magic, that might have been it. Haveldan said something happened when Della treated him. He should be dead, but Della somehow saved him. Valdir saw her use it and lost it."

"He killed Ragnfast," Steiner said.

"And he burned his wife that night," Kordan replied. "I won't kill him."

"Hang him," Steiner yelled.

"He stays in the Tower," Sir Solveig said.

"You don't have a vote here," Steiner yelled. "You asked to be at the meeting, and that is all."

"We will not vote on the death of the man. I speak for Gaut too." Orn said. He held on to Gaut's shoulder who slumped in his chair staring at the fire.

Steiner stared at Kordan.

"My will says no, Steiner," Kordan answered.

Steiner hit the table and sulked away staring at the Tower.

Footsteps scraped up the stairs. Herrick ascended, wrapped in a thick blanket.

"Hello, all," Herrick paused at the top of the stairs. "Forgive me. I think I'm better now. Just give me a moment." He dragged himself to the table, out of breath. "I've sat at this table for a year. We've discussed starvation, death, and revolution." Herrick sat down lost in thought. "This week ... this day, we've lost too much." Herrick's lip trembled. "Aurdr told me a lot, not sure that I understand any of it."

"He was going to kill your wife," Steiner said.

"The forest god protected her," Kordan answered.

"Forest god," Herrick looked at Kordan, pleading to understand. "You say that like it's a common occurrence here, Kordan. The magistrate, the grainery, this thing in the forest, these last days are unlike anything that's happened in Elta's history. Magic is everywhere and we can't use it." He paused. "Aurdr said

Della commanded the lightning."

"Your wife worked very close to Lofn, Mayor," Sir Solveig said. "Valdir was the one who told about the magic Lofn used to bring back Aurdr's baby. Della was there taking part in it. The magistrate was very interested in her after …"

"Say it, you *meinfretr*," Kordan said through gritted teeth, his hand reaching for the chair.

"I have no quarrel with you, Kordan. Stay your hand. I am unarmed," Sir Solveig continued, hands open on the table. "I was there when Ivanar was questioned by the magistrate. I will admit I was never a fan of him or his brother. We knew that they hated the Tower, but who came to treat the dying knights in the Tower?"

"Now is not the time for this," Steiner said, pacing erratically. "The monster in the Tower, do we hang him?"

"No." Herrick stared at the fire.

"Ivanar died with her name on his lip, Mayor." Sir Solveig said.

Herrick sat at the head of the table, then his head went into his hands. Silence overtook the table until Herrick stood. "The council disbands without a vote on Valdir."

The non-believers crept into Shrinehall and took Orn and Gaut leaving without a word. Steiner ranted through Shrinehall casting curses in the ruins. This lasted several moments until Sir Solveig quietly stood from the table. It gave Steiner a foil for his anger and he left, barking at Sir Solveig all the way downstairs.

Kordan stood, watched Sir Solveig leave, and sheathed his sword. He walked to the edge of Shrinehall, gazing at the Tower and the burned-out area next to it. Fires still smoldered in the forest with an occasional flare up, but the main threat had ended. He walked around the ruins and watched the valley. "Herrick, that thing you refer to near the Witches Forest is a god. His body remains there and I suspect the White Citadel is responsible. The magistrate laid a trap for Him, just as they did for Bera. If Della went into the Witches Forest, she is safe." He nodded to Herrick and walked down the stairs.

As he descended the stairs, he heard Herrick weep.

CHAPTER 32

During the night watch, Sir Hakon and Sir Solveig marched Valdir back to his shop. Smoke billowed from the forge and within hours, the ringing of the anvil echoed through the empty valley. The winds shifted, blowing in warmer ocean air than the cold mountain's breath. A sign that the coldest winter nights were over.

Kordan slipped into Ragnfast's shop to check on the meat stores. He stared too long at the old white oak block Ragnfast used to cut up game. Old cleaver marks pointed every which way, scarring the wood. He stepped forward and touched it.

"I'm sorry, old friend," Kordan whispered. "I can only wish that on my death the forest god appears and takes my soul. I will mourn you but celebrate you too."

Kordan stood in silence, checked his bow and sword, then exited. He had another broadhead arrow in the quiver just in case. He left the shop, asked a few hunters to prepare a pyre for Ragnfast, then moved out into the valley. He stood at the foot of the forest god. A tree that had grown as large as those surrounding it in a day. He sat against it and faced the blacksmith shop. He sat there for hours, letting the constant dings and clanks lull him to near sleep. He noticed a form approaching the Witches Forest. Herrick, still wrapped up in a blanket. The mayor called for his wife, but the words froze in his throat. They sounded angry and lost. He paced back and forth like Valdir before he entered the Witches Forest, and it brutally defeated him. Herrick stopped and stared down at the snow. He wrapped up in his blanket and left.

Kordan pulled a blanket out of his bag. He wrapped up and leaned against the fallen god's body. The clanging continued from the forge as it belched smoke. Kordan watched, protecting the village against his old friend.

A group of carts lined up near the Tower the next morning. Orn stood near them, against his oldest daughter. "I will come."

Steiner walked up to the cart and dropped a bag into the back of it. He glared at some of the true-believers as he talked to Liam. The great-grandson of Gaut worked for him as an apprentice before Liam realized he didn't have the back for stonework.

"It's smoked meat and I don't care if you want it or not," Steiner said as he gave the man a tight hug. "You got a long road in front of you, don't make stupid decisions on hunger."

Gaut sat in a chair surrounded by his kin. "I am too weak and old for this journey. The bed death will claim me soon enough." Of his original 14 children, only 6 were still here. The descendants of his family took up the majority of the 46 that were ready to go.

Valdir appeared in the Tower's white cloak. He wore armor underneath, and his sword appeared at his side, complete. Steiner saw him from a distance and walked away.

Sir Solveig and Sir Hakon also approached, saying their goodbyes to the crowd. Herrick Blanchfield stood with Kordan near the Tower.

"They are marching to their deaths," Kordan said.

"The knights have medallions that protect against the forest. They would never let a commoner have one. I need to say my goodbyes." Herrick approached Orn.

"Is there any way we can talk you and your families into staying?"

"There is no food here for us and magic is about. We don't

belong here anymore, Herrick. Our temple is destroyed, and other gods walk out of the forest. We go with Asagrim."

Herrick looked over at Valdir. "Is he going with you?"

"Yes, he will take us to the trailhead and on to the Delirium Forest. It's burned all the way to the trailhead. Our faith will keep us strong."

"If I had a way to go back home, Orn," Herrick sighed and put his hand out. "I might go back home too, but the village needs me. May the Allfather bless your pilgrimage, my old friend."

"You have a chance to go home now, Herrick." Orn took his hand, shook it, then embraced him. "Blessings unto you as well."

To Herrick, Orn felt as brittle as tissue paper.

"Grandfather, it's time," Liam said. Herrick noticed that Liam hid something in his mouth as he shook Herrick's hand. The other true-believers said their goodbyes to the villagers. Herrick talked to a few more that looked him in the face, but many others stared at the ground when he approached.

Valdir approached the mayor with the bearing of a Theim. "Orn, I will help you into the cart." He lifted the old man into the cart next to his great-granddaughter, ignoring Herrick.

Valdir adjusted his armor and approached the forest's burnt opening. "May Asagrim guide us all," he said before taking the lead horse. He steadied himself. Then took a long look around that stopped at his shop, the remnants of the mill, and finally his wife's ashes. Without saying more, he turned and walked in.

Kordan moved over next to Herrick. "Will we ever see him again?"

"Liam said he's taking them to the White Citadel, but I wouldn't be surprised if he stays with them."

"If he doesn't walk into the forest first."

"Good riddance to the savage," Steiner said behind them.

The three stood and watched as the caravan went deeper into the forest. The true-believers strolled out of view as the trail took a right. Steiner meandered, then left with a quick nod to Herrick and Kordan.

"There is something I wanted to show you," Kordan said.

Herrick and Kordan walked to the large field near the Tower.

"This is where we fought the creature from the Delirium Forest. What do you see?" Kordan asked.

Little stems rose out of the ground with leaves covering them.

"Are those weeds growing up through the snow?"

"No," Kordan answered. "They are saplings from the Delirium Forest. Everywhere that creature bled after we shot it, these grow. It flew over Elta."

The hunters searched combing Elta for the saplings and digging them out from the frozen ground. Kordan scoured the trail imagining the thing's flight. The hunters spread out, searching the area to make sure all saplings were gone. It was warmer down in the valley near Ragnfast and Valdir's shops. The aromatic smell of the ocean flowed heavy down here. As the hunters searched, their boots broke through the soggy snow. Kordan found a sapling. Further than where the blood should have flown. The snow felt slushy in his hands as he cut the last.

"We search the entire village. I may have been wrong about the blood." It was time for a thaw and spring to come to the valley. They had survived the season of darkness. Now the magistrate was silent, the knights quiet in the Tower, but the Delirium Forest would soon grow into Elta, and they may not be able to stop it.

CHAPTER 33

inders fell like snow in the forest whenever a gust whipped through the trail. Ashes surrounded a broad path where five oxen wagons could easily pass side by side, but one simple horse-drawn cart drove up the middle. The pace of it was damning enough for Valdir.

Odd shadows followed through the trees but never drew close enough to engage. Valdir warned the pilgrims not to lose sight of each other in the smoke. Even with the swords and a couple of bows between them, they were sheep out in these woods. He fanned them out in a pattern with torches to provide the most light in the near pitch-black forest.

Valdir scouted, glancing back to see if the trail magic worked on them or if anything followed. The slowest walkers' torches were almost out of sight. Valdir stopped the horses and let them catch up. The elderly sat in the carts, but the starving adults shuffled on, tripping over the roots on the burnt trail. They had walked for over an hour. The Tower stood a brief run away, but Valdir would not abandon them.

Old Gulbrand, first son of Orn, taught Valdir how to smith thirty-two winters ago. Gulbrand taught how to make the fire hotter, how to truly make the metal burn and char out the impurities. In hushed tones, the villagers said Gulbrand and Valdir's swords were natural magic, stronger than those created by the White Citadel.

Valdir built a pyre for Gulbrand and took over his business not long after that apprenticeship. These true-believers took him in without knowing his past sins. He met Bera not long after. She had a way to calm him down and kept the beast at bay. In the darkness of the long winter nights, he told her history that left her in shocked silence, but she still accepted him. Bera forced Skofnung away, buried into the floor and out of his life. It stayed quiet for so long until the birth of Austri, Aurdr's child. Then the sword replaced the quiet of the long nights with old battle hymns.

Skofnung hung at his side. Valdir's constant companion remained silent. He pulled the sword. Those around him stirred. "It's okay. I'm just checking it," Valdir said but noticed those nearby stayed on edge.

The torchlight reflected no blemishes in the sword's mirrored surface from the reforging. Before it broke, twelve berserker souls inhabited the sword. His battle brothers' souls were in there and the strange outworlder that was the original inhabitant and name of the sword.

The sword was a present from his master, King Hrólf. Valdir had taken an almost fatal spear in combat meant for the king, and it healed poorly. His days as a warrior were done. The king presented the sword, a gift from the strange outworlders, the Rhylkos, and the king whispered its name to Valdir.

Valdir repeated the name. Within days his wound healed and Valdir became the greatest of Hrólf's warriors. As his brothers fell in combat around him, parts of their souls came to Skofnung. Now, he wasn't sure if any remained. He reforged the sword under watch of the Tower's knights and found a magical stone embedded in the pommel, unharmed. Combat would be its test. If it failed, hopefully Asagrim would find him worthy to sit at his table, since he had become a kin-killer.

On the trail forward, the path split. Light trickled into the forest, but Valdir knew it was not the sun that still hid behind the mountains.

"Liam. Take the horses until the others catch up. I'm scouting ahead."

"It splits off ahead and to the ..."

"What is it?"

Liam steeled himself. "It's the grainery roof, where the fire started."

Valdir ran up the road.

The roof's thatch had burned away and probably set the fires when it landed. The charred skeletal timbers reached out to the four winds. One long timber seemed to point up the trail where he led the pilgrims.

Valdir kneeled in front of it. "I know, love. I know. Even from the shining hall, you still ride my ass." He listened to his heartbeat and the wind as it moved through the trees. "Gods. I will take them," Valdir whispered.

"Where is she?" Whispered back on the wind.

Valdir ran back to Liam, who stood half asleep next to the horses. Valdir counted those he could see, forty-two.

"Liam, where are the others?" Valdir shouted.

"Where is she?" came another whisper from the woods.

"Pull your weapons!" Valdir shouted. "Skofnung, awaken," Valdir said. Odd bits of electricity shot up his arm, then one odd jolt kicked him in the heart. "Skofnung, show me." He glared deep into the Delirium Forest. Back in the trees around two hundred lengths, a shepherd watched them with the four missing true-believers.

"Swords to the front of the group, bowmen to the back. Our attack will come from here."

A few of them stepped back from Valdir. Skofnung's voice was still there, the alien presence.

He rushed, moving those with swords and bows to the proper place while hearing the shepherd above the panic. "Where is she?"

"Where's Siv?" someone asked.

"Tornunn?" another yelled.

"Silence," Valdir shouted.

The shepherd drew the lost forward. He touched their foreheads as if anointing them and each collapsed. Valdir thought they died on the spot until strange voices called out through the

WILLIAM BRIAN JOHNSON

forest. The bodies jerked, their skin unnaturally stretched as something sought release within. Long cuts formed in their skin as barks, yips, and howls erupted around them. Wolves ripped and emerged from their skin. The shepherd pointed back at the cart. The wolves circled the shepherd and shot out through the woods to the trail.

"Bowmen! Fire as soon as they clear the trees!"

They were startled, confused, and untrained. Ranveig and Ranhild were two brothers, great-great-grandsons of Gaut that would go out with Kordan and the hunters. They both knew how to use a bow, but that was against a doe they startled in the woods, not against a pack of wolves attacking from the forest.

"Liam, protect the bowmen."

Valdir surged forward as the first wolf broke through the woods.

Ranveig and Ranhild took shots, hitting one of the four in the haunches and slowing it down. Valdir caught one with the sword and severed its backbone. Skofnung proved again to be a viable sword. Liam shouted as a wolf attacked him. It leaped and took him down before he even brought his sword to bear. Ranhild shot at it, narrowly missing Liam's head. Liam yelled as the wolf bit his arm and dragged him into the trees. A high-pitched scream came from the cart where a wolf had pulled down a young girl.

Valdir sprinted to Liam, skidded in the ash, and ran back to the girl. Skofnung easily removed the wolf's head. The girl still screamed, jostling out of its decapitated maw. On the other side of the cart, Ranveig took out the other injured wolf with a quick arrow to the eye.

Sigr and Yngveig were two older men with swords, both in the service to Asagrim that settled in Elta after their service was done. Two old men who lost their chance to sit at Asagrim's table while in service, in other words, lucky enough to survive their wars without dying. Their wives, Hilde and Turid, held on to shields, protecting their men. Turid and Sigr's son, Siv was lost to the forest and held Liam's hand in its maw. Valdir did not have the

202

heart to tell them.

Cautiously, the four approached. Sigr swung at the wolf. It let go of Liam and backed into the trees, growling. Yngveig drew close to the woods. Valdir ran over to Sigr as Turid dragged Liam back, checking his wounds.

"Be careful, old man," Valdir shouted to Yngveig as he drew close to the trees, sword ready. He looked up, groggily, as a large, hairy arm grabbed him and pulled him into the forest.

"Get back," Valdir yelled. Sigr dropped his sword and grabbed Liam. Valdir sprinted at them as the monster stepped out of the forest, flanked by two wolves. Valdir stared into the shepherd's yellow eyes.

"Where is she?" the voice roared in Valdir's head. It made his vision swim as he almost dropped Skofnung. As his grip hardened, he heard himself say, "Shepherd, return to the forest and leave us."

Valdir's eyes cleared. The beast was missing an arm, which appeared gnawed off. Its face and bearing had familiarity.

"Nol?" cried Ranveig as he approached with his bow ready. Ranhild stood at his side, arrow nocked.

Valdir snapped to his senses. "Aurdr and the child have gone to the White Citadel, Nol."

"Lies." The beast snarled and the two wolves attacked. The swordsmen and bowmen were ready. Ranveig and Ranhild shot true. One arrow hit a wolf in the chest, taking it down, as the other arrow struck the second wolf's hip. Sigr rushed forward and stabbed it through.

Valdir searched the path. The monster had disappeared.

"Skofnung, show me," Valdir called, but no visions came back to Valdir. The sword was silent.

One of the elder women, Orn's daughter, Freydis, helped Liam into the cart and examined his wounds. She was part of old Elta, the healer that gave her business to Della when her fingers ached too much to apply bandages and unstopper healing potions.

"We need to move quicker," Valdir said. "Nol will be back."

The panic woke some of them up from their starvation. Some of the slower pilgrims were loaded into the cart as the others wept at the loss of five of their own. Valdir's eyes caught Freydis and Turid attending to Liam as they cleaned and bandaged his shoulder wound.

"Watch for madness," Valdir said. He had already killed a couple villagers in the last couple of days, he wasn't excited to see that number rise.

The sun hit its apex for the day but still crested below the mountain. In the Delirium Forest, that tiny amount of sunlight somehow magnified as the brightest of summer days. They journeyed for four hours at this point. Valdir doubted that Liam had walked this entire trail in a day while starving. At a glance, Liam looked fine. As Valdir watched him, Liam's hands trembled and sweat poured from his brow. His bandaged wounds still bled. Orn tried to comfort his great-grandson, but Liam ignored his words. Valdir gave the reins to one of the pilgrims.

"Liam." Valdir tried to hail him. "Liam, how much further does the trail go?"

Liam only stared ahead in a strange gaze.

"Liam?" Valdir asked again.

Liam sat up like Scraps hearing his master whistle. "Do you hear him, Valdir? He's near again. He's calling to me."

"I hear nothing. Stop this talk, or I will have you tied up.

Liam laughed. It started as a child's malevolent giggle and grew in intensity and volume.

"Give me a rope," Valdir asked Orn.

Liam sprung from the cart and within four leaping steps, ran into the trees.

Orn cried out.

"Are we going to survive this journey?" Turid asked.

Liam disappeared into the forest, heeding the call of his new master, and was anointed to become a wolf.

Dusk swallowed the Delirium Forest. As darkness encroached, the forest came alive. Through the trees, hot spots from the fires still burned. Some appeared as normal flames, others reflected a fire nearby and burned with different colors. Valdir lit more torches and passed them out. Lightning flashed overhead, but there was no rain. Thunder rolled through the forest but seemed muted, changed. The forest trail tapered to where the horse had a narrow path. Valdir met with Ranveig and Ranhild and had them follow the cart and the stragglers from behind. Sigr, Hilde, and Turid marched at the front of the cart with Valdir. They mourned for their losses but cleared the trail if the branches drew too near. Burning leaves covered the path, sometimes blocking the way ahead until Valdir crossed through. The forest weighed on him.

Dense smoke surrounded them. Valdir was unsure if the return trip to Elta remained a possibility. Ragnfast's memory held heavy on him. Sharp images assailed him as if in a fevered dream. His previous berserks left him fatigued with no memory other than occasional scars. This last one caused glimpses of Ragnfast's murder to haunt him.

He shook his head trying to clear the visions. From the corner of his eye, he thought he caught a reflection of something staring at him.

"Jahan."

The word weighed on his soul. His friend's last word and possible request.

Smoke filled the path. It choked and slowed them down. Valdir's eyes watered as they passed this part of the burning forest.

Now only the torchlight led the way. The occasional lightning flicker left images of someone watching them just out of reach.

Exhaustion crept into Valdir. Knowing that the starving would soon fall behind them. He thought about making camp here, but it would be suicide.

"Jahan."

Ragnfast's battered remains stood near him in the trees.

Valdir heard it again and wanted to yell out. To scream to make it stop. When he felt a hand on his shoulder.

"Valdir."

Valdir almost struck when Sigr said his name.

"Look ahead. Torches."

Valdir shook the fog of his misdeeds from his head. Several torches passed ahead.

"Come quickly, this must be the trailhead," Valdir said.

He ran forward, leaving the pilgrims behind. A unit of soldiers marched on the south trailhead.

"Heilir, blessaður!" Valdir called out the old traditional greetings. The soldiers passed stone-faced.

"Please help us, we are pilgrims from Elta. I have starving men, women, and children."

There was a quick tempo in their march that completely ignored his pleas.

A commander on horseback passed, ignoring them.

"I am Valdir of the Hamrammr. I served under King Hrólf of Kraki, and you will have an audience with me."

The commander stopped his horse and circled Valdir several times. Soldiers and knights broke rank and surrounded Valdir, swords and spears drawn.

"The Hamrammr are dead and disbanded after the death of King Hrólf. Any trained soldier knows that story."

"Then you know there were two survivors."

"Give me your name again."

"Valdir of the Hamrammr."

The commander pulled a horn and blew three quick notes into

it. Up the road, a wagon broke rank and sped toward them. The driver hopped down and dropped the ladder from the wagon as its door opened. Valdir fell to a knee as a high-level warpriest of the White Citadel descended.

"Commander?" the warpriest asked.

"Apologies for your summons, Warpriest Edwin, but this man emerged from the Delirium Forest and claims to be a Hamrammr," the commander said.

"Delirium Forest, you say?" The warpriest pulled a simple gem from his pocket and spoke a word of power into it.

Valdir stood and felt a familiar crawl up his spine.

The warpriest whispered, "show me" as he held the gem to his eye. He almost dropped the gem. "Commander, call your soldiers back at once and help this man in any way possible. What needs do you have?"

"I come with forty-one of Asagrim's followers from Elta who are fleeing chaos that magic has brought down on the village. They are starving and on a pilgrimage to the White Citadel." On the trail behind them, Sigr, Hilde, and Turid emerged.

"By the Allfather's hand, you brought them through the Delirium Forest?" Warpriest Edwin asked.

"A fire burned a trail. The Delirium Forest affected us at the end. We need rations, they are starving." Valdir turned and watched them come out. He had succeeded in his mission. The cart emerged followed by eight more, visibly shaken. Valdir walked past the elders and children in the cart. He took his torch and ran back, watching the empty trail.

"Ranveig," he yelled. "Ranhild?"

He ran to where the smoke filled the path.

Tears filled his eyes. "Skofnung, show me."

The smoke cleared, but down the path, no one remained. Deep into the woods, he watched a child fall, and a wolf emerge from its skin.

CHAPTER 34

Darkness plummeted in Elta as a storm emerged over the mountains. It crawled over its peak like a great wyrm, fell down the mountain, and roared thunder into the valley. Kordan stalked the treeline of the Witches Forest wary of its presence. As lightning flashed overhead, he searched for any sign of Della. The storm's wind hit, howling through the trees like a pack of ravenous wolves. Many of Elta's villagers didn't take chances with the weather after the last major disaster, so the streets were bare. Kordan sought shelter in the beggar's shack wondering if it would be strong enough to survive the wind.

He forced the wood plank door open, and as he entered, his ankle caught a simple tripwire by the door. Kordan fell in and hit the dirt floor. Someone jumped on his back and held a dagger to his throat. In the corner of the dark room, illuminated by lighting, Lofn stood cradling her belly. Kordan relaxed.

"Della?" he asked.

"It's me."

"I thought you were lost to the forest."

Della got off his back and sheathed the knife. "I'm sorry, Kordan. I didn't know who was coming. I also didn't know what you would do when you saw me."

"When I saw you?" Kordan stood. Della wore one of the old leper's robes from the shack. Long black strips of shroud fashioned into robes. Her skin seemed luminous from where it showed. Her eyes glistened like the stars on the stillest winter night.

"Gods, woman. What's happened to you?"

"The forest transformed me when Valdir chased me into it."

"The forest god is dead, Della."

"No, not dead. Weakened for a moment, but His fire still burns. If a single tree in this forest survives, He is with us. He will be reborn."

Kordan gazed at Lofn. "This?" He pointed to Lofn's belly.

"No. This is His son."

"Your sacrifice to save the village, woman, was to have the forest god's child?"

Lofn stood still and whispered, "In the simplest of terms."

"How are you so far along?"

She stood stoic, like when she faced the overseer and the magistrate, but pain washed over her. Her stance changed, and she doubled over grabbing her stomach. Della whispered a strange language, red lights flickered from her hands, and Lofn relaxed.

"Kordan, my waters have already broke," Lofn said. "The baby will be here soon, I need help."

"Anything."

Della touched Kordan's shoulder. "It will be a difficult delivery. Go get my bag from my office. I also need potions and herbs."

"Herbs I collect out in the wild, but your potions will be strange to me."

Della sighed. "That was what I was afraid of. Lofn cannot be left alone. Will you stay with her?"

"Yes." Kordan nodded.

"Will you protect her, even from the knights?"

"I pledge my life to protect you both," he said without hesitation.

"I watched you fall asleep at the forest god's feet, and that tells me volumes. The Tower will soon know. They want the baby, and this may end in bloodshed, old friend."

"I welcome it," Kordan said.

Lightning struck nearby, light filled the beggar's shack, and rain fell within.

Della was gone. Kordan stepped back.

"Magic will take some getting used to," Lofn said. "For now, we are too exposed here. Take the blankets and cover the walls with them. The longer we hide, the stronger we will be."

"Why not have the baby in the forest?"

"He is weakened and there are things dangerous in the forest without his protection. This oddly is the safest place."

Kordan moved around, stuffing the blankets into the cracks of the walls. He knew it would not be enough. "What about Della's house?"

"Too close to the Tower. Here we have time to see them coming." Lofn moved to the single cot in the shack. "I saved the village and give birth on a bed full of pox."

"We had our rules here, Lofn. You went against them to save the village."

Thunder rumbled through the valley.

"I didn't know the cost to the village. I thought it would only be on me."

"The knights have forgotten about us. The true-believers led by Valdir are on the way to the White Citadel or dead in the Delirium Forest.

"That's suicide," Lofn said.

"It's his penance," Kordan said with a sigh. "For Ragnfast. We've lost a lot here. I'm sure Della has relayed the names."

"Ivar, Ragnfast ... Bera."

Kordan nodded. "Ragnfast still lays on the pyre."

Lofn sat up, gripping her belly.

"Another?"

"Yes," she said through gritted teeth.

Kordan walked over and held her by the shoulders. "Sir Solveig said I'd have to use new skills to survive."

"I don't think this is what he meant."

Kordan embraced her. Lofn held on tight.

"This should have been ours."

"I know, at one time." Lofn said through the pain.

Red lights flickered in the shack once more, and Lofn's body relaxed. Della was back in the room. Kordan released Lofn and wiped a tear from her cheek.

"I didn't know Valdir damaged my office that badly. I apologize for taking so long."

"Your magic and the fancy lights will attract the attention of the Tower. Should I organize the hunters?"

"They know." Della placed her potions in the center of the room. "If you asked before the magistrate came, we would have organized the Tower's end. Now, I realize my actions have cost too many lives. The only thing I ask is to keep them from burning down the shack while I deliver the baby."

"What about Herrick?"

Della paused. "Tell him to stay with Allistril. Hopefully, this will all be over soon. Is he better?"

"I saw him at the council meeting we had on Valdir. He's okay."

Della drew circles on the floor. "Tell him ... I'm okay. Luck be with you, Kordan. Go quickly."

"Luck be with you as well." He stood at the door and watched Lofn, then went out into the night. The streets of Elta were empty. Too much has changed suddenly, the storm, the magistrate, the true-believers deserting Elta. The sun was to rise and set, seasons came and went, elders passed and babies replaced them. This was too much change for Kordan.

The sky boiled, and the thunder trailed through the valley.

He woke Cody first, rousing the young man from bed. Next, Haveldan seemed too willing to protect his saviors, one that saved his life and the other that brought food back to the village. They moved through the wet streets, armed and ready to start a revolution.

Near the beggar's shack, a strong bolt of lightning struck the god tree. A large branch fell, and the very ground around it glimmered in a soft green glow. Lofn's scream echoed through the valley.

"We're losing time. Cody, rise the rest of the hunters. Haveldan, you are with me," Kordan said.

They descended Dead Man's Trail as the horns from the Tower moaned. A large pulse of red light emanated from the shack. The sky itself swirled above the beggar's shack and absorbed the color as if it burned.

"So much for having the baby without the Tower knowing," Haveldan said. Another scream echoed through the valley, pinpointed by rolling thunder.

They made it to the end of the road when the Tower gates opened. A large, armored warwagon flew down Tower Road, dangerously tipping through the mud. Kordan and Haveldan ran to the shack.

"We're outside, Della," Kordan yelled, knocking on the side of the shack. "And they are coming."

"What do we do, Kordan?" Haveldan asked. "Are we killing the knights?"

There was no answer from inside other than Lofn's moans.

Kordan investigated the shack. His gaze was met with a red light that grew in intensity until he had to look away. He blinked, trying to get the bright spots from his vision, unsure of how far to go to protect those inside.

"If they attack, we slaughter them."

Wagonmaster Thron sped by the village square, whipping the horses into a frenzy. Sir Hakon followed close on his mare. The Tower's bells clanged the gale warning as lightning struck in the village. The clouds above the beggar's shack appeared bloody and ready to drop.

The villagers watched through the cracks of the storm shutters and between draped windows. Afraid to step out but fascinated by the sight of red light pulsating and bleeding from the beggar's shack. When the warwagon sped past, it emboldened some and enraged others. Six hunters notched arrows, ready to fight Sir Hakon and whoever was in the warwagon.

There was a standoff. The villagers of Elta emerged like wolves following the scent of blood. Some for vengeance against Lofn, some to protect her. Lofn's scream echoed through the valley, followed by more pulses of red light.

Mayor Herrick Blanchfield told his daughter to stay in bed, but she was already up from the storm and aware of what was going on.

"That's Lofn and Mommy," she said

"Something is going on, and it's not safe, Allistril. Please, stay here."

Even before he was downstairs, Herrick knew Allistril would sneak out.

"Please, Allistril. By all that is holy in this house. Do not leave." Herrick saw the fear in her eyes, and it broke his heart. "I'll do what I can for Mommy, but I can't be worried about your safety."

Allistril sat back on the bed and wept. Herrick moved downstairs and grabbed a short sword, bow, and quiver of arrows.

Outside, the sky burned red like the sunrise of a bad-omened day. The clouds swarmed overhead in a maelstrom. Down below, the warwagon parked in front of the hunters and the beggar's shack. As he reached Dead Man's Trail, Herrick checked his arrows and sword, then his eyes never left the warwagon.

As he drew close, he knew Kordan and the other hunter's eyes were on him. Sir Hakon stood in front of the open door to the warwagon, hand on his sword. As Herrick approached, Sir Solveig climbed from the warwagon. "That's close enough, Mayor."

Villagers loosely lined around them. Through their murmurs, Lofn's cries escaped the shack. Herrick heard Della's fatigued voice inside.

"Last chance, Mayor. Don't make a mistake that you'll rot for," Sir Solveig said.

"Please, Mayor Blanchfield," Sir Hakon said. Fear crawled across the knight's face. Herrick pulled his sword and headed toward the shack.

Lofn screamed inside, and another pulse of red light exploded from the shack. The god tree pulsed with the same red energy that bled from the shack. Several unseen voices whispered through the valley. The groans of the trees from the Witches Forest answered them back. Herrick looked into the center of the maelstrom and onto the determined faces of the hunters. They wanted revenge this night.

"I'm here for you, Della. They won't stop you." Herrick said as he gripped his sword.

For an hour the standoff continued. Villagers emerged from their houses, some brought their farming implements and labor tools for weapons. They lined up on both sides. The knights unsheathed their swords. They stood by the warwagon as something remained in its darkness, watching and patiently waiting.

Silence sunk into the valley. The clouds slowed overhead and fell apart, revealing a somber moon. The pulsing lights of the tree and within the shack slowed and ebbed to darkness.

"Della?" Herrick called out.

The softest whisper escaped the shack, a mournful "No." It reverberated through the trees and was answered by the forest. A wind blew through the forest, slightly rustling the leaves. Leaves from the god tree fell like snow as they abandoned their branches. The trunk groaned and cracked. The top branches split and fell, causing the tree to fold upon itself and collapse.

"Gods, no!" Kordan exclaimed.

There was a tap on the warwagon. Thron hopped down, lowered the steps into place, and kneeled.

For moments, the villagers held their breath. From the darkness of the warwagon, Overseer Daniels limped out. His crimson robes were replaced with black, the sign of a dying overseer. He leaned hard on his burnt staff as he descended the stairs. His strong arm wrapped around his staff as his left arm fell lifeless at his side. When he stared up at the shack, his hood fell from his withered face. It appeared as if Asagrim had smeared the left side of Overseer Daniels' face. He stepped down ignoring the villagers' stares and moved off toward the mayor.

"Is she dead?" he asked, lips only half functioning.

Overseer Daniels' single cold, blue eye stared through the mayor as his left calloused eye set upon the shack.

"How dare you?" Herrick answered.

"Go fetch the child, Herrick." The overseer croaked.

"Continue to burn in Hel, Overseer."

"Broken your control, pet?" he asked. "Then you will join her. Knights, why isn't that shack burning?"

Sir Solveig sheathed his sword. He grabbed a torch from the warwagon. Several arrows notched in his direction and it stopped him. Overseer Daniels gripped his gnarled, blackened staff and struck it against the ground. It produced sparks but nothing else.

A small cry came from the shack. The overseer closed his eyes and muttered a quick curse. When he finished, his blue eye blazed with an inner fury. The cry picked up in volume. The infant's cry was strong.

"Knights to arms," the overseer commanded and stepped back.

Sir Solveig swung the torch, staring at the hunters surrounding him. Overseer Daniels commanded, "Burn it. Burn it down before it's too late."

Herrick pointed his sword at the overseer. Sir Solveig dropped the torch and pulled his sword.

"Pity." Overseer Daniels said. "Then you will burn with your daughter on Ragnfast's Pyre. Cut him down."

Sir Solveig froze.

The baby's cry continued through the shack.

"Hunters, aim for the overseer's heart," Herrick yelled.

The bows pulled around him, all zeroed in on the knights and the overseer.

"Leave, Overseer Daniels. Your temple is in ruins, there is nothing for you here."

"Really, Herrick. There is everything here." The overseer stamped his staff once more. Fire burned from his staff.

"I beg you to stop. There's a newborn in there," the mayor pleaded.

"Step aside, Mayor, or die."

Sir Solveig's wide-eye stare fell on those around him as sweat poured from his face.

"Listen to me, Sir Solveig. You don't have to do this," Herrick said.

Sir Solveig's eyes set upon the Herrick. "No, Mayor. By the White Citadel, we do."

The baby's cry moved through the shack and to the front door. The old plank door flew open. A black-robed figure held a baby to her withered chest. The wind moved over the old plague robes giving them a life of their own. An age-spotted weakened arm presented the baby to the crowd.

"It is over," she moaned. "This is Lofn's child."

Herrick spun around. "Della?" he asked.

She trudged out from the door, unsteady in her gait. She grabbed for the door as she moved through. Herrick barely recognized his wife. In the dark, she looked like the Magistratus. As Della stepped into the torchlight, she glared at Overseer Daniel's burning staff. It sputtered and died.

"You seek to kill this child, Overseer? The very gods you ignore, protect it," she said.

"Hand over the child, crone." Overseer Daniels said. "Your forest god is dead."

"So is your Allfather, fool." The old woman laughed harshly.

She removed her hood. Della's brown hair had turned stringy white and fell with her hood. Her skin stretched over her skull.

"I have seen the future, Overseer. This child will be the White Citadel's ruin, and you, you will not live past this night."

Her taloned hand stretched toward the moon. In a harsh guttural language, she muttered a spell that ended in the word "Aristid." The wind changed direction as a heaviness descended on all that were there. Then silence. The villagers panicked and fled, Sir Hakon moved to protect the overseer. Sir Hakon's mare panicked and bolted through the crowd.

Overseer Daniels leaned heavily on his staff and shouted a rune. Energy spread out around him and the knights. "Now, Sir Solveig."

Sir Solveig rushed forward, knocked Herrick to the ground, and stabbed Della through. Arrows sought out the overseer and Sir Solveig but fell to the ground as if they hit a barrier. She cradled the baby, sliding down the sword.

"With my death, this child is protected!" Della wailed.

Sir Solveig took the baby from Della's dying grip. As he handed the baby to Sir Hakon, Herrick spun over and struck Sir Solveig's groin with his sword. Sir Hakon dropped his sword, grabbed the baby and Overseer Daniels, and dove into the wagon. As the overseer's barrier retreated, Sir Solveig took an arrow to the neck and fell on Herrick. The warwagon's heavy door slammed shut. Wagonmaster Thron whipped the horses forward, trying to duck below the armored sides as arrows plinked off the armor. Haveldan rushed forward, jumping on the wagon, but not finding a handhold, fell and tumbled.

"Shoot the horses!" Kordan yelled.

"I refuse," Cody said as he dropped his bow. Haveldan

scurried and reclaimed his bow. Kordan fired. Arrows plinked off the horse armor as one embedded into a thigh.

"Go help Herrick," Kordan shouted at Cody as they chased.

The warwagon took a long path up through where Ragnfast and Valdir's shops stood empty, past the burnt down grain bins, and up through the village square. Kordan eyed the path and loosed an arrow. It struck Thron in the shoulder as he furiously whipped the horses past the village square. They lost the wagon as it went behind Shrinehall's ruins. Kordan and Haveldan ran up Dead Man's Trail as the warwagon hit Tower Road. Kordan blew his horn. The other hunters followed but left Cody behind.

They figured the wagon would shelter in the Tower, but it flew past the gates and across the outer walls.

"They're taking the path through the Delirium Forest," Kordan yelled. He stopped in the village square as the wagon entered the burnt remains and disappeared.

"Gods, we lost our prey," Kordan said.

Herrick wiggled out from Sir Solveig and Della's bodies. Cody arrived and helped him move Sir Solveig's heavy-armored form away. Herrick cradled Della, the sword angled up through her chest.

"These are my last moments here, love," Della said.

Herrick cradled her form. He went to remove the blade.

"If you do that, my time is ended. Wait."

"What happened?" He touched her face, brushing the tears that dashed from her eyes.

"It was a difficult birth. Lofn died before I delivered," she gasped her words. "I put everything into that child. Just like Lofn did … for Allistril. Just like Allistril." Her form went slack in Herrick's arms. She was gone.

Herrick glared at Sir Solveig. A small pool of blood had formed underneath his neck, but he too was gone. Herrick stood and kicked the arrow embedded in Sir Solveig's neck. He picked Della up. Cody walked over to help.

"Please. Let me," Herrick said.

He carried Della up Dead Man's Trail. Allistril watched him from the path and ran to meet him. She stared at the form in his arms, lost somewhere between terror and sorrow.

"It's Mommy, my dear. She sacrificed herself for Lofn's baby."

"Where's Lofn?" Allistril asked, her voice smaller than her frame.

"She's gone."

Allistril wept, holding Della's limp hand.

"I'll go get her," Steiner said.

Through his tear-stained vision, the villagers followed him up the road.

"Sir Solveig?" someone in the crowd asked.

"Leave him for the ravens," Herrick shouted.

They followed him up to the house. Herrick entered with Della and Allistril inside. He would not send her to the next world in leper's robes. He found her favorite dress among her simpler clothes and dressed her in it. Then he went to the cupboards and pulled out his idol of Einridi the Thunderer.

Aurdr appeared at the door. "We need to dress Lofn in something fine as well."

Steiner stood at the door with her body. Lofn appeared at peace. Herrick picked out another of Della's dresses, maybe a size too big for Lofn, but one that Herrick loved. He handed it to Aurdr. Steiner laid Lofn's body on the couch and stepped away as Aurdr prepared her. Herrick dropped to his knees in front of Della's body.

"Della?" Aurdr asked.

"Yes," Herrick tearfully answered as Allistril and he stared at Della's withered body and wept.

"Steiner. Go to my house and ask my oldest for the basket of pressed flowers," Aurdr said as she finished dressing Lofn.

Steiner turned and left.

Aurdr touched Lofn's cheek. "Gods, Herrick. Could we have done more to save them?"

"Only given our lives, and it wouldn't have changed anything." He sobbed.

Steiner returned with the wildflowers. Aurdr went to work creating two crowns from the pressed flowers. She placed the first on Lofn's head, the second on Della's.

They stood in the house for a while, letting the tears flow. Several of the villagers came and waited outside. Kordan stared at Lofn's body from the doorway.

"Form a party of hunters. We will find Hakon's horse and I will get that warwagon to stop," Kordan said to Haveldan. He entered and knelt before Lofn. He placed her hands over her belly and removed a small idol from his pocket. "In the next world, I will find you at the table. We will drink and laugh at the feet of our gods." He knelt in silence until Haveldan came back.

"Kordan," Haveldan called from the door.

He leaned forward and kissed Lofn's lips. "We will have our revenge." He stood and faced the gathered hunters. "I will ride, have the hunters follow on foot. If the forest affects them, retreat. Stay to the middle of the trial and arm yourselves well."

Cody was with them, and there was a long stare from Kordan. It was broken when he spoke. "I'm sorry, Kordan. I follow Asagrim and will not attack a horse or the overseer."

Kordan passed him quickly. "Stay and watch the village. They will need help with the pyre."

Hooves galloped down the road.

"It's time," Herrick said to Aurdr. "Get Steiner to lift Lofn." Herrick lifted Della and, with Allistril in tow, walked to the village square. The villagers had extended the pyre, but still, the ravens came and had to be shooed away. Ragnfast's body had been picked at by the birds. He carefully placed Della's body on the pyre next to Ragnfast and placed the idol of Einridi in her grasp.

"Take care of her in the next world, Einridi. For I failed her in this one," Herrick said. He lifted Allistril to the pyre and let her have her last words. Steiner brought Lofn's body and laid her down. Next to Della and Ragnfast. He knelt and said a quick prayer before moving off. Allistril sat next to Lofn and held her hand.

"It's not right, Daddy. The way they died."

Herrick could only nod.

Kordan flew up the burnt trail in pursuit of the warwagon. The wagon led him but was slowed by weight. The swiftness of Sir Hakon's horse instead of the team might give him the advantage. He held the torch low and ahead of him, trying to use moonlight to see. Smoke obscured the path ahead. Kordan slowed for a moment before kicking the mare forward. If the path suddenly veered to the left or right, he could unknowingly gallop into the trees and be lost. He still sprinted down the trail. The deep ruts in the wet earth showed they were about thirty minutes ahead. One of the horses, the one they hit with the arrow, was having trouble and dragging a leg.

A growl behind him took his attention. A large, white wolf chased him on the trail, spots of blood covered its fur, and the beast had no tail. Kordan spurred the horse to a faster gallop through the smoke and soon the wolf following him disappeared.

Something was ahead on the trail. Kordan slowed and in the moonlit dark found a group of dead wolves. Spear marks covered them, probably from the wagonmaster or Sir Hakon. Near the trees was a human body. One of the true-believers from Elta, Gaut's great-great-grandchild.

Kordan pulled up to the body and jumped down. He

unsheathed his sword as he approached the dead wolves. Lack of tails told a story of them not being natural.

The boy was dead. Marks of a heavy wagon wheel trailed over his throat. The two wolves were dead by sword and arrows. He watched as one arrow moved and fell out of the body.

"This is a foolish mission," he said as the wolf's yellow eyes popped open and stared at Kordan. His sword removed its head.

He ran and jumped on his horse, urging it forward. He had to do this for Lofn, but if lycanthropes were here, it could be worse than Valdir's berserk bear form roaming around Elta. The wolves hunted in packs.

He galloped through several smoky areas going faster than he should. The trail narrowed as bodies of true-believers and wolves lie in the trial ahead. Kordan kicked the horse forward and made him jump over one of the true-believer's bodies.

"Bring her to me, brother."

Kordan barely heard it over the horse's labored breathing.

"Where is she?"

He glanced side to side, then watched the shepherd walk out of the trees onto the trail ahead. Smoke billowed around the shepherd, obscuring the trail ahead. He pulled back on the reigns, making the horse stop. Wolves stepped out of the trees and surrounded the shepherd like it was their alpha.

"Where is she?" it demanded.

Kordan stopped the horse and turned around. He goaded the horse forward and rose in the saddle, narrowing the distance between the horse and his head. The horse misstepped and started to fatigue. When he passed Gaut's great-great-grandson's body, the wolves next to it were gone. In the moonlight, deep within the trees, he could see them running after him. They ran in a V-formation like a flock of birds seeking warmer weather. Kordan counted twelve.

On the current path, he would take them straight into Elta who already mourned enough dead. He stopped the horse once its breath turned ragged and panicked. He turned again deeper into the trail and his pursuit of the warwagon. He waited as the wolves came closer. Behind them was a figure running on three legs.

Kordan pulled his sword.

"Where is she, Kordan?"

"Damn you, Berstuk. The dark forest lady surrounds me with issues," Kordan yelled to the forgotten god, one that his father only whispered about in his madness. The lady of evil brought the dark things to the forest. If Lofn brought the forest god, the old religions talked about their duality. The dark aspect of the god could surface as well. Where the forest god healed the crops and brought the migrating animals back, Berstuk woke the darker, more horrific aspects of the forest.

He jumped off the horse ready to take on what he knew would be his last fight. The horse galloped off and crashed through the trees. Its screams echoed through the forest as the wolves and the shepherd surrounded Kordan.

The next morning, all that remained of the pyre was charcoal and a few bones. Herrick Blanchfield went through the piles, carefully separating them as they fell into ash. Once collected, they moved down to the graveyard. Three new graves were dug by the hunters that remained. In the first were Lofn's favorite books, a game set, combs, brushes, and her drinking horn. Della's had similar items along with her medical bag and a couple of potions and medical books. Ragnfast had his favorite cleaver, one that Valdir had made, and a ridiculously sized drinking horn made from some long-forgotten animal. Cody arrived with a smaller basket.

"What is it?" Herrick asked.

"An old friend," Cody said as he laid a dog's skull and a few bones at the base of the grave. "Farewell, Scraps and Ragnfast. May your hunts be legendary in the afterlife." Cody sat there for a moment in silent prayer. He rose, touched Herrick's shoulder, and hugged Allistril before wandering off.

"So many new dead," Herrick said. "We live a life that celebrates an early death that sends us to the arms of Asagrim. Sometimes I think the gods punish those left behind with memories." He roughed up Allistril's hair. They sat in silence for a while as the sun almost appeared from behind the mountain.

"Allistril, there is one more thing we need to do for your mother. Are you ready?"

Allistril wiped a few tears from her face and took one last look in the grave. "Yes."

"The hunters said they will fill these in later. Come on, let's go to the Tower."

They walked from the graveyard, across Elta, and up Tower Road. The gate remained open. Herrick entered, fearless. There was no Magistratus or Overseer Daniels here. Their reign was over. If they came back, Herrick would make sure that they would never leave again.

He opened the large door leading into the Tower and walked into the great room and over to the throne. Two large fire pits sat in front of them, cold and unlit. He climbed the small stairs to the throne and sat down in front of it.

"Aren't you supposed to sit on the throne, Daddy?"

"No. I am a mayor, not a king or tyrant. This was the overseer's overstep. He fancied himself as a king or maybe worse."

Allistril searched the room, looking at the various tapestries on the wall, each telling a spectacular story about a war.

Herrick sat back, head relaxing against the throne when he heard an odd scraping that echoed out into the hall. He got up, took Allistril's hand, and left the great hall. A long hallway stood before them.

A short girl with dark skin and brown hair, and the whispy beginnings of a light beard swept the stones. When she saw Herrick coming into the hall, she immediately bowed her head and stepped back until her back touched the wall. Herrick knelt in front of her.

"My name is Herrick Blanchfield. I am the mayor of Elta. Do you know what that means, child?"

The girl shook her head, still staring down at the floor.

"I am the new ruler here. Not a king or an overseer, but a person that the people of the village asked to lead them."

The girl continued to stare at the floor.

Herrick bent his index finger and put it under her light-whiskered chin. She flinched as he slowly raised her face. "I am the ruler of this village, and we decided a long time ago that slaves are not allowed."

The girl screamed, shocking Herrick. Flustered he quickly changed his words. "No, child." Herrick grabbed her. "You are free, you are no longer a Theim. If you come with me, I will remove your shackles."

Another girl came running down the hall. A blonde, slightly taller than the dwarven girl. She held a mop ready to fight.

Herrick held out his hand. "Please. I am here to free you."

"Did Della send you?"

Herrick smiled. "I'm Della's husband. She spoke of you both very often."

The blonde girl squared up against Herrick. "We cannot leave, we are Theim."

"I am the ruler here, and I say you can't remain slaves. I want you free, to live how you want."

"The overseer?" A look of hope came over her young face.

"Gone."

"Sir Solveig?"

"Dead."

"Good," the blonde girl said and spit on the floor.

"Della promised us freedom," the little brown-haired dwarf said.

"And that is why I am here. I am fulfilling that promise."

"Where is Della?" the dwarf girl asked.

Herrick hesitated trying not to sob. "She died last night bringing a little baby into the world."

The dwarven girl looked at Herrick. "She was very kind."

"She was," the blonde girl added. "So, you will be our new master?"

Herrick smiled. This was going to take a while.

The four left the Tower. They walked down Tower Road. Several villagers stopped and stared at the mayor followed by Allistril and the thralls as they passed through the village square. They moved further in the valley to Valdir's smith shop. Herrick entered the shop and found the tools he needed. The wrist restraints came off quickly, but the neck collar took a little more time. The little dwarven girl was the first to be fully unshackled. When Herrick removed her collar, her hands quickly went to her throat.

"I'm free," she whispered.

The blonde girl did something similar. Herrick took the shackles and threw them away.

"What now?" Allistril asked.

"A new life for us all," Herrick said and smiled.

CHAPTER 35

T he horses complained at every whip crack, screaming and straining against the cruelty of Thron. Wolves chased the wagon for the last two miles, and Sir Hakon's defense of the warwagon was sloppy.

"White Citadel can't be made in a day. You're mad, Overseer. Mad," Thron said as he cracked the whip. He knew there would be no retort or punishment. Overseer Daniels was sealed within the warwagon, protected by armor, only susceptible to a baby that would not stop crying. The cargo unceasingly wailed and made every wild thing in the hillside investigate. "Shut that thing up."

His shoulder burned where he pulled out the arrow. His angered whip cracks drove the nearly hysterical horses to exhaustion. Their sweat glinted in the occasional smoke-stricken moonlight. Thron cursed under his breath as it also revealed wolves giving chase and something standing upright, howling.

"Sir Hakon!" Thron bellowed over the wails from the carriage. This had already been a tense journey transporting a demon child from the village of Elta to the White Citadel. Wolves added to it, chasing them for the last two miles. He gazed into the forest, watching for the monstrosity he knew waited to attack.

"There, you dolt." Thron pointed from the edge of the trees as Sir Hakon climbed into the seat with a spear. Two wolves ran along the left side of the warwagon, a third ran to the right. The third tried to cross in front of the warwagon, but Thron steered into it. The wolf fell under the wheels with a thump. Thron let out a quick laugh. Sir Hakon stabbed at both wolves on his side. They collapsed on the trail. Sir Hakon relaxed and sat with Thron as the wolves slowed. On the trail behind them, something crawled out on the trail and watched them flee.

Thron cursed under his breath at the spent horses. The fresh horses were still miles away and one of his had an arrow to the flanks causing it to tire out long ago. Now another stumbled and regained footing. The wolves gave up the hunt and whipping only added to their torment. Thron wiped the sweat from his brow. He pulled a flask and took a heavy drink of spirits to warm his body from the chill night air. The horses slowed their pace.

"I'd offer you some, Sir Hakon, but I'm not going to," the Thron said.

"Thron, talk like that to a knight at the White Citadel and you will be hung," Sir Hakon replied.

Thron laughed.

A small hatch opened behind the wagonmaster's position. Overseer Daniels gazed out. "Why in the name of the Great God are you slowing down."

"Horses are half dead, Overseer. I'm guiding this trail the best I can. One wrong move and the horses are in the Delirium Forest. The trailhead is still several miles from here. There isn't much left in them or me."

The infant wailed and the entire forest surged with real and imagined foes. Several wolves howled in the distance.

"Gods, man. Force them on until they drop," Overseer Daniels pleaded.

"And leave us stopped and waiting for death? I think not, Overseer. You wanted us to make the White Citadel as soon as possible, we will have to reserve their strength. You get that damned thing to stop screaming and I'll worry about the horses. You sure they are bringing fresh horses on the southern trail?"

The hatch slammed shut, and the baby continued to wail.

"There will be fresh horses," Sir Hakon said.

"Gods. We're all cursed." Thron muttered as he took another drink.

The next hour went too quiet. The baby must have fallen asleep, or the overseer put it out of its misery. Thron pushed the horses but not past a fast trot.

Voices crept back into Thron's head. Shouts of laughter and mirth belittled everything he did. It mocked his stature, calling him a dwarf, told him he wouldn't live through the day, and promised a slow death. Out here on a haunted trail, it seemed impossible to make it. The load was too heavy and the horses too weak. They needed to stop and rest. Maybe make camp and sleep. Even with the White Citadel's magic allowing them passage, bits and pieces of the forest made it through.

Up ahead an old man stood.

"Hakon, look," Thron said. "Am I seeing ghosts?"

"Is that … Yngveig?" Sir Hakon asked.

Thron remembered the old soldier kindly and should have gone to wish him well on his journey when he left. He stood near the trees.

"Does he need help?" Thron asked. He slowed the horses.

Overseer Daniels opened the hatch again. "What are you doing, Wagonmaster?"

"Yngveig is up ahead."

"Yngveig of Elta?" Overseer Daniels stammered.

"Yes."

"Do not stop. It's a trap the Delirium Forest has set for us."

"It's Yngveig, though. What if he needs help?"

"Sir Hakon, take the reins."

Overseer Daniels aimed his staff at Thron. Thron handed the reigns over. Sir Hakon drove the horses forward past a silent Yngveig who stared and watched them pass without gesture.

"Gods, the forest claimed him," Thron said.

The hatch slammed shut behind him, and Sir Hakon drove the horses on.

"Watch yer left," Thron said. "No! Your other left. That's the edge of the Delirium Forest, do not enter it. How did you learn to ride a horse, boy? Underneath it?"

Thron snagged the reigns back. "If we are to die today, it will be by my hand. That way I know everything was done correctly and it was against all odds."

He whipped the horses and got them to a brief gallop. For the next hour, they rode in silence. The smoke drifted in a little heavier, and the same stretch of road seemed to repeat.

"Are you seeing this, boy?" Thron's voice echoed back to him.

Sir Hakon stared ahead, silent. He touched the magical amulets that guarded their travels. It felt cold and lifeless.

Drive into the trees and let the forest embrace you. It was the clearest voice in Thron's head. He whipped the horses faster. The rear brake horse groaned. The arrow still chewed up muscle as he ran, and there was no way of getting it out unless they stopped. He guessed they had a mile to go on the trail.

"Hakon, wake up," he yelled.

Sir Hakon slowly stared at him, eyes wide, face blanched pale.

"All these years of listening to my own voices gave me a leg up in the insanity," Thron said.

Thron slowed the horses to a fast trot and watched the rear brake horse. Although groaning and tired, the pace seemed better for it. The smoke choked Thron and the horses. He brought up a small piece of cloth over his nose and mouth and didn't worry about Hakon.

A light emerged up ahead. Thron adjusted the seat. This might be the first beacon of hope on this journey. A lit torch was posted to a tree. The warwagon reached the end of the Delirium Forest. Thron felt his head clear as soon as he passed the last of the cursed trees.

Rut marks littered the south trail with horse and human tracks. He turned the horses to the trail and sped to give them more distance past the forest's exit. His knuckles raked the hatch, and Thron decided not to risk waking the demon child. An army marched through here and the path was well marked.

Sir Hakon stared at him trying to make words.

Thron smacked him with his gloves.

"By the Allfather, what happened?" Sir Hakon asked.

"Delirium Forest, boy. It took you down hard. Our amulets failed, but we made it. We're on the southern road to the White Citadel."

"Why all the torches?"

"Troop movement and it's a big one. I'll watch for a side trail to move around them."

Thron kept a steady pace on the team. The trees thinned out as the area became hillier. Thron found a side road. It appeared less damaged and they wouldn't have to pass an army.

"Better check on the overseer. I haven't heard him yet." Thron said to Sir Hakon. Sir Hakon crawled over and climbed down through a top hatch.

Thron didn't care about the overseer but wanted the time to clear his head and drink. After the Delirium Forest, his flask wouldn't last to where the next team waited.

He exited the trees and now was on an open rolling plain. The moon above gave him ample lighting to see several miles around. The cold wind helped his panicked sweat dry and Thron relaxed. The team was almost exhausted. Thron forced them up a tall hill, but there was not much left in the horses. At the top of the hill, something signaled at the crest of the next hill.

Thron smacked the hatch.

"What is it?" Overseer Daniels asked.

"Knight!" Thron yelled. He tried to goad the horses faster, but they refused. He didn't know if they would make the hill.

Thron paused. It was an odd location to meet, but the knight might save them all. Sir Hakon climbed back out and pulled a magical golden circle up to his eye. He said a command word and looked into the distance. "By the Allfather," he whispered.

"Is it another trap?" Thron asked.

"No. Not at all. It's Sir Gregory." Thron watched the excitement in the young knight's eyes. Sir Gregory, Champion of the Cause, Leader of the Western Army, had arrived with fresh horses. A stopping point for this damned journey that allowed them a chance to survive, but it would be a treacherous place for a team exchange. Uneven footing and a sharp drop off would prove disastrous with an already spooked team. The wolves were not far behind.

The next hill proved laborious. The tired horses crawled the trail pausing dangerously at the top of the hill. Thron whipped them until marks appeared at the top of their flesh. The horses were done and doubtful to survive this night. They had made it and Thron pulled to a stop.

Sir Gregory's armor reflected moonlight like a beacon in a stormy port. He stood his ground with fresh horses grazing.

"Gregory," Thron called out, daring familiarity.

Sir Gregory ignored the wagonmaster and dismounted. He removed his war helm and rapt on the wagon. Overseer Daniel undid the locks from inside.

The metal door flew open with a clang causing the baby to wail again. Sir Gregory peered into the carriage.

"This is it?"

Sir Gregory watched the child squirm in its loose blanket. The overseer sat back, not wanting to touch it.

"This is the child of the witch," Overseer Daniels said, pointing at the baby.

"You fools fear an infant?"

"The child's father was a forest god."

"Or a horny villager. Look at it."

Sir Gregory picked up the infant as stool fell from its loose swaddling.

"Driving all night with a demon child and you packed no new swaddling? Idiots." Sir Gregory turned to Sir Hakon. "Thank you for your support on this fruitless adventure. The path ahead is clear with soldiers waiting. I release you to go back to Elta."

"I have no passage through the Delirium Forest, the Allfather's amulets have failed," Sir Hakon said.

Sir Gregory paused. "Very well then, assist with the horses.

Wagonmaster, are you waiting on a sign from the Allfather himself to begin?"

Thron swallowed the last of his flask and paused. He thought of great insults to tell the great Sir Gregory, but imprisonment at White Citadel wasn't worth it. He jumped down from his seat and stretched his road-weary bones as Sir Gregory watched.

"Overseer," Sir Gregory called out.

Overseer Daniels glanced out of the wagon.

"Give me your cloak."

Overseer Daniels seemed surprised at the request.

"Give me your cloak, now."

The overseer undid his cloak and tossed it out to Gregory. Gregory cleaned the baby the best he could with the old swaddling, then wrapped him tight in the old cloak. The infant, now clean, relaxed and drifted off into slumber. He took the old swaddling and threw it down the hillside.

"It's an infant, superstitious fools."

"The High Father requested I deliver it. It was born from an active witch, and an old crone provided the midwifery. She cursed us all."

"You pushed with all abandon through the cursed forest at night, running almost unobtainable lengths to get this baby before the High Father."

"He requested it."

"The babe is human. Congratulations, Overseer Daniels, your piety is beyond our simple reproach. Does this babe have a name?"

"The crone was using old tongue, but I did hear one word of power in it. Aristid."

Sir Gregory patted the baby, repeating the name as the

overseer continued.

"She called it out on her curse before the knights stabbed her. Unfortunately, she initiated a death curse to protect the child."

"You allowed a death curse?"

Overseer Daniels settled back into the warwagon, attempting to escape any more scorn from the knight.

Sir Gregory looked at the infant. Thron and the young knight still worked on the horses. Gregory pinched the baby's leg causing it to wail. Howls out past the darkness of moonlight answered it back. The tired horses whinnied and paced about as the Thron struck one and told it to settle down. One howl echoed closer. The horses stomped the ground causing Thron to stand between them attempting to calm them down while the young knight worked on the yoke.

"Sir Hakon, you may need to move," Thron said.

Gregory walked to the warwagon's door and slammed it shut. The overseer called out.

"You take forever to exchange these horses, you buffoons," Sir Gregory said.

Thron glared at him. "I've been driving all night and am exhausted like these damn horses. If you want it to go faster, help … and shut that child up.

"You haven't unbuckled them yet?" Sir Gregory quietly loosened the break.

The wagonmaster didn't look up. "We're working on it."

Sir Gregory pushed the arrow deeper into the rear brake horse's flank. The horse screamed and leaped, causing the other horses to gallop. They knocked Thron and the young knight down, dragging them by the yoke brace. The team headed straight to the cliff and over. Their screams reverberated from the hills. A smile crossed Sir Gregory's lips as he gazed at the infant struggling in his arms.

"May the blind eye of the Allfather be turned to this as I deliver you, little one. Aristid. You are too grand of a prize to be handed over by a common overseer."

Sir Gregory scanned the area and found a lone figure far down the southern trail near the Delirium Forest. It sniffed the air and smelled recent death. Gregory knew about the shepherd spotted near Elta. At least he wouldn't worry about disposing of the bodies in the wreckage at the bottom of the hill.

CHAPTER 36

Sir Gregory galloped through the heavy night air. The pace put the infant to sleep. It took days to make it from here to the steps of the White Citadel. A large contingent of soldiers flooded the southern trail on a slow march that would delay him longer. Sir Gregory touched his amulet.

"I need a gate to the frontier. Steed and two riders."

He had to be cautious as magic had been unreliable as of late. Their clerics and wizards lost abilities at an astonishing rate, only the most zealous priests maintained their connection to the Allfather, and their life forces waned. The magic users became the true power and that was why the White Citadel hunted them or controlled them.

The air shimmered down the trail. The path ahead contorted and shifted to a land several days away. Dry air flowed through the gate, making the humid air compress to the ground. Fog formed at its foot. He waited a moment to make sure the gate stabilized.

This was the reign of the 43rd Allfather. This one known as Allfather the Long-lived because he had endured longer than his previous incarnations by over 250 years. The deathwatch had continued for the last five winters, but he refused to rejoin Asagrim, his godly self. When he did, a new Allfather would appear, confused and wandering the countryside until found and anointed with power. Between the Allfathers' reigns, his daughter, Lady Eira, would lead the White Citadel.

Blasphemous thoughts crossed Sir Gregory's mind. The

Allfather had become a *haugbui*, a burial mound monster. Surrounded by his finery and his followers, feeding off them to stay alive.

He passed through the portal. The heavy valley atmosphere gave way to thin, high mountain air. He took a couple of deep breaths, leaned in, and kicked his steed. Falthomir, his potion and magic-imbued stallion galloped down the trail faster than any known horseman could catch him. In the next several days, Falthomir would be useless, fending off spell and potion fatigue and the effects of this long journey.

The last gate took a day off his journey, the next would be less, but magic was uncertain the further transported in. Too much chance with chaotic magic and ending up in another place or another dimension. He needed to get away from the last gate and separate the rift by a few miles. Some said that it was the latticework of magic the Allfather had created. His followers used and drew power from it. Now it had become chaotic, twisted, and unknown. The mangata, the magical scholars, attempted to shore up the power, then decided to remake what was once perfected by a god.

It was a fair system, but the old practitioners had to be wiped out. Those that drew power from the old system caused ripples in the new. As the old system faded, they found forgotten old defenses, those placed by the Allfather to keep his hand on power. As it waned, old gods and new gods appeared in-country and caused chaos.

The combination of so much change would cause a new age to soon develop. Lady Eira will take the throne, and the bundle in his arms would be his wedding gift to her, a child of remarkable power.

Herrick awoke to the sounds of the hunter's horns. Allistril and the two thralls were asleep. He moved around the room, got dressed, and ran down the stairs. The horns sounded again, something wasn't right. He grabbed his bow, quiver, and sword and headed for the door. It was early morning or late night. The horns sounded again and came from the Delirium Forest. Haveldan stood at the burnt trail's entrance. Steiner, the stonemason, ran up Tower Road with a heavy cart. Herrick followed.

Herrick caught up to Steiner by the middle of the road.

"Haveldan's got wounded," Steiner said.

They broke the crest of the hill. Haveldan half-carried Kordan. When they got closer, Kordan's wounds were more apparent and vital. Behind them, Yngveig stood, appearing lost in thought, but unharmed.

"We lost another to the forest," Haveldan said. "We don't dare return."

"Get Kordan down to Della's office," Herrick said, then realization kicked him in the gut. "Maybe we can find something there."

Haveldan laid Kordan down in the cart. Steiner and Herrick pulled it to the road.

"Yngveig, what happened to the pilgrims?"

There was silence. Herrick looked back to see if Yngveig had heard him. Tears freely streamed down his roadworn cheeks. Herrick let the question go. "Haveldan, do you know any healing?"

"Natural first aid, but not enough."

Kordan's face was etched with scratch and bite marks. Ripped pieces of bloody clothing promised more wounds. Cody caught them coming back from the Tower. He stopped and stared, seeking someone else.

"We lost Klas in the Delirium Forest," Haveldan said. "Wolves attacked with a shepherd. He was right behind us in the smoke."

"Did you see any sign of the pilgrims?"

"Just Yngveig." Haveldan motioned. "Standing near the trees like he'd seen something awful,"

"One of Gaut's boys. The cart ran over him," Kordan whispered.

"The shepherd, Mayor. Gods, I think it was Nol, but he was missing an arm, and he has changed." Haveldan said. "We took out most of the wolves, but they overpowered Klas when we tried to back away from the Shepherd. If it was Nol, we better prepare in case he follows us back."

"I'm going to take Yngveig back home. I'm not a good nursemaid," Steiner said as he led Yngveig away.

Herrick nodded and stopped in front of Della's destroyed office. The village's best protector lay in the cart half dead. The other warrior with any ability was lost to the Delirium Forest leading a group of true-believers to the White Citadel. They moved through the rubble and back into the beds. Cody helped Kordan from the cart into a nearby bed. Haveldan rushed around the remains of the office searching for what they needed.

"I think one of Della's kits are in the house. I'll be right back."

Herrick moved over to his house. He found one of Della's kits, near it on the floor was a red velvet bag. He took it with him and hurried back to the office.

He gave the kit to Haveldan, who already tended to Kordan's wounds. He poured the contents of the bag onto a table. Dried leaves, flowers, a rolled-up scroll, and a rock fell out. Herrick unrolled the scroll and read it.

"Haveldan, do you know how to make potions?"

"Like a bad cook burning water. Why? What do you have there?" He wiped the blood off his hands and read the scroll. "This could be useful. Where did Della brew her potions?"

Herrick moved past some of the rubble to a small closet in the back of the office. He opened it and immediately the smell of old herbs and leaves wafted into the office. "I helped her a few times.

Let me get it going."

Spying the mortar and pestle, Haveldan ground the leaves and flowers. "These are exotic plants. I've never heard of some of these, wonder where she got it?"

Herrick lit the alcohol burners. "I don't know. She didn't tell me much after I was attacked by the Magistratus. I was so busy in village business that I was unaware of my wife plotting a rebellion."

Haveldan stared at the fire. "It wasn't just her, Mayor. A lot of us were involved. I almost took a shot at Overseer Daniels when he tried to burn Lofn."

"Sir Solveig told me that Ivanar mentioned her when he was being interrogated."

"It wasn't just Ivanar and Ragnfast." Haveldan stopped and put his hand on Herrick's shoulder. "We all had our hands bloodied at one time or another. The magistrate discovered us, but other than Ivanar's loss, seemed not to care."

Herrick shrugged off Haveldan's hand. "They left in a hurry."

"Maybe they decided that our village wasn't worth it."

"Or they realized something else was about to happen."

The last gate malfunctioned. The strange warping of space made Sir Gregory feel like he suddenly stopped, then catapulted a great distance. The sudden pain caused the infant to wail. Falthomir was leg deep in noxious water. The air felt as if it had not moved in centuries.

"By the Allfather, Mangatas. You will be the death of me."

"You are miles off target, be prepared," the amulet said. "Knights have been dispatched from the nearest watchtower."

"Location."

"You are very near Bluozan Bog. Travel with extreme

caution."

His army encountered a tribe there once. They were backward people, praying and giving sacrifice to land weights and local spirits. The muck slowed the horse to a steady crawl. The horse begged to run and squealed in protest. The muck tried to suck his hooves back down into the swamp. Sir Gregory pulled Egil, his sword, and awoke it. The sword flashed to life. Gregory scanned and stared at the rocks and petrified trees with scorn.

"You there, I seek safe passage," Sir Gregory said.

The stone lethargically rolled and stood up.

"You bring sacrifice?" it asked.

"No. I am from the White Citadel, and I demand safe passage."

"White Citadel means nothing to Bobo. You bring sacrifice?"

The baby's wails continued. "By the Allfather, you will give us safe passage."

Falthomir stopped.

Sir Gregory pointed Egil at the creature. Its squinty obsidian eyes stared back at him.

"Bobo will ask the father." The troll meandered to the remains of a large ancient tree.

"No." Gregory kicked Falthomir to move. The steed pulled one hoof out struggling.

The troll went to the base of the tree and touched what Gregory originally thought to be part of a large branch, until it moved. "Father, knight won't give Bobo sacrifice." Wisps of yellow light formed around the swamp. "Father, the knight has a baby offering." The vines on the tree undulated and crawled down into the murky water. Little wakes formed in the stagnate water as the vines closed in on Sir Gregory.

"Falthomir, if you don't move, we are doomed."

Falthomir let out a deep neigh that ended in a squeal. He leaped, almost knocking Sir Gregory from his saddle, then trudged through the mud. He whinnied as he gained momentum.

A figure stood on impossibly long legs. His branch-like arms crossed down in front of it. It lurched forward, breaking away from the tree, while its smooth eyeless face scanned the bog.

"Bring me the infant." Its voice boomed in the swamp.

The troll reached up and took its twig-like fingers, leading it toward Sir Gregory. With its other hand, it reached out toward Sir Gregory. Long vines draped from its arms and moved under the brackish water. The vines, covered in sharp thorns, broke the surface of the water. They moved closer to Falthomir.

Falthomir continued out of reach as movement bubbled in the waters around them. Odd little lights escaped from the tree and flew like bright firebugs. They flew in odd circles near the trees and disappeared in the water. The bodies of the past sacrifices rose from the swamps stood, their gait unsure. One fell over and crawled toward Falthomir. Sir Gregory pulled the wailing infant close to his chest and struck. The blade sliced through the corpse, searing the wound as it passed through. Another stumbled near.

"I have no time for this, bog spirit. Give me safe passage or die."

"Give us the sacrifice." Its deep voice roared through the swamp.

Gregory sliced the bog corpse in half as it drew too close and then sheathed Egil. Gregory's hand broke the amulet around his neck.

"Mangata, reign fire."

He threw the amulet at the bog spirit. The small troll caught the amulet and handed it to the bog spirit.

There was a satisfaction in its voice as it said, "Bobo earned sacrifice?"

Gregory kicked Falthomir forward. The horse struggled, then hit firmer land. Something whistled in the air high above them, screaming louder as it approached. The horse found a small trail in the swamp and galloped away. Gregory glanced back, then leaned forward to shield the baby and Falthomir's head as a large burning boulder fell through the trees and landed on the bog spirit and troll. The explosion pushed Falthomir forward and almost threw Sir

Gregory off his steed. Falthomir galloped up the trail finding a drier and safer surface to run as the swamp burned behind them.

Portals appeared around them as knights emerged on horseback and on foot.

"Make sure nothing follows," Sir Gregory called out.

"We will have a gate ready at the watchtower," one of the knights called out. They whipped their horses to follow Falthomir, who outpaced them.

Gregory ignored it and left the knights behind. The mangata had put him in an old sacrificial bog with a screaming newborn. He might pass the gates for a while and let Falthomir run.

Gregory examined the infant wrapped in the overseer death robes. He knew it was hungry and had hoped to be closer to the White Citadel at this point. He covered the infant a little better and held it to him, galloping through the night. Magical fires jumped from the watchtowers in the distance, calling his way home. As he progressed into the night, the baby settled into an uneasy sleep.

"I've never brewed anything that glowed before," Haveldan called out.

Herrick attempted to bandage Kordan but from his grunts and winces decided to leave him alone. Haveldan entered with a potion bottle and a cup. The bottle pulsed with red light and had a heartbeat of its own. "I tried some, it's good stuff."

He poured some out into the cup and held it to Kordan's lips. He stared at it with his good eye, then greedily drank. His head sunk back to the pillow and his breathing slowed.

"Della gave me some of this after the Magistratus attack. It takes a moment," Herrick said.

They listened to Kordan's breathing. After a few moments, Haveldan pointed to Kordan's mauled leg. The claw marks and cuts sealed themselves, and the redness of the wounds faded. The more significant open cuts of his face came together, scarring, but the swelling around his eye did not abate.

"Looks like we will have to deal with a one-eyed leader of the hunters. There goes his bow aim," Haveldan said.

"Could we give him more?" Herrick asked.

"The power of the potion can only do so much. Too much might poison him," Haveldan said. He watched Kordan. "Eh, he's a strong boy." Haveldan poured another cup. He lifted Kordan's head to drink, and he finished another cupful. The swelling around the eye only slightly healed.

"Too much," Kordan said. Then retched over the side of the bed as Haveldan grabbed a bucket.

"Even Kordan has his limits," Haveldan said. "Go do what you need to do, Mayor. I think we are over the worst of it. I'll keep watch on him," Haveldan said. "Go take Cody up to the Tower and see what you can find. Nol may be close by, and we need to be ready."

The brown-haired dwarven girl climbed the trail with them. She was silent, head kept low, not looking at either Herrick or Cody as they ascended the Tower Road. As they hit the top of the road, she stopped.

Herrick reached out and touched her arm. "It's okay. The Tower is empty." She flinched at first, then relaxed at his touch.

"I can take you to the armory," she whispered. "Come this way."

They walked through the grand hall, down the hallway, and into a large room. Cody and Herrick stared at the armor and weapons that lined the wall. Sir Geir and Sir Torstein's armor sat displayed ceremoniously. "Cody, I think Geir's armor would be a good fit. I may have to really pad Torstein's armor to get it to fit."

"What about Solveig's armor?" Cody asked. The way he said it, Herrick knew the words came out of his mouth before he could stop it.

"Maybe for Steiner if he wants it. Otherwise, let it rot where it lays."

Cody stayed silent as he wrestled the armor down.

"The knights made it look so easy wearing this. How?"

"Training, I guess. I never thought I would be organizing a small army for Elta and raiding leftovers from the Tower."

"Mayor? Where is your dwarf?" Steiner asked.

They searched the room and found nothing. In the hall, they grabbed displayed weapons off the wall. A long sword for Herrick and a short sword and axe for Cody. A light escaped a room down the way. They snuck down the hall with pilfered weapons in hand.

The room was lined with several war banners, armor and weapons of other races, and trinkets from other countries. The girl sat cross-legged in front of a display of dwarven armor and weapons, staring at it.

"Sir Solveig made me polish my grandfather's armor, then he would wear the helmet and gauntlets and beat me. I thought about putting my father's axe through his sleeping face many nights."

"He took a lot from us, but he's gone."

"He was a battlefield scavenger and nothing more than a vulture. The White Citadel army killed them. Solveig just took their relics."

"He never did much here either."

She sighed and stared at the floor. "I want my people's keepsakes."

"Then they are yours." Herrick sat down next to her. "Take what you can. If we need to come back, we will."

She smiled and slowly looked up. "I never want to come here again, Herrick. Thank you."

"What is your name?"

"Theim."

"No. Your real name, your clan's name."

The girl sighed. "For thirty years I have been known as Theim. Unlike the other girl, I had twenty-four years with my family before we were defeated at the battle of Clan Eitri."

"You're fifty-four winters old?"

"Still a young girl by dwarven standards."

Herrick laughed. She rubbed her neck where her collar used to be.

"Nóri," she said quietly as if she waited for someone to punish her. "My name is Nóri of Clan Eitri."

"I'm sorry I didn't ask earlier, Nóri of Clan Eitri," Herrick said and patted her on the back. "Is there anything else that might help us?"

"Have you searched Overseer Daniel's quarters?"

Herrick stood in the doorway of the lavish room with his jaw hanging open.

"Don't touch anything, Cody."

Shelves of books lined the walls, some in languages that danced across the cover, inviting him to read and get lost in. Bottles of strange glowing things, odd wands, and bags lined desks and stations. There were similar appliances that Della brewed potions with, but much grander, with odd columns, windows, and adjustable flames. "This is far beyond me." He reached out and touched a wand laying on a table. A small arc of electricity shot out and hit his finger. "Nope. We're done in here."

Nóri pulled a cart into the great hallway, and they loaded up the loot. There were no horses left in Elta, so Cody, Herrick, and Nóri eased it down Tower Road. Steiner rushed up the road when the cart threatened to run away and helped them stop it.

"Wow. Plundering the Tower?" he asked when they caught

their breath.

"Nol may be on the hunt."

"Oh, and let me guess, we are the stand-in army now? We have armor and weapons that no one knows how to use. At least our deaths will be efficient," Steiner said.

"It might allow you to feast with Asagrim," Cody said.

Steiner chuckled. "Herrick, Aurdr is looking for you. She wants to feast before the grain is ruined."

CHAPTER 37

Falthomir breathed heavily in the night air. He had outdistanced the Bluozan Bog by a day's journey at least. Even the greatest of Sir Gregory's steeds, enhanced by magic and potions, had his limits. Sir Gregory was hitting his limits as well. They were entering the outer borderland of the White Citadel. Instead of watchtowers being small dots of light on the frontier, they were closer together. Several towers pinpointed the distance. He slowed Falthomir to a trot, then into a walk. A nearby tower had archers walking around with knights. A short man in red robes worked on some odd brass apparatus around the base of the watchtower.

He looked at the infant. How could this babe be responsible for so much fear and hatred? A child of a witch and forest demon remained a simple babe in his arms. The thought brought a smile to his lips. The baby shifted in its swaddling. The night was chilly, too cold for an infant of this age. Aristid. A word Gregory had heard from his betrothed's cousin as he rained fire down on distant armies.

"Hail, Sir Gregory approaches," someone yelled in the distance. Familiar horns echoed from the tower. In the distance, the knights mounted horses. Sir Gregory stopped, grabbed his horn from the saddlebag, and blew three quick notes in response. The baby wiggled and cried. Before long, the riders galloped toward him. Gregory put the horn back and pulled his sword, Egil. With a slight whisper, the sword glowed and Gregory waved it over his head. He stopped, waiting for the approaching knights, and watched the infant.

"Ho, Sir Gregory!" the lead rider called out, a stout man wearing heavy plate and a ceremonial helmet with Ram's horns.

"Sir Thormund, hail to you."

Behind him, Sir Holt rode, glowing and over-armed with magical trinkets. Sir Gregory glanced to his sides. Even though he paid some attention to the rider's approach, he was unaware Sir Njólborjn followed him.

"You traveled with the babe through the Bluozan Bog? Impressive." Sir Njólborjn emerged from the trees, quiet as a breeze.

The riders surrounded Gregory, his own personal captains.

"What of Overseer Daniels?" Thormund asked.

"Their caravan came under attack of wolves as they were changing horses, took the warwagon off the cliff."

"You saved the cargo, Helsa!" Sir Thormund cheered. "The great god has smiled on you once more. The child, is he as fearsome as told?"

Sir Gregory held the baby up.

"Normal," Sir Njólborjn said.

The other riders cheered him on and sounded their horns once more. The baby erupted into a full cry. Sir Gregory watched their reactions. This child was foretold to be a monster but was as human as any other child born in the citadel. There was fear from hardened soldiers Gregory had personally seen commit atrocities. This child could be raised as a warrior and an omen to enemies.

"Call a gate, Sir Holt. This road has left me weary."

"Sir Gregory, a mangata from the very tower of magic is here. They were a little upset that some junior wizard sent the special cargo to a sacrificial swamp. He is working on a very special transport for you."

"Is that Soren?" Sir Gregory asked, squinting in the darkness.

"When you have something of interest, they sent the best." Sir Holt pointed to the small man in red robes.

The four trotted through the night to the base of the tower.

The trees stirred around them. The animals woke up, disturbed by the wailing baby. Flocks of birds exploded from the trees and disappeared in various directions.

"That's interesting," Sir Holt said.

Howls sounded in the distance, echoing back closer. The knights scanned the surroundings for a threat and continued toward the mangata.

"Sir Thormund, let the horse rest but he needs ran back. Be warned, he's full of potions, and the shoes are enchanted. He's a little road-worn now, but if I stable him, he'll kick down the walls."

Sir Thormund pointed at the man with the mangata. "We brought Torin, just in case."

The young man looked up and walked toward them as they approached.

Soren stood in front as a young Theim helped him put the apparatus together. Soren drew something on the ground in front of it. When he finished, he stepped into it, arms moving in some fashion of dance while speaking words that seemed to echo back with more intensity. The apparatus flashed to life, and thunder rumbled throughout the area. Inside the apparatus, a green-cloaked version of Mangata Soren gave a thumbs up and stepped through. Behind him, the White Citadel stood in all its glory.

"Almost home," Sir Gregory said.

Past the apparatus, a line of knights and warpriests lined the entrance. Sir Gregory dismounted and walked the horse the rest of the way. "Hello, Torin." He handed the reigns over to his squire. "Potions are active, beware."

Torin nodded. "I want to hear stories when I get back."

Sir Gregory bounced the wailing baby. "Oh, there will be stories."

"Wolves on the perimeter," Sir Njólborjn called out. The whistle of arrows soon answered.

"Helsa, to you Sir Gregory. Give our regards to your betrothed, and may the great god watch you on your journey," Sir

Thormund said.

"Always the sentimental one, Sir Thormund."

Gregory turned and looked. In the darkness, several dozens glowing eyes watched and paced.

"Now, Sir Gregory. I believe they may attack soon," said the green-robed Soren.

Sir Gregory walked through the apparatus. Unlike the previous gates, this felt like walking through a door. There was no sense of movement over great distance. The crowd watched him nervously as he emerged. The red-robed Soren said some word, and the scene dissolved behind him as he stepped through, the green Soren already halfway through an incantation.

Warpriest Aldwin stepped forward and greeted Gregory. He wore his finely jeweled ceremonial robes. His pale eyes fell on Sir Gregory and then went to the baby.

"The Allfather requests your presence immediately."

"I will take the baby to him."

There was a pause in Aldwin's demeanor. "I will take the infant."

"I've just rode a seven-day journey in a couple of hours, and you stand before me demanding this? I will take the baby to Lady Eira, and we will approach the Allfather together."

Aldwin half-bowed. "As you wish, Sir Gregory."

Sir Gregory stared at Aldwin as he took a half step backward.

"You had your chance to be the voice of the Allfather, that is over."

The dense wood doors of the White Citadel's Grand Hall opened. Citadel guards, knights, and squires rushed into the great hall to capture a glimpse of the child as Gregory entered. Aldwin walked several steps behind. Rumor had circulated about the child after the magistrate sent reports, but he didn't think it created this much interest.

The inhabitants of the White Citadel lined the halls, whispering to one another. Gregory clutched the baby and moved past to the Allfather's Hall. The walk was not a short one in the immense citadel and thousands crowded around, straining to see the bundle that squirmed in his arms.

The closer to the temple, the more the throngs of people squeezed in to catch a glimpse.

"Enough of this. Knights to ranks, squires to ready!" Sir Gregory's voice demanded.

There was an eruption of chaos as the knights and squires pushed others out of the way and attained battlefield precision.

"Clear a path," Sir Gregory ordered. Several knights stepped forward, moving the younger priests and their followers out of the way. Now a path stood before Sir Gregory that the warwagon would fit through. His knights stood guard.

He turned and watched the crowd and felt Aldwin's heated stare.

"Look!" Sir Gregory said, removing the swaddling and held the baby up naked in the cold air. "It is a normal child and nothing else."

The baby shrieked and cried. A few of the Allfather's prized wolfhounds loose in the great hall whined.

"That remains to be seen," Sir Aldwin said.

Lady Eira stepped out from the temple doorway. Fatigue from his journey drained away when Sir Gregory saw her. He marched to the temple doors, went down on one knee, and presented the baby to her.

"Welcome back home, Sir Gregory," she said. She seemed puzzled by the old overseer robes that swaddled the baby, adjusted them, and covered up the infant. "Follow me."

Sir Gregory stood, turned to the gathered crowd, and found a commander. He simply nodded, then the commander announced dismissal.

Sir Aldwin stood before the doors of the Allfather's Hall, eyes settling on Sir Gregory.

"You are dismissed, Aldwin. We will call for you if we have need," Sir Gregory said.

Sir Gregory turned and walked through the doors of the hall as Aldwin protested. The doors shut with a loud boom. Several of the High Priests looked up from the Allfather's bed.

"Was that necessary?" Lady Eira asked.

"More than you will ever know," Sir Gregory said and smiled.

The Allfather lay in the center of a large white circular bed like in the middle of a great womb. His head priests circled him, head's down in prayer. They were connected to him, touching his hands, feet, and head. Sir Aldwin should be here among them, connected and dying.

Sir Gregory and Lady Eira approached the bed. One of the Allfather's priests stood. His face wrinkled and tissue-thin like ancient parchment, lined runic tattoos covered the right side of his face, they constantly moved, changing their meaning and spells. He sacrificed his left eye to the Allfather to become a high priest, his right eye rolled back to the point only viscera showed. It always chilled Gregory to see them.

"I am called The Wanderer, son of War Wise," the priest said.

They sacrificed their souls to the Allfather, each one's life and memory joined and shared with the Allfather's essence.

"I am Sir Gregory, commander of the Einherjar forces of the White Citadel. I return from Elta with the witchborn child."

"Give the witchborn to me."

Lady Eira placed the infant in the priest's arms. He walked over and placed the infant at the head of the bed. Then crawled back in with the other priests, joining their outstretched forms. The Allfather remained in the center of these wraiths, an odd biology of skin-draped skeleton held together with the life force of twenty priests that surrounded it. He lay in a fetal position, but as the baby moved on the bed, a noticeable chill slithered around the Allfather and his priests.

Fragments of words came from different priests. Their heads rose from the bed like drowned men seeking air at the surface. They cried out like children having a nightmare.

"Ragnarök!"

"The doom of everything."

"The doom of the god."

"Prophecy!"

"Fire and famine."

"Defeat of the Einherjar, death of Sir Gregory, the disappearance of Lady Eira."

"Allfather?" Lady Eira whispered.

She walked over and took the baby.

The priests raised their heads, all fixated on the baby and yelled, "End it."

Lady Eira stepped backward.

Two of the priests stood and stumbled towards Lady Eira.

"Gregory," Lady Eira said.

Sir Gregory bounded to the bed and picked the Allfather up, breaking his connections to the priests. The priests scrambled after him, some too weak to stand. Gregory rushed off the bed and moved across the room. Lady Eira's hand went up, and she commanded a runeword. Silence rolled through the room. The priests silently shouted after Gregory, but he moved through the room, calculating the movement to be trapped by the priests, but they were weak, exhausted by the strain of keeping the corpse in Sir Gregory's arms alive. They collapsed to the floor, and some crawled. The odd rune-like messages faded from their faces and their remaining eye rolled forward. They gasped for breath like salmon plucked from the rapids.

It didn't take long. Lady Eira feared the Allfather's death could go on for an hour and poison would have to be used, but in three minutes, the last of the high priests' heads hit the floor.

Gregory placed the fragile Allfather back in the center of the bed. He gathered the high priests from the floor and placed them on the bed as the great horns sounded from the White Citadel.

Someone pounded on the door.

Lady Eira answered. Quick panicked voices on the other side of the great door shouted questions.

"My father, Allfather the Long-Lived, has passed beyond the vail. The Allfather is dead," she answered coldly.

CHAPTER 38

Herrick sat in the village square. His raw hands scrapped at the pyre's burn marks, trying to remove them from the stones. A small fire lit the ground enough to show his work wasn't particularly fruitful. He sat on the edge of the stone seat, red-faced, sweaty, and beaten. He looked away from the fire, gazing down into the valley. The moon lit the valley well.

Sir Solveig's corpse rotted in front of the beggar's shack. Every time Herrick's gaze went to the place, it burrowed like a maggot into his nerves. It was a reminder of past failures. A place where the diseased went to die. With more recent failures, Lofn's entrapment, the birth of Lofn's child, Overseer Daniels stealing it and fleeing to the White Citadel, and the death of his wife. The place itself was a sickness. A scab on this village. If it burned tonight, the ashes could be worked into the soil by next week. As soon as the ground thawed, he would plant a garden, maybe an apple tree.

Herrick rested until the sweat stopped dripping from his brow. He got up, his body silently arguing as he stood, then walked to his office. He hadn't set foot in since the attack and stared through the window at the bloody desk. Della saved him, yet he did nothing during the birth.

He took the torch by the door and lit it.

On his walk to Dead Man's Trail, he relived it. Aged and near death, Della emerged from the shack, protecting Lofn's baby. Sir Solveig made her pay for it.

"Gods, Della. Come back to me."

It was late enough that no one was out, save a few hunters who maintained watch. Herrick walked down Dead Man's Trial towards the shack when something caught his eye. Far down in the graveyard, a shadow dwelled among the graves. A black spot in the moonlight.

"Della?" he asked aloud.

Herrick moved across the field and held the torch behind him to get a better look, straining to see. Some gravestones stood out in the moonlight, but something blocked the others in shadow. The center of the darkness seemed abyssal, not allowing any light to filter in. Herrick stared at the scene like a dog hearing a whistle. Another figure lay near a grave. Herrick thought about the torch in his hand. If he drew any closer, the light would give him away.

Running up the trail, Herrick waved the torch in the air but did not get the hunters' attention. He ran through the cold night air until he passed Valdir and Ragnfast's shops, the ruins of the grainery, then finally the bakery. There was a steep trail into the graveyard. At its bottom, false darkness spread out.

A cold chill ran up his back, up through his neck, and wrapped around his head. Icy tendrils dug into Herrick's brain. He wanted to scream.

A body lay near a gravestone with a robed figure standing above it, reaching down through his chest.

"Magistratus," Herrick howled as his voice cracked.

The figure in the black robes pulled his hand back and stood, collecting the inky blackness around him. The robes billowed out in a ghostly wind that Herrick did not feel.

"Magistratus!" he yelled again.

"Herrick, what is it?" Haveldan called above him from the hill. "I see it." Haveldan notched an arrow and let it fly.

The arrow flew in front of Herrick and down to the graveyard. The arrow passed through the robed figure and broke on the gravestone behind it. Cody ran behind Haveldan with a torch. Haveldan shot a couple more arrows with the same result. Cody threw his torch, and it landed near its shroud, driving it back.

In the light, the shadowy form looked different. It didn't have the wide-brimmed hat of the Magistratus but still had tight skeletal features. When it floated back, it revealed the body at the foot of the grave, Gaut.

"Oh, gods," Herrick said.

For a moment, as the creature backed off from the fire, a flicker of light crossed its darkened cowl and revealed a shock of red hair.

"Ivanar. Cody, go get more torches. Run, boy," Haveldan ordered.

Cody ran into the night, but the creature below stood in place, slowly raising its arm. A shadowy digit pointed at Haveldan and Herrick. Then the creature collapsed. The entire graveyard filled with darkness and then like morning fog, it dissipated.

Haveldan and Herrick stood on the hill scanning below for any movement. Cody returned with more huntsmen and torches. They lit the torches and eased down the hill. Gaut did not move as they approached. Haveldan and Herrick stared at each other until Herrick finally relented.

"I'll check him out," Herrick said. He approached as the hunters fanned out behind him. "Don't the Tower weapons contain some form of magic against this?"

Haveldan drew his sword. It was once Sir Geir's. He approached Gaut and touched the blade to his forehead. The blade did nothing.

"This is ridiculous." Herrick waved Haveldan off and bent down. He touched Gaut's forehead. "He's cold and has been here for a while. I wonder if his death attracted the wraith. Oh, gods, Gaut. I'm so sorry."

The torchlight revealed his family marker. Gaut had added several names to the stone. The stump of charcoal remained in his hands.

"We have no priest," Haveldan said.

"Why does it matter? The overseer hasn't been around for the last several deaths," Cody asked.

Herrick sighed, "I think Gaut's been dead for a while. If Gaut was killed by the wraith, there is a chance he will rise as one. That's what happened to Ivanar. Gods, it almost happened to me." Herrick looked at Haveldan. "Go get Yngveig. I don't know if he was related or not, but we have to burn Gaut tonight."

Haveldan turned to the hunters. "Go gather more wood. We'll burn him in the square."

"I don't want to chance it. We will burn Gaut over there," Herrick said, pointing to a patch of bare earth not far from the graveyard.

"It doesn't seem right, Mayor," Cody said.

"Right or wrong, Cody, I'm not taking a wraith to the middle of the village for sentimental reasons."

Cody stared at the body a moment longer before running off to gather wood. The hunters hastily built a pyre in the field. Herrick picked Gaut's small, feeble frame off the ground and placed him on the wood as Yngveig emerged from the shadows.

Herrick lit a torch and carried it to the pyre. Herrick looked off into the Witches Forest. "Does anyone have anything to say?"

"I'm out of words for the dead," Haveldan said.

Herrick nodded. He held the torch out to Yngveig, but he shook his head. Herrick took a deep breath and lit the pyre.

"To the arms of the Asagrim," Yngveig said as the hunters surrounded the pyre with bows at ready.

The fire took, and the pyre lit up the night. They watched Elta's oldest inhabitants burn.

"I only remember him old," Haveldan said. Yngveig nodded but said nothing. They all watched the shriveled body for any strange movement, waiting for Gaut to rise as a monster. Cody stood on the wrong end of the pyre and had to move once the smoke overtook him. He coughed, looking away from the pyre, trying to rub the smoke from his eyes.

The Tower bell sounded through the village, and Herrick looked at Haveldan.

"No one is up there," Herrick said.

The gong sounded odd. The bell didn't ring but vibrated into a low moan. Lights filled the village as its inhabitants rose. The bell continued its haunted notes, and purple lights erupted from the Tower.

"Gods, they're back," Herrick said.

Several villagers left their house, confused and panicked. They gathered in the square, then seeing the pyre, moved down into the fields next to the hunters, Yngveig, and Herrick. The villagers chattered to guess what was happening. Did the overseer return? Was the magistrate already there? Then Yngveig, quiet for most of his time, looked up. Tears streamed down his already swollen red face. "You all don't understand," he said, then looked at the crowd gathered around. "When I was a soldier, they taught us the meaning of the bells. The Allfather is dead."

CHAPTER 39

Days had passed since the Allfather died. The crowd attending spilled out through the entrance of the White Citadel. Silence commanded as Queen Eira ascended to the Allfather's throne. Once at the top, she turned and inspected the legions of knights, the surviving priests, and the emissaries gathered before her. Her new Kingdom. Aldwin stood in the back of the great hall, his order decimated. The passing of the Allfather left the high priests dead and enfeebled the warpriest ranks. Aldwin, head of the order, stood alone in their ranks. Queen Eira's cold stare settled on him. He refused to become a high priest at the Allfather's beckoning and disconnected himself from the Allfather's magic to survive.

The emissaries stood close to her throne: the monk priests from the eastern countries in their bright red robes, warriors from the allied Elysion, druids from Yggdrasil, and the odd, outworlder callers from Rhylkos. The dwarven emissaries stood out, led by Nilsdorf Ogdben in his fine-jeweled, earthen-toned robes. Nilsdorf had her attention and bowed deeply. The war between the White Citadel and the dwarves had continued for over 100 winters, it was quite brave for them to be in attendance. Queen Eira hated how well they interacted with those gathered.

Sir Gregory climbed the steps of the throne, bowed, and presented Gungnir, the Allfather's mighty spear. She took it from Sir Gregory and stared at the crowd gathered before her. It had been over 30 years since the Allfather welded the spear, and now, Queen Eira held it aloft.

"Gungnir, design provided by the monks, blade forged by the dwarfs, wooden shaft provided by the Druids of Yggdrasil, imbued with magic of the forgotten ones, proven on the fields of Elysion in battle." Queen Eira lowered it as the blade illuminated the room, touching all. "Let it be known that the Allfather has passed into darkness and you witness the transition of power. I, Queen Eira, have ascended to the throne. I will rule until the next Allfather has been found."

The emissaries bowed as a roar went up in the great hall and outside into the White Citadel. When it died down, Queen Eira continued, "A new age has begun. The last age has been fraught with war and fear." She gazed down at the dwarves. "May the next age be one of enlightenment and peace."

Hope flashed across Nilsdorf Ogdben's heavily bearded features.

"As the Allfather becomes one with Asagrim, let the great hunt begin." She slammed the haft of Gungnir to the floor of the throne. As the light from the staff extinguished, a rumble grew and spread through the hall. "Knights are dispatched throughout our country of Valrborjn, the sprawling cities, the towns, and villages to keep watch. May the blessings of Asagrim shine on us all."

She slammed the haft of the spear once more, signifying her speech was over. Once again cheers and roars filled the great hall. With the last slam of her staff, the Allfather's passing ritual began. At the foot of the holy grove away from the great hall and the attendants, young priests loaded the frail Allfather's body on the pyre.

Queen Eira looked around the great room. Aldwin had disappeared. Her ranks of soldiers dispersed from the great hall, leaving the emissaries from the different countries. She descended from the throne and met with those from Elysion first, who claimed the old alliances were still strong. The monks presented beautifully written scrolls outlining the life of Allfather the Long-Lived and continued their hope to keep trade open. The Druids approached, bowing slightly to Queen Eira, and asked to visit the sacred grove before they departed. When the druids left, those from Rhylkos faded from view, then blinked into existence in front of the throne. Queen Eira took care not to stare into their dark cowls as their gurgling voices pledged allegiance to her throne, for insanity could even claim her. Mangata Soren of the Yellow Robes approached and took the ambassadors to the magic tower. Finally, Nilsdorf Ogdben and his dwarves stood before the throne.

He approached as Sir Gregory stepped in front of him. The palace guard stepped up and surrounded the group, swords sheathed, but at the ready.

"Ah, Sir Gregory," Nilsdorf smiled and bowed. He presented a highly jeweled scroll case. Sir Gregory glanced at the mangata standing near the throne. He nodded, showing it was clear of any magical traps. Sir Gregory took the case and opened it. He removed the scroll, unrolled it, and discarded the case. Nilsdorf's eyebrow arched, but he said nothing as the case tumbled and rolled on the floor. Sir Gregory nodded as he read, then handed the scroll to Queen Eira.

"The Dwarves offer a cycle of peace."

"We wish for the scouts to be allowed into the dwarven-occupied lands," Queen Eira said.

The request left Nilsdorf's jaw hanging. "We're at war, and you want to just simply come over?"

"You offered peace. We only want to search for the Allfather."

"Absolutely not. Dwarven blood has been spilled there."

"We also ask that you let our knights accompany them to secure their journey."

"As terms of a total peace treaty?"

"No," Queen Eira said. Her denial echoed in the great hall.

"Then no knight will walk on dwarven land. Simply we offer a reduction in hostility due to the loss of the Allfather. As you said, we approach an age of enlightenment. The war is still fresh in our long-lived minds, but for your people, it has lasted generations."

"I was there at Mount Theo when the Allfather flooded the mine," Queen Eira said.

"We are aware, but Sir Gregory's grandfather was a young squire at the time."

"A squire who grew to great standing." Sir Gregory shifted, hand moving to Egil.

Nilsdorf closed his eyes and sighed. "This has been a long, costly war for both sides. We offer a temporary truce for both sides to breathe. We cannot forgive the creation of Lake Laogi over the surface mines and will not allow your knights to roam where they please."

"You mined the land without the Allfather's permission," Queen Eira said.

"And he flooded the mine by his godly might and cost us thousands of kin. No dwarf will touch the water, no surviving dwarf will forget."

"So here we are. A hundred cycles later not forgetting the start of the war," Queen Eira said.

"King Thum of Clan Brokkr proposed the deal itself. As you said, Great Queen, a time of enlightenment."

"Never trust a dwarf if land or gold are being bargained," Sir Gregory said.

"That was your grandfather and his generations." Nilsdorf took a couple of deep breaths. He bowed to Queen Eira and said, "We ask for this Age of Enlightenment. Not for the decrees of a demented elderly god-king who spoke in fevered dreams."

Gungnir's metal sunk into the stone at the Nilsdorf's feet. The dwarf stared at Queen Eira, picked up the jeweled scroll case, and looked at the guards around him.

"We are glad to see a new ruler of White Citadel on the throne, Great Queen. May you be on the throne for a long time." Nilsdorf's smile showed beneath his beard.

"Send them away," Queen Eira said as Sir Gregory pulled Gungnir from the floor. The guards marched the dwarves from the Great Hall. Queen Eira took Gungnir back from Sir Gregory. Her hand caressed Sir Gregory's face, and she cast a quick spell between the two so only Sir Gregory heard her.

"Lake Laogi, they named it Lake Death in their own tongue. I was unaware of that. Go find Aldwin, he's scheming something. I must attend the pyre."

Sir Gregory charged through the White Citadel. He walked among the high priest's bodies stacked in their quarters. Younger priests stopped and bowed as he passed through. The warpriest quarters had healers running back and forth taking care of the fallen. He toured the towers, looking out at the crowds gathered below, but did not see Aldwin. Sir Gregory walked through the barracks, the Allfather's Hall, and finally went to Queen Eira's residence. He knocked on the beautifully carved door, a carving of Queen Eira and the Allfather, and waited. Usually, a thrall instantly opened the door. He tried to open the door but found it blocked. Egil jumped from the scabbard and in a bright flash sliced clean through the door.

Two thralls lay dead on the cold floor. Sir Gregory rushed through the residence. In Queen Eira's bed chambers, he found Torunn, Queen Eira's hovfröken, or honor maid, dead with a dagger wound to the back. Sir Gregory rolled her over and looked for any sign of life. Her arms carried wounds as if she protected something with her life.

"Queen Eira, hear me," Gregory said. "Aldwin has Aristid. Torunn and two house-thralls are dead in your chamber."

Sir Gregory felt woozy as air and space flew around him. He was in an ancient grove on the White Citadel grounds. The startled Druids stepped back.

"Check the sacrificial groves. I have a feeling he is there," Queen Eira's voice rang in his head.

The northern altar stood in the shadow of the White Citadel. A consecrated place where the more unsavory aspects of worship and religion were carried out. A grove of ancient oaks circled an altar carved from the felled body of what was once the oldest tree in the grove. If the warpriest had brought the baby to this location, it may be too late.

Sir Gregory broke past the hanging trees and past the eyeless war criminals and thieves hung by one leg in the branches high above. Their fleshless faces screamed at those below. The fat ravens called this forest home, casually striping flesh hanging in the trees. They stood on the high branches looking down like large black leaves. Sir Gregory walked these woods at night. He was fearless, his motives were always just and on the side of the Allfather. Until now. A dark pit formed in his soul. They had gone against His will. Aldwin may have known the will to destroy the infant. If they were in this grove, Aldwin carried out the Allfather's final order.

A baby wailed from the center of the grove. He rushed forward and heard a rune song. The old language's vibration whipped Gregory and his brothers into frenzy and victory. Now, it made his heart ache. The grove hummed with power and the ritual was underway. The promise of a child to his barren betrothed would be broken.

Gregory emerged from the woods. Aldwin did not waver concentration as he approached. Pitch written in destructive runes covered the baby. The slight red light encircled the baby and pulsed with its own life. Aldwin held a dark dagger above the baby that pulsed with the same intensity and beat.

Aldwin brought the dagger down towards the baby's throat. Light flashed, and thunder filled the grove. Aristid wailed at the light and sound. Aldwin shouted and dropped the shattered dagger.

"The third time I performed the ceremony on this abomination and the third time this happened, Gregory. This baby, this abomination, that you and Eira seek as your own will destroy us all. I know you are aware. He prophesied this long before. It was his last request of me when he died in your arms."

"You lie," Sir Gregory growled. "You broke with the Allfather."

"I know what you and Eira did, and I am lost for that knowledge." Aldwin's eyes went wide. "I cannot fulfill the Allfather's last request. Not now. I am far too weak. So, I will leave this kingdom in the hands that sought its destruction."

With Egil in his hands, Sir Gregory charged. Aldwin turned to the side, almost to intercept the blade with his heart, and disappeared. Egil screamed through the air.

Dark Magic, the sword screamed in his head.

"Queen Eira, hear me." He waited for two heartbeats. "Aldwin used magic to escape, can you locate him? Aristid is on the altar but is safe."

One of Queen Eira's ladies-in-waiting faded into the grove. She approached Aristid, picked him up, and disappeared in one step.

Gregory felt a rush of air again, his footing unsure. He looked around the room. Things had been hastily grabbed and discarded. Maps, books, and scrolls lay scattered across the floor. Light exploded in the other room, and a pop echoed. Gregory rushed in as the portal disappeared.

"Queen Eira, hear me, he is gone."

Once again, Sir Gregory moved at an incredible speed. When the world stopped, he regained his balance. A mangata stuck his head in. The mangata had white hair piled up and gathered into a topknot, his beard dropped down to mid-belly in a long braid. His robes shimmered in a mix of silver and white, just like his cloudy pupils.

"Ah, Sir Gregory, Queen Eira announced your arrival. What can we do for you?"

"Mangata Dimas, I need you to find Warpriest Aldwin."

The mangata looked disheartened by the request. "That's it? Very well, follow me."

They walked to a map of the room surrounded in copper and bronze rings, other metals were here, but Gregory did not recognize them." He looked around the room, so much here seemed foreign. His eyes stopped at a mage talking to a dark-robed figure. The visitor from Rhylkos had its hood removed. The rainbow men of Mangata Soren surrounded him, happily chatting. Gregory had to look at something else suddenly. Fear crawled up his spine threatening to take over. The being the wizard talked to looked straight out of a child's nightmare. Its face constantly shifted. Its eyes dropped, replacing its nose, as its teeth were like a crown. Its mouth opened wide and swallowed its face as the eyes emerged from the mouth to stare at Sir Gregory. It spoke, and its honeyed words made him forget why he was there.

"Ov'Tolep, could you pull up your cowl?" Mangata Soren of the Red Robes said. "We have an uninitiated in the room."

Something slithered from the back of its head and pulled its cowl down low.

Egil glowed and vibrated until it took Sir Gregory's attention. He grabbed the hilt and closed his eyes, trying to ignore what he just saw.

Calm, Gregory. Clear your mind.

"Sir Gregory."

His name slapped his attention. Gregory shook his head, trying to clear it. Mangata Dimas stood while two small, golden orbs levitated above the map.

"He's not at the White Citadel." The orbs suddenly multiplied and crawled over the map. Mangata Dimas's blind eyes focused into the distance. "Not the major cities. Wait ... I have a trail. Did he teleport?"

"A couple of times, but the last was a portal."

"A-ha." He looked surprised, his head tilted to look at Sir Gregory, "That's not within his usual abilities ... he had help."

"I sensed a foul magic," Sir Gregory said.

The orbs broke apart, splitting into several small spheres that rolled over the map. Finally, they lined up at the White Citadel.

"He is not within the border of Valrborjn." The spheres continued south. "Oh no. I don't believe it."

Gregory looked at the orbs. "What is it?"

"Use your sight, Sir Gregory, and tell me, what sea did Aldwin cross? What lines did the orbs pass?"

"By Asagrim, he crossed the River of Blood. He is in the home of the giants. Send me."

"It's certain death," Mangata Dimas said shaking his head.

"Now, Wizard!" Gregory's voice echoed through the hall. All conversation stopped. Mangatas Dimas' white misty eyes darkened to storm clouds.

"The laws of magic, the very laws passed by the Allfather, prohibit any magic to that area. We cannot. The chaos of the area prohibits our spells."

"Chaos?" The voice sounded like a drowning. "We go to the Ütan …" Ov'Tolep's voice trailed off. It clouded Sir Gregory's thinking.

"Sir Gregory, it is forbidden. I do not know where Aldwin is," Mangata Dimas said.

"We can't lose him now," Sir Gregory said, trying to clear his head.

"Our sacred maps do not go deep into that territory. Where I think he is could be feet or thousands of miles from his location.

"Show me," Ov'Tolep's voice gurgled.

Mangata Dimas reached out. His hand went into the darkness of the cowl. The cloud covering his eyes disappeared, and strangely elongated pupils looked at the map.

"Connected, searching …" it said.

Sir Gregory watched the cowled being. Its shadow grew darker, then crawled from the floor and stood up. Sir Gregory's hand went to Egil. The shadow flew from the room and through the wall. Mangata Soren of the Red Robes walked up and touched Sir Gregory's sword hand.

"Sometimes magic can be unnerving to those that don't fully understand. Please stand down."

Sir Gregory looked at him and nodded.

"Come with me." Mangata Soren took Sir Gregory's hand like a parent handling a scared child. They walked into a room full of pillows, chairs lined the walls. Sir Gregory sat. "Think of what you are willing to do, Sir Gregory. The Allfather fused their king with the mountain, and he still lives. We don't dare enter the Ütan frontier without the chance of giants invading ours."

Sir Gregory nodded. A shadow flew past him and into the other room.

Ov'Tolep howled "Ütangard" like a sick wolf. The capital city and at the foot of King Skrymir and Mount Duris.

"You would be by yourself in the city of the giants at the foot of their entombed king."

"Queen Eira, hear me. I have a report."

The room shifted and spun. He was in the Allfather's chambers. Queen Eira stood, holding Aristid.

"Aldwin has fled to Ütangard."

"I will have the mangatas set up trackers immediately. We will alert the watchtowers on the frontier."

He scanned the room. Other than a few ladies-in-waiting dwelling in the background waiting for Queen Eira's summons, no one was there. Sir Gregory stepped forward and whispered in her ear. "He knows." He pulled back looking into her eyes. "Aldwin knows."

"If he steps into Valrborjn or our allied cities, he will be put to death."

"So be it, beloved. I was so close to ending him."

She moved Aristid between them. "We will be safe, and our reign will begin. Before long, Aldwin will be the least of our worries." She paused for a moment, staring at Aristid. "The hunt for the next Allfather has begun."

CHAPTER **40**

The bell rang throughout the night. The villagers gathered around Gaut's pyre until it fell into ash. They stared into the embers but remained silent. Several villagers kept looking at the Tower, fearful that a knight would emerge, ready to attack.

The stars winked out of the sky, and a light pink dawn appeared over the mountains. As the sky brightened, the villagers trudged to their houses. Steiner arranged the stones of a new grave as the hunters shoveled pyre ashes into the dirt. Cody placed the last scoop of ashes in the grave, and Haveldan covered it with dirt. They stared at the names written on the tombstones in Gaut's scrawl.

Herrick walked down and joined them.

"The bells stopped," Steiner said.

They looked at the Tower, waiting for something to happen.

"Finally. It was giving me a headache," Herrick said, breaking the tension.

"All the armor and swords have been relocated across the village. Aurdr has the kids plus your two Theim," Haveldan said.

"They got names. Nóri for the dwarf girl, and the blonde girl is Iona."

"Iona? That was my grandmother's name," Haveldan said.

"She spent some time wandering the graveyard. It may have been your grandmother's name."

Haveldan laughed. "My grandmother was a good woman. May her name serve the thrall well."

"She was a slave for so long that she didn't know her true name. Iona's name will serve her well."

Haveldan looked over at the houses.

"How is Kordan?" Herrick asked.

"Recovering." Haveldan took a deep breath. "And angry that I won't let him out of his house. I'm surprised he's not standing out here staring me down."

Herrick yawned and stretched. "Let me know if you need anything. It's been a long night. It's been a long day. It's been a long time."

The Tower bell rang.

"Gods, what now. Are you sure no one is there?" Herrick asked.

"Go check out the Tower or go wait at Shrinehall," Haveldan said.

Herrick waited, looking at those around him. "Everyone. Go to Shrinehall, we will meet whomever there." He moved among the villagers, trying to direct them.

Haveldan watched the Tower. Before long, Kordan hobbled up to the steps of Shrinehall, using his longbow as a crutch.

"Hear the bells?" Haveldan asked.

"All night. Couldn't sleep. Leg hurts and my face hurts," Kordan said.

"Your face hurts me too," Haveldan said. Kordan stared at Haveldan, his good eye glaring at him.

"Let's go to the top, maybe then we can see who we're dealing with," Herrick said, trying to stave off a fight.

Most of the village was there. Many had been lost over the winter, and a few hid in their houses. The bells sounded once again in their summoning tone.

Two knights passed through the Tower's open gates on horseback. A few whispers went through the crowd, questioning if they were magistrate. The words echoed in panic.

"Please, everyone. I don't think this is the magistrate. It appears to only be two knights. Please be calm."

Steiner and Haveldan stepped forward.

"That's light armor, not full plate," Haveldan said.

"Scouts?" Steiner asked, squinting to see.

"White Citadel banner."

The knights themselves did not hurry. They trotted to Shrinehall without ever taking their horses to a gallop.

Herrick looked around. "Haveldan, Cody, and Kordan, stay up here. Steiner and I will meet with the knights.

Herrick calmed down as they came into better view. The knights' tunics were bright white with the black raven, the standard of the White Citadel. These were not the various black and red cloaks of the magistrate.

"Góður dagur!" One of the riders yelled out an old language greeting as they approached.

"Hello," called back Herrick. "I am Mayor Herrick Blanchfield of Elta." The two knights stopped their horses in front of the Shrinehall. Steiner took the reins, allowing them to dismount.

"Hello, Mayor. We want to bring news to the people and address them. The Allfather has passed this world. We seek the next reincarnation, and we have other news for the village."

"We currently have no overseer. He went to the White Citadel several nights ago," Herrick said.

"Yes, we are aware. The village awaits," one of the knights replied.

Herrick stepped to the side and allowed them up the stairs.

The two knights ascended. They stood, staring at the toppled statue of Asagrim.

"The witch did this?" the knight asked. "Gods, the temple is in ruins."

The other knight approached the statue and touched it. Herrick stood uneasy, eyeing the hunters. The knight that went to the statue turned from it and approached the broken altar.

"Villagers of Elta, hear me." His voice quaked with anger. "The Allfather is dead."

Herrick looked over the crowd. Yngveig was right. He stood near the back of Shrinehall head hung.

"We search the initiation of the new Allfather. Then we come to this," the knight continued, hands gesturing to the statue. "Overseer Daniels has died. There was an accident on the way to the White Citadel."

Whispers murmured throughout Shrinehall.

"What of the baby?" Herrick asked. Kordan hobbled forward next to the mayor.

"Sir Gregory, commander of the armies and the champion of the White Citadel, delivered the infant to the Allfather. I saw it with my own eyes."

Herrick felt the anger building in Kordan.

"What of the pilgrims?" Yngveig yelled from the back.

"Word is that a pilgrimage joined one of the armies marching to White Citadel. There are survivors, but there were also heavy losses.

Yngveig's sobs echoed through Shrinehall.

The knight looked over the group of villagers. "You are without an overseer or knights in this village. The White Citadel cannot guard this village. The priests are recovering from the Allfather's loss so one cannot be dispatched. This temple is in ruin and is an affront to Asagrim." His eyes settled on Herrick. "Mayor, you will organize your people and clean this up. When we return, we expect to see this hall in better condition. When a priest comes, the Shrinehall will be in proper condition to receive him."

"We've been responsible for the protection of this village since the knights left—" Haveldan started, but Herrick's hand on his shoulder stopped him.

"The magistrate ordered to quarantine the food." The knight looked at those around him. "You all look well fed. I see you've already tripped the grainery safeguard. Gather all the food and grain, it will burn in one hour."

Herrick's tried to think of a peaceful resolution to this, but

Kordan blurred past him. He moved to the knight addressing the villagers. Kordan's hand snapped in a broad arc across the knight's throat. A knife gleamed in his hand as it slashed between his leather chest plate and helm into the soft flesh of his throat. The knight stumbled, hoarking for air as blood spilled from the wound. Haveldan shot two arrows at the other knight as he clumsily pulled his sword. One hit left of his heart, slowed by the leather armor. The other hit under his left eye, driving the knight backward into the statue. He fell against Asagrim's hand and died. The villagers panicked and ran for the exit.

Herrick yelled for calm, but the majority were running down the stairs. Some tumbled from them and fell as the mass fled.

Kordan stood over the knight he took down. "Haveldan, as soon as the villagers clear, take the bodies to Ragnfast's shop."

Steiner walked up to Herrick. "So, I guess we are now at war with the White Citadel?"

Herrick looked at the knight. "We were already at war. We survived winter without their help, and now they try to take the food that sustained us. The overseer and knights will not return. These were scouts too. With the search for the Allfather happening, I doubt they will turn up missing for some time."

"By Asagrim, Herrick. What if you're wrong?"

"Tonight, we will ransack the Tower for anything useful, then the hunters will set traps and snares for anyone that comes back. We will make Shrinehall our new defense."

CHAPTER 41

L ate afternoon settled into Elta. Herrick and a group of villagers combed through the Tower. They searched for anything of use and value but stayed away from anything magic. Haveldan and the other hunters kept watch in case anyone else showed up.

Kordan felt better, unnaturally. The healing potions helped his wounds, but another fire roared in his belly. The fire emerged when he spoke Berstuk's name, the dark forest lady. She was there when Nol attacked in the Delirium Forest. When Nol stood above Kordan's beaten and prone body ready to kill him, the dark lady stopped him and whispered something in the shepherd's ear. Nol went rigid and wandered off with his wolfkin.

Berstuk stood over Kordan, a look of mirth on her face. It was the last image of his ruined eye as Kordan gave into darkness.

He understood now. Berstuk had warped him, made him a thing of the Delirium Forest. He was a danger to Elta.

When the knight died at his hand, Kordan had an idea. Butcher the bodies and let the wild take care of it. Their armor grew the village's hidden armory. Then cut the knights up like meat and distribute their bodies in various places within the quiet Witches Forest. The White Citadel never crossed into it, and he had a place to feast.

He looked at the bodies on the floor. Cody had helped him remove the armor and tunics. "Burn the tunics, restore the armor, then leave the rest to me," Kordan said. He cleaned Ragnfast's old, white oak stump that he had used as a butcher block with a bucket of water. "There are things in this life you don't need to see." Then Kordan turned and stared at Cody until he left.

He laid down the first body, the one he killed with a blade. He hung it upside down and drained the blood through a trough to the back of the shop. Kordan repositioned the body on the block. Four quick chops separated it at the major joints. Then Kordan lost his ability to stay human.

"You okay, Kordan?" Haveldan knocked on the butcher's door an hour later.

Kordan placed the last leg into the cart. He was water-soaked but clean. Empty buckets lay scattered on the floor.

"This is poor, bloody work, Haveldan. Will you fetch more water?"

Haveldan grabbed the buckets and left. Kordan hid the knight's thigh bones. They had teeth marks in them, but he sliced up the meat enough to conceal his feast. Kordan had never felt so full, so meat-drunk before.

Haveldan returned. They finished cleaning up, removing any trace of what was done.

"This is grim work," Haveldan said, passing a bucket to Kordan.

Kordan washed off the butcher block. "More than you will ever know."

Herrick sat in the house, the girls and Jahan sat close to the fire.

He reviewed the hunter's plan for traps and snares at the Tower. It seemed good enough, but what size force would come into Elta looking for the lost scouts? He hoped that between the White Citadel's search for the Allfather and their continued wars, two lost scouts were an insignificant loss.

"Herrick. Could I go walk the village?" Iona asked.

Herrick got up out of his chair. He had sat too long, too deep in thought. His legs ached and his back hurt.

"Maybe it would be good for everyone. It's not dark yet."

They left the house, walking past the damage of Della's office. It stopped him for a moment. Out of sadness and yet another cleanup Herrick needed to organize. He gave Iona some room as she roamed around the village square and walked down toward the forge and butcher shop. Kordan left the back of the butcher shop with a cart.

"Kids, let's go this way instead."

He moved the children. Children? The dwarf was older than he was. He knew nothing about dwarven societies, something the White Citadel had been at war against for generations. How could he raise a dwarven girl that would become a woman in the years when Herrick was an old, enfeebled man? He shook the nonsense from his head. They moved past the vendor stands that had closed. They needed a rallying point for the village. The next yearly observance was Highsun, still months away.

"Herrick!" Aurdr called out from across the village square. She carried Austri, her other daughter trailed behind her.

"Hello, Aurdr." Herrick reached out and stroked Austri's head. "Growing like a bean pod."

"Yes, she is. Hungry too, which has me thinking." It was always dangerous when Aurdr said she was thinking. "We need to have a festival. That grain's beginning to turn."

"I've talked to several people in the village willing to help me bake, but since the grain's wet, we need to use it. I've already had to throw out some of it."

"I've thought the same thing. We need something that will

bring the village together."

"I talked to Haveldan earlier about the meat stores, there is plenty. He also said he spotted elk returning, Herrick said.

"Praise be to Lofn. She saved us," Aurdr winked.

The name shocked Herrick. Constantly he heard prayers to Asagrim or the Allfather, who did little but bring grief to them this last cycle. Herrick felt the tears fall and took him a moment to speak.

"There aren't many true-believers left. I think we should have a festival to honor Lofn, what she did for us."

"Girls, take Jahan and Austri to my house. I'll be there soon." Aurdr gave Austri over to Nóri. The children walked off, and Herrick continued to look at the ground. Aurdr embraced Herrick. "We've all had loss, and we need to remember and to call out their names among friends and family."

Herrick nodded and wiped away the tears. "I'll talk to all the vendors. What do you think, three days to get ready?"

"I'll have help, let's do it in two."

"Can you watch the children for a couple of hours? I'll go organize."

"Already planned on it," Aurdr smiled. "It will be a nice break from everything."

Herrick went house to house talking to families and vendors. The villagers answered their doors, long in the face and waiting for some sort of calamitous news. Each villager relaxed as Herrick laid out the plans for the festival.

He went to the Tower and checked on the work. The hunters had done well. Cody and Haveldan offered to stay on watch. Kordan seemed distant.

"Kordan? Kordan?" Haveldan smacked his shoulder.

Kordan looked up, boiling in fury.

"Whoa. Sorry, you were lost there for a moment."

"I'm … I'm not feeling myself. I pushed too hard today."

"It has been a long day, and a lot's happened. Can I walk you to your house?" Herrick asked.

Kordan took a moment. "I'll make it home." He stood and left.

"Is he okay?" Herrick asked as he watched Kordan leave.

"He's acted a little shaky since he cut up the knights. I guess that could affect anyone."

They walked to the Tower. Haveldan went into the gates and pointed out the traps.

"Do you think it will work?" Herrick asked, looking at a drop pit.

"Depends on how many come. A small force, sure." Haveldan looked around and quietly said, "Large army, we're doomed."

Herrick looked down at the sharpened stakes. "We need to make sure children don't come up here."

"Like Allistril and Jahan?" Haveldan smiled.

"Allistril would walk into a bear den if you told her not to. Jahan doesn't do much anymore," Herrick said as he brushed the dirt back onto another trap. "Make sure there are clearly marked maps. We'll distribute to the villagers in case we have to shelter here.

Haveldan nodded. "Tomorrow we start fortifying Shrinehall. What do you want to do with the statue?"

Herrick thought, his hands rubbing his temples.

"Yngveig is the last of the true-believers. I don't want to do anything that insults his beliefs or anyone else's."

Haveldan nodded. "It can be added to the defenses. No bolts or arrows will pierce marble."

They walked to the top of the Tower and looked out.

"That's odd," Haveldan pointed out.

"What is it?" Herrick asked, trying to follow his finger.

"Kordan's walking out into the Witches Forest," Haveldan said.

CHAPTER 42

Allistril woke up in the middle of the night. The fire must have gone out because the upstairs was freezing. Nóri and Iona huddled together in the bed, daddy lay in the other bed flat on his back, snoring. She sat up, shivering, pulling her quilt up around her, and tried to hug herself to get warm. Frost had formed inside the window, and the cold moonlight barely filtered through.

Her body tensed from the cold, and her stomach spasmed. She tried to say something, but her jaws clenched shut, and her teeth chattered. Something stood near her father, not quite casting a shadow in the room. It stood over him, a hand on his shoulder.

"M-mom-mommy," she stuttered. Tears welled in her eyes as the figure moved toward her. As it drew toward her, the form changed. The mist seemed to fall apart and rejoin as a soft hand and went through Allistril's hair. "Oh, how I missed you." The voice was far off, but familiar. "Hello, little firehead."

"Lofn?"

The mist flowed and formed a familiar face.

"Your baby, Lofn? Where is it? How are you here?"

"That is not important, little one. Come to the forest, your mother and I need you."

"Mommy is with you?"

"Allistril?" Herrick sat up. "What is it baby? Is it a nightmare?

"Come to the forest." The voice hung in the air as the mist evaporated.

Herrick got up. "Why is it so cold in here?"
Allistril only looked at her father and cried.

Herrick slogged to Shrinehall as dawn winked over the mountains. It was a long night. Allistril had a nightmare and refused to leave his side. They slept downstairs after the fire went out and it took some time to warm up the house. He slept fitfully in his chair with Allistril the rest of the night and decided to get up early. Work echoed from the Tower. The hunters chopped down a couple of trees from the Witches Forest and used the lumber used to fortify Shrinehall.

He watched the work for a while. Some of the vendors returned to their stores, prepping for opening today and the festival tomorrow. He passed through the vendor market saying his hellos and asking if there was anyone needing help.

Steiner wandered down and caught up with him. "Anything from White Citadel?"

"Silence. I'm okay with that," Herrick said.

"Good, good. I was afraid the village would be crawling with soldiers this morning."

Herrick looked over at Shrinehall. "Just the ones of our making."

"Setting up Shrinehall as a defensive point?" Steiner asked.

"It's high ground around the village. I'd hate to set up a defense where knights suddenly appear."

"I hate to break it to you, Herrick. Overseer Daniel's would just appear up at Shrinehall all the time. I don't think he ever walked from the Tower." Steiner patted Herrick on the back as they walked.

"Didn't think about that. I don't do good with the supernatural."

"I can understand. You survived the Magistratus."

"Ugh, saw Ivanar's wraith too. Too much for this lifetime."

Steiner nervously laughed. "So supernatural ... did you do something with Sir Solveig's body?"

"No. Gods, I didn't think about it if the scouts had seen the body."

"It would not have ended differently."

"We should go move the corpse. Did you get the armor?"

"Um, I'm not taking armor off a man that's been dead for a while. I'm not that level of adventurer. I don't think you get my point. Walk with me." His strong hand redirected Herrick back to the village square and down to Dead Man's Trail.

"Allistril woke up last night. The house fire went out, and we had frost upstairs. She swears she spoke to Lofn."

Steiner looked serious and nodded at the right points, but Herrick didn't believe he was listening.

"I'm glad Overseer Daniels is gone, but there are days I wish there were a priest around," Steiner said.

They stood above, looking down. "I want to burn the shack during tomorrow's festival."

"I understand. Now look again." Steiner said, pointing down toward the shack.

"Where is Sir Solveig's body?" Herrick asked.

Steiner fell behind as Herrick rushed up Shrinehall's steps.

"Kordan? Haveldan?" he shouted as he climbed the stairs.

Cody stuck his head over a fortification, "They're up here, Mayor. Is there a problem?"

Herrick had to catch his breath as Haveldan walked over. "Sir Solveig's body, where is it?"

"Catch your breath, Mayor. I don't know. I'll ask Kordan."

Kordan sat in the corner of Shrinehall away from Asagrim's statue. He worked on a long branch, sharpening it, oblivious to Haveldan's approach. He looked worn, sweaty, almost burning with fever. Haveldan said his name a couple of times to get his attention. Kordan glared up when Haveldan spoke. His glare moved to Herrick and Steiner. Then he shook his head and went back to his work.

Haveldan walked back over. "He knows nothing about it."

"Is he okay?" Herrick asked.

"I think he's infected with something but won't take anything for it. Says it will burn out on its own."

"Did you ask where he went last night?"

"Started to. If you didn't notice, he's not up for conversation today. I may send him home soon, so he's decent for tomorrow's festival. As for Sir Solveig, let's figure it was an animal."

"Armor and all?"

"I didn't take it, and I forgot about the body. I'll check in with Kordan later when he's better."

Herrick nodded and left. He walked down the steps, peering into the forest and the shack as he went down.

"You want to burn the shack today?" Steiner asked.

"Would you give me a hand?"

"Destruction's the favorite part of my job," Steiner replied.

Allistril woke up and felt for her father in bed. She sat up and looked around the room surprised that she was back upstairs. Nóri was awake, looking at her, but Iona was still asleep. Allistril pulled her knees to her and rocked a little in bed.

"What is it?" Nóri asked.

"I don't know. I had a dream last night, but I think I was awake."

"What happened?" Nóri got up and sat on the corner of the bed.

"Lofn came to me," Allistril said.

Nóri laughed. It triggered some tears from Allistril. "Oh, no. I'm not laughing at you. Don't cry. My culture has all sorts of ghost stories. I didn't know Lofn, but I knew your mother." Nóri put her hand on Allistril's shoulder. "Before your father released us, she was the only one to show us kindness in some time. From what I heard, Lofn was a powerful warlock and saved the village."

"What's a warlock? People called her a witch, but that's not right."

"My people can't work magic well, so we have to go about it a different way. My grandfather was one of the most powerful warlocks in the dwarven kingdom, but the Allfather took his power."

"The Allfather could do that?"

"The Allfather was too powerful," Nóri said.

"But he's dead now," Allistril said.

A slight smile crept over Nóri's lips, and she nodded.

Allistril hugged her legs a little tighter. "Lofn came to me last night," Allistril said in a small voice. Tears fell again.

"An *aptrgangr*, an after-walker in your language?"

"I don't know what that is," Allistril said. She rested her head rested on her knees, looking at Nóri.

"Sometimes us dwarves are determined. When the Allfather flooded the mines, the story goes that the dwarves were so determined that they kept working even after death."

"That's terrible," Allistril said.

"Yes, it was. It's now a lake in my homeland. One that no dwarf will go near. I'm glad the Allfather is dead. Maybe now my ancestors can finally rest." Nóri looked deep in thought. "Sometimes with the after-walkers, they need closure. They took her baby, right?"

"Yeah." Allistril buried her head.

"Maybe that's it. I don't think we can get her baby back."

"She wants me to go to the forest."

Nóri stared at her for a while. "My father always said never give a ghost what it wants. It lives in the past." Nóri walked over to her pile of armor and weapons. "With something so simple, maybe we should. Your father plans to have this huge festival tomorrow. I say we sneak out of the festival and go while the sun is up. I don't like that many people to be around, and Iona doesn't want to go at all. When the festival is going, after your father introduces us, we'll go look in the forest and see what we find." She put on her grandfather's helm. It looked too big at first, then shrunk to fit Nóri's head. It made her look like a fierce warrior.

"What if we find their ghosts?" Allistril asked.

"She asked that you come to the forest. Maybe that's it. We stay away from them and come back."

Thoughts ran through Allistril's head like the wildfire that ran through the Delirium Forest. Lofn and her mother would never hurt her, and this party was for the adults. Aurdr already had plans for them if they wanted to leave, which meant Austri would be with them. Go to the Witches Forest. One of the first warnings her father sternly told her was to stay away from the forests that surrounded Elta. They were both dangerous. Lofn went there, and so did mommy. Now, it was time for Allistril to follow.

CHAPTER 43

Work in Elta happened at a feverous pace. Cody and Haveldan laid the Tower's final traps while the other hunters built Shrinehall into a defensive position, and the vendors cooked and prepped food for the big day. Herrick felt useless, to the point that Allistril, Nóri, and Iona asked him to stop checking on them. The day was warm, and the sun stayed over the mountain peak just long enough to warm their faces. From the melted snow, green exploded into the valley. Herrick sat at his dinner table looking over plans for the festival as the girls marched downstairs and out of the house to play.

"Stay out of the Tower and Shrinehall. I mean it. There are traps there now, and you could get seriously hurt. Okay?"

"Okay," Allistril answered in her sing-song voice of not paying attention to anything Herrick said.

He looked at Nóri, and Nóri nodded back. "We're going to get Jahan and Austri so Aurdr can work."

"Thank you, girls. Find me if you need anything." Herrick said.

They shut the door and were off. Herrick sat back and thought. The beggar's shack destruction would be a dark spot on the festival. Why bring his feelings into it? This was to celebrate the village's freedom. He pinched the bridge of his nose as that long deep feeling of woe surfaced. Gods, he missed Della. He missed Lofn. He even missed the endless bickering of Valdir and Ragnfast, Bera's dirty looks, and Ivanar's boasting of his hunting abilities.

He rose from the table and left the house. The girls had already disappeared in their adventures, so Herrick walked through the vendor tents and down to the graveyard. Something pulled at the pit of his stomach as he walked near Gaut's new gravestone. The supernatural was an open threat, and he had no defense to this village. He walked over to Della and Lofn's markers. This pulled at the pit of his stomach worse.

"I am a raven-starver," Herrick said as he kneeled at the site and wept. Everyone in the village had something to do. He had a moment to himself without doom ready to invade. For once, time seemed abstract. He touched the marker and thought of asking Steiner to make something better for them. Several things raced through his head, but one thought stood out. Something that had nagged at him for too long.

He stood, wiped his tears and nose on his sleeve, and walked the long way around to his office. No one stopped him on the street, no one said hello.

He took the torch off the office front, lit it, and marched down Dead Man's Trail. Blood was still on the porch and in the dirt. Sir Solveig's body laid there long enough to leave an imprint, but oddly there were no drag marks. If an animal did take him, he didn't drag him to the forest. Herrick examined the dirt. A set of footprints trailed into the forest. It sent chills up Herrick's spine. He held the torch in front of him as he stepped over Della's blood and entered the shack. So much blood covered the mattress where Lofn died. "I am so sorry." He lit the mattress on fire, then held the torch up until the thatch roof caught. He looked around as the smoke filled the room. He stepped out and kneeled to touch the blood at the door. "Rest well, my love."

It didn't take long for the flames to consume the shack. He stepped back and took a seat on the ground and watched it like all the recent pyres. This wasn't releasing a body to Valhöll but removing blight from the village.

The work in Shrinehall stopped, and hunters gathered, looking down at him. Soon, there were footsteps behind him.

"I thought you needed help," Steiner said.

"I thought I might, but I didn't," Herrick replied, still staring at the fire.

"Hmmm. I thought about a memorial stone here ... once we clear it. Maybe an herb garden for healing potions."

Herrick smiled. "I like that idea. I also want some nice headstones for Della and Lofn."

"Don't be shortsighted. I've already got those made. I know this place doesn't sit well with you, Herrick. But, you forget, this is where the Tower left us. We inherited the village."

"I think we may need a wordsmith to come up with something better for a marker."

"By Asagrim, to think I count you as a friend," Steiner said. He sat next to the mayor. "Steiner, I'd like to do this by myself."

Steiner rummaged through his bag and pulled a bottle of Valdir's mead. "Yeah, I know."

Herrick watched Steiner eye the cork, fumble for his dagger, and try to dig it out. He stood and grumbled. He spotted a rock and used it to break the neck off the bottle.

He brought the bottle back over and held it out to Herrick. "Watch the glass."

Herrick took a good draw from the bottle as the thatched roof collapsed. The walls of the shack fell in, and the fire leaped into the sky.

Steiner sat down and raised the bottle, "To those that died here." He took a drink and handed it to Herrick.

"Except for Solveig. That *meinfretr*," Herrick said. He stared into the fire a bit longer, took a big drink and spit out a glass shard.

Several of the villagers and hunters stopped by to help the wood burn, to make the place nothing but ash by the festival. Some brought ale, some brought mead, others brought tools to keep the fire going. More bottles arrived and soon everyone gathered had a full cup or drinking horn. Herrick looked around as the smell of spiced bread filled the valley. "Take a bottle to Aurdr. She's working too much."

Herrick looked over at Steiner, who was already laying back drunk. Cody finished a mug of ale. "I'll do it."

He walked up Dead Man's Trail and over to the grainery remains, then to the bakery. When he entered, someone yelled in the back, "Bread's not ready, come back later."

"But I bring refreshments and nothing else."

Aurdr walked out, covered in sweat and clutching a mixing bowl.

"The gods have answered. Did the festival start? Are we late?"

Cody smiled and showed the bottles. "Herrick burned the beggar's shack, and the village raided Valdir's mead and ale. I think everyone is about half in, so yes, the festival began."

A look crossed Aurdr's face, Cody couldn't tell if it was anger from exclusion or sheer exhaustion from the heat and cooking all morning. Four other villagers plus Aurdr's older daughter moved and prepped in the baking area.

Cody popped the cork and poured Aurdr a mug. "I want my mug back."

"Then get to work youngin'."

"You get to tell Kordan and Haveldan you took me." Cody sat the mead and ale bottles down as Aurdr drained the mug and slammed it on the table.

"Gods, this was Nol's favorite. Another."

She downed another and slammed it on the counter. This time she sat down the floured bowls and took the bottle.

"Ladies, this strong, young man has offered to help and brought ale. Take a break, drink up, and let's finish this so the festival can start."

The heat inside the back was stifling, even in the cold season.

Several of the older ladies from the village hailed and clapped as he came in. Cody's sight settled on Inkeri, a villager that he liked since she could draw a bow. Her long brown hair was pulled back in a knot. Back by the ovens near the grinding stone, she had stripped down to undergarments.

"Well, hail to you, Inkeri," he said as he approached with a bottle and a smile.

"You hush and open that. I'm thirsty. We need to finish grinding this wheat to flour."

A chimney slightly moved the air, but the room boiled.

"Ugh, it's like Highsun in here. How can you work?"

She ignored Cody, gulping from the bottle.

She paused to breathe. "That's what I needed. Now, boy. Aurdr said to watch the grain. Look for spoil."

"Spoil like mold?" He looked at the bags still needing ground.

"Yes, I think it looks like black flecks on the grain. If you see any, we need to throw it away."

Cody hefted a bag and dumped it. He looked at the yoke where Bera's pet donkey used to stand.

Inkeri laughed. "You're the ass now. Get in the yoke."

Cody went under the yoke and fit under it uncomfortably. "This is fun," he said as he strained but moved the grindstone.

"Now you know why I'm in my underclothes," Inkeri said.

By a few revolutions, Cody had soaked through his shirt. Inkeri had pulled some spoiled grain off and threw it into an old barrel. As Cody passed her under the yoke, she slapped him on the hip.

"Faster, beast," she said.

"I'll show you a beast," Cody said.

"Maybe after the festival," Inkeri smiled.

They worked until the sun fell. A hunting horn sounded from the village square.

Aurdr stumbled back into the grinding station. "Go clean up, you two. The festival is about to start, officially. I'll work what's done and bring them out," she stammered.

A pleasant feeling of numbness carried Aurdr's tired steps. Too much ale, too much heat, but the end was near. Each helper worked at a station: they processed, mixed, kneaded, and cut. When their job was done, Aurdr excused them. The first baskets of bread were delivered to the tables. Outside a nice wind blew in from the South Sea, and the warm smell of salt and sea life filled the air.

Tables surrounded Shrinehall. This number of villagers had not been together since the magistrate rounded everyone up in the village square and read the new laws. Now, they had control of the village.

She watched the kids at the far side of the revelry and approached. "Everything well?"

Little Nóri answered, "It's fine. Austri is a little fussy and hungry."

Aurdr took her baby. "I'll feed him. I've still got a helper in the bakery, then I'll give him back if you can watch him during the festival."

Nóri smiled and nodded. Aurdr reached in giving a strong hug. Maybe it took the dwarf a while to warm up. Jahan and Iona stared at the ground. Allistril ran circles around the group and gazed down into the forest. "You be a good girl," Aurdr said and intercepted Allistril with a hug and a kiss to the top of her firehead.

Another horn blew from Shrinehall. Aurdr stood and smiled at the children. "I'll be back."

Nóri watched Aurdr and Austri leave. The sun was still up, but time for the forest was quickly running out. "We shouldn't trust a forest at night," she said to Allistril.

"There's still some light. We won't stay past dusk."

Herrick walked up the steps of Shrinehall.

"Hear me people of Elta. Today we celebrate our freedom!"

The villagers roared, some toasted with ale and mead, others with bread and meat.

"We survived the winter, and the Tower has finally left us."

More cheers drowned out the last word.

"I want to introduce two new villagers imprisoned in the Tower and have been released. Nóri and Iona stand up and be recognized."

Nóri walked over to Iona and took her hand. Cheers again, some confused.

"Well, that was awkward," Iona said as she stood.

Nóri waved to the crowd. "Yeah, enough of this. Iona, go get the pack out of the house and take it down to the forest, I'll meet you, Jahan, and Allistril there. I'll grab some meat, so we're not starving."

The three walked back up to the house as Nóri walked through the crowd. Several smiled and patted her on the head or shoulder, except for an old man who glared at her with a mix of hated and disdain. She avoided him like the undead.

Herrick spoke more, but she ignored it until he called out Della's name. It stopped Nóri, and she looked at Herrick. He was paying tribute to the dead. She had never seen how humans did it. Their lives were so quick and brutal, but the love was there. Her people were long-lived, so death was an oddity unless from war or disease. Herrick announced the names of Lofn, Ivanar, Bera, and Nol. There were several others she didn't know. Someone called Yngveig out for being a sole survivor. She noticed several people walking up to the hateful old man. It broke his stare for a while. No one called out the knights' names or Overseer Daniels and it was fitting. Rumor was they were dead and Nóri hoped so.

"Sorry, hon." Aurdr rushed up and handed Austri to her. "Bread's about to burn. Sorry. I'll get him soon."

She took Austri, a dwarven namesake, and hugged him. He was tightly swaddled and near sleep. "It's a little much for Jahan and Iona, so they went back to the house. I may go too."

"Get some meat and bread, dear. I'll get you a basket quick."

"I'll get it. Go take care of the bread, Aurdr. Stay with the village, this is a little too much for me anyhow. I don't like crowds outside."

Aurdr embraced the dwarf and kissed her on the top of the head. It was quick and awkward, but nice. Better than a slap across the face and a push to the floor like in the Tower. Nóri smiled and hugged back.

"Thank you, Aurdr. Now, go. Your bread is on fire."

Aurdr rushed off as Nóri snaked around the tables. She took a handful of meat kabobs wrapped in wax paper.

"Dwarven godless scum." She looked up. Yngveig stood on the other side of the table. His face was burning red, his hand clenching and unclenching.

She looked down. "I'm sorry, sir." It was automatic. She waited for the hit.

"Unhand me," the man yelled.

Nóri looked up. A man with a half-mauled face held Yngveig's arm.

"I will not … ever hear you say something like this to a child. If I do, you're on the Delirium Forest's trail," Kordan said, releasing him.

Yngveig took a big bite of the roll, turned, and spit it at the dwarf. Kordan slapped it down, and it landed at her feet. Kordan forced Yngveig up and pushed him away, glaring at him as he walked off.

"He's a drunk and an old soldier. He lost most of his family in the Delirium Forest. If he ever gives you a problem, let me or the hunters know," Kordan said.

Yngveig took a few steps forward and stopped. He looked at

the Delirium Forest as if he heard something. Then slowly turned.

"Berstuk calls you, Kordan."

Kordan looked confused. Nóri stared into his ruined eye. She finally shifted to the other part of his face, but something didn't seem right.

"Thank you," Nóri said.

"You have friends here, little one. Don't be afraid."

She nodded, took the meat, but didn't want to wait on the rolls. The people around her talked once again. A few reached out to touch her and tell her welcome as she glided through the crowd. She made it to the edge with Austri and the meat, finally feeling able to breathe. Herrick still spoke from the Shrinehall and the words melded together. She walked through the houses, down through the empty vendor tents, and into the graveyard. The village was on the other side of Shrinehall and no one saw them here. She wrapped Austri tightly and checked that no one followed. The pack and the other children stood near the edge of the forest.

"Everything okay?" Iona asked.

"Found out one of the villagers hates dwarves. Otherwise, everything is good. Take Austri."

Iona took the infant while Nóri opened her pack. Allistril looked into the pack. "All that armor should have been really heavy."

"But it's not. Dwarven smithing at its finest." The armor was large, her grandfather's. As she put it on, she felt the armor flow and shrink, to give her a perfect fit. Allistril put on the helm, but it remained too large.

"Aww. I wanted to wear this."

"We will find you another one," Nóri said as she put it on and it fit her face.

At the bottom of the pack was her father's axe. She touched it, trying not to cry.

She pulled the bearded axe out, twisting the shaft. The long axe head shifted and became double-bladed. "Bless you, Eitri. It still works."

"Who is Eitri?" Jahan asked.

"He's my family's god," Nóri said. "If you want, you can follow him too."

Jahan smiled unevenly. "Okay."

Nóri closed the pack, gave it to Allistril to carry and asked, "Which way?"

Allistril smiled. "This way," she said as she skipped into the Witches Forest.

Aurdr didn't feel well. Almost as if the rolls she ate and the ale she drank didn't sit right. She was so hot, almost like Valdir used to get at the forge, but she had several plates of rolls ready to go. Her eldest daughter had taken some but several remained.

"So hot," she said and walked over to the bucket of water. She pulled the ladle out and poured the rest over her head. She looked in the bucket and swore there was a fish in there. She shook her head. "Too hot."

She grabbed a platter and stumbled out of the bakery. She carried it a couple of steps and dropped it. Her hands were bright red, sore, and clumsy. Her feet refused to hold her up anymore.

In the distance, wolves howled. She laid on her back and looked up. Several wolves stood near the Tower, looking down on the village. One stood between them. She stared as it stood up. It only had one arm, and its features looked familiar.

"Nol?"

It jumped down from the Tower's lofty hill and landed near a couple of houses. She watched it approach, human-like, but wild eyes reflecting in the late sun. She reached out for him as he approached. Her husband had returned.

Herrick made the last hoarse proclamation of the evening. He had a headache from the constant applause and shouting and was ready for more ale, meat, and bread.

Allistril and the kids were at the house getting away from the crowds.

He kept an eye on Yngveig after his outburst and Kordan as he sat back, troubled by something. Yngveig left after his last fight with Kordan. Unease seemed to cross some of the tables. A few revelers had consumed too much ale, mead, meat, and bread.

A fight broke out among the tables over old land rights, who owned the abandoned true-believer's land, and it caused fists between some of the farmers. A couple of hunters stood near the outside of the group, stumbling through the crowds unable to control them. Someone screamed from behind Shrinehall.

"Aurdr?" Herrick cried out and tried to get through the villagers. A lone wolf howled at the edge of Elta. Herrick looked to Kordan, who stared forward in his chair talking to no one. Haveldan sat across from Kordan with his head on the table. Blood seeped from his throat.

"Kordan?" Herrick asked as a fleeing villager nearly pushed him down.

Then around the back of Shrinehall, wolves flowed into the village. Herrick grabbed for his horn. His hands burned, his legs tingled, and he fought to stay upright.

"Herrick Blanchfield," someone growled behind him.

He turned to find Yngveig in his White Citadel armor.

"For the downfall of the Tower!" His arm came forward. Herrick felt something stab him.

He tried to focus on Yngveig as time slowed. Wolves streamed out around them, taking villagers down, but Herrick felt deep underwater, his limbs cold and empty and his reflexes dulled.

Darkness closed around him, but among the crowd, standing in a shaft of sunlight, stood a tall beautiful, blonde warrior. In full armor, she walked easily among the chaos. Her armor shone like a beacon in the setting sun. Then all sound left the village. She looked at him and reached out.

Herrick reached out for her. "Battle-Maiden?"

She took his hand and led him. The light around him darkened and tunneled. They continued through the sudden night as distant sound returned. Laughter and mirth surrounded them. A sound rang out among them. The laugh was a low one, an odd chuckle for a woman, and he identified it from far away.

"Della?" Herrick Blanchfield said as he died.

Yngveig ran the mayor through. He sat there on the end of his sword, muttering before falling dead. Yngveig looked around. Kordan sat motionless. "Awaken, monster. Where is your wolf-skin?"

There was a stirring within Kordan. He stood wrong, off balance. His hips broke and collapsed, sending him to the ground. His skull popped and lengthened, then the monster roared among the villagers.

Wolves flowed around Shrinehall like a flood. Some villagers stood and ran. Others found their legs no longer worked, fell, and were trampled. In their madness rushing up Shrinehall, some fell from the high steps. Others sat in a stupor, drooling from the poisoning of the bad grain. The shepherd walked among them, driving the wolves from their skin with his touch. Beside him, Kordan crawled on the ground, still becoming.

At the top of Shrinehall, Cody looked over the edge with Inkeri. They quickly dressed as the masses rushed up to Shrinehall. Cody grabbed his bow and shot several of the wolves below him. Several villagers yelled and screamed, some fighting the invisible around them. Inkeri grabbed a spear from the weapon pile, keeping several of the villagers back. Their burning, red eyes screamed madness as they tore at each other. Some fell, clutching their hands or legs. Shrinehall filled with a throaty growl, and those still standing went for cover.

Slowly, the beast climbed up the side of Shrinehall, his claws piercing the rock. When he emerged at the top, his ruined face scanned the crowd.

Cody spun around from shooting wolves and sent two arrows into the beast's chest. They hit, then fell from its thick fur. Cody felt the low growl reverberate through Shrinehall. He turned and grabbed Inkeri's hand and ran to the back. The steep drop-off fell to the valley by the Witches Forest. Cody shot another arrow, coming close to the beast's ruined eye.

"Kordan. Is that you? Can you hear me?" He sent another shot to the knee. Worthless.

Cody grabbed the spear from Inkeri. Behind the beast, Nol rose from the steps. He touched those that had fallen. Some lay dead, and some shuddered and fell away as a wolf emerged from their bodies. Large wolves attacked and tore at the remaining villagers, and soon Shrinehall's floor flowed with blood.

Kordan paused and looked at the shepherd. It touched Kordan. "Take the raven's soul." Kordan collapsed and screamed. His shoulders cracked and pushed through the fur on his back. Long, bloody bones emerged like battle flags, and long feathers unraveled and straightened like horrific banners. Kordan pushed himself up, his muzzle twisting and breaking. He opened his mouth. His fangs seemed to crowd together as they formed a bony point. His eye stared at Cody, almost pleading for him to end it. Cody rushed forward with the spear, trying to hit Kordan but his fur stopped the blade. Kordan slashed forward and broke the shaft of the spear.

Cody dropped the broken shaft. He looked at the weapon pile and knew they were all worthless. As Kordan approached, Cody stepped backward. His arms wrapped around Inkeri, and together they fell into the empty air behind them.

CHAPTER 44

llistril ran through the trees. Jahan kept up with her, but Nóri and Iona with Austri struggled to keep up.

"Allistril, slow down," Nóri called.

"It's this way. Hurry!" Allistril yelled, running deeper in.

The sun dipped below the mountains, and the shadow now filled the Witches Forest. Light drizzled through the canopy, but soon, even dusk was hard to see.

"We're going to get lost in here," Iona called.

"It's this way, please. I know it." Allistril stopped, letting the others catch up, but then sprinted ahead and even Jahan fell behind. Nóri yelled for everyone to stop. Allistril ran through several of the branches ahead and disappeared.

"Stop here and wait for her to come back. Jahan, stay there. Iona, take the baby and go back about halfway."

Muffled shouting came from Shrinehall, but the forest broke it up.

"Still partying it up, I guess," Nóri said.

More branches broke around her. "Allistril, you coming back?"

Nóri looked through the gloom of the forest. A large looming figure stood.

"Hello," Nóri said.

It seemed startled, and it stumbled through the trees, groaning.

"Eitri, protect me." Nóri gripped the axe as the head illuminated.

Sir Solveig crashed through the trees. His neck fell at an odd angle, his head twisting to look at her.

Nóri closed her eyes. She was trying to remember. She hadn't done it since her grandfather taught her, but the words were etched into her soul.

She opened her eyes and stared. Sir Solveig's cloudy eyes fell upon her. She held the axe out in front of her. "In the name of Eitri, builder of life, creator of the gods, drive this haunted soul away." She plunged the handle into the ground, the coldness climbed her feet and up her back. Nóri felt anchored with the ground below. She felt the dead knight's presence near her, felt Iona, Austri, and Jahan. As she reached out, she felt Allistril's presence in the forest. There was something else. Something that slept and at her intruding presence, awoke.

She repeated the prayer. "In the name of Eitri, builder of life." Her voice rose with power. The grand light emerged from the axe, crawled into her hands, and spread through her body. "Creator of the gods, drive this haunted soul away." The light focused on the axe's head and shot out. It struck Sir Solveig and took him from his feet. He fell to the forest floor and didn't move. From the center of his chest, a shadow emerged and floated back into the trees.

"In the name of Eitri, the builder of life ..." she continued. Firebugs rose around Nóri, their lights driving through the holy light that Nóri channeled.

Iona yelled, "Do you see them? They're everywhere." Jahan stared at Nóri.

The bugs pushed past Nóri, going after the shadow and pushing it further into the forest. The shadow howled. Other bugs circled the children.

"Iona, come to me, now. Jahan we're coming to you," Nóri yelled. As Iona ran through the trees, Nóri broke her connection to Eitri. She took a defensive stance behind Iona and pushed forward. Jahan stood in the trees, screaming. They grabbed Jahan and moved.

"I think that was my father," Jahan said.

"Let's get away from him as fast as possible. Allistril's that way," Nóri said. The firebugs followed them deeper in. Muted shouts and screams from Shrinehall made the children run faster.

"This is becoming a nightmare," Iona said.

The firebugs moved past them and flew into a grove ahead. Allistril stood as the firebugs flew above them, lighting up the grove.

A mist formed between Allistril and the group. "It's okay. They're my friends," Allistril said. The mist dissipated into the forest floor. A small creature approached from behind a tree. It looked like Allistril, but also looked like every other child there, even Austri, but was half of the older children's size. Its skin glowed a simple pattern that started up its fingers, radiated through the body, and exited the toes. The light entered the trees and pulsed.

"It's okay. We won't hurt you," Allistril said, kneeling before it. It approached slowly, taking Allistril's hand but kept a wary eye on Nóri.

"Sir Solveig was back there."

"And you forced the wraith away, child." A voice boomed through the forest.

Nóri readied her axe.

"I mean you no harm. Allistril of Della and Lofn was summoned here. You all will be welcomed."

The children gathered around Allistril and this strange child of the grove. The forest closed around them, protecting them from the horror that occurred in Elta and what could soon come from over the sea.

Outside of the Witches Forest, as the villagers of Elta died, trees sprung up from the tiny sprigs that grew throughout the village. They grew like unkept vines, taking over spaces, crashing through the houses and meeting places, and strangling Shrinehall. From Tower Road, Berstuk surveyed her new land, right to the edge of her brother's forest. The Delirium Forest filled in that night. Berstuk, the dark forest lady called Nol, Kordan, Yngveig, and their pack of wolves home. The ravens picked clean the remaining corpses.

The next morning, Steiner woke up. He had too much drink at the festival's beginning and someone carried him home. His cursed stomach screamed for food to soak up the remaining alcohol. "Oh, my head," Steiner said. Maybe someone on the street would bring him something. He opened the door. At the entrance of his house, on the edge of the village, Steiner stared at the tree trunk that had grown through his porch.

"What in the name of the gods," he said.

CHAPTER 45

Far from Elta, the stranger walked until the sun dropped on the horizon. Distant mountains seemed no closer after walking all day. Signs of war were all around him, divots in the ground, fortified positions, and old siege weapons. If he stopped long enough, their stories sang to him in poetry. He knew their history, their battles, their ruin, but did not understand why. The stranger didn't want to stand and listen, he wanted civilization, not ruin. Cold settled in and he sought a place to camp for the night.

A distant fire appeared down the road. For the next hour, the stranger walked toward it. A wagon full of provisions sat next to a single form huddled near the fire trying to find warmth.

"Hello," the stranger said.

The figure jumped at the voice. When he looked up and realized it came from a human, he darted for his pack and produced a small axe.

"Boy, are you on the wrong side of the river."

"I mean you no harm, only wish to warm myself by your fire."

The little man looked puzzled as he slapped his axe against his hand.

"What are you doing here?"

"Walking. I think I live near the mountain."

"You think your home is near the mountain? How long has it been since you've been home?"

"I don't remember. I woke up this morning, and here I am."

"You got any weapons on you, sir?"

The stranger held out his walking stick and looked at it.

"I've seen sticks poke out eyes and bash in skulls before."

"I don't know you. Why do you think I would cause you harm?" The stranger threw his stick away. "It's helped me walk. I've traveled a long distance today."

The dwarf stood and approached the man. He lowered his axe but still held it tight if needed. His grip caused the leather handle to creak.

"This is the wilds. You never know who you could meet on the open road."

The dwarf walked around the man, looking him up and down.

"No memories past this day?"

"No."

"Are you hungry?"

"Not really." The stranger shrugged. "I don't know the last time I ate. If you wish, I could keep walking."

The dwarf walked several circles around him. "You are more than welcome to join me, friend. Tomorrow, we'll walk to the mountain. We're about three days away. There is a war going on."

"Anything serious?"

"War always is. Nothing should bother two travelers like us. We will stay away from the soldiers."

The stranger felt the dwarf smile under his thick unruly beard.

"I know some quieter ways inside the mountain. We will be safe from the war. I also might know some people who know you."

"Within the mountain?"

"Oh yes, it's very safe. Violent people are trying to take our land away. Hard-fought land that dwarves have paid for with their lives. But I know paths. Yes, I know how to get into the mountain and not draw attention to us. We have very wise people who live there, some very long-lived. They might know who you are."

The dwarf rummaged in his pack and brought out a blanket. The human walked around the fire, and it made him nervous.

"Stranger, come sit by the fire and warm yourself. I have good food and drink. We will dine this eve, so tomorrow our pace will be sure and well."

The dwarf went to his cart and plucked some of the supplies out of it. He had an important guest, even if it cut into his money. This was the unfound Allfather. This one chance encounter could hand the war to the dwarves. Rumor was the dwarves made a false treaty since the Allfather passed.

The dwarf looked at his wines. This young man, this stranger with no memory, was he the new incarnation? Why else would a human be in the dwarven territories? He could drug the man, tie him up, and bury him in the cart. How much poison takes down a god? Too little, he knew. Too much and he dies. Then he would be reborn, maybe this time on the correct side of the river.

"Come join me for some drinks, friend. Tell me everything you remember," the dwarf said.

"I don't even know who I am."

"Then we will start with a name. I am known as Thedrick Thunderbelly."

The stranger nodded at him "Well met."

"Now what will we call you?"

"What is the name of that peak over there on the mountain?"

"That's Obdinspire." The dwarf hesitated after he said it. It was too close to one of the Allfather's old names.

"Obdin, I like that. Call me Obdin."

"Well, then Obdin. Set down and have an ale."

The dwarf watched him. This was the Allfather, Him. Thedrick Thunderbelly, the name made him laugh. Thedrick Thunderbelly was the fat gnome whose heart gave out when the dwarf robbed him and stole his cart, heading for market. He didn't want to head to the dwarven kingdom because of his past. His name was Baleseager. His last name was shed years ago to lose contact with any surviving family deep in the mines. He was a slaver, a thief, and an assassin. That didn't matter. The dwarven king will pay handsomely for such a prize, and possibly forgive old sins. After the Allfather was secured deep inside the mountain, he could sell information to the humans. This land would be open for the victor. Allfather the Long-Lived's reign was too brutal on the dwarves. Now, it was time for retribution.

The dwarf drained his mug and went for a refill before the stranger even lifted his glass. His weapons were in a satchel case by the keg. He snuck a pair of cuffs, a poison dart, and a sap into his back pocket just in case he needed them later. Might as well make a friend rather than an enemy this early in the game.

"I think we may develop one great friendship, Obdin. We have a bit of journey ahead of us."

ABOUT THE AUTHOR

Like a crow in a field of glass. Brian Johnson is a teacher, writer, photographer, storm chaser, and adventurer. He's kind of an evil version of Robert Fulghum. His first novel, Hell to Pay, is available on Amazon. Brian has also been published with short stories and poetry.

Questions, comments, concerns for his eternal soul? Check out his websites:
https://fatherthunder.blogspot.com/
https://talesfromthehauntedtypewriter.wordpress.com/
and see his storm-chasing adventures at
www.ruminationofthunder.com